Children of the Flame

Book Two of
The Chronicles of Avinol

MIKE ATCHLEY

Children of the Flame

For Ian.

I'll always be grateful for the time we had, my friend, and look forward to being together again someday…

…where we will ride on the backs of dragons,

and when we can make up for the time we lost.

Based on the Award Winning Podcast
"Dice Tower Theatre presents Dawn of Dragons"

Written by Mike Atchley

Cover Art "Kartilaan and Sophie" by Matthew "Little Bird" Baker

Part 1 Plate- "Ivory Library" - Mike Atchley
Part 2 Plate- "Vix" - Storm S Cone
Part 3 Plate- "Elona" - Mike Atchley
Part 4 Plate- "The Widow" - by Matthew "Little Bird" Baker
Chapter Art Part 1 and 2 by Crann Casta Studios
except Chapter 7 "Vix" by Storm S Cone
Chapter Art Part 3 and 4 by Matthew "Little Bird" Baker

Editing by Cindy Henderson and Susan Thomas
Proofreaders Cindy Henderson and JD Rose
Layout by Daniel Nichols

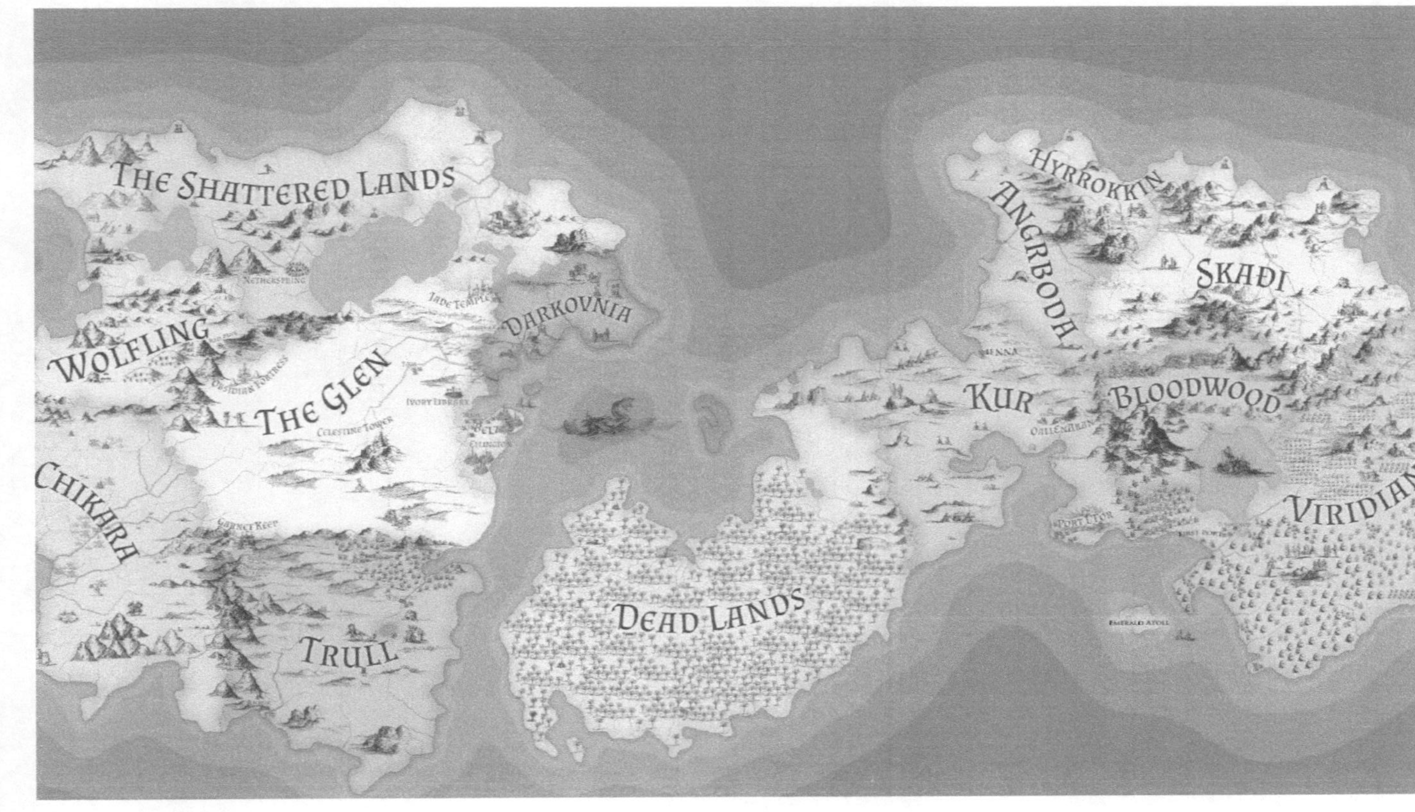

The Shattered Lands
Wolfling
Chikara
The Glen
Darkovnia
Trull
Dead Lands
Kur
Hyrrokin
Angrboda
Skadi
Bloodwood
Viridian

CONTENTS

PART 1 — 1

Chapter 1 – Shield Of Faith — 3

Chapter 2 – Phoenix Rising — 19

Chapter 3 – The Celestine Tower — 45

Chapter 4 – The Dark Army — 65

Chapter 5 – To Absent Friends — 83

Chapter 6 – Through A Glass Darkly — 101

Chapter 7 – Shaken Ground — 119

Chapter 8 – Tide Of Winter — 135

Interlude — 143

PART 2 — 147

Chapter 1 – Chasing Destiny — 149

Chapter 2 – The Guardian — 167

Chapter 3 – Applehead — 189

Interlude — 201

PART 3   205

Chapter 1 – The Plan 207

Chapter 2 – The City Of Fire 225

Chapter 3 – The Arena 243

Chapter 4 – Blood And Dragons 265

Chapter 5 – Lost Secrets 283

Chapter 6 – The Expedition 311

Interlude 331

PART 4   335

Chapter 1 – Unexpected Allies 337

Chapter 2 – Wings Of Fire 355

Chapter 3 – Thorn Of The Rose 371

Epilogue 389

Acknowledgements 393

About the Author 403

"Nightblade."

The name passed Dabria's lips out of habit as she caught herself looking at her best friend.

"I mean...Una." She sounded tense and frustrated, perhaps a little embarrassed. Though they had always been close, Una did not carry her heart the way the dark-haired swordmaster did. She sighed and tucked her feelings behind her cold golden eyes before continuing.

"Look at this map and tell me what your...friend...means by 'the skull mountain of a great prince.' You claim it's a place, but I never heard of it."

Dabria tossed the rolled up parchment onto the dark ironwood table in her chamber. Dust curled up from underneath it. The dark-robed figure stepped forward and pulled her hood back to reveal midnight blue-black hair and two slightly different colored eyes - one hazel, the other gray. Una was quiet unless she had a reason to speak, and at this moment she chose to do so.

"Yes. That's what she says, my dark sister. A mountain of a great prince. Maybe it ties to another name. Dwarvish possibly? I don't know. Hmm, let us take a look. Yes?"

As she answered her own question, Una untied the thin red leather cord that held the stiff parchment tight. As she rolled it out, she saw the cord had been very successful in protecting the red and black inks that danced elegantly across the cloth-like paper. Elvish or draconic, no doubt. No human hands were this skilled at fine detail. The map should be framed, not tucked in the corner of the room. Likely, this was stolen at some point. Spoils of war, perhaps, or possibly from their army's occupation of this city of fire.

There was a heavy knocking on the door; the sound of a mailed hand, thudding and dull. Una quickly lifted a book from one end of the map, allowing it to remember the curve of its roll and close itself up on the table. Dabria nodded at her before calling.

"Enter!"

The thick oak door swung to the side, allowing a guard to enter the room. The heavy dark plates of his armor clanked, grinding together at the joint as he walked. The leather that bound them was oiled, and his helm was wickedly shaped under his dark eyes. Hooking outward, it made him look like a bird of prey. A personal guard of Dekkion, she knew.

As if in answer, the dark cleric himself stepped in, flanked by a bald man in dark robes and a black-haired woman with glowing blue eyes.

"Ah. There you are, Una."

Dekkion's thick boots clung to his thin calves as he walked toward her. His smile was a cheap imitation of caring as his thin chapped lips pulled taut under his cruel eyes.

"I need you to help us see what only you can see, child." His voice was raspy and hoarse, and his stare held everyone in its gaze under thin wispy white strands of hair that draped and framed his gaunt face.

"Now."

Una looked at the bald priest. Sighing, she pulled the hood back over her head as her lip curled back..

"Fine. I'm coming, Mortas."

Mortas snorted as he smirked at Una, following her out the door. His skin always glistened in the heat of this city, and his face and neck were covered in creamy red-rimmed boils that threatened to pop or ooze at any moment. Watching them leave, though, Dabria didn't care. Her eyes were on the woman behind Dekkion. Noticing, Dekkion's eyebrows raised slightly.

"Oh! I apologize for getting in the way of you two. Do say hello."

"Nightblade?" Dabria said gently to her lover, knowing there would likely be no answer. Nightblade's skin was pale now, her eyes filled with the glow of the undead. Dabria lowered her head as she clenched her fists at the agonizing silence. She held onto her anger like a lifeboat in a storm, a storm which threatened her to shed tears. She had sworn those tears would never be seen by him.

Dekkion smiled, sensing her struggle. Drawing up a single thin hand, he sharply snapped his fingers and the silent Nightblade turned to walk out the door. Pausing, he placed a hand on the door and drew it across the wood gently, a cruel smile once again slicing across his papery face.

"So much for love's flame, I suppose."

Chuckling, he shut the door behind him. Silence and dust settled as the sound of their feet began to fade.

Dabria waited a moment before daring to move. Then, with a sigh, she quietly let the tension pour out of her body, as silent as the love of her life had just been. Stepping over to the rolled map, she drew it open again with the glide of her hand. She paused, staring at a point just south of the Shattered Lands, north of the Celestine Tower in the center of the Great Glen Valley.

"I swear I'll free you," she whispered to herself, looking at the ceiling. She imagined open skies and the smell of ocean surf. Remembering for a moment, she plucked it from her heart like a golden rose to treasure forever.

She closed her eyes, allowing a tear to form and draw a line across her cheek.

"My sunbeam."

I

SHIELD OF FAITH

My legs burned slightly from days spent on the road. My eyes felt dusty and my skin was cracked. The smell of the horses and, frankly, our unbathed bodies surrounded us. But all that meant nothing to me at that moment.

"Keldor. Look."

I heard Elloveve's voice break the gentle whisper of the woods as it mixed with a bird's call. "Hmm, look. There's Bemil. I remember it now."

After two decades, we were together again. The warmth of that realization mixed with the warm fall sun on my face. My eyes opened and looked for Benedict, the young squire in training. He was the son and heir to my lord and longtime battle brother, Lucilius. I thought also of his mother, Elona the Fair, as dear to me as a sister would be.

My glance then fell upon Cordelia, thumbing through her book with her head bowed in study. She was so much like her mother Lorahana, who served with us so many years ago alongside her husband, my great friend Erebus Shieldheart.

Oh, how I wished Elloveve and I could show those four missing members of the six winds how their children were becoming heroes. My heart now truly soared alongside the path that day.

Elloveve called my name. "Keldor?"

"Yes, my love?"

"After Garnet Keep fell, we fled to the old country and took an oath to hide the children. What became of our order?"

I looked into her questioning eyes. Beautiful pools reflecting deep oceans, I thought. Again, nothing would take me from this cloud today. I took a deep breath and looked in my mind for the facts, not the feelings, of those dark days which I tried never to recount.

I cleared my throat. "Well, the Knighthood was already clinging to hope like the sails of a sinking ship when we served it. But we all knew that, right? I headed into Trull to serve justice and...well... the coin more often, honestly."

"Hmm, so Trull..."

Sophie's soft voice interrupted my chain of thought. I didn't blame her for being inquisitive. She was smart, too, just not the best of decision makers. Very impulsive; it was a trait that she carried on her own.

She must have lost a bit of her manners because she chuckled.

"What?" I asked, curious as to what I had said that was so humorous.

"You mean the blood pits? In Enruk, right?" Sophie said. I laughed loudly before bursting out with a hearty, "What? Me?"

My voice must have carried more venom than intended, as I startled her with my response. Her eyes, though strong, couldn't hide a hint of the chastised puppy in them. I even saw a faint tremble in her lower lip. We had slowly been making amends after I was called out by her yesterday for keeping my past a secret. It was a secret I was still having issues letting go of but, again, we were together. We were all together and this conversation was actually welcome and, I thought, surprisingly needed.

"No, no!" I laughed a little more warmly this time, "no offense taken, dear Sophie."

My laughter eased her jaw from the locked tension I had seen on the face of so many other soldiers. Other warriors. Other friends.

"Actually, Sophie, I have been helping in small deeds over the last 20 or so years."

"Oh! Well, I heard you did well at the games so I figured you were used to pit fighting." Sophie shrugged, laughing. I just shook my head, chuckling.

"I appreciate your faith in my skills, but no. I'm not good at starting fights." I smiled. "I was more accustomed to ending them." Sophie nodded at me with a smile. I continued. "Much like you, I was living town to town. Living by the sword, helping those in need."

I saw Elloveve's eyes soften. I feared what she might say, so I continued more earnestly. "I had turned my back on my vows to the Knighthood. After all, Garnet Keep was lost, as were you all."

That rushed statement ran through my heart like a blade of fire. The guilt of losing them all, and then almost losing them again was—and still is—a bitter pill to swallow.

Benedict looked up at me from his plate armor, sensing the stumbling in my voice. I looked directly at him, hoping he would understand my next statement.

"...or, so I thought."

Benedict's eyes tore into my heart.

"Did you not want to know if we were still alive? Did you not want to seek us out? Did you..."

"Not care?" That voice wasn't Sophie's. The words may have come from her lips, but it was clear the voice belonged to Zane. I could hear him; they truly had become one person. I braced for yet another hit to my heart, another statement designed to cast me down from flying in the clouds of my happiness today.

"No, Benedict. I remember Keldor loved us all. He was like an uncle to us."

I felt the blood slowly begin to throb in my veins again. My face flushed, almost betraying my fear and distrust of moments earlier.

"Well…thank you Zane. Er…I mean, Sophie." Sophie laughed at me, struggling to refer to them in the proper sense. It was going to take a bit of getting used to. "Whatever!" I laughed as I smiled at them. I felt Sophie and Zane's friendship again.

"Both of you," I added, before turning to Benedict on the other side of me. I winked, a big smile crossing my bearded face.

Benedict's eyes relaxed and he smiled in return. The pleasant fire in my chest rekindled. I would protect and serve this young man, pledging the same oath I gave to his father.

I heard Elloveve chuckle as I felt her gentle touch on the dull, hickory-colored pauldron covering my shoulder. She smiled, and though she seemed to be enjoying the conversation, I found it was her expression that unconsciously urged me to continue, as much as her words.

"So, you went to Trull," she coaxed.

"Yes, yes. I'm sorry," I replied, a bit embarrassed at the distraction. "In my travels there, I heard rumblings. Rumor had it that the Celestine Tower was still as central to operations as before." I paused, remembering the grand tower that reached toward the heavens, more than a thousand feet, made of bright blue and white stone. I could picture the graceful spire itself as though I stood there once again.

"The Celestine Tower?" Benedict said excitedly, "I always hoped to see it, Keldor. Does it still stand?"

"It does!" Lorvana, next to me, stopped playing her little lute and turned toward Benedict with huge, excited eyes. "I've seen it! Tallest I've ever seen! A huge tower stretching into the clouds in the center of the Glen Valley. I would love to see it again." She smiled, tossing her red hair behind her shoulder, then turned back to her instrument and began humming happily. Benedict cleared his throat.

"Do the knights still..." Benedict stopped himself and shook his head.

I sensed he was both craving and fearing the answers to his questions. I sighed and smiled at him reassuringly. If we were careful, we could both help each other avoid falling off our respective mountains. Mountains of good feelings were fragile now, at least today.

"It's truly magnificent, son. The pride and joy of the Knighthood. The steward was, last I heard of course, Lord Alvar." I chuckled, looking at Elloveve as her lavender eyes lit up with a grin of recognition.

"Alvar?!" She laughed happily. "Our mentor is now the Knight Commander of the Tower?"

"Yes! Ha! The same." A wave of fond memories burst into my mind. I saw Elloveve, Elona, and Lorahana. We were talking in the hall as we heard a roaring man's voice yelling down the hallway, followed by a madly laughing Erebus.

"Run! He's coming!" he cackled as he sprinted past us with a pair of shining silver-plated boots. I laughed as Elloveve chuckled, not knowing all I saw in my mind's eye.

"What?!" she asked with a smile. I saw others were interested too.

"Remember how Erebus used to hide his sabatons, or mismatch them, or…" I looked at Elloveve, gesturing with my hand, as if I were passing the memory to her. She easily took it, as if the memory had played itself to her as well.

She laughed. "Or when he swapped them for a size…"

"Slightly smaller!" I finished.

Elloveve and I laughed, and I noticed the children laughing too. Well, they weren't really children anymore. I had no right to call them that, though my heart wanted to.

I looked at them in that moment, grown up. My eyes fell on dear Cordelia, the youngest. I remembered that her mother had just had her not three months prior to the night that drove us all away from each other. When Garnet Keep fell and we lost our family and I lost my way. I thought for sure that the child had also perished with her mother, with everyone else. It was so good to see her laugh. The forge-fire eyes of Erebus and the raven hair of Lorahana Shieldheart. It was like they were both there with us again, too.

"I apologize, I needed that laugh. He was quite the prankster." I smiled before continuing."Well, of course, the Jade Temple and the Obsidian Fortress still stood abandoned, as much as they did when we served the Knighthood. Not much changed there."

"I heard that those were supposed to guard the way north, into those accursed Shattered Lands." Skotmir looked a little shaken by his own statement. I had heard that the culture of the dwarves was very superstitious, and one could possibly say that was all he was struggling with at that time. I wasn't as sure about just brushing it off as that, though. He wasn't wrong.

"Well, Skotmir, they still guard the way north, for what good that did. It's only a wasteland in that direction from what I hear, though. Uninhabited. There's more life in the ghost stories about those two places than is actually there."

Elloveve spoke up. "The Jade Temple was always just a ruin to me, but the Obsidian Fortress... that was menacing, empty or not." She then nodded slowly in thought as she processed what I had just said. She, unlike dear Sophie, was not impulsive.

Zorin tensed his brow in thought. "Hmm. That's four, but I always heard references to five."

"Five?" Benedict questioned.

Zorin smiled wide, embracing his found wisdom before continuing. "Yeah! You know. 'Five bastions of the knights will protect forevermore the' ...wait."

"What?" Benedict could sense a level of sarcasm from Zorin and he braced himself for what may fall from his lips. Whatever it was, it was likely not to be pleasant.

"I...just want to...savor this moment."

Benedict sighed deeply. "And what, pray tell, is..."

Zorin's roguish character got the best of him. He saw his opening and struck with no hesitation. "I know something *you* don't... about the knights?!"

Vix the Chaotic looked up from under his blue-hooded robe. "Feels good, doesn't it?"

"Actually, it really does," Zorin chuckled as we all burst into laughter. Even Benedict joined in once his hurt pride relaxed. Honestly, it was good to let Zorin have that victory. After all, the poor boy had Lord Pallus as a father. Well, however much of a father the man dooming the civilized world to enslavement under a dark goddess could be, I supposed.

When the laughter died, Cordelia broke in. "Actually, Benedict, the fifth bastion is guarded by my order. The Ivory Library."

Everyone nodded in understanding as we continued to walk the dusty northern road.

Little Lorvana pulled her lute from her backpack and began to sing a traveling song that she told me was a halfling favorite.

> *He called for them to help them bring*
> *Back the power of a ring.*
> *They travelled there from worlds so far*
> *To find the crown with moon and star.*
>
> *Ho-ei-oh! Here we go!*
> *We dance across the skies,*
> *We are the heroes over space and time,*
> *There are no graves in which we lie.*
>
> *No graves in which we lie!*

I listened to her strum gently in time with the trotting hooves of our horses and the rolling cart, as we moved south into Bemil. Her simple song lifted me up, and I floated in happiness alongside my restored family.

THAT EVENING, FOR THE FIRST time in what felt like an eternity, we found our first real beds at the Slow Match Inn. Not the best place in town, but far from the worst. I knew it attracted a younger crowd and, frankly, that always helped me relax.

Everyone had gone to bed pretty early, after a dinner of roasted potatoes and flaky baked fish. Lemon and rosemary lingered on our lips. The minstrel that night was intent on playing old, slow ballads. Not bad, mind you, but nothing energetic enough to really hold the wandering attention of most of our tired group. One by one, they politely retired to their chambers.

All, except Skotmir. He simply belched and walked away in a drunken stupor, his belt unbuckled and dragging behind him on the smooth wooden floor. After a moment, we realized that it was only Benedict, Elloveve and I seated at the large table, which we now had all to ourselves. Benedict had just pushed the pewter plate away from him when he looked at me with curious but demanding eyes.

"So tomorrow we return to Ellington. What then?"

"Well, we will meet with the Duke and explain what we found. And, I suppose, see what's next," I stated briefly, off the top of my head. Elloveve furrowed her red eyebrows at my comment. She looked more concerned than I expected.

"What of the rest of the order, or the trade barons?" Elloveve asked.

She drew us closer to the center of the table as she lowered her voice cautiously. "We can't seriously expect to be the only ones who are in this fight?"

"I…" I stammered without looking at her, "I know of no other supporters, yet."

"Yet?"

Her voice was curt and angry which spurred my response. I snapped my eyes back to hers, "I realize what happened in Port L'For was a catastrophic event to you all, but word of it has barely reached this land. I believe it could be downplayed by those in support of Pallus."

She was sitting directly across from me and turned her head to the side to face away from us. A long lock of fire-red hair fell from her shoulder to the table. I could tell she was frustrated. I wanted to brush my hand across the alabaster skin of her soft cheek and tuck that stray lock behind a single pointed ear. Even in this place, she glowered at me.

"Can we reach them?" Benedict's voice snapped me back to the discussion. The cloud of joy that had carried me through the day was finally fading, I realized. I drew in a deep breath as I ran a calloused hand through my dusty and dry beard. I wondered how many gray hairs were from conversations just like this one. Clearing my throat, I began.

"The order...the knights, I mean. It's small but it's not empty, right?" I leaned across the table, drawing them in to do the same, instinctively matching my distance. Nodding at my own statement, I continued.

"Benedict, we have been hiding far away from the order for so long that..."

"Oh, come on!" Elloveve's fist came down hard on the oak table, startling me. I looked at the love of my life, weary and tired from the road. Most importantly, I noticed, she was angry.

I shakily tried to begin again, wary of her building wrath.

"Well, by 'We' I meant..."

Elloveve's voice pierced through the calm evening like one of her arrows.

"You know well enough that we can find others in the order. You've just been hiding behind that...that...stupid beard for so long. Just hiding who you really are!"

Her words found their mark as they ripped into my chest. I felt a wave of anger rise, but every retort died on my tongue before escaping my mouth as I realized none of them would bear any fruit.

Not to mention, she was right. I looked at my blackened armor and faded tunic. My hand went to my beard. It was a hand bearing the scars of many battles. Proud battles.

"If you can find him, that man I knew. *That* Keldor could find an army that believes in this cause in a desert full of nothing but sand and cactus."

Her hand swiftly scooped up the dented pewter goblet for one last gulp of wine. Sighing in the still silence she had created, she nodded and stood up. Her lips were pursed in strong defiance, both at the conversation at hand and, I imagined, to keep herself from saying too much in her fury. She stared a hole right through me, and I could feel the disappointment corroding every word.

"I'm sure of that. On that note…good night."

As she left, my mind and heart beat themselves against the brick walls of guilt raised over years by embarrassment and dishonor. The seemingly endless wellspring of anger didn't protect me that night. I looked at Benedict before bowing my head in shame.

THE NEXT MORNING, WE RE-SUPPLIED basic food provisions and added a few luxuries like cured meats and a waxed cheese. Then, loading into our cart, we continued south toward Ellington. The journey was only three days but, in my mind, it felt like forever. I kept thinking about what Elloveve had said to me and, for the majority of our travel, I remained silent.

On the last night, we camped off the road in a grove surrounded by several hundred yards of golden maple trees and rosehip bushes. Not far away, a small creek ran past. Soon it would be joining with the river that flowed back through Bemil on its way to the sea. Once we finished the bit of unsavory hardtack and jerky we were snacking on for a last meal, I went to the creek and pondered.

The creek was only a yard or so wide at this point. As the water lapped, the night air brought a crispness to the smell of pine trees just beyond the grove of maples. I gazed up at the nearly-full moon, which drew higher above the trees and cast shadows amongst the short ferns and grasses that lined the bank.

After a few moments, the soft crunching of leaves under heavy plated boots told me that Benedict had come, likely to check up on me.

"Keldor? Are you alright?"

"Ah, Benedict. Please sit with me for a moment, my friend."

Wearing steel plate armor will wear anyone down after a while. I believe we all wish for and dread sitting down when the time finally comes. Benedict was no exception. I could hear the plate shift and chain scrape as he groaned to a seated position. As he sat upright, he pulled off his leather gloves and laid them in his lap, turning his eyes to me. I took comfort in knowing I had a friend's ear for a moment.

"The Knightlord protects us as the Maiden holds us. Is...that still true? To you, I mean?"

My stammer had returned, betraying my desire to remain calm and collected. Benedict smiled reassuringly.

"Yes, that is what is written in..."

"No," I interrupted. This wasn't what I meant. I wasn't looking for a sermon, I was looking for answers to the questions in my own soul. I sighed, smiling politely, and continued.

"Not what is written, milord. I mean, do you believe it?"

"Yes."

"Hmmm...that's my problem. If you, my young lord whom I've pledged to, believe it to be so then why do I not?"

Benedict paused for a moment, thinking. The moonlight reflected off the top of his head as he answered. "But what do you believe you should be doing?"

"Well, to that, often I wonder what *they* should be doing."

This made Benedict raise an eyebrow. A smile crossed his lips. "Our faith shouldn't be because we believe the gods will do anything we want, Keldor."

Groaning again, he stood up and looked at me, his blue eyes resolute and proud.

"It is our belief that they will guide us to do what is right." He paused as yawned, stretching backward slightly to adjust the thick breastplate across his chest. It was later than I had anticipated, and now the moon had risen higher in the sky, growing smaller as well.

He looked back at me. "What do they tell you, my friend?"

"They tell me that I...I mean *we*...need an army." I chuckled slightly. How was I going to help raise an army? I had no idea where to start. I had abandoned my post and lost my station so long ago.

Benedict chuckled in response as he smiled. I felt a reassuring peace, then. Like he knew my feelings.

"Then let's find one. Goodnight."

As he went to bed, a wave of realization washed over me. I smiled at the young paladin's words. How simple, yet it was exactly what I needed to hear. A clear path lay before me now, and we needed to act.

THE EARLY MORNING SUN WARMED the dew on the wild raspberry leaves as small, blue-green speckled birds chirped gently in the breeze. The stream continued its babbling in the distance as the smell of cooked eggs filled the campsite. Zorin mopped his beard with a damp cloth, brushing it briskly at the end in case any remnant of his breakfast had become trapped in the soft, dark brown whiskers.

"Well, that breakfast was pretty good, Elloveve!" He sat back and rubbed his belly with one free hand. "I missed those eggs."

Elloveve chuckled. "There's not much magic to them, Zorin. You just have to move them quickly and plate them while they still look creamy."

"Creamy or not, they were better than those beans a few days ago," Skotmir said, with a mouthful of egg he had mixed with some crumbled hardtack biscuit.

"That wasn't my fault." Vix narrowed his eyes at the dwarf as he dug into his plate of eggs with a twin tined silver fork. "They were not soaked like you said they were, and I anticipated you wouldn't salt them. How was I supposed to know you were taking it upon yourself to become a world renowned chef with nothing but salted, DRY beans."

Skotmir laughed, a mouthful of food spraying a few loose chunks into the fire pit. "You always salt the beans while they are dry! Everyone knows that."

The group went silent for a moment before Cordelia cleared her throat, breaking the silence. "Ahem. Um. No, you don't."

"No?" Skotmir's puzzled face gave away that he was genuinely stunned by the comment.

"Nope."

"Oh."

"Well, I think it was…" Elloveve began, until her eyes fell on me as I entered the camp from my meditation in the woods. I had been missing from the rest of the group during breakfast that morning, having been up early with new preparations. New to them, at least. My memory had faded some, but as I worked it had come back to me like a gentle tide. I saw everyone look at me, their eyes wide in disbelief at my new appearance. And amongst those eyes I found myself standing there, bracing against the unknown in anticipation for what they might say.

Sophie stepped forward as she pulled her swordbelt up to drape over a red-armored shoulder. Her blonde hair was pulled back and away from her face.

"Your beard?"

"Yes." I put a gloved hand to my newly smooth cheek. The scraggly long beard had been replaced by a trimmed and oiled salt and pepper goatee.

"It's gone," I continued.

Elloveve set the pan that was in her hands on the ground and stepped toward me. Her eyes were wide, and a gentle smile tugged at her lips.

"You…you look like you did 25 years ago. And your armor…"

I had shaved the beard off, but had also polished my armor. Once appearing dark, almost black, it was now free of the dull tarnish it had gained over the years. As a holy knight of the order, I wore a suit of brass to denote my station. It now gleamed golden in the morning sun. My cream tunic was scrubbed and bleached. I had even brightened up the faded threads of the embroidery to show the crimson sword and crown of our order. It sat prominently over my chest, as I had returned it to display right side out.

I looked at my friends sitting in the camp, and felt a forgotten fire rekindle in my belly. I saw Benedict smile in silent understanding as we both nodded, excited to see what lay in store for us in Ellington.

CHAPTER 2

PHOENIX RISING

The late morning sun baked the into the back of my plated shoulders as we walked through the busy marketplace. Merchants shouted from behind wooden carts and through the occasional open window of buildings as we passed by. Soon, a familiar smell wafted past my nose, bringing back memories from a little over a month ago. I questioned the passage of time as I walked it back in my head, recalling the events day by day to keep it straight. Yes, I thought. It had been 33 days, if I was right, since we were last here in Ellington.

The city was timeless. It was a sprawling metropolis, the largest I had ever been in, comparable only to a few that I could recall. Time had, of late, truly seemed to move as though suspended in a sweet baker's syrup.

I grew up in Belz as the son of a fisherman, and found my faith honestly at the end of a reel. Staring up at the towering statue of the Knightlord in the harbor every day can have an impact on a young man like myself. Leaving a smaller town like that to come to this city was a shock. Even after nearly five decades of being on this land, I still found it awe-inspiring. This smell, though...it was everything pleasant after the road and our simple rations.

I turned to Skotmir, who happily waddled alongside me with his greataxe over one furry shoulder. The ivory of his chipped-tooth grin split his shaggy beard as he smiled up instinctively in response.

"Ho, Skotmir! Do you smell that, my friend?" I gestured to the cart at the end of the row.

Skotmir sniffed through his bulbous nose, then laughed. "Those pies!"

I laughed. "Yes! Come, friends. Let's treat ourselves. Skotmir and I had these during the games, and they are delicious."

"Not as delicious as my victory that day," Skotmir teased.

It was hard to stifle a laugh at my friend's remark. "That's...not how I remember it."

Vix cleared his throat and, without looking at anyone in particular, grumbled. "It's not how *any* of us remember it, for that matter." He walked with a proud stride in his blue robes, protected by his own pride as usual. No one loved Vix more than Vix, after all.

"You weren't even there! Where's your owl, by the way?"

Vix looked at the dwarf, then. He was not angry, simply annoyed at the smile on his face that rarely dimmed. He thought about the owl and, at its mention, instinctively felt for the small winged statuette in his pocket. He smiled, knowing she was still with him. Still safe. He turned his head to the warm white clouds billowing in the sky above and felt a slight breeze touch his golden cheek.

"Happily soaring the skies...far from you, I might add."

The sudden negative comment silenced us. The dust of the road began to turn to sparse stone, a red brick edge marking the next area of the marketplace.

"Wow. That was cold." Benedict spoke, his eyes narrowing at Vix before warmly turning to Skotmir and I, "Lunch sounds great to me as well."

Sophie laughed. "Ha! Yes. As does a tall glass of milk, I'm sure!" she teased.

"Very tall," Benedict chuckled.

"Not as tall as me, though!" We all laughed at Skotmir as he skipped slightly, the axe on his back slapping against bare, powerful shoulders.

It proved everyone was in high spirits that day. Even Vix was chuckling to himself, a faint smile creasing the corners of his smooth, elven face. The journey into town had only been a couple of hours from our camp by the side of the northern merchant road. We had followed that road from Bemil through the forest to the jeweled city of the New World known as Ellington. It was a bustling metropolis of trade and the arts.

Cordelia stared upward, drawing her raven-black hair away from her face and letting it fall about her shoulders.

"Who is that?"

She pointed to the statue of a regally-dressed man holding a quill in one hand and a scroll in the other. The hand holding the quill was resting on his chin in thought. The faint outline of a close-cropped beard trimmed his jaw and his eyes looked back toward the market as if willing it to spring up before him. Surprisingly, no name was found. However, Vix quickly found a quote.

"Trade is meant to serve the people, not the other way around," Vix read smoothly and precisely before he continued. "Ah, yes. Angelos Vasilakos. The first Duke of Ellington. Or the New World, for all we know. It is a *very* rare title to be called Duke, after all. Might as well be called King."

"He led the rebellion," Benedict recalled from his studies.

Vix looked into the young man's blue eyes. "Rebellion is a pretty strong word, I think. Rather, it is more that they just left, really. Something about different ideologies."

Vix stared at the statue rising 20 feet from its 10-foot pedestal. A slight smile cracked the corner of his mouth.

"He was also the predecessor to Vlassis Andreas, the current Duke of Ellington."

The Duke of Ellington was known as a fair and just man. Fifty years ago, a civil war had taken place which had separated the land of Belz from the Trade Baronies of Darkovnia. In the last 20 years, he had healed those wounds and created a city that was a legend in its own time. Angelos led the people of Belz and was elected to the rank of Duke. Dukes were unheard of in the land of the Trade Barons. The people, collectively with Angelos, offered this title to help impose responsibility rather than to establish power. It was a responsibility to look after the people in their care, a responsibility that both Angelos and Vlassis took very seriously.

As we drew closer to the market, the sounds of carts rolling and hawkers yelling became louder. The smells of dust and food cut through the air, as handheld legs of chicken and turkey roasted over rotating spits next to fires charring wooden skewers of seasoned beef and lamb.

It was obvious by the longer lines that these carts were the local favorite. We even saw a few of the older crowd bring their skewers of meat to a baker selling toasted garlic and cheese bread. Here, they would combine the two into what I had heard referred to as a "Rogue Sandwich." Although this looked delicious, I was brought back to the task at hand by the familiar sound of Miloslava Mugwort calling out her wares.

"Meeeeeat pies! Get yer meat pies!"

"There she is, Skotmir!"

"Don't have to tell me twice!" he yelled over his shoulder, as he broke into a happy trot toward the familiar red and cream striped cart. The cart was steaming, warmed by stacks of small handheld packages wrapped with cooking parchment and tied with bits of colored twine. We knew the different colors were her way of keeping the broad selection of flavors straight.

"Meeeeat pies! Get yer meat pies! Steeeeak! Onion! Even chicken!"

The rest of us made our way to the cart and saw the familiar sign for Miloslava's Meat Pies, weathered from the elements. It leaned slightly on the right corner to face the crowd that bustled by and stood nearly as tall as the halfling behind it.

"Greetings! My, don't you all look happy today! Please, step right up!" The vendor smiled at them genuinely, slowly turning some of her flaky wares over on the hot iron table that she used for browning them. The smell of sweet onions, as they sautéed in sherry and blended with the beef, was prominent. This aroma practically danced as it mixed with the scent of buttery pastry gently frying on the side. I could sense Skotmir vibrating with happy excitement next to me, as Cordelia stepped forward.

"Thank you! May I have a..."

"Beef and Onion!" Skotmir interrupted, with a grin so wide his eyes were closed.

"Wha...? But..."

Skotmir pointed at the surprised Miloslava. "Nothing but the best for my good friend here!" He turned back to Cordelia, whose face showed a bit of confusion. "Trust me. The beef and onion, you won't regret."

Cordelia sighed."Oh,ok. I guess I'll have the..."

"Waaait a minute!" Zorin grabbed her shoulder and pointed. "Look, Cordelia, there's a chicken and parsnip one."

"Ooh, I do love parsnips. Hmm."

Cordelia put her hand on her chin in thought for a moment. Both sounded equally delicious. After a moment, she pointed toward one with a purple ribbon.

"Hmm, ok. I'll take that purp…"

"There's dessert pastries, too? At this time of day?" It was Vix's turn to interrupt, and something about his tone implied that he took great pleasure in doing so. Benedict tapped Vix's arm and pointed past Cordelia at the short stack of pies tied with yellow ribbon.

"I'm leaning more toward the venison, there. Cordelia, you would probably like that, too."

Miloslava looked as confused as Cordelia was. When I saw the look on her face I was sure she thought this group of so-called friends was being rather rude.

"Uhh…oh boy," she mumbled, nervously wiping her clean hands with her apron out of habit.

I'm not sure why I didn't step in at the time to try to get everyone to relax instead of piling up on poor Cordelia with demands. I myself may have looked too embarrassed to intervene, but in reality I was simply hoping she would stand up for herself. Friends, after all, especially the closest of friends, should know and respect boundaries.

Miloslava began to pull the pies from the cast iron warmer, trying to keep up with the deluge of inquiries pouring at her all at once. I had to take a step back, as Cordelia was trying to wrest control of the conversation. I could see her emerald eyes darken slightly as they narrowed.

"So, I'll-"

It was then that Sophie angrily raised a gloved hand, whistling to get everyone's attention. It shocked everyone, including Cordelia.

"Hold up, all of you! She can make her own decision, and doesn't need you…"

Cordelia's eyes grew wide as she stamped her foot and raised her voice.

"Would you all SHUT UP!"

We all froze, wide-eyed and awestruck as we looked at the young woman who was now clenching her hands into balled fists. Her chest heaved slightly in frustration. Skotmir approached his furious friend.

"Hey. I get it. I get pretty hangry too."

She shot him a look that would have burned a hole through any other warrior. We all stared at each other, concerned about being so close to the wrath of a fire mage. Skotmir, on the other hand, simply shrugged and turned back to the wide-eyed Miloslava, who was peeking sheepishly from behind the stack of beef and onion packages tied in red string.

"I'll grab a beef and onion, and whatever my friend here wants. My treat."

WE ALL MADE OUR PURCHASES and continued through the street market toward the grassy park that held the Games we had participated in. The grandstands were permanent structures, as were many of the platforms and stages. Sophie turned to Zorin.

"Look at that!" She smiled. "What an arena! The games are quite the production. I bet performing in an arena like this was a lot of fun!" She trotted a few steps ahead and held her arms out like a champion.

"Heh, yup!" Zorin smiled at his friend. She turned back to him.

"I would have loved to perform in a place like this, people cheering my name. Wow, that would feel great!" She beamed at Zorin before looking up at the flanking grandstands.

Zorin took a moment to look around, glowing with pride. He had fought here before and was marked a rogue champion by Elias Silvertongue, the king of bards himself. He had heard people calling his name, and had even been asked for signatures. Sophie was right. It *was* a great feeling.

"You are a master with the sword, Sophie! Seeing you in an arena like this would be awesome!"

He grabbed her in a hug that almost tackled her. They laughed together as we all continued on our way toward the sweet-smelling grass.

We could see the Duke's Keep on the other side of the stadium, about a hundred yards from the last stage. Built 2000 years ago, it was formerly a fortress, its high wall designed to protect the citizens in case of an invasion. That was before the fall of the stone, a time of warlords and raiders who struggled to conquer or, simply survive. Now, the Keep was reduced to only its central tower, which overlooked the city from over 300 feet above.

It was very likely that the baron rarely ascended higher than halfway up the Keep. There was no need to, now. Dozens of giant ballista, last fired over a millennia ago at some airborne flying beast, were now just fixtures on top of the wide battlements. It was unknown if they were still operational and, more importantly, it was hoped that they wouldn't have to be.

In addition to firing upon huge creatures like dragons, these armaments hurled 25-foot bolts of steel and ironwood that could be cabled together in a line, like a wicked bola, to wipe out entire armies. I shuddered at the thought.

That was a long time ago, though.

The gray and rose colored stones from the former outer wall had been repurposed to build the stages and stadium seating. A bold move, it was part of the Duke's plan to fight back against discourse and an actual need for defenses. By providing simple entertainment that was accessible to all, the people were kept happy, entertained, and busy. There would be no need for further defenses. This was a strong and well known philosophy of the dukes.

"Stop! Someone stop that thief!"

The raspy, nasal shrieking startled me from my thoughts. I saw a young girl running from a baker with a loaf of bread in his hand. Her face was terrified as she looked back at him stumbling toward her. Not watching where she was running, she slammed into the broad chest of a man with salt and pepper mutton chop sideburns.

"Oof!" she shouted, as she fell backwards. Her tattered dress hit the soft grass on the side of the road, cushioning her fall slightly.

"Ho there, Lassie! You shouldn't be just stealing," the man stated. He reached down with a scarred arm to help her to her feet. "Now, let's just..."

"I demand she be p-punished!" the shopkeep furiously stammered, his round face beet red. The jog had winded the man to the point of exhaustion. He bent over and placed a thick palm over the blue and gold knee of his velvet breeches to catch his breath.

"T-this is an outrage!" he continued. "What am I supposed to do with a riff-raff like her running around?!"

A crowd was beginning to gather, and it soon became apparent that the shopkeep wasn't alone.

"Yeah," yelled a man with a curled mustache, from behind a dark chestnut cowl. "She's just scum. Look at her!"

A woman stepped forward, her teeth ripping into a roll with a chunk of greasy meat. Scowling at the young girl she added, "Obviously crawled from some trash heap. Or, possibly... the sewer."

The girl was now wide-eyed and trembling. She held out her hands palms up, tears welling in her green eyes.

"But I…I'm so hungry. Please?" She was shaking with fear. The crowd was escalating, their voices rising as they began to circle her like a pack of wolves cutting a calf from the herd. Their mumbling became statements, and those statements were becoming war cries as they fed off of each other.

"What is that smell? Is it her hair, or her clothing?"

"She's probably got diseases and…"

"Diseases?! Oh, no. Send her away! Away, I tell you!"

"Yes! Before we all catch our death, or…whatever that was she's rolled in lately."

The man with the sideburns stepped forward and held out his hands. "Now, everyone, calm down. No need to…"

"You all need to stop!" A young woman walked toward the man to stand at his side.

"Priestess Jessica?" a voice exclaimed. More murmurs ran through the crowd, some in doubt, perhaps. Most, though, ignored Jessica and the white and gold robes that identified her as a priestess of The Maiden.

"Hey, we know her!" Zorin said to me, as we made our way to the crowd.

"Yes, Zorin. From the games, correct? Let's help her and her friend out." I placed my hand gently on the shoulder of a young man craning to see around the others. I'm not the tallest person, mind you, but here I was thankful I could see over the heads of most. He stepped aside, a bit of surprise in his dark-rimmed eyes. Leading on, I parted person after person as we made our way to the center of the crowd.

"Lice. At least she would have lice. Look at the dirt and ABSO-LUTE uncleanliness!" The crowd murmured in response to this latest accusation.

The young girl shook her head. "Please." Her voice was becoming softer as she began to lose her will to survive this. She was beginning to accept her fate, whatever that may be. Matted locks gently brushed the front of her dirty clothes and her dust-caked face as she shook her head.

"Shameful. How are we supposed to eat in the market when she's around?"

"I say we just take her to the pond and give her a bath."

"No! Don't do it!" Jessica shouted, lunging toward the crowd. A large man with a black beard and dark eyes pulled her away from the girl.

"Of course! A bath would be a gift for the poor creature!"

"Yes! Bathe her! Yes!"

"Bah! Such scum should be drowned!"

"The only way to be sure!"

Jessica's friend held a hand to the man in the dark beard. "Ho there! Let her go!" The man reluctantly released Jessica, who immediately drew light into the palms of her hands. This took the audience aback, as they began to challenge themselves about what they were doing. As her palms pulsed and glowed with holy radiance, the man pointed at the crowd closing in on the young girl from the streets.

"No one will touch this girl." His voice was calm and cool before he took a deep breath to shout, "Hear me?!"

The crowd responded defensively. Not surprisingly, the collective spirit was refusing to change course. Voices erupted all around me as I finally drew close to the front of the line.

"Move, or you'll get the same!"

"Yeah, drown him!" a young man said as he took off his triangular red and white cap and mopped the brow of his forehead with a dark blue cloth. I saw a handful of ivory stars embroidered on it.

"Drown them both! He's probably infected, too!" he continued. More of the crowd began to speak up, and the voices ran into each other.

"Out of the way, you fool!"

"Yeah! Filthy, all of them!"

"Drown them! Drown them all!"

I drew my sword and held it toward the sky, briefly reflecting the sun's light into the eyes of the crowd.

"Hold up!" I shouted, as I entered the center of the bloodthirsty group. Everyone paused for a moment out of surprise, taking the time to find out if I was friend or foe.

"I'll pay for the bread," I offered to the man originally chasing the girl, who was still holding the loaf. This *was* a stolen loaf of bread, I assumed. I heard a few murmurs in the crowd.

"Who's the fancy one with the gold armor?"

"PSSH! Looks horribly gaudy. And heavy, too."

The shopkeep smirked behind his mustache and narrowed his eyes. "Humph! We don't need charity from him! In fact...NOW it's not for sale. Begone!" He waved his hand in dismissal. The crowd responded in support of him with cheers and mocking laughter. I stood my ground. I had no intention of letting this shopkeep or the mob of wild dogs potentially take this child's life.

I had seen vigilante justice in other situations, and the outcome rarely was righteous. I also saw the other man's face, Jessica's friend. His head was bald, save for a ring with two thick salt and pepper mutton chops to either side. His hazel eyes went wide when he recognized me and though I sensed I knew him, too, this wasn't the time for a reunion. Someone's life was at stake.

"No," I stated plainly to the shopkeep, driving the point of my greatsword into the ground. I draped an arm over it, both in defiance and to keep from seeming a threat.

These people were wrong and misguided, sure, but from what I could tell they weren't evil. They were just frustrated, dealing with their own ignorance and insecurities. It's easy to attack those who are different from yourself, especially when others help pave the way with their own actions. They were feeling justified and righteous in the moment, feeding off of each other as they drew close to what they believed to be a common foe.

Unfortunately, the foe was only a young girl who had attempted to steal a loaf of bread. But now, in this crowd's eyes, she represented so much more. To one person, she was the cause of the disease that had taken a close family member. To another, she was the same thief who had mugged a friend one night, bringing them close to the point of death for only a few gold coins. Yet one other saw her as just another leech on the pursestrings of society who wasn't willing to work like everyone else.

She symbolized these traits. Though she was guilty of none of them, this crowd was going to make her pay regardless. That is how evil can rise, and how even the kindest people lose their own humanity.

"Get him!" The crowd was wide eyed and feral now, fueled by its own cycle of rage. There was little common sense left, only a common goal that had me at the center of it. This is what I had hoped, to draw their attention to me. *To protect those who can't protect themselves,* I repeated over and over in my mind. They were the words of an oath I hadn't said in a long time.

"We don't need you outsiders!"

Above the din of the mob's shouting, I heard the shopkeep huffing as he drew up a short cane to swing at me.

"I said BE. GONE! AHHH!" To his surprise, I easily caught the man's wrist. My eyebrows raised as I shook my head, looking at the cane clutched in his trembling hand. An arrow had split the cane's shaft inches above our entwined arms. His eyes, once wild, were now wide. Elloveve stepped into the now-frozen crowd, notching another arrow in her bow. Behind her, I saw the rest of my friends fanning out to support if needed. The crowd murmured.

I could hear voices of disbelief and hope. Eyes that were angry now seemed ashamed, and others smiled as if in recognition.

The shopkeep was again not alone in this feeling as well. His eyes grew wide.

"Wait, you are..."

A chuckle came from behind me, interrupting him. The happy voice of the man with the salt and pepper mutton chops defending the girl rang out.

"Keldor Ironfist."

I watched him, looking for a sign of recognition. Time was against me, after all, and worse than that was my memory. He sheathed his sword and stood with one balled fist across his chest. I suddenly remembered him in an archer's dark leather armor, similar to Elloveve's. It was an armor that also had the red Sword and Crown worn by our order.

Smiling, I dropped the shopkeeper's limp wrist and approached my old friend.

"You. I know you... don't I?"

"Lamprey, sir. Sixth Archers of Garnet Keep." He smiled, showing a missing tooth that I remembered well. "I served with you in the battle of the Cheerless Swamp."

"Yes. Yes! Well met, old friend." We clasped each other's wrists in a strong warrior's handshake. The years were gone, but not our strength. We nodded at each other with a warm smile.

"Uh..."

The shopkeep rubbed his wrist with his other hand, trying to ease out some of the ache. Both his physical pain *and* his hurt pride, I imagined. "You are Keldor Ironfist? Th... Then you must be Elloveve Haw...Hawklight?"

The man with the red cap stepped back, his eyes growing wide. "From the 6 Winds? From Legend?! Oh...oh my."

The large man with the dark beard stepped toward Elloveve, offering his hands in surrender.

"Please...forgive us. We only..."

Elloveve threw her hand between them, but he ignored it, approaching her. Sighing, she nocked another arrow and trained it on his broad chest, halting him in his steps. Her eyes went cold as she continued.

"You ONLY meant to take an opportunity to direct your own anger on this...hungry child? Who else would steal a loaf of bread, if they were not simply hungry?"

Elloveve nodded in the girl's direction. She was shaking slightly, and her eyes blazed with anger and determination. It was a familiar sight for me, but from long ago. She continued.

"It shouldn't take me, a stranger to your city and your culture, to protect your own people."

The shopkeep nervously nodded and brought his hands up. His face was laden with guilt as he surrendered to his apparent wrongdoing.

"I...I concur. This is an embarrassment. I...sincerely apologize. Please. Please forgive me. Forgive us."

Elloveve and the baker looked at each other directly. With a tense exhale she lowered her bow and, seeing the look of guilt spread across the crowd, nodded before walking to Lamprey. She clasped his forearm in a soldier's handshake. The crow's feet in the corners of his eyes cracked with a wide smile, glistening slightly.

"Good to see you again, Captain."

"A blessing to see you as well, Lamprey!"

The angry mob had largely dissipated into the bustling streets, leaving me with a very embarrassed shopkeep. I reached into the small leather pouch tied to my belt.

"Hmmm. Here are two pieces of silver for the bread." The shopkeeper was embarrassed by my intentional overpayment, but didn't challenge my offer. Bowing, he took the money with one hand and held the bread out to the girl. She took it quickly.

"Thank you. My apologies," he said as he walked away, his shoulders rolled forward and his head held low.

I turned to the girl. "And two silver for you, Lassie. Get yourself another later."

Her smile was like the noon sun on a welcome cheek, and infectious. We couldn't help but smile in return. Even Vix gave at least a smirk of approval.

"Oh, thank you! Thank you so much…Keldor." She said my name, and turned to trot off under the stone archway leading to the residential area of the city.

"Wait, child!" Jessica called after her. Turning back to us she said hastily, "I'm sorry…but I need to help that one, I think."

She smiled at Lamprey and clasped his hands with her own. "So wonderful to see you again, my friend. Don't let me get in the way of such a grand reunion! Goodbye, Keldor! Good to see you, as well!"

Skotmir smiled. "Good to see you, Jessica!"

She paused. "Wait, is that Skotmir!? And Zorin! Wow! Ok, come and visit me at the temple. It would be good to catch up! Goodbye!" Turning abruptly on her heel, she quickly ran after the young girl.

"Well," Vix snorted, with a sour look on his face. He crossed his arms. "Good to see she remembered YOU all, I guess."

"She was a bit busy, Vix," Zorin said sternly, with a touch of frustration.

"Yeah, she's got a real job there, fancy pants," Skotmir joked with a chuckle. "Unlike us."

"Speak for yourself," Vix said coldly.

A pause of confusion passed across Skotmir's face as he struggled to understand. Casting a glance to Zorin, he saw they shared the same confusion. After a moment, they shrugged and walked behind the rest of us as we resumed our march toward the Keep. Lamprey adjusted his pack over his shoulder.

"Elloveve, are you heading to the Duke?" he questioned.

"Yes, we are." She was happy to change the subject away from Vix's complaining.

"I have news for him, as well. Mind if I join you?"

She smiled. "Not at all. Come, tell me what's become of the company since I last saw you."

"I THOUGHT I WAS CLEAR."

The booming voice of Lord Pallus echoed against the glossy obsidian walls, accompanied by heavy footfalls. A powerful man stood across the table from him, staring at the ancient map that was permanently carved in the granite. Deep, grooved lines were filled with the dust of bright, blue-green agate and set to appear natural. The millenia had been kind, and the map showed no wear.

The man's dark black beard was a single braid falling from his chin. His eyes, so dark blue they were black, were surrounded by dark tattooed circles. He looked at his sister. She, too, was raven-haired and had eyes of darkness. They were both dressed in blue leather scale armor, the cruel jagged pauldrons over their shoulders falling to black velvet capes. Capes like wings.

The silence in the room was thick. Smokey incense that smelled of sweet roses danced gently from a soapstone tray on the table. He looked back to Lord Pallus.

"You were, my lord. It is my duty to-"

"I DECIDE YOUR DUTY, AZURE!" Pallus roared, slamming a fist on the table. They felt the impact, though the table showed no marring or dust where the heavy gloved fist had been. Behind him, a man with flame-red hair leaned against the wall with his arms crossed, an amused smirk on his face. He enjoyed watching Azure squirm.

"Yes, my lord." Azure bowed. He balled his hands into powerful fists that were almost twice the size of Pallus's. His sister placed a hand on his shoulder. Cobalt's touch caused him to relax and shake free. He couldn't oppose Lord Pallus. To do so could be fatal.

"My brother believed we should bring Dekkion to witness the assault. He thought he would like to oversee it."

Pallus laughed.

"He would, Cobalt. Yes, he would. But he is needed elsewhere. He will be sending a detachment of his undead legion from Enruk to meet you there." He pointed to a city far southeast of the continent.

"Led by Dabria."

Cobalt scoffed, "So, we get the Mistress of Pain? Fine."

"And we will be there, as well," hissed a new voice as two more figures entered the room. Squib the Crusher walked in with confidence, flexing a bicep of mossy green skin that pulled tight over her powerful muscles. Long braids fell down her back, swaying across the fur and leather armor as she stormed into the room.

"I will love nothing more than to see these self-righteous knights tremble before my family. Right, Ebon?"

Squib was followed by another orc with jet-black skin and blood-red eyes. He was massively built, and clad only in black boots and a matching warskirt of thick black leather. Ebon's chest heaved and flexed like a gladiator anticipating a fight, though he carried no weapons. He was a foot taller than Squib, but it was clear she was in charge. He nodded in agreement with a crooked grin pulling at the corner of his mouth.

"Good, Squib. We will crush them together," Cobalt said with a smile. Squib caught the sarcastic jab at her name and chuckled. They weren't friends, but each was a means to an end.

Azure laughed as sparks danced in his black eyes like lightning in a storm.

THE DARK WOODEN WALLS OF the Duke's meeting room were familiar, pleasant and rather cozy. The Maiden and Knight carvings in the fireplace caught the light from the fire within, casting shadows that danced across the walls and ceiling. As night fell, a chill became more prevalent in the stone halls, and warmth was welcome. I could smell the sweet birch log burning slowly in the hearth.

"That truly is unfortunate. Most unfortunate."

The Duke was taking the news about the destruction of the artifact as well as could be expected. His hands gently cupped the bowl of a copper goblet as he searched his mind for options.

"Hmm. Well, no use grieving over that which we don't understand." He paused, looking briefly at Sophie. "What was it called again?"

"The green heartstone," she answered.

"Yes...a green heartstone." He repeated her words, but it seemed they were nothing more than just that: simple words for a very complex problem. He turned to the handsome bard leaning against the wall with a hand on his chin, also in thought.

"Does this mean anything to you, Elias?"

Elias Silvertongue sighed deeply before shifting his weight to stand evenly.

"None. I can only hope our friends in the Ivory Library could tell us more, but-"

"Eh, it's no matter." The Duke held up a hand, dismissing any further action. "The more I think about it, it just seems better off having been destroyed than in the hands of Lord Pallus. I know I wouldn't know how to use such a thing."

Silence shifted across the room as we all took in his words. "You...you make an excellent point, your grace. Not to mention, as well, that the return of both Keldor Ironfist and Elloveve Hawklight is an edge we had not foreseen. Such legends. I'll admit I'm a little embarrassed I didn't recognize you before." Elias smiled sheepishly at me.

I shrugged. "I wasn't exactly wishing to be noticed, Elias. I take no offense."

Elias laughed. "True! True that, good sir. But I did write a song about you, after all, and I..." he smiled, winking at me, "...I really should have paid better attention." We both laughed, and the Duke chuckled warmly.

"Regardless, we are happy that you have come to our aid, my friends." The Duke stepped toward us. "Keldor and Elloveve, what do you know of the current state of your order?"

We looked at each other briefly. Her face gave me guidance that I should start.

"Truth be told, we disappeared after Garnet Keep fell to the marauders and didn't look back." I hesitated before continuing, trying to choose the best words to avoid any confusion. "We... believe-"

"We have received word from the Celestine Tower, your grace," Elloveve interrupted. My shocked face showed that this was news to me.

"We have?" I whispered gently into her ear.

"Yes. Trust me," she said briefly under her breath before turning to them again. "May we permit Sergeant Lamprey Kandler to enter this meeting?"

"Oh?" The Duke was particularly interested. "The gentleman with the rest of your group in the parlor?"

"Lamprey?" Elias chimed in. He sounded happy, as though mentioning an old friend. "The owner of the Toasted Frog?"

The Duke smiled in recognition. "Oh! I thought he looked familiar. Wonderful establishment!"

Elias nodded with a smirk. "Absolutely THE best mead, your grace."

"Yes. The same," Elloveve said, taking a step backward and bowing with her arms outward. I recognized this as an elven gesture of respect toward a correct decision.

"Yes. If you so desire." The Duke clapped his hands three times, quickly. The door creaked open and a guard peeked through.

"Your grace?" he asked.

"Viktor, can you fetch Mr. Kandler?"

"Right away, your grace."

The tall, strongly built guard walked heavily away from the door into the next room. I'll be honest - I hadn't paid much attention to the conversations between Lamprey and Elloveve on the way to the keep, but apparently they were catching up on more current events than I had thought. Ha. She was always a step ahead of me.

As soon as the guard's steps had faded I heard them return, with Lamprey marching alongside him. Both had a stride indicating purpose.

"Your grace. May I introduce Lamprey Kandler, sole proprietor of the Toasted Frog."

Lamprey turned to the guard with a quiet voice. "Thank you, sir."

As Viktor closed the door, Lamprey cleared his throat.

"I am at your service, truly noble one."

The Duke smiled and motioned for the kneeling soldier to rise.

"Well met, Mr Kandler. Elloveve told us you may have word of the order currently within the Celestine Tower? Is this an accurate assumption?"

Lamprey dusted off his knees before continuing, and there was urgency in his voice.

"Yes, sir. I received word from an old compatriot and friend of mine that in recent weeks there were rumors spinning 'round. They were reporting a lot of activity northwest of the Tower." He paused to catch his breath. Lamprey had worked himself up some, and it seemed he was trying to de-escalate himself. Drawing a slightly smoother breath, he continued. "Well...when scouts were sent out, they reported activity coming from the...um...Obsidian Fortress."

My heart dropped as I heard its name.

"What?! That's...that's not possible. It's been abandoned for centuries!" I was horrified, thinking about my next words and what they could mean. "Guarded by-"

"Guarded by the curse!" My heart sank as Elloveve looked at me, finishing my statement.

The Obsidian Fortress was a bastion supposedly cursed by the Knights of the Glen centuries ago, to never allow anyone in until the order was restored or required. Powerful magic would be needed to negate that curse. Not to mention that, as I understood it, the people of Wolfling were neither hospitable nor receptive to anyone living in that tower. Ever. If Pallus was setting up his base there and not in Enruk as we originally thought, it would be very concerning.

"Yes...the curse..." The Duke paused for a moment, recalling what he might know about this. It was a legend, but not a widely known one this far east of the fortress itself.

"Forgive me for not recalling specifics." He looked at Elias.

"Allow me, your grace. The legend has it that when the order began to lose members, following the mutual separation of the forces from Bloodwood and Veridian they decided to put in place magical wards to protect the five bastions. Well, since the Obsidian Fortress was so close to the Wolfling barbarians and the Shattered Lands, it was decided upon to use an old dark magic to seal it...and seal it as close to permanently as possible."

Elias suddenly stopped pacing, his mind hanging onto his last words. Realization set in.

"Wait. Oh, no."

"What?" the Duke responded, as we listened with an anticipation so thick you could hear the air moving against the walls of the room. After a moment that seemed an eternity, the Duke stepped toward his advisor and put a hand on his shoulder. His voice was quiet, careful and reserved as he continued.

"Elias...what did they use to seal it?"

"Blood. The blood of the original Six Armies from the War of the Stone. The blood of those that formed the alliance that made their order in the first place."

"He could have collected blood from Viridian and Bloodwood. He had conquered them at least partially by the time he attacked Port L'for," Elloveve offered the room.

The Duke nodded.

"And If he's been set up in Trull for as long as I've heard tell, then he's had access to the blood of the dwarves, elves and men of that region, as well. I assume that would help complete this grim portfolio."

My hands were cold now, despite the fire. My head throbbed with a deep worry as my brow furrowed. The people within the original armies were lost to time, but the legend stated it consisted of six armies. It was the Hammer and Ax armies of the dwarves, the Tree and Stream armies of the Elves and the Stag and Wolf armies of man. I sighed before turning to Elias and the Duke.

"The only organized army in these times that could oppose him is The Knights of the Glen, but the Celestine Tower is the last remaining outpost of my order…last I heard."

"That's true, sir. The knights slowly faded into antiquity, they did. Heh. Only us old salts remain. They are still training there, though, and it's not a small force. Maybe not as big as in the days before…but they are still there."

Elloveve turned toward Lamprey.

"Lamprey, if the word you received is true, then the Celestine Tower would be his strategic next step."

"Of course." Elias's voice became slightly darker. "If it should fall, then the free people of the world can expect no assistance from an inevitable doom."

"Hmmm." I stepped toward the mantle of the great fireplace and rested my hand on it. I saw the Knight bowing to the Maiden as she held out a chalice, offering life. Gliding my hand across the carved wood, I felt the Knight's sword under my fingertips. I remembered my vow, my promise to Benedict. I knew what we must do.

"Your grace, I will set out with my party in the morning. We will march to the Celestine Tower."

The Duke nodded and placed his hand on my shoulder.

"Sir Keldor, yes. Please do go with haste. I can only hope this is a false alarm, but we should plan for a storm. Godspeed, my friend. And may the Knight and Maiden watch over you now."

CHAPTER 3

THE CELESTINE TOWER

Mud and slush sloshed in the courtyard as horse-drawn carts moved thick posts and timber. The sound of drivers shouting at each other as they navigated the crowd was dulled by the stained glass window of the library.

Ayla Forsythe sat in a smooth, ancient chair made of rich purpleheart listening to the work being done outside. The smell of a beeswax candle burning added a hint of honey to the pine in the fireplace several yards away, warming the room of knights and knights in training. She rubbed her palms together, coaxing blood back into her fingers before picking up the quill from the inkpot. She gently smoothed the pages of the open journal on the table as she leaned over to write.

> *"1523 First Snowfall. Squire Ayla Forsythe, 4th infantry pikeman. This journal I hope to pass on to my father so he may see the deeds of his daughter and feel he sired something other than another plowman whose hands were raw from the lines of the ox under a yoke. This is far from that life, and rarely does something here remind me of it. Reminders or not, I do miss*

it. I miss our rolling fields of corn and the groves of tomatoes and-"

She paused to chuckle to herself.

"The knight as my witness, I even miss mucking out the stalls in the morning before the sun gets too warm. I miss the sun. These days have been over-cast in a milky white and gray haze both from the clouds far above and the large bonfires ablaze to rally around behind these cold, high walls.

They keep us warm as they stay lit through the night. A light that gives us a false sense of security, like the candle in my baby brother's room. Something to chase back nightmares and shadows so they may rest. But the tower behind me does far more to scare away any shadow, I could imagine.

For anyone who has never seen it... it is truly a sight to behold. When I first came within a day's journey from it I could see it in the distance, silhouetted against the setting sun. Almost menacing.

After that evening's camp in the soft grasses by the side of the central road, I rose and began the morning ritual of preparing the coffee. The breeze was gentle as I prepared the coals from the evening with the small kettle. I was startled by the chirping cry of some small birds fluttering a bit close to our camp.

I looked up and saw that tower in the dawn's golden light behind me. My breath was lost in the morning dew cast about on the tall grasses. The distant ivory color, I imagined, was glowing in amber and gold as if warmly in greeting, or welcoming us. As we traveled closer, the details became more clear.

The central tower ascends 1200 feet into the sky, easily providing the assisted eye with the ability to see the whole valley - I imagined - from its flat top. The mere thought of standing that high on a simple 20 foot wide platform- the feeling of soft wind at my back- well, it made my head reel.

Six relatively smaller towers stood alongside it, about half that height, surrounded by a 60 foot high wall that encircled them for almost a half mile in any direction. The wall was made of creamy limestone with parapets, walkways and accents of a deep blue travertine. As we ascended our cart up the hill to the large central gate I noticed the ground it rests on is majestic as well.

Standing in the center of the flat glen valley are twenty miles square of hills, with the Staghorn river running from them north to Tova, then into the south of Darkovnia where it enters the sea north of Bemil Bay. The hills are covered in the soft velvet of thick grass common to the whole glen, covering them like a carpet, though this time of year they were laid flat and browned from the first frost a few weeks ago.

When I first arrived here six months ago, the soft emerald grass and sweet yet tart-smelling violet and white meadow flowers were calming and delicate despite the sense of the overwhelming power they lived near. Now, they lay below a shallow layer of snow, a snow that in our camp churned up the cart ruts to a cold mud that clung to our clothes and smelled of dust and rot."

Ayla flipped a few pages back in her journal to glance at the crude map she had made from her first days. It showed a simple overhead drawing of the central tower and its six supporting ones, each now named. The two at the top were marked as The Knight and The Maiden. These were the towers originally for the galley and armory, she had noted. The two in the center that stood on either side of the central tower were marked as the Judge and the Hag. The library she was in was also within the Hag's tower. The tower of The Judge held meeting rooms and the large ceremonial hall they had all taken their vows in. Finally, the lower towers were The Prince and The Ferryman, where they found sleeping quarters and the infirmary.

She smiled at the organization and how the building honored the six gods equally. Ayla sighed then, thinking of the changes to the organization and how the rooms were changing. Everything was being repurposed, even herself and the other troops. Dipping the quill she prepared to write again, imagining her day as if reliving it all over.

"Earlier today I was reviewing my notes in this journal during a break when Silvie approached me.

"Ugh... hmm... Hey, Ayla?" she grunted. I admit, I was a bit lost in thought.

"Huh... wha?"

"Put your book down and help me with this platform, will you?" Silvie was straining to lift a five foot disk of wooden planks herself. I was embarrassed to have ignored her need for assistance as long as I had.

"Oh! Yes. Yes, of course, Silvie."

Setting down my book on the edge of the barrel I was standing next to, I took a few short steps to grip one end of the thick oak and steel bound disk. It was easily as heavy as one of the stones we had unloaded earlier and I marveled that she was able to get it as far as she did without any help.

"That's it... Just a little more to me here- Yes!

"Whew! Is that the last of it?" I turned to Silvie while still panting. She smiled proudly.

"Yes. This will now be the base of the war machine." She chuckled, thumping it heavily with the heel of her palm. *"They will build it tomorrow. Ha! Not us, this time! You just get to run it."*

I laughed nervously at this. I was feeling very anxious about this new change in plans but I trusted her judgment. If she was confident, I should be too.

"You will do great." She paused to sigh before kicking a stone off the platform. *"Not the same as being up front like we trained for, but you just show them what we can do!"*

I nodded at her as she turned to walk away. Silvie is my company's Captain and a great leader. The whole company respects her as if she were our mother, but she is more the older sister, I think, and thankfully so.

"Gustav! How are you?" I heard her voice change to a jesting tone. "Too heavy?"

Laughing, she clapped Gustav on the back. I saw her then greet another brother in the company who was drinking from a waterskin, resting after setting up his own barricade. She had a genuine smile we had come to expect and look forward to. I looked back at my barricade. The 5 foot wooden stakes were sharpened to points and arranged in a menacing spiral down the 8 foot length of it.

"Ayla, looks good! " Gustav laughed while walking over. "Hahaha! Ah... I think these positions are about as good as they are going to get."

"Gustav... Do you think this will stop them?" My question caused Gustav to pause for a moment. I could tell we all were a little unsure of ourselves.

"Hmmm. In theory it should at least slow them down from reaching the gate."

I looked back at the main gate behind me. The massive twin doors were each 40 feet high and 40 feet wide. Made of oak bound with heavy iron beams, they were designed to swing outward...although that was a rare occurrence.

Gustav pointed at the smaller door to the right.

"Especially the pet doors," he chuckled.

*We all had nicknamed the 12 foot square portcullis
on the right door the "pet door". This was the gate we
actually used to enter and exit the tower courtyard.
The main gate, to my knowledge, was rarely used.
In fact, once I thought more on it, I had NEVER seen
it open.*

The echoes of dinner plates and the neutral conversation of a few hundred people filled the stone halls as we walked. The familiar smells of roasted meats and bread soon followed. Skotmir hastened his step toward the front of our party.

"Mmm... now THAT smells pretty good to me, Keldor. Let's hurry up."

Replacing him I saw the blue robes of Vix stride next to me.

"Do you honestly think we will be welcomed as some 'great help?'" He sniggered quietly, his voice thick with doubt as usual. Looking around, he raised his eyebrows slightly before he continued. "It seems to me they have everything under control."

Sophie shook her head and chuckled, slightly exasperated.

"Anyone can need help, Vix." She looked away in thought. "Many times those that appear to not need it are those that actually need it the most."

Elloveve smiled. "Well said, Sophie."

"Wow. This place is beautiful," Cordelia said in wonder, running her hand along the smooth limestone in the hallway as she walked.

She pulled her hand away briefly so as not to disturb the threadbare old banner hanging on the wall. The crown and sword were embroidered with a thin gold thread against the deep blue heart of the emblem. The resident Knights obviously took care, for the blue had faded slightly in places. She smiled in curiosity as a question arose in her mind.

"Does anyone know why the knights use a crown and sword for their symbol?"

Benedict shrugged. "I was told it was to show how power should be protected. That law needed something or someone to ensure it was followed." He looked at me. "Right, Keldor?"

Truth be told, I was always uncertain of the origin of our order. There were no kings to serve, as we served the people, and not all knights carried a sword. I looked at Elloveve as she smiled gently and shrugged, chuckling. I smiled too.

"I'm not sure" I began, "but I suppose we are in the right place to find out. I can tell you the obvious. The reason it's blue is because this is the Celestine Tower. Every tower has its own color that is worn."

I looked at the faded red sword and crown on my chest and sighed. I wasn't sure what to expect when others saw it. Silence followed for a few moments until I heard Vix speak to Cordelia as she again marveled at the walls as we walked.

"The flow of magic here is strong. Raw, almost primal, isn't it?"

She looked back at him. "Is that the-"

"-dragon magic?" He interrupted with a smile. "Absolutely. Ancient and powerful, but untamed."

I watched Vix take a moment to let the feeling of power course through him. I imagined the ancient flow of magic that was hidden within the walls probably wasn't something he often came across. We knew he was well accustomed to the chaos of wild magic. In fact, it's what gave him his nickname: Vix the Chaotic.

"You see - I cannot wield the magic of the dragon, little mage. To do so I would need to become a librarian, like you." He couldn't hide the bitter jealousy on his tongue, I noticed. I raised my eyebrows at him, hoping to quell the rising tension. Vix's eyes locked with mine for a moment, and he sighed,before shaking his head free of some unknown dark thought.

Clearing his throat, he continued.

"It's perfect, to be sure. These halls echo with the power of creation itself, Cordelia."

I saw it was Cordelia's turn to raise an eyebrow at the sorcerer.

"Indeed," she said, as the hall filled with a cacophony of voices. We had begun to open the doors to the dining hall.

We entered the dining hall for the west section of the Central Tower, located on the second floor. The first floor was divided into quadrants, consisting of four Armories and supply storage. The vast dining hall was originally built to cater to four thousand individuals in three rolling shifts. Upon entry we could see this was a poor expectation to have. Benedict's smile faded as he saw the room.

"Um... is this all that remains of the Knights posted here?" He leaned over to whisper to the puzzled dwarf next to him.

"Skotmir, would your people answer the call if we were to reach them?"

Skotmir turned to Benedict. "If we had a month to reach the Garnet Mountains and another to come back...maybe."

I saw the look on Skotmir's face. This request troubled him and I knew it wasn't an easy journey for him. He held his ghosts of war in the past, as well.

"I could try, but I doubt I'd be able to-"

I interrupted briskly. "Unfortunately my friends, time is something I fear we do not have."

Skotmir looked at me, despite my message affecting our cause, with a thankful smile on his face. His ghosts would have to continue to wait to find peace, I supposed.

I turned toward the crowd of my shield brothers and sisters and felt their eyes on us. Whether they were sitting down at the long wooden benches or making their way through the meal line they turned toward us newcomers in the doorway who had invaded their dining room. Spoons hovered for a moment as an army of eyes stared at us first in curiosity and then in some disbelief or even confusion. I saw them start whispering to each other.

Heads turned and hands shielded lips from betraying their words and as the silence took hold over the room I heard a familiar voice ring out from the crowd, accompanied by plate steel boots, called sabatons, striking the concrete as he walked.

"Hail Keldor! Lamprey, you did more than deliver our message I see!"

"Hail Lord Alvar!"

We clasped each other's wrists in greeting. Lord Alvar was formerly our instructor within these very walls almost three decades ago. Many memories of that time flooded over me. I could see the six of us sitting in this dining hall near the door. I bet if I looked hard enough at the grain of that table, it would tell our stories better than any book. The same could be said of the wooden swords in the squire's training area. I couldn't help but smile at the feeling of belonging somewhere again.

"Hail Lord Alvar!" Elloveve said with a broad smile like a daughter greeting her father after a long time.

"Elloveve! You look the same as when I last saw you." He chuckled, taking her wrist in the same greeting. "Pity. I seem to have misplaced my supposed elven heritage many years ago. These wrinkles keep appearing each day!"

"Well you still look as strong as ever." She laughed.

"Ha! You speak such wonderful lies my dear." He nodded as his smile faded, his tone growing increasingly darker. "Elloveve if you would please, bring your friends and follow me. We need to talk."

We walked through the seating area past the familiar long wooden tables, the reddish tones of the wood oiled and polished though they shared their own darkened battle scars from years of use. They faithfully served those stationed here as a place to rest for a moment, converse and take in a meal. The hall's smells echoed with citrus, steamed rice and smoked trout. Arriving at the far end of the room we came to the second entrance to the great war room of the Celestine Tower.

Alvar motioned us to enter ahead of him as he held the door.

"Now I realize you're probably wanting a bit of refreshment following your journey. Let me ask one of our returning folks to assist." He turned to shout out the doorway at a few soldiers that had just entered the dining hall themselves. "You there! Private!"

"Hail Lord Alvar!" The young squire called back, her voice carrying well over the room. She approached Alvar after twenty paces or so. I noted she was quick. Likely a great foot soldier if she could close the distance like that with an enemy. Alvar was still a great trainer.

"How may I assist you?" she said

"Can you request a spread for…let's see," He turned counting out all of us in the room, "eight, nine… ten! Ten from the galley?"

He halted for a moment looking at Skotmir's face, "Second thought, better make it eleven."

Skotmir beamed his chipped tooth grin.

"Absolutely, consider it done sir!"

"Thank you, uh…" He hesitated trying to recall her name. No one could fault him though, there were many of us in his service.

"Ayla sir. Ayla Forsythe." She said with a polite chuckle.

He smiled, "Of course. Forgive my memory. Thank you Ayla."

As she walked out of the room Lord Alvar shut the heavy door behind her. I chuckled as I sat down at a sturdy oaken chair around the wide table with the rest of our group. Benedict, Sophie, Skotmir, Vix, Lorvana, Eralin, Zorin, Lamprey, Elloveve and myself made quite an impression in the small room I hoped for.

"Well you are still sharp as ever." I joked. Alvar smiled back at me

"Ha! Usually I got that treatment from Erebus. How is he?"

The mention of our old friend stung more than I thought it would. Especially the genuine smile on Alvar's face. He didn't know. Elloveve gently put a hand on my shoulder, her eyes mirroring the ache in my heart.

"He's gone, Alvar. As are Lorahana, Elona and-"

Lord Alvar's sigh was heavy. "Ah... Yes I... heard about Lucilius. I had hoped, though."

Elloveve lowered her head for a moment. Looking up, her eyes went to Cordelia, Sophie and Benedict and she smiled slightly, her purple eyes brightening.

"But they are their children."

Lord Alvar beamed.

"By the Knightlord's hand." He gasped walking to Cordelia with a broad smile.

"I can spot the look of Lorahana with you child. Am I correct?"

Cordelia nodded. "She was my mother sir."

He laughed, "You seem to carry a similar- sacred fire about you as well!"

Lord Alvar was keen at spotting people's strengths. His gray eyes were never the best at seeing the physical world and now I could see the pupils hazy with the fog of age. His proud beard looked coarse and wiry. The former blonde cast a slight gold at the corners of his mouth and his head was now greatly thinning on top. The long hair pulled back from the temples and sides in proud warrior's braids still. He was once tall now the weight of the world had pressed our old mentor down slightly. Though I could tell none of this had dampened his valor and spirit.

He walked to Benedict.

"Hmmm... You are- ah!" He gasped and clapped his hands together like a schoolboy answering a quiz. "You obviously carry the blood of Lucilius with that chin and the hair on your head. No mistaking a Kettlebane there but your eyes- Those eyes are none other than Elona the Fair to be sure!"

Benedict smiled and stood up from the chair only to bow to the Lord of the Celestine Tower on a single knee. Pride filled my heart at this humble display of chivalry.

"My lord I wish to serve you and this order as my parents before me." Benedict said with his head bowed.

Lord Alvar smiled as he turned to me. There was no sarcasm in his eyes, only the question I expected him to ask.

"Your take on this potential squire Keldor? Or of course you, Elloveve?"

"He is a valiant warrior. Young but righteous." She responded and I nodded.

"I echo Elloveve's assessment. Benedict's service I believe can benefit the order and his goals are noble." I hesitated with my next statement but knew it was the right time, whether or not I was ready for the answer.

"I.. I wish to assist him in reclaiming his name and rightful place at Garnet Keep."

Lord Alvar looked at me seriously as my heart rose in my chest.

"We shall see, Keldor." He said, emotionless. "But now there are more important matters to be dealt with I'm afraid."

His answer wasn't what I hoped for but it also wasn't a no. There was still hope we could prove ourselves and restore Garnet Keep. This was all my heart desired–to find redemption–but for now it had to wait. Lord Alvar turned to Lamprey who was cracking a peanut he had found in a center bowl of mixed nuts.

"Lamprey I see you delivered our message and thank you for bringing everyone here. As you can see our situation is grave and all of you are needed I fear."

Alvar looked worn down. More so than his years told. Then there was a rapid knock followed by the door bursting open.

The welcome and familiar smell of salty chicken steamed with local spices and root vegetables entered the room before the soldiers accompanying them did. We turned to find three young knights and their Captain bringing in four large serving bowls of the steaming stewed chicken with four large loaves of fresh bread. Memory flooded over me.

I remembered Erebus laughing at the table with Lucilius over some joke. Elona easily laughing alongside them. Lora was a bit quieter, like myself, but we still needed and enjoyed the company of our friends. This was the day Elloveve first joined our unit as scout archer. I looked at her now and she smiled knowingly.

"Ah! here it is. Familiar to some of you I'm sure." He chuckled as he winked at Lamprey who was laughing. "He hasn't changed."

"And I'm sure it is just as welcome sir."

"Welcome back friends." The powerful young man next to Ayla as the group bowed to us.

He was in his early 20's, I gathered. Even the Captain wasn't much older than Benedict.

"Thank you. For your hospitality." Vix nodded to them politely.

I recognized the embroidered ball crowned in flames that graced their tunic's left breast. I turned to their captain,

"Captain?"

"Silvie, Sir"

"Captain Silvie," I motioned at the emblem they all wore. "Trebuchet. Correct?"

"Yessir. Newly formed." She answered.

Elloveve shifted in her seat slightly. She met my eyes with a look of worry. She knew why I was asking. This meant one thing.

"What unit were you with before?"

"We were part of the 8th Infantry." Captain Silvie answered with a note of hesitation in her voice.

Elloveve nodded with a smile in acknowledgement. I cleared my throat before I continued.

"Well, my brothers and sisters. May the Knight and Maiden guide your hand on the battlefield."

"Thank you sir." The Captain answered as they turned and left the room. When I heard the door shut I turned to Alvar, this time with more urgency to help my old friend expedite to the point.

"Trebuchet, Alvar?" He nodded with a sigh. Now confirmed this was indeed dire times, I pressed further.

"Then tell us my friend, when are you expecting a siege?"

THE CAMP WAS ANKLE DEEP in thick mud churned up from the invaders' activity. Heavy carts laden with crude swords, lances and shields passed between the various tents and campfires. These were made by dwarves they were told but they seemed less quality than most would expect.

The air was cold and the breath froze for a moment in slow fog when leaving their mouths. There were faint scents of dirt and wet ground with occasional foul and rancid overtones. The units all had set up their own base of operations. The infantry were primarily orc and human units. There were also several blue dragons at the far end of the camp leading with their riders and an undead legion. The sounds of jogging feet and the slap of chain links against leather cut into the night air.

Rogmesh panted as they jogged through the slush of the mud and muck between the tents. The encampment was organized into rows and they drew close to the end of the orc legions now. Looking to their left they caught glimpses of a blue dragon crouching over a few sheep it had collected during a scouting flight to the northeast. Its horns were swept back and jagged, allowing it to fly faster than most despite its size.

Rogmesh huffed as they took a right at the last tent in the row and continued jogging. One stray orc stepped in front of them but was surprised to find his body skidding on the ground when Rogmesh barrelled through them.

"M...Move!" Rogmesh shouted as they passed the soldier clamoring to get back on his feet.

There was no time to stop unless they wished the wrath of the mistress of pain. A few more yards and they came to the tent they were seeking and dreading.

"Hooooold... Staaate your Naaame and Puurrposssse..." The wicked voice hissed out as the tent's guardian, a skeletal warrior clad in dark armor, raised its glowing blue green eyes.

"Rog.. Rogmesh Tuskborn with-" Rogmesh struggled to catch their breath. "A message for Mistress Dabria."

A deep silence became apparent. Rogmesh for once could feel a chill race up their back as reality set in. The soldiers here didn't move. They had no need to. They were already dead, including the guard, Rassler, before them.

There were stories about Rassler circulating in the darkest corners of the barracks, away from the officers' ears. Some said Rassler was once a powerful warrior that was cursed for betraying a powerful necromancer. Others said she was the product of an experiment on herself. Whatever the story was, Rogmesh was positive they didn't want to get close enough to find out. Rassler stared empty at them now, taking their time as only the dead can appreciate.

"Enter." Rassler hissed like steam escaping a rusty kettle and pulled the curtain back revealing a room with two figures. They stood around a table talking quietly.

One was cloaked in the shadows of dark hooded robes, a vibrant spear in one hand. A faint jawline was all that was visible. They were talking to a young woman who was leaning over a map on the coarse wooden table. A finger place marked the discussion from an anticipated interruption. Her canary blonde hair was cut short to the scalp framing her taut skin around the high cheekbones. Her thin lips were emotionless as her gold eyes looked at her new guest.

"Yes? What brings you here, swordsman?"

Rogmesh gulped air instinctively in fear, "Umm... a letter. A letter from our spies on the front lines, Mistress Dabria."

"Excellent. Put it here."

She motioned with her other dark gloved hand to the table. As he placed the envelope on the table with the black wax seal facing up, he paused. Rogmesh noticed her dark black armor was fitted with a skull at the center. This was just below a single goat's horn that swung from a length of cord around her neck. The armor hugged closely to her torso with short blue-black pauldrons at the shoulders, accented with small wisps of smoke that seeped from it disappearing in the air only an inch or two above. She bored her eyes into him without. Saying a word.

"Are you still here?" Una chided musically, "Or is there something else my little carrier pigeon?"

"N..No mistress Una I meant no disrespect I-"

Dabria dropped her hand heavily to the table, "But yet you give it. Leave us, NOW!

"Oh! Y..Yes! Forgive me!" Rogmesh scrambled over themselves fumbling with the heavy canvas tent flap before finally running as fast as they could back to the orc encampment to celebrate being alive.

Dabria chuckled as she smirked. "Well what DO they have to say in this letter my dark sister?"

"Let us find out, shall we?" Una handed the letter to Dabria.

Dabria ran a sharp fingernail along the wax seal shaped with a stylized D. This was a common symbol used by some merchants to mark their documents when they were too cheap to have their own seal made. Unfolding the letter, the corner of her lips pulled back in cruel satisfaction.

"Well it seems his heir is now in the Tower itself."

Una clasped her hands together and smiled behind the dark hood.

"Excellent news, my Dark Sister. She will be pleased." She looked back at the map on the table and pointed at a few green and blue lines clustered together.

"Our assault in the morning should prove most interesting."

THE DARK ARMY

Voices yelled in the distance as their breath heaved together in unison. The sun hung low in the morning's still air as the metallic scent of blood mixed with mud and wet snow wafted around them. A black bird's harsh cackle came from the branches of a lonely broken tree twenty yards away. Captain Morren adjusted her silver helm, pulling the topknot of blue horse hair away from her face and adjusting the chinstrap.

"Ah. The ravens feast early this day."

"Yes Captain." The dark-eyed Bryce was out of breath and leaning on his long sword. The crumpled body of an orc soldier lay face down in the mud where Bryce had driven him just a few moments before. He wasn't celebrating his action, but was still happy to be alive.

"Quite so... hmm." he spoke more to himself than to her. She looked to the rest of her unit. They were a smaller infantry unit, drafted to hold the hill to the south of the keep. Not the expected location for a frontal assault but an important flank nonetheless.

"Benedict." Her gauntleted hand rested on his armored shoulder a moment. He didn't stir or react, she noted. He simply stared at the ground leaning on the battle worn two handed greatsword.

His armored chest heaved for a moment while he was resting and trying to slow his breathing.

"Three." Benedict sighed between breaths. "Three. Oh wait- we've lost four." His voice cracked at the sudden realization of the loss of four comrades. Four new friends who had smiled just hours earlier as they took their position on the battlefield. Now their bodies lay lifeless, no longer joking about the meager breakfast of oats and eggs or about Captain Morren's unwavering attention to detail.

A slight breeze once more carried the smell of iron and blood across the icy cold air of the field. He could see other units and skirmishes still battling, the closest 100 yards away. They were in a position far to the south of the attack's center, primarily fending off or intercepting small units of Orc and men that were attempting to flank the order's outward defense on the battlefield. He noted the sun's position still low in the eastern sky and hidden slightly behind the tower at his back. It felt like it had been hours, but it was merely the beginning.

The cold air shattered with the sound of warhorns again and the distant thunder of another wave of boots stomping towards them. He looked back to his Captain as the roar came from the invaders to the west.

Bryce stood up and shouted to the dwarven shield maiden ten or so yards to his right. She stood staring into the distance, on the end of a toppled cart they used for cover from archers earlier. Studded with a few dozen feathered shafts stuck into the oak and iron underbelly.

"Ridley, can you see anything left of their vanguard?"

"Nay! They seem to be all gone. This is fresh for us sir! How bout you Mallius?" she laughed teasingly to her friend, "What do your pretty elf eyes see?"

The slender elf laughed as he drew his longsword again. "Same as you!"

As Ridley confirmed with her Shieldbrother, Captain Morren didn't take her sharp green eyes off the newest member of the 5th infantry. She needed to make sure he was as ready as he could be for what may come. The battlefield holds no mercy after all. She smiled at Benedict as she eased him to his feet.

"Come, another wave is approaching Benedict." The smile of resolve creeped across her sunkissed and chapped lips as she looked out to the approaching army. "Hmm, another dance I suppose."

Benedict nodded and as he saw the approaching horde of wild faced enemies he drew up his sword to meet them. Morren drew an ax and sword in each hand as she called back to what remained of her brave team.

"Shall we then?"

In unison the five warriors roared a battle cry as they waded into another wave of the Dark Army.

THE TORCHLIGHT CAST A WARM glow in the heavy iron sconce on the wall. The oil soaked rags were cupped in the end of the rusted iron cage at the end of the hardwood rod. They smelled of rancid kitchen grease thought Cordelia as she scrunched up her nose. They were old, as were these halls they knew. As the warmth grew she looked toward the end of the stone hallway towards the next room.

"Vix, is that a library over there?" She said, pointing to the soft glow of what appeared to be bookshelves bathed in multicolored light from above.

"Ah, yes. Yes it is. I shall see what it holds that may give us a clue," he said calmly as they made their way towards the room.

"Please do, we need any clues at this point. Oh wow!" she exclaimed as she looked around the massive central hall they now stood in.

This was the tenth floor of the central tower and was a massive mezzanine styled area. It was also unused. She found herself remembering watching the army with Lord Alvar only a few hours ago.

At that time, they had stood on the massive wall overlooking the battlefield. Legions lined up on the vast white plain, tufts of browning grass poking up out of the snow at intervals, casting a dirty hue to ground. She noted the small armies at this distance seem less real and more like a game for a sinister child. The sun cast the tower's shadow in a long hand across this field of battle stretching a few miles, landing finally on the faint invaders encampment in the distance. Lord Alvar turned to her with deep worry in his eyes, the facade of strength finally crumbling away as he watched the impossible unfold.

"I never thought I'd see such a sight. An army daring to advance on the Celestine Tower." Lord Alvar said with a heavy sigh, the wind whipping his hair and beard to the side as he looked across the valley.

"It's so aw-"

"Horrifying." Sophie interrupted, placing a hand on her best friend's shoulder. The padded friendship bracelet rolled between her wrist and Cordelia's robe. Internally she felt a calm wash over her even in an instant, here they were together and not alone.

"Yes." Lord Alvar continued pointing over the high battlements that protected them and downward, "And our forces are bare as you can see. I fear some are not as ready as others. Too young. The local farmers have offered up arms to assist but I've decided only as a last resort. Do-"

Lord Alvar looked at Cordelia. His gray eyes and kind face were still proud, but unable to hide a glimmer of hope behind them.

"Do you truly believe the portal still exists?"

"It sounds like much of the tower is still a mystery even to you, My Lord," Her eyes twinkled with understanding, "but from what I know the five towers are connected with a portal that can be used to teleport between them in times of need. I've seen the one in the Ivory Library."

Vix cleared his throat and leaned into the conversation. "I concur with Cordelia as I have heard the same thing. In times of old it was used to assist in help... or message as well as moving people and resources."He sighed allowing his characteristic self-doubt to color his next words, "Although to be clear, it may be rendered unusable. I cannot guarantee it still works of course."

"Of course." Alvar nodded, "Besides we- haven't ascended past the tenth floor for centuries. There's been no need to. After enough time there became superstitions and legends that kept any secrets it held safe. I know not if they are true, but there may be guardians that I don't know about."

Eralin and Zorin looked at each other, anticipating Alvar's next words.

"Who knows what ghosts roam those halls above?" Alvar shrugged. "I believe you though and it may be our only chance to link up with our allies in the Ivory Library after all."

Cordelia nodded, "If we can find the portal we could bring the Librarians here to assist before all is lost."

"Agreed, and again I must rely on that hope." He paused a moment, looking into her eyes before finally nodding and raising a hand of blessing.

"Hurry, my friends, and may the Knight and Maiden guide you."

The sound of Zorin's voice stopped Cordelia from revisiting recent memory.

"You sure they said they came to this floor? It looks like it's been empty for a long time. I mean between the dust and the yuck." His voice dripped with disgust before his eyes were drawn upward in the center of the chamber. "Wow… look at that."

They all gasped as light poured in across their faces from outside. The sun had risen in the sky far enough to cast bright beams through the large, ancient, stained glass panels in the central hall. There were six panels, each a different set of multicolored glass depicting a figure surrounded by several smaller scenes. The reds, blues and greens danced across the five story high walls, diffusing the image but making it no less beautiful. They noticed this chamber branched into six directions, no doubt spanning into the other six smaller towers. Sophie's eyes fell on one in particular.

"Hey! Back here is the path up to the next floor." Eralin called out to them from behind the large central desk flanked by the circular rows of books. Cordelia thought this reminded her of the Ivory Library, only much smaller of course but organized similarly.

"Race you there!" Lorvana called out from behind a table she had been standing on just a few moments before. She had been trying to get a peek at what might lie on top of the bookshelf.

"You go ahead. I'll be right there." Sophie told them as they made their way towards the exit.

Once alone, Sophie stared at the images. One figure in particular carried a staff and wore a long black robe. Under the robe, the face was a grim visage of an ivory skull holding a staff in one skeletal hand and a single coin in the other. She thought she saw the eyes glow with an internal blue light, like sapphires. "I haven't forgotten my promise, or what you have given me."

Sophie glanced at the other stained glasswork of the gods Benedict knew so well. Sophie, and Zane for that matter, had never carried religion in their hearts but they knew of the Righteous Knight, Life-Giving Maiden, Law-Bringing Judge, Primordial Hag, Vengeful Prince and the Ferryman of Death.

The panel to the left of the Ferryman was a young man sitting on a blackened throne, a hand on his chin and a crown on his head. The crown was emblazoned with a star and moon at the front and set with five stones above his brow and dark, serious eyes.

To his right a knight's profile in full golden armor knelt offering their sword upward in service, a clear blue sky above and a field of meadow flowers below. As realization set in she looked at the others briefly, in quick confirmation of what Zane and she had always known.

Standing with an arm outstretched was an old woman holding a wheel of earth, air, fire and water. Wielding a dark gavel a man sat emotionless, behind a pulpit graced with a pair of scales. Finally a young woman surrounded by butterflies of many colors, stared softly in prayer to the chalice in her hand.

Sophie turned back to the skull faced man, setting her jaw sternly with courage as she looked up at the image of the Ferryman. The god of death. She took a deep breath and bowed.

"I… I haven't forgotten our promise. We will find your daughter."

AYLA SAT ON A HEAVY oak barrel of grain outside the tower of the maiden. The warmth of the sun had faded here by day's end. Soldiers and cooks alike carried similar barrels by her to prepare for supper. She was taking a moment to herself to reflect on the day. She looked at her hands. They were tarred from the rope and sore but not too damaged she noticed and was thankful for.

She had tomorrow to do it again, she sighed. She reached into her pouch and retrieved her journal and a short stub of a plummet. Seeing the dull end she drew a small knife and whittled the end of the wood and lead pencil to a sharper point.

As the smell of cooking fires started to roll out of the kitchen, she began to write.

> *Today was a great day though so much happened that I must write down what I can remember.*
>
> *I remember heavy stones as they ground deep into wood, rolling into place on the platform. Thick rope of rough hemp ended with a four foot disk of heavy leather. Our eager hands wrapped this against a rough cut stone ball. The huge ball was barely contained by the wrap as they strung the other line to a heavy hook at the end of the trebuchet's arm. There was a brief silence in the cold air. The smell of oiled steel and leather lingered on my hands as we waited. In the distance my focused hearing started to pick out guttural war cries of the dark army. I felt the line in my hands, it was taut and ready. I steadied my breathing to make sure the adrenaline of battle wasn't making my hands shake too much and possibly fire prematurely.*
>
> *"Fire!" As if sensing my worries, Silvie's call ripped through the silence as I pulled the line free. A deep rumble of air whipped around the stone as the arm groaned into action, sending the stone sailing. I slipped and fell to my knees. I was unable to see the stone's mark but I heard Gustav cheer.*

"Yeah! Good shot!" He called me from a few yards away.

"You too, my friend!" Though I didn't see his shot either, it seemed like the appropriate thing to say. I grunted, while standing up and could see him nodding with a smile.

"Load them up! Let's show them what we can throw back at them! For honor!" Silvie called out to us as we began the cycle again.

I turned back to the rope attached to the long arm of the trebuchet and took a cursory glance to make sure I didn't see any tearing. I joined my team as we turned the multiple wooden spokes of the war machine, winding the 30 foot arm down and lifting the several tons of counterweight off the ground simultaneously.

Based on our last shot we would keep everything the same as much as possible. I could smell the burning bonfire behind us and it helped ensure we couldn't smell the horrible smells of battle. This time the heat of the fire was more welcome.

"Captain!" Gustav called out, "Cavalry fifteen degrees west, nine hundred yards and approaching."

Silvie smiled, "Well hurry up and prepare to welcome them!" We all laughed at her jovial tone. "I don't mind late comers to my party, do you?!"

"NO!" we all shouted in unison.

"And we still have gifts for our new friends?!"

Silvie knew. She knew as she looked across the battlefield at the charging cavalry of a mix of human and orc mercenaries that no doubt served this Lord Pallus. Their dark armor was cruelly cut to angles at the shoulders, horns curved wickedly in different directions. And their eyes! Even from here we saw their eyes flare with an intense bloodlust as they drove towards the front ranks of our infantry. Those brave souls set out to anticipate and intercept our enemy, but Silvie just knew from the still and tense air behind her we were ready.

"YES!" we shouted back in unison.

"Then may the knight guide your hands," She held this statement as she raised her and took a deep breath, "FIRE!"

The roar of the trebuchet in concert releasing was welcome. We heard the groan of the ironbound wood planks heave and the whistling of stones in the air ending with cheers erupting from us once again as the 200 pound stones cut through their advancing ranks. Despite having our duties changed at the last minute it felt as if this truly was our calling on this glorious day.

Our barrage continued as the sun drew low in the sky; until the last of the advance pulled back at the end of the day. They would return to their camp on the other side of the distant hill and we would pull back opposite them to the southwest of the tower. It was then that something happened I will never forget.

I saw a rider coming back from the front line after retrieving a body. I had avoided this following the day as I was afraid of what I might see, but something struck me this time. I had to know. I looked at the rider.

"Make way! I need a healer to help them please!" Her face was wide-eyed as she sought help. "He's not dead yet! Please!" she screamed.

"I saw the blood matted blonde head loll to one side displaying behind the grim look of a very much alive knight and more so, I knew him."

"Ho there, Arsinia!" Gustav ran to the rider to help. "Is that-"

Dread filled my heart as I recognised my friend.

"Mallius!"

Arsinia slid to the side of her bay-colored horse to dismount. Gripping the cracked leather reins in her left hand she placed a calm right hand across our friend's badly hurt head taking care not to touch any of the wounds hidden in the mass of hair and blood. The pointed tips of his graceful elven ears helped us to identify him even when the rest of his face was in such a state as to be unrecognizable.The iron and mineral smell of the horses sweat and the blood was the first real smells of warfare we had all day.

Gustav and I realized this as we looked at each other shocked as if just then it dawned on us this battle was in fact very real.

Mallius groaned as one bloodshot eye tried to open, "Ay..Ayla? I can't see you, my friend, is it you?"

I put my hand on his thigh as I tried to see the best way I could assist carrying him. My voice trembled,"Yes I'm here... Mallius... Please.. stay with me."

Mallius could sense my worry and his cracked lips pulled back in a weak attempt at a smile. "It would take more than that lot to take me out, my friend."

His bloody smile told me this was true and my heart settled a little, as his head rolled to the side again as if he were a child's rag doll. Looking up from the back of the horse as we pulled him to the ground, he groaned. If Mallius was a human like myself I'd say we were about the same age, around a quarter century. His elven bloodline was ancient in the land of Trull, more specifically his family were nobles within the Silver Maple woods at the northern border from what he had told me. Before now, tanned skin on his face wore a proud badge of those sunlit groves of the sweet purple apples. They native to that land and held tart apricot notes within the crunchy fruit itself. Golden hazel eyes, though filled with pain, showed much life still to be had and I prayed we could help him live it.

I had no choice but to smile in relief at both my fearless friend's condition and more importantly his attitude towards it. A more seasoned soldier than I probably would have made a joke and walked away, simply planning on when to meet him in the infirmary or even just waiting in the barracks for news of what may come, but I wasn't that cold yet. Truth be told I hoped I never would be.

I heard a gentle voice clear their throat behind me. "Excuse me Sergeant Forsythe." The voice came from a cleric of the maiden dressed in golden armor and the white and blue tabard of our order. "I must tend to his wounds now."

"Yes…of course." I stammered, stepping away.

Hearing my formal title was to be honest a bit jarring as here we didn't refer to them directly. Our positions and roles at the great war machines that towered before us revealed enough. Everyone loaded the machine, but only we Sergeants pulled the release. Even then, only after the Captain called for it. We left Mallius in the hands of the cleric as we made our way back into the great wall that surrounded the Celestine Tower.

Now, the great doors were open.

A FEW HOURS HAD PASSED since our forces had returned to the keep to refresh themselves from the battle. Eight hundred and twenty five young soldiers was what we had left. There were a handful of veterans such as myself fighting alongside these brave young people but the odds were staggering. The more we repelled the more we felt them double in size like a great hydra.

Benedict had enlisted much to my delight though I wasn't surprised. It was at the end of the day I saw him helping tend to the wounded with hopes and prayers. I felt something in them though, not just the rhetoric of faith, simply recited from the practiced tongue but an actual power in his words. A calming power. I noted how the knightlord must be truly guiding him as I saw him kneel next to a Dwarf whose arm was battered and bloodied. I saw his father's dark, raven colored hair on his bowed head. There was no doubt this was Lucilius's son, the heir of Garnet Keep.

As I walked the parapet I came across a lone guard. "Evening, how is the watch?"

"Good... Knight Captain."

Her nerves were tight from the tension of the day's events. I could feel the coiled spring of readiness tempered with panic.

"Excellent. I hope you don't mind if I join you here." I chuckled to ease the tension a bit. "I'll have a hard time sleeping tonight."

She chuckled, making me smile, "Sure. Be my guest. Though I don't have much to offer in the way of refreshment or-

I laughed at her jest, "Well then! I would have to leave this embarrassment to my station. Obviously!"

We both laughed with our eyes smiling, both of us happy to be alive in that moment. The cold air was filled with the smell of the bonfires below that kept little heat but much needed light to ensure there were no raids during the night. We had received a cease of action from their army's commander, Cobalt, that they would not be pressing into the night as that was viewed by her as an act of cowardice.

She stated they wanted to see our dead faces in the sun as well, was what Alvar told me behind closed doors. A grim code of chivalry it was.

"Excuse me, Knight Captain?" She spoke, breaking the silence we were lost in.

"Keldor. Please, call me just Keldor, and your name is?"

She looked at me with a different look then. The hard gaze softened her deep brown eyes. The rich mahogany of her cheek shone a tint of scarlet where it met the gleaming helm of her polished silver armor. A long plume of midnight blue dyed horse hair poured out in the gentle breeze gracing her pauldrons.

"Daria. I noticed, Keldor, your-" She paused, taking in my name as she looked at the tunic. "Your tunic's emblem is red, I've never seen that before."

I considered the old, worn tunic over my armor, now restored somewhat to its glory. Originally white as was hers it was now more cream with the holes of wear about. The crown and sword at my chest along with two wide bars at the base denoting my rank were in fact originally crimson. Now they faded to a pale red, the colors lost to time as with what they symbolized to me in those lost years. Daria's emblems, as the rest of the knights here, were blue.

"It's the mark of those protecting Garnet Keep with their life." A voice called out, one that was all too familiar to me. I glanced to see the knight approaching, his uniform a blue mirror of my own rank and his face curled back in a satisfied grin, like a wolf who had come to the end of his hunt. White hot lava of guilt poured over my heart, the ashes of his sister's memory surfacing in my mind.

"Garnet Keep?" She sounded slightly confused and surprised. "but I thought the keep was-"

"Lost?" Sir Caleb's voice dripped with venom and hatred. "Heh, as did I Watchmaster. As did I."

I turned to him, my voice attempting to veil my embarrassment and fear. "Caleb! How are y-"

"Oh stop with the pleasantries, Keldor!" He cut me off with a hand raised, trembling with a barely held fury. "We both know there is no time for that, especially from you…deserter."

Daria straightened up, "I beg your forgiveness Knight Captain. He's… he's no deserter."

Caleb's eyes widened as did his sneer. "Oh? Did you not know the story of the brave Sir Keldor?"

My heart sank. "Please, Caleb I-"

"Please? You ask me to forgive you for abandoning your post? For abandoning your so-called friends?" He closed the distance to me in an instant to hiss in my face. Spittle bounced off my cheek with every anger-filled syllable. "You let my sister die in that fire, didn't you?"

His words struck home like a lance draped in a holy flame. I felt the white hot lava of guilt pour over my heart remembering his sister Elona, bravely diving into the flames of the burning building to defend her family. Pulling off his helm I saw his auburn hair was still cut close to the head as he always preferred. Ice blue eyes peered through the dark rimmed slits like a predator preparing to strike. Hot breath held remnant smells of a hasty meal as he took a deep breath.

"Answer me!" He shouted, his voice cracking. "Didn't you?!"

"Caleb!" Lamprey roared from behind me as I heard his black boots step quickly towards us. "Caleb! You are no judge!" He stood between us now with his hands on each of our chests holding us apart. He continued

"YOU have no idea… WE have no idea what he's been through."

His hazel eyes were strong and locked on Caleb. I looked at how his black tunic whipped in the wind against the leather armor he wore underneath. A streak of mud cut across the tunic's four fading red bars at the base denoting a Sergeant Major of Garnet Keep. Caleb's white tunic depicted two blue bars indicating a Knight Captain like myself, but based out of the Celestine Tower. Lamprey's left eye was bloodshot from the grit of the day in the trenches with the pikemen who were repelling infantry and cavalry alike from a centralized attack.

He was a respected member of the infantry but at this moment he stood between two officers. A bold move to be sure but I was thankful for the cooler head to be his in this situation.

He softened his voice as he lowered his hands, "Now is not the time to relive that which we cannot change."

Caleb still shook with rage. A rage I imagined was well rehearsed and practiced since I abandoned my post so long ago. "My quarrel isn't with you Lamprey."

"It is now."

Lamprey's words became cold as the ice on the carts in the courtyard and Caleb froze for a minute, assessing the situation. The wind on the parapet blew by as I could feel the tension in the air approach a zenith. My hand unclenched, leaving deep indentations in its palm I was unaware of until now. I could smell birch and pine in the blazing bonfires out at the perimeter 50 feet below, the arms of the several trebuchet lined up just at the edge of the firelight another 50 yards or so, from the wall. The moonlight aided in a blue-white glow that reflected from the walls of the magnificent tower behind us.

One thing to note for some such as myself, when tension rises I've found you become more aware of your surroundings and in many ways more alive. I suppose that is why some of my shield brothers and sisters grew to love battle.

Shouts came from below, breaking the stalemate between the three of us. Daria sighed..

"There is no time for any of this! Now calm yourselves!" She stepped to the edge of the wall.

"Ho there! State your name and business!" She called out into the dark shadows. Standing there by a horse was a single figure at the edge of the torchlight. Teal warpaint surrounded his eyes and pulled his alabaster face down into twin points like assassin's daggers. His copper hair was straight and hung to the shoulder. It was pulled back to reveal the pointed ears of the elves. He wore a midnight tunic emblazoned with what appeared to be a smeared dark blue teardrop, but inverted as if flowing upwards. I looked at Lamprey. His furrowed brow and eyes confirmed he had never seen it before either. The unknown figure's lips curled cruelly back.

"I am Loukas! I carry a proposal of great importance to one of your own."

The creak of the small gate opened as two heavily armored sentries walked out to hear the visitor's proposal. They looked at each other with shock to find one of the generally good-natured sons of the forest staring at them with a crazed look on his face. But he was an elf in the ranks of the dark army. The mysterious teardrop shape now revealed a grim skull looking as if it were melting down the front of the tunic in a deathly blue green.

"Speak your words stranger. Speak them and be gone!" Our sentry demanded from behind a steel helm training his spearpoint on Loukas's chest. "Your lot killed many of my friends this day and I wouldn't mind burying you here."

Loukas laughed as his face became a mockery of disappoint-ment. "My only wish is to speak with my brother's son... Is that so much to ask for?" He chuckled cruelly, "Tell my dear Mallius to meet me in the center of the battlefield at dawn before our first sorties. The fate of the Silver Maple Woods rides on it. He will know what I mean." He mounted his steed.

Bursting into laughter he yanked the reins of the horse hard and galloped quickly into the night as the wind picked up, dusting light snow against my cheek. Lost in the same cold shadows from which he had appeared.

CHAPTER 5

TO ABSENT FRIENDS

The dining hall was surprisingly quiet that evening, as members of the order sat on their oaken benches largely in silence. A single reminder of the siege was the pasty thin broth they were rationing tonight. This taste would likely not change for as long as they were trapped inside the halls of the great tower. For some they felt it could be their last. Altogether, the wear of battle was driving spirits downward. One Squire sat with his company staring at the last bite of the provided food balanced in his spoon, carved from a single golden horn.

"Oh," he sighed as he slurped the liquid slowly, imagining the precious fluid entering his blood and nourishing his body, " Well Morren I hope you have a good evening." He stood up, easing himself off the shared bench with both hands on the table for balance.

Captain Morren smiled. Her sandy blonde hair was free of her helm now showing the tight warriors braids that fell to just above her shoulder. "Yes. You as well Benedict. Rest well."

"Hey Benedict?" Benedict turned to Bryce looking at him through dark eyes while chewing on a piece of hard biscuit.

"Yes Sir. I mean Bryce."

Bryce chuckled, "You fought well today kid."

Bryce smiled. The blue crown and sword on his black tunic was darkened in spots as was his attitude prior at the table. But, at least for a moment, the normally brooding Corporal relaxed the tension in his face and eyes. Ridley the dwarf also looked up at Bryce. Seeing him smile caused a big grin on her face.

"Real well."

Ridley beamed as she slammed a fist on the table. "You were great! See you in the morning." She grinned mischievously back at Benedict with excitement, "and we'll send more of them back to the shadows from where they came! For Mallius!"

Benedict nodded smiling, "Sounds good Ripley, and thank you Bryce."

Benedict made his may out and into the quiet hall of the tower. The tower here was separated into sections much like the cross section of an orange. Each of the six smaller towers flanked the central tower while being adjacent to each other. They were, in their own right, impressive. The central tower may be a staggering 1200 feet high but the side towers were still 400 feet if he were to guess at them being a third of the height from a distance.

He looked to his right and saw the curving high walls were covered in ancient paintings and flanked by faded and worn tapestries. Once vibrant colors over time had faded to their pale pastel counterparts in the stale air that reverberated down the halls. He imagined the pale periwinkle was once a strong blue as seen on the newer tunics of the soldiers stationed here. The mint green could be a bold turquoise or even deep jade. Imagination was taking hold in his mind and he began to focus on one painting in particular.

"Woah... this is the War of the Stone. Wh.. where it all began."

Benedict stopped in front of a tapestry depicting a battle around a towering monolith shaped eerily like an anvil. Though black, there were numerous colored threads woven inside to show multiple colors shimmering on the surface. It was impossible to tell how large it was but in the embroidery it certainly felt like a small mountain. The foreground was filled with banners he didn't recognize. Axes, wolves, trees, elk, hammers all were in battle against the standards of a raven or an eagle. He wasn't sure.

Erebus hadn't shared much of this time in history, just the legends. Which honestly were probably more fun and entertaining to a 10 year old. He was aware this ancient order had existed since the war of the stone, and this Tower was built in the years following it. But that was over 1500 years ago. These banners and those that followed them were established well before that he was sure.

As he walked past this glimpse into the past, an opening in the long wall became visible where the hall curved gently towards it revealing the central sanctuary. He smiled recalling the events a few hours ago as he slipped into its warm memory, falling deeper as he took each weary step.

He remembered that the sanctuary was filled with white tunics of the Knights and the Black tunics of the soldiers. The blue crown and sword rippled across every chest like gentle waves as they sat watching the procession. Benedict knelt and bowed at the front of the room with five others dressed in only a simple white robe. They didn't waver. Steadily balanced and calm before the large crowd of witnesses. This ceremony was not a mystery to them as they had been a part of it themselves at some point in their career.

The knight known as Caleb stepped forward.

"Members of the Order. You have witnessed their actions today and wish to welcome these initiates to our ranks as Squires. Lord Alvar, Knight Commander of the Celestine Tower, it is my honor to bring them to you." Caleb stepped back offering his position to his superior, "May the Stone now guide your judgment, milord."

Lord Alvar stepped forward. His wiry beard seemed more full and strength seemed to return to his gray eyes. Alvar wore no ceremonial outfit, just the same white tunic he was accustomed to wearing. Complete with four blue bars at the bottom to show his command was above all others.

"Initiates, you proved valor this day on the field. When in battle only YOUR heart will know if your intentions were honorable. In our tenets there are guiding words. Words we use to guide our tongues as well as our sword. Our actions are still our own.,but now they will also carry with them the collective will of the knighthood. In all your days, give not into anger or seek revenge. Show kindness and generosity. Forgive the unforgivable. Keep your word in all things... Always, always defend those who can't defend themselves."

He stepped forward and drew his longsword. The brass pommel and cross guard was polished to a high sheen. The well-used blade had been carefully ground to remove the deeper nicks and blemishes but many remained to tell their story. Many watching knew that story from their own sparring with the old veteran.

Fatigue sapped at Benedict's legs, snapping him out of the pleasant memory and back to where his body was calling him. He took a last look in the wide room. Benedict could still smell the rich incense and sage from the braziers, hear and feel the cheers as they welcomed him to their ranks. Keldor and Elloveve had proudly embraced Benedict following the ceremony as his Commander Morren while Bryce and Ridley led the rest of their group in a rousing huzzah.

This was everything he had dreamed of. Soon his footsteps came to the stairway that ascended to the floor above which led to the barracks. The stone steps were kept clean since the cavalry could wear their smooth sabatons and those could act more like skis on these stairs with one wrong step. Agonizing gently over each step his legs screamed as he climbed the two stories to the next level. This huge room branched to several rooms. Each contained twenty cots covered in tufts of straw bedding and topped with a tanned, large animal fur. It was surprisingly comfortable and a step up from the hard ground of the road or the turn in the wagon.

Benedict sat on the edge of the bed for a moment before pulling his boots off. Only one thing was missing today. Sighing he bowed his head in a quiet prayer in the hushed night.

"Knightlord, please watch over my friends tonight. Though we are separated I feel we are all still together. May the maiden guide those in the Tower seeking its secrets that may help us- and please help brave Skotmir in organizing the volunteer militia tomorrow. I know I shouldn't doubt him, he's a strong and likable person..." He hesitated trying to think of more to say. With a shrug he decided to keep it simple. "Well I guess...please help him to see that too."

Benedict couldn't help but smile thinking of his awkward but caring friend. Skotmir was rough but if he just believed in himself, Benedict knew he could do great things. Then, laying down on the bed, his eyes drifted off to sleep.

DAWN CAME TOO SOON FOR most, especially those in the 5th Infantry. Captain Morren looked at her company once they reached their point at the front of the line behind a long line of entrenched pikemen. Long black tunics donned most of her soldiers. Elves, humans, dwarves and an orc or two had served by her side. Northern Darkovnia, Bellz and parts of southern Trull were all represented in the ranks. Blue crown and sword emblems blazed across the chest of all including the four veteran knights, who wore white tunics like herself. She was Captain, or how she liked to think of it, they allowed her to be captain.

They let her wear the twin blue stripes on a white field. It was her honor to lead them. Like a dog preparing for a hunt she sniffed the air from habit. She had grown up in the land of Wolfling and her people were taught to hunt this way, smelling the air first and tasting the breeze.

Her pale green eyes shone behind the visor of her steel helm. The ends of dark, ash colored locks from her temples fell from behind its edges. These were braided and kept shorter than the shoulder. This was a common length for Infantry and Cavalry she had noticed, though many wore their hair in different styles befitting their own personalities. They wore the same plate armor, though emblazoned with the Sword and Crown emblem, but it was left to personal taste or preference whether they would don a helm.

They were down a few soldiers from the prior day. One of note was the corporal Mallius, who was recovering from a serious head wound. The elf was struck next to her by a great club, the wicked knot digging deep before sending him reeling by the leering man in dark armor.

She remembered swinging her back in an arc behind her just seconds too late.

The dark army soldier fell at that moment but so did Mallius. The skirmish had cooled and she dropped to his side. She wiped the pouring blood from his brow to find its source. It was grievous. Warhorns sounded an end to the assault and, as they had hoped, also the end of the day.

"Hold on Mallius." She shook the concern from her voice. It was the last thing he needed to hear. "You hear me? There is no dying in the 5th, not on my watch!"

Mallius groaned softly. He was still conscious, but barely.

"Come on Mallius, stick with me! Say it!" She hissed at him seriously.

"Nn..no d..dying..." he stammered. Morren nodded quickly.

"Close enough!" she turned to shout for another soldier in her ranks to help. "Benedict! Flag that cavalry returning for us! We need to get Mallius back to the camp."

He nodded and jogged to where he would be better seen. "HEY! Over here!" Benedict stood with his arms outstretched waving enthusiastically to get their attention. They were returning from the front line back to the tower as the battlefield cleared for the day.

"What do you need, Squire?" An elven knight called back. Long black hair was tucked behind her pointed ears and held by a silver clasp.

"We need help with the wounded!"

Arsinia looked at her major who nodded in agreement before quickly galloping over.

"He's over here, hurry!" Benedict pointed at Captain Morren, tending to a crumpled body on the ground. Arsinia spurred her horse to gallop to her side. Pulling the reins and driving her heels forward, the horse obeyed and swiftly came to a stop as commanded.

"Captain Morren I'm here to..." As she swung from the saddle she paused in recognition, "Oh no! Is that you, Mallius?!"

"He's hurt badly, Arsinia. Bring him back to the clerics at the gate immediately. I'm afraid we may lose him if we wait for them to come to us."

"Yes of course." She nodded, her eyes wide with concern.

Benedict turned to Arsinia with urgency, "I'll help you get him on your mount."

Arsinia mounted her horse as Benedict and Morren lifted his limp body to drape over her lap. Holding him and the reins she drove her heels into the ribs of Flyte, her gray mare, setting them off in a gallop back to the tower looming in the distance.

That was yesterday, Captain Morren thought. She hoped he was still fairing alright. The Infantry felt an impact yesterday but their Cavalry and Archers had kept the majority of Pallus's dark invasion back on that first day. Those that had made it past their lines only fell to the heavy stones flung by the trebuchet and more archers. They had been covering the left flank but today was different. Lord Alvar moved them closer to the center this time as he anticipated they were just testing the defenses as before. The long shadow of the tower stretched across the battlefield as the dawn waned on.

The warhorns sounded in the distance.

"Well, here we go again," Captain Morren told herself as she drew in a deep breath to call out loudly, "Archers! Nock!"

Bryce repeated this command to the Archers on their backline. The tops of the distant hills wavered and rippled slightly as masses of darkly clothed figures creeped like a slow dark tide across the earth. It seemed the night itself was wishing to return from an early banishment. Once they drew within the furthest range of their longbows something unexpected happened; they halted. The grinding drone of heavy boots went silent in the morning breeze.

Benedict was confused. "Why?" He whispered before shouting to Morren, "Captain? Why are they holding?"

Captain Morren was silent as she too was seeking answers in the still line of blackened swords and spears. She sniffed the air, the smell of the wet mud and snow carried across the battlefield as did the oiled leather and steel. The wind was dulled to a gentle breeze in the early morning, and when she looked up the overcast sky held nothing to fear from what she could see. She remembered what she was briefed on this morning as she saw a single rider appear in a fast gallop to the line. She was told about the vain threat of a dark uncle of Mallius and it seemed this mysterious man may be making good on his promise.

She held her hand up to her warriors and shouted, "Hold!"

"Mallius! Where are you boy? Do you not remember me? Do you not remember your beloved uncle? Come now! Don't hide!"

The black leather armor was emblazoned with the same blue green skull smeared like an inverted teardrop seen last night from the parapet. Benedict was looking at him intensely. There was something sinister about the man besides his words.

"Mallius!" His tone was nasal and patronizing, "Don't keep your uncle waiting! I know you are scared. Well, WE all know that, don't we Mallius?"

"I REALLY don't like this guy." Benedict huffed under his breath. The insulting tone of one of his allies who he saw fall was infuriating to him.

"Mallius! You coward! Face me now and you can keep your precious silver maples!" He was screaming now, drooling in a rivulet down a smooth elven chin, "Prove to this world you deserve them! Not just because you were born to them but that you earned them! Earn them by defeating me? Hahaha! Yes! earn them with MY blood! Hahahaha!"

He broke into maniacal laughter that was echoed by the dark army behind him. Hundreds of jeering voices filled the void from the tower forces to the hill at that moment. Benedict turned to Bryce.

"Corporal Bryce! Permission to-"

"No! Stand your ground Companion!" Bryce shouted.

"Corporal I can-"

"I said no!" Bryce shouted but he wasn't entirely sure.

He didn't want to be held responsible for the private's death but this seemed a straight up match and frankly Benedict had proven to be a formidable warrior one on one. Morren's jaw trembled with rage as time began to slow. Taking in a deep breath she closed her eyes to cool the anger that was building in her chest. Cooler minds must prevail, she told herself. Sighing, she whispered.

"I really hate that guy." She shook her head and shouted. "Corporal Bryce!"

"Yes Captain!"

"Is there someone you recommend to answer this… gentleman's demands?" she spat the words with a thick, syrupy contempt.

Bryce looked at Benedict. The young man appeared to be, for the most part, successful in holding back his anger. Bryce couldn't help but smile a bit. He knew what that meant.

"Benedict Shieldheart!" he shouted proudly. He saw Ridley raise a fist with a huge grin on her face.

"Thank you." Benedict nodded solemnly to the corporal as he left the line. He strode from the line drawing his great sword as he passed the line of bewildered pikemen. Benedict looked at Morren as he passed. Her lip curled in a proud smile.

"Bless you Benedict." she whispered before turning to the twisted uncle of Mallius. "Loukas! Your demand on this battlefield to meet with Mallius cannot be met, but this man will gladly stand in for him.

"Why?!" he screamed, "Where is my rat chicken of a nephew?"

"All that matters is he is not here, and as is our custom on the field of battle, a demand on a member is a demand on the order itself," she smiled a little as she drove home the point, "and must be fulfilled, thus we must honor it to be met."

This infuriated Loukas who swung off the horse. The green daggers of face paint around his eyes curled at the points from his wicked grin. Drawing an ebony longsword in his hand the dark oiled Damascus rippled in the dawnlight. He pointed one at Benedict's approaching chest and laughed cruelly.

"It doesn't matter! This whelp shall lie slain in the mud regardless. To become a feast of worms for my dark lord." He paused for a moment as he sized up Benedict, "You, Benedict… You only prolong the inevitable and Mallius will… still… DIE!"

With a shout Loukas lunged at the young knight swinging the longsword in a flurry of blows looking for any weakness in his armor. Benedict kicked him away, buying some time to take a swing with the great two-handed sword he wielded. It sailed over Loukas' head as he ducked and again drew closer.

Loukas dove at Benedict, lashing out with a quick arc to the midsection that he dodged by jumping back slightly on his heels. He answered with a high strike downward to be met by Loukas's parry.

"Weak!" Loukas shrieked, "I could fight you all day!"

As they circled each other Benedict calmly drifted his focus to the crowd behind them. He was confident this would not disadvantage him. This was a learned behavior from his days pulling Zorin or another friend off sticky, beer-soaked floors during a tavern brawl. Always someone waiting to drive a tankard into your skull if you weren't looking. He took note of two individuals who now stood out against the dark horde.

They wore no helm and their polished leather scale armor was a midnight blue rimmed in gold. Not gold paint but real gold leafing. The male stood behind the woman, their dark rimmed eyes containing Irises the same color as the pupils. Black as a starless night. They both had cruel one sided grins as they stood at the front of the army with their arms crossed, watching intently. They were the ones holding the army back, enjoying the spectacle.

Benedict panted slightly, "As could I… but I have better things to do!" With a shout and clang of steel, they locked blades, staring at each other. Benedict could tell he could drive his blade through the other's guard easily but it would open him up to a possibly deadly counter. Loukas kicked free and swung in a series of wild blows that drove Benedict backward several steps, finally stumbling to a knee. Bringing his sword up into a high guard Loukas drove a single chop to the shoulder.

Benedict groaned in pain as Loukas struggled to laugh through clenched teeth. Benedict grabbed the blade in one hand holding it in place at the top of the shoulder where it passed through the black muslin tunic he now wore. It had entered his armor between the pauldrons and the breastplate itself. Dropping his own blade, he stood up and swiftly kicked the side of Loukas's knee. As the man dropped his weight in pain, Benedict grabbed the crossguard and drove Loukas's blade with both hands back into his opponent's face. Two well placed blunt hits cracked into his nose leaving it bloodied.

With a groan, Loukas loosened his grip enough for Benedict to disarm him as he stumbled backwards from the blows. He thought briefly about dispatching Loukas. Benedict saw the looks on the knight's faces; largely smiles. They knew he had won this battle honorably and Morren nodded, smiling. He remembered the guidance of his Knight Commander, and the oath of his order to "forgive the unforgivable". Looking over his shoulder back at the horde behind him, the dark haired woman stared at him with her cruel smile. The blue scarf around her head gently tossed in the breeze. She leaned back to the man behind her and whispered something.

Benedict could tell they both expected Loukas' death. Loukas, their own soldier. This disgusted Benedict.

"Bah! Get out of here!" he shouting, kicking mud into Loukas's chest. "slither back to the rock from which you came!"

Tossing the black sword to the side, Benedict began to walk back to the ranks.

Defeated and insulted, Loukas's rage reached a boiling point, "Don't you turn away from me!" He shrieked as he leapt to his feet. Drawing a curved blackened dagger from the cracked leather scabbard at his waist, Loukas dove at Benedict's exposed back. He drew it back to strike, the tip dripping with the dark ichor of an unknown poison, his eyes wide in maddening anger.

Loukas was cut short as lightning ripped through his body. Screaming, he toppled forward as sparks danced across his lifeless body in the mud and snow.

Benedict turned and saw the dark-eyed man's hand extended towards where the now blackened body of Loukas once stood, his face twisted in a cruel lopsided smile. The woman was nodding though she was no longer smiling.

"I am Commander Cobalt and no one in my army stabs backs like a thief in an alley! Let that be a lesson to you all or face the same fate!" There was a silence that carried. Cobalt nodded as she turned to the Man who had struck down Loukas. "Come Azure. It is time."

Leaving the still body of Loukas on the ground they turned on their heels, walking back into the crowd as the warhorns sounded and the battle began all over again.

Deep inside the tower Vix stood staring. He was failing to see what Cordelia thought was so important.

"Well this... is worthless."

"No it's not." Cordelia narrowed her eyes at his dismissal.

"Oh?" He chuckled sarcastically. "You figure it out then. I'm going to make sure Zorin and Eralin don't do something equally stupid." He walked away with his blue robes trailing behind.

A large oval, the height of two people high, stood in the center of the large chamber. The steel frame was five feet wide and depicted relief sculptures of dragons tied in intricate knots. Cordelia was positive there was a meaning to this and the chamber itself.

"Fine." She sighed, "Sophie, can you help me?"

"Sure. What do you..." Sophie paused as she stared in thought at the archway. "What do you think we should try?"

"Well, I think to start, we just need to dust it off, especially the gems."

Sophie chuckled "Is that why Vix took off? Afraid you might conjure a dust bunny?" The two friends laughed at each other. Vix turned glowering.

"Real mature of you both!" he shouted as he walked away. Chuckling, Cordelia looked back at a smiling Sophie.

"I think there is no power in them right now. So if it's a magical apparatus there should be nothing to worry about if it... wait." She paused, realizing something in the dusty room. "That's what we have to find out actually. What powers this or how? It has to be around here somewhere."

Zorin, Eralin, and Lorvana began looking around the room as well. Scanning the ceiling, Zorin spotted something in the darkness above the arch.

"Hey Eralin. You see that up there?"

Zorin spotted an area in the high ceiling that hung within reach of the steel oval, where a ring of stones was framing something. Eralin pulled back his hood, revealing the platinum hair and deep blue grey skin he kept veiled. His eyes scanned the ceiling but saw nothing at first.

"No. Where?" he coldly mentioned to Zorin.

"There! See it just above that archway thing." Zorbing pointed in a tone like a parent would a child. Eralin nodded.

"Yes... Is that a-"

"Yes of course." Vix interrupted with a condescending tone, "A trap door." Eralin glared at Vix while Zorin just shook his head.

"Obviously." He looked at Cordelia smirking. "Now this is important."

Zorin was flabbergasted, "Wh.. Really?!" Cordleia sighed deeply as Sophie just shook her head in disbelief, "Didn't you just say it's worthless?"

"Well, not anymore." Vix said matter of factly. Zorin slapped the palm of his hand on the back of an old chair, sending a cloud of musty smelling dust into the air.

"Bling bling! That went from worthless to priceless faster than anything I can remember."

Leaning back in a similar chair Lorvana laughed at Vix sarcastically while tuning up her lute.

"You really do have all the magics!"

"Yeah I was wondering if this little spot I polished held some sort of magical power." Sophie chuckled, "Everybody stand back while Vix whips out some spellwork! Give me a moment and we're going to see some-"

"IF you're quite done!" Vix shouted, exasperated by the group chuckling at his expense. "I can explain to you ignorant fools how it works." The group went deadly silent. No one had seen Vix that angry since the Underworld and it was frankly a little unnerving.

Vix cleared his throat, smoothed the cuff of his robes and collected himself before continuing.

"Not all magic can be summoned from yourself or the immediate surroundings, you idiots. That's why some spells require a little extra push, like spell components or maybe a focus like a wand or staff to assist. This is also true with very powerful magic. Ancient magic."

Vix paced to the steel ring. As he drew closer, he saw in addition to the five gemstones there were inlays of brass, bronze, copper, silver and gold spread throughout the artwork, gently glinting from behind the dust and tarnish. The smell of the musty air and dust in this room proved it had lain untouched for many years. No windows graced this central chamber that was placed many floors above the stained glass mezzanine from before. The only source of light was the torches in the sconces or in their hands. Vix leaned back and looked up at the trapdoor.

Cordelia looked at him, puzzled. "What is it?"

Vix smirked with realization. "This aligns perfectly to the opening above. If I were to guess, there's a very powerful spell component at the other end of this trap door to activate this archway."

Cordelia clapped her hands together happily, "I told you! This is it isn't it? The portal between the towers!"

Vix nodded, smiling.

Zorin chuckled, "Well then! Hey Eralin, help me up so I can find out where this goes."

CHAPTER 6

THROUGH A GLASS DARKLY

Ayla looked at her journal blankly waiting for words to come to her tired mind. Sighing, she massaged her brow in an attempt to coax the letters to form words and sentences from the fog of memory. She looked at the stained glass window again. She had memorized every bend in the leadwork and knew every piece of glass that pieced together the image of the red rose and purple lily surrounded by gold knotwork.

She smiled, looking at the familiar chip in one piece of kelly green tinted glass as the words began to form. Drawing the quill again from the small pot of ink she began her ritual, recalling time from memory to the pages before her.

Year 1523, Twenty-three days after our First Snowfall. Twenty-two days we have been under siege, day after day. The first week they seemed to toy with us, giving the illusion of grace. But soon these were slowly broken by small sorties and some sporadic skirmishes. Making us believe we were winning, but then came the real terror as undead legions started coming at dusk, evening or even the middle of the night.

*The dead didn't need to sleep, and though their
wasted and fragile bodies could be easily broken,
they never ceased coming and that was slowly breaking us more effectively. Wearing us down until we
were walking shadows ourselves. Soon we didn't
know the last time some of us had slept. We lived in
a constant state of high alert. Hearts raced when we
lay down as if there was too much tea or coffee prior.*

*That all said, the last few weeks have been a blur.
We've lived in a rotation commanding the trebuchets
in sparse teams with only one leader to control the
barrage. Father-*

AYLA PAUSED FOR A MOMENT thinking of the grey haired man
sitting in a chair at home reading this journal in the future. A future
hopefully with her in it but in case he wasn't maybe he needed
to remember how she never stopped thinking of him. Smirking
mischievously she dipped the quill back in the pot and began again.

*Father, you'll be pleased to know my mousey hair
is luckily not matted as it hangs to my shoulders. I
agree this is amazing, given the fact bathing hasn't
been a luxury we have afforded ourselves as regu-
larly as we probably should. My team is very forgiving of the rancid symphony of odors. We just try to
do our best to ignore them. Honestly once it is mentioned it can take hours to forget it so we prefer to
not torture ourselves.*

*The day started with their new normal vanguard of
skeletal warriors. Shambling bones of the restless*

dead eagerly cascading into our weapons, as if hoping for some sort of respite from the torment of undeath. This was followed by sorties of mercenaries all from bloodthirsty Trull if I were to guess.

They are all orcs and men mainly, though we have heard of more elves and possibly dwarves in their ranks. I'm personally not surprised, after all the lust for gold cares not about its victim as it corrupts the soul of the mercenary. I'm one of the few of us from the farms of nearby Tova I believe.

As luck would have it, Grayson, the boy who used to tease me for my tom-boyishness in school, is here. We actually rode in together. He's different now; more mature, no doubt from his time at the front line.

There may be more of us in the local militia being mustered as a backstop. We fear putting these untrained farmers, bakers and laymen into the battle. They claim they are all willing to protect the free world against the growing power of Lord Pallus. But father, I do not have the stomach for just sending them to slaughter.

I can see the pain in Lord Alvar's eyes when he looks at them. There is a dwarf berserker among their ranks, one of those who joined us the night before the first assault. I remember him really enjoying the provisions we brought to their meeting. He's probably the only seasoned warrior among them, and that only means they will be like a mob on the battlefield.

I should stop; it sounds like I'm complaining. And as you taught me, father, there's no good in doing that. It's just that morale is very low. We lose some of our own every day but it seems no matter how many we kill they come back the next day as if nothing happened. We started noticing some of their dead coming back in the unholy vanguard, or it could have been our minds playing tricks on us.

Well today started as the other days have, and as the day progressed it seemed today would be more of the same as before but- well I would be proven wrong yet again.

AYLA LEANED BACK AND CLOSED her eyes, willing her memory of the day back into her mind. That time was indeed unique and she wasn't the only one trying to recall what took place.

The deafening sound of swords scraping on steel plates trailed with the ringing of their blades and the screams of the wounded. The coppery smell of warm blood striking their faces was now easily ignored as they cut through the line of the attackers. It was even welcome today as they could tell they were fighting the living, at least in this moment.

"Yah!" Benedict drew back his sword from the chest of a mercenary, the links in the chainmail split where the blade had skewered the man seconds before. His eyes returned to the surging flow of dark clad bodies clamoring towards them.

"Captain Morren! The center is pouring towards us!"

Morren stepped back a single step, feeling her heel strike solid ground from the slippery shield Benedict had set foot on previously. Without looking to confirm she shouted to the line of long spears to her left.

"Pikeman, hold your line!" She turned forward just in time to catch the rusted blade of an orc warrior in the crook of her sword's crossguard inches from her helm.

"Time to die scum!" It cackled mercilessly before ending in a gurgle and slumping backward.

"Not today." She said through clenched teeth as she pulled her longsword from the thick leather over his chest.

"Benedict! You and Bryce push forward with those pikemen!"

"Yes Captain!" They both shouted in unison as they locked eyes with each other.

The battlefield had churned mud for almost a month in this area till now the mud was in 2 or 3 foot mounds throughout where their feet had pushed them from the originally solid, flat earth. The moist sound of sludge under boots was muffled by the din of steel, leather and flesh clashing violently. Morren's face was caked with mud on one side, matting her ash colored hair to her cheek back to her left ear. The battle sounds faded in her head for a moment as she took a breath leaning on her worn longsword.

"We will persevere. The Knightlord guides us."

Perched on the other side of the battlefield four riders sat on dark horses. Cobalt and Azure with their blue and gold trimmed scaled armor stared at the battle intently. Dabria, the mistress of pain, and the seer, Una flanked them. Una raised her head from her deep concentration and opened her gray and green eyes.

"Ah... it is, as I have foreseen, the most honored Cobalt. Their faith... is fading. Breaking... Yesss."

They were overlooking the battlefield towards the east. At the far end only a few miles away was the Celestine Tower glinting in the noon sunlight. Una's eyes were closed behind her dark hood but Cobalt knew she didn't need eyes to see. She was a seer and a gifted one considering she served the dread Lord Dekkion. It was also good she had somehow stayed alive all this time, like the golden eyed Dabria who rode next to her on the far right.

Only a handful of living Centurians such as Dabria, who then commanded hundreds of undead on the battlefield, led his Undead legions, but Una was different. There was something or someone inside the young woman. Her hair fell like ravens feathers framing her face from behind the dark hood. She held a blackened spear in her hand.

Cobalt laughed at Una's words. "Hmm... now as they are frozen in fear we must SNAP them." She hissed, squeezing her clawed hands into fists.

"Snap them?" Dabria growled, matching the intensity of the commander's "And how will you do that? Using our undead ogres perhaps? How about the banshees? We can send them out this evening."

"No Dabria. No banshees." She narrowed her midnight eyes in thought briefly before looking at her brother. Azure nodded with a cruel smile. The twisted braid of his beard dancing against her broad chest. "I believe it may be time to show them the true power this army possesses."

Dabria recoiled slightly from the veiled insult. Una drew a hand of warning to her lips while staring intensely at Dabria. She nodded and calmed herself, bringing her back into control of her emotions. Cobalt didn't seem to notice as she clapped a hand on Azure's shoulder.

"Tell me Azure," she spoke musically with an equal amount of grace and sinister intent, "How are you feeling today?"

He chuckled as his deep voice boomed, "I would *love* to stretch out a bit."

Cobalt smiled, "Be my... guest" she hissed.

"Gladly!"

Azure slid off the horse and took a few steps forward through the clearing down the hill. Taking in a deep breath he threw his arms out and down to the ground, groaning in the short burst of intense but welcomed pain.

In mere seconds he was on all fours with a reptilian head the size of two houses on top of each other towering into the sky. Stretching out from his body were great mustard yellow and blue wings. His human form was now replaced with that of his natural magnificence.

Dabria felt her skin crawl as she saw the deep sapphire blue dragon pull its head back towards the sky with a terrifying roar.

THE ANCIENT AIR WAS MUSTY and silent except for the sounds of living breaths being drawn in soft rhythm. The smooth, medieval stone reverberated with the sound of hardened leather heels climbing polished steps in time, creating a symphony of life that had not been heard here in over a millenia.

Cordelia brushed a raven black lock out of her face as she looked at Zorin's lightly veiled and puzzled look. "Are you sure?"

Zorin smiled back, proclaiming a level of confidence that didn't get past his old friend.

"Yes. Of course I'm sure!" He scoffed as Cordelia threw her hands up and chuckled in a mock defense. After a few steps he sighed to himself, "After weeks of this I better be sure."

Eralin sighed, emotionless. "He's not sure."

Zorin's head spun towards him, "I am and you should be too! You were with me!"

"Not that much with you." Eralin shrugged as Vix sighed deeply with disappointment.

For weeks Zorin, Sophie and Eralin had been exploring the upper section of the central tower. Meanwhile, Cordelia and Vix had been keeping busy investigating the selection of leather bound tomes in the great mezzanine with Lorvana. The bard would help by recalling stories and songs of long ago as the fire mage and chaos sorcerer searched the more arcane listings. Though the selection was relatively much smaller than that of the Ivory Library she was used to studying in; it still was very impressive on its own.

After the first 10 days Zorin decided that he and Eralin would find a way up into the shaft itself. It was then that he realized it did not run parallel with the stairwell going up but had two 90 degree bends before continuing straight up into the darkness. They were now following this leg up a long spiral staircase that seemed to climb forever.

"Well. It still doesn't make sense why it would go this way." Vix panted in frustration. "But I suppose I will trust in your expertise."

"Well-" Zorin's proud smile stretched across his face. He looked back at Eralin with a smug chuckle.

"Vix- did you just concede to Zorin?" Sophie asked thoughtfully

"I... in fact did." Vix shrugged.

"Wait. Really?" Cordelia was stunned.

"Absolutely." He announced with a thin smile.

"At least someone gives me some respect around here." Zorin said under his breath.

Vix continued, "Expertise in his field after all- includes hiding lockpicks in uncomfortable places."

"Hey! It..." Zorin's pride that beamed moments before lay shattered at his feet as he scrambled frantically trying to piece together enough to protect his fragile honor, "it... it was my boot!"

"Oh sure it was," Vix's eyes narrowed as he smiled, "Whatever you say... Expert."

"Oh, shut up." Zorin huffed as they continued their ascent.

After the better part of an hour in silence, the party came to the top of the stairs where, after a short landing of 10 feet, a door lay in front of them. A strong wind pushed against the iron bound oak of the door. Shards of sunlight around the frame was a noticed warning of what was likely to lay on the other side. They guarded their eyes from the forgotten daylight as Zorin and Eralin lifted the oaken bar and opened the door.

Sunlight blinded them as they walked out onto a wide circular platform that Zorin noted was ringed with a waist high battlement. Not for repelling any kind of arrow at this distance but thankfully for something to hold onto from this height to avoid tipping over into the expanse below. Clouds rolled close and even some smaller wisps stretched out below their level. Realizing this was the absolute summit of the tower, Sophie felt a little sick, Zane's voice echoing that feeling deep within her mind.

"Well... this is the top." Zorin looked back at the group with wide eyes, "How high is this again?"

Sophie closed her eyes and Zane's voice internally cut through the roar of the wind at this height. "Oh... oh no. Is that me feeling sick or you Sophie? I'm sorry if its-"

"Stop Zane," she spoke, leaning on red metal scales armoring her thighs, "You aren't helping."

Cordelia looked at Sophie questioningly, "What's that?"

Sophie burped into her own mouth leaving a bitter taste, "Oh this is. I'll ... I'll wait for you all inside."

With several quick paces the powerful swordmaster retreated back to the door from where they came. Zorin put his hand on Cordelia's concerned shoulder.

"She'll be ok." He took a deep breath and smiled, "Look at that. You can see forever."

Zorin and his friends looked at the battlefield before them a quarter mile below. The wind was whipping by in gusts that seemed to threaten to pull them from their footing, but only in their mind. The fresh air smelled clean from here and though it felt icy it was dry. The roar of battle seemed to be a dull rumble from this height. As everyone looked out, Cordelia went to the center of the platform where she found a similar ring of tile that matched the one in the ceiling of the portal room.

"Hey Zorin, look at this."

"Uhhh....mm Cordelia?" Zorin was distracted it seemed.

"What?" She sighed, before pleading, "Come here it's only a second. "

His voice was slow, "You want to come here actually."

She huffed impatiently as she stormed over to them looking over the battlefield far below.

"Fine. What is it? it better be-" She froze as her heart dropped, "Oh.. oh no!"

Horror sank in her heart as Zorin was pointing to the swift blue shape of a powerful dragon flying close to the ground, screaming towards the troops guarding the tower.

THE QUILL IN AYLA'S HAND trembled as she took a deep breath, closing her eyes to focus, unaware of anything else around her. She recalled how Gustav's eyes had grown wide and, shaking the fear from his chest, he yelled, "Ayla! Look dead ahead!". Exhaling sharply she placed the quill back to her journal.

> *Father, I looked out across the battlefield and saw*
> *a blue shape in the distance approaching quickly.*
> *Once it reached our front lines fear cut me to the core*
> *as sparks ripped a swath through our ranks. I was*

frozen, wide-eyed and terrified. Gustav ran to reload his trebuchet, as Silvie's voice cracked through our paralyzed fear.

"Dragon!" she screamed over the clash of the battle and screams of terror, "Don't just wait for it! For the love of all that is holy, load! All of you, now!"

The familiar grind of stone on wood filled our ears but all we could see was that dragon and its massive, serpentine form coming our way. By the gods themselves a real dragon, father. I drew in a ragged breath and turned back to the rope attached to the long arm of the trebuchet and took my usual review to make sure I didn't see any tearing.

I called out to my team, "You heard her... Load!"

I joined my team as we rapidly turned the war machine winding that massive arm down and lifting the several tons of counterweight off the ground simultaneously. Based on our last shot I knew where our arc was, knowing it was too risky to adjust now. I imagined the arc and the line where the stone would be thrown. I know how long the whipping motion took. I knew the feel of the leash in my hand...

I was one with this machine now.

"Ready and holding, Captain!" I heard Gustav call out.

"Well this is a big one today!" Silvie laughed, then looked at me and smiled.

"Ayla, you can't rely on me for this one. You know where your shot will fall, just get it there! Right Gustav!"

"Yes Captain!" I heard him call as I nodded to Silvie.

Captain Silvie knew she would slow it down, that our disciplined formation this time needed to just act quickly.

"May the knightlord guide your hands," Silvie said as she shouted, "FIRE AT WILL!"

We held the trebuchet line like coiled snakes waiting to strike. The dragon let out another blast into supply wagons at the edge of the river and I breathed slowly noting it was almost in range. I began to hear our war machines launch.

"Steady." I found myself checking the palm of my hand on the leash for sweat. It came closer and I heard Gustav call out followed by the whip and grind of the massive trebuchet springing into action. I closed my eyes and counted.

"One... two... three... now!" and pulled my line as well. I watched the three remaining stones sail through the air towards the dragon. First the dragon cut hard to the left, then barely missed the second stone as well. My eyes grew wide that in doing so it over-corrected into Gustav's stone and finally mine found its mark across its head, driving it towards a heavy skid into the ground.

*Our team erupted into deafening cheers as Gustav
lifted me off the ground. The dragon had fallen!*

"THAT'S." VIX SHOOK HIS HEAD, staring down at the battlefield below and more importantly the crumpled blue shape lying prone in the mound of earth it had plowed up from its impact. Even from this height the dull boom had been audible as was the crowd cheering but soon was drowned out by his companions offering their own cheers as well.

"That's impossible," he snorted.

"Yeah! Look at that! That was…" Zorin paused and looked at Vix, "wait, what do you mean impossible?"

Vix looked at Zorin indignantly, his voice dripping with condescension, "You idiot. A trebuchet can't take down a dragon." Zorin was stunned as Cordelia and Sophie exchanged a bewildered look. "But...?" Zorin wiped his face in frustration. "Vix. It just did."

"I refuse to accept this-" Vix fumbled trying to search for the right word to express himself.

"Magic." Sophie offered with a smirk.

Vix didn't hesitate to continue, "Absolutely... There must have been magic involved."

"Tons of it!" She snickered.

"Yes." Vix nodded with a sigh of comfort.

"All the magics!" Lorvana chimed in.

Vix sighed, "Stop."

"In the form of a trebuchet I guess!" Lorvana shrugged, drawing more laughter from her friends. Sophie was laughing hard, obviously not feeling sick anymore, her bravery overcoming Zane's memory of falling from *The Sun God*'s main ship mast a few months ago. Vix huffed and stormed to another edge of the platform, shaking his head in anger.

Chuckling, Cordelia grabbed Zorin's sleeve and escorted him to the center of the platform.

"Hey... so Zorin, check this out," she said pointing to the ring of tile she had found moments before the dragon appeared.

Zorin's eyes couldn't hide his excitement, "Well, that's gotta be it!" He placed a hand on his bearded chin before passing it through his hair in thought.

"Hmm... I wonder if it opens from the same gear we used down-stairs so I could crawl in? Looks like there's some mechanism to open it."

Cordelia's smile faded slightly, "But it still doesn't explain what the big spell component is."

"Wait a moment." Vix turned towards them as the knots of a puzzle unravelled inside his mind. He looked around the platform and then at the sky itself. Snapping his fingers he turned to the others with a proud grin on his face.

"Ha! That's it." he proclaimed, proudly placing his hands on his hips.

"That's what?" Zorin responded coldly.

"The largest, most powerful spell component my salt crusted companion." Vix chuckled as he slapped a hand on Zorins shoulder, "One we can't hold, Zorin. The sun."

Cordelia's eyes lit up as she looked at the sky, a smile again beginning to form. Sophie raised a single eyebrow, not showing the same level of trust in Vix's assessment.

"How did they get it down there if there was a bend..." Suddenly realization hit. "The mirrors!"

"Yes, mirrors but the sun changes all day doesn't it, so there must be something set up to control it from down below." He narrowed his eyes as a thin smile tautened his lips. "It would take ages to come up here to adjust it manually, they would have to be special, specific mirrors I would guess."

Zorin flipped a tile on the north side revealing a double gear. He studied it briefly.

"This appears to change two mechanisms independently on the same shaft. Now we should look for some mirrors that have a hexagonal shaft to mount in this hole."

"Hey, I may have found where they are in the room next to the portal. It looked like a lab but it was filled with all kinds of large lenses, I thought. Without taking the sheets off to look, I suppose they could actually be mirrors!"

"Why didn't you take off the sheets and look?" Eralin shrugged his tall broad shoulders at this statement.

Sophie sighed, "You don't get this far in life just lifting up sheets in spooky places, Eralin. Just seems to be against the rules."

"Seems like a silly rule." he said coldly.

Zorin chuckled, "You are a strange man, Eralin. A brave man but certainly a strange man for sure."

The group returned to the room Sophie described. Cordelia lifted the tan and dusty sheet which fell apart in her hands from centuries of no use. It revealed a polished silver disc, concave towards the middle and covered in a clear thick glaze that retained and protected the reflective properties of the silver. Lifting the other moldering sheets, they found two more identical discs.

Zorin and Eralin then went back into the tunnel above the portal, taking the disk with them. Finding Identical points in the floor hidden under a loose tile they placed the mirrors with snap as they aligned to the ancient gear work. Over the next few hours, all were in place. Everyone made their way back to the portal room for a final test where Cordelia stood at the front of the archway walking through a checklist in her head.

"Ok... so there are no fancy words or spell work. I believe and Vix correct me-"

"Oh I will." Vix happily interrupted.

"IF I'm wrong. Correct me IF I'm wrong." She answered a bit impatiently.

"Gladly.:" Vix smiled curtly.

Cordelia sighed before looking at the others.

"The sun will be the power source and we can use the gems to talk to the other towers. Provided-"

"Provided they still have theirs activated as well." Vix finished.

"And it's not in parts everywhere like this one." Zorin added.

Cordelia nodded. "Ok here we go."

Cordelia absently played with the tied ends of a simple yarn bracelet on her left wrist. A twisted red and orange colored cord formed her faded and treasured friendship bracelet. Sophie noticed and smiled, raising a single muscular arm. There, barely visible next to the thick vambrace on her forearm, was a matching bracelet. Cordelia smiled and nodded at her friend.

Meanwhile Zorin and Eralin turned the large gear on the wall that opened the hatch in the ceiling. As it opened, small aquamarine gems glowed next to the crank. The light increased in intensity; something they hadn't noticed before. As they turned the two smaller cranks would select which gems were glowing in an arc. They noticed there was a second arc with a faint glow between two stones: one to the right and another at the center.

Zorin shrugged at Eralin, "Lets line them up. I wonder if it's a guide to the sun's position."

Turning the wheels the glowing light moved across the arc of gems until they lined up. As Eralin finished his adjustments the room slowly began to glow until it was bathed in light.

"Yes! that's it!" Cordelia's face glowed with excitement and anticipation.

Vix looked at the young fire mage. "Cordelia, you were not wrong."

She almost saw a smile from the elf's face but she brushed it off as wishful thinking.

Cordelia grew serious, "Ok... Here we go."

The blue sapphire glowed brightly at the top in the sunlight. The various metals on the arch glinted and shone, almost bringing the dragons depicted from their frozen state. To the left of the sapphire was a coal black jet and then a deep red ruby. To the right of the sapphire was an emerald and finally a diamond. She reached for the diamond and pressed in on it. The diamond locked in place glowing brightly and instantly.

Cordelia jumped back as the gate began to hum and streak tendrils of light across the frame like the tuning of a drum. Once the glow subsided she could see another room. It was similar to the room she stood in only with white marble with rose quartz. Several benches and a table were spread across the floor. Looking back at her friends they all stood frozen in place and wide eyed.

Zorin shrugged slightly, his eyes wide in disbelief.

"Can.. Can you step in?" His eyes became more concerned, "Is it safe?"

Cordelia sighed, "Well, only one way to find out."

She reached down and picked up a small fragment of an old white candle from the ground and tossed it into the room.

"What is that?" A curious voice rang from the room. She tried to place it and hoped but another voice rang out, one much more familiar, especially to Cordelia.

"Huh?" Rue cleared his throat, "What is it Moira?"

"I thought I heard something over there, by the portal." Moira's voice questioned.

"Let's see." The deep voice of her order's leader called out. Cordelia heard footsteps approach the portal. A tall man came into view, his deeply toned bald head topped the deep blue robes he wore and was riddled with the familiar tattoos she remembered.

Rue's eyes were wide and he smiled at his student, "Well... hello Cordelia. Welcome back to the Ivory Library, though your method is far from expected, my friend.." He saw her friends and sensed the urgency in the room. His voice became more serious.

"How can your fellow librarians assist you?"

CHAPTER 7

SHAKEN GROUND

"What's wrong Bula?" the reptilian voice hissed from beyond the small campfire.

The cold night air at their back, the orc centurion known as Bula stared into the fire. He glanced at the small humanoid, no taller than a child. She was known as Sharptooth, red orange scales swept across her toothy muzzle under concerned eyes.

"Hmm-hahaha The skeletons scared them! HAHAHA! Scared big tough Bula! Hahahaha!" the voice cracked and shrieked slightly as it cackled into the crisp night air.

Bula ignored the laughter of the crueler of the two kobolds, known as Broadflare. They both shared similar body types and leather armor common to their kind, but these two were the leaders of their units. Sharptooth was the calmer of the two, less barbaric in nature. He was the better one to talk to.

"I believe there are boots to lick back in your camp little Broadflare." The orc flexed a strong arm revealing a balled bicep they cupped with another hand, as their lips pulled back revealing worn tusks in an unamused snarl, "Leave."

Broadflare threw the empty tin plate he held in his clawed hands. "You fat, pompous, ugly troll! you don't tell Broadflare what to do! I-"

"Don't."

Bula hissed as they drew a long battered blade from their waist. It was stained dark and had been hammered into a crude shape to serve a hasty purpose. Broadflare suddenly hoped that purpose didn't involve his throat. He frantically began stepping backwards in the cold mud.

"I... I uh-"

Bula stood up, towering twice as tall as the small, cowering, wide-eyed creature, red brown eyes filled with a deep rage.

"Leave!" Bula shouted.

Bula watched the kobold scamper through the mud between the wide makeshift alleys of their tents. The orange glow of fires broke the dark midnight air, dancing off Broadflare's scales as he darted by.

They took a deep breath as Bula picked up the tin plate now leaning against the leg of a wooden camp chair covered in thick, stained ivory canvas.

The smell of cooking meat of unknown origin was heavy in the low smoke. Likely local venison. They looked at the pot before them. A mash of beans and a single large ham bone floated as the ladle broke the surface. They gently began circulating it in a false hope it would make the stew taste better.

"Sharptooth," Bula spoke gently over their shoulder as they stirred the bland but nourishing thin broth. "Do you miss home?"

"Enruk?" Sharptooth looked at her plate in thought. The memories came to the front of her mind. Laughing with some of the ladies who were talking about the golden eggs they were caring for. She remembered how excited she was to first put on the armor of a warrior, and the stoic but proud look on the elders of the city nodding at her as she marched away. That was long ago.

She had since lost many friends. She grimaced as faces of the fallen sprung to her mind unexpectedly.

"Yes. I miss it very much." She brushed a tear from her eye before anyone could see. "But we are many miles away now."

"I miss it, too. My home that is." Bula sighed heavily thinking of his brother from long ago, who now lived far away. After a few stirs of the pot in the quiet camp, they continued, this time looking at Sharptooth. "I have something I need from you and your team."

Sharptooth nodded, "Yes Bula. What do you need?" She grinned slightly.

Bula wasn't a cruel leader of the kobolds under their command. They had honored the command passed to them from Dabria when she was made a centurion in Dekkion's army and allowed to command a dead legion. Leading the kobolds was a job no one wanted. They were wild and unpredictable. Hordes of teeth, claws and spears swarming the battlefield. A living nightmare.

Bula thought of the time they had the kobolds under their command, and realized they had never moved on to another command because this is what the tall and muscular orc wanted. For all their faults the kobolds were living, and they didn't feel comfortable leading mercenaries or other orcs. They were a living nightmare, but at least it was that. Living.

Sharptooth looked at Bula, her dragon-like snout cocked to a side questioningly. Her fangs were longer than most and hung over her lower jaw slightly giving her namesake.

There was a level of trust between them that Bula needed to call on now. Sharptooth was a great leader and invaluable on the battlefield but there were more important things at stake.

"Take three with you and make your way south towards home but I need you to go into the mountains to deliver this," Bula held out a letter that had been folded up and stamped with a "D" wax seal on it. She took it from them and after putting it in her pouch Bula continued.

"Take it to Dubok of the Mistgard clan. Only Dubok. The rest are not to be trusted. Then make your way back to Enruk."

They reached into a pocket and pulled out an iron disc the size of a large coin with an inlaid copper dragon claw on it. Bula gave this to Sharptooth as well.

"Take this coin and show it on your way out of the camp to show you're not deserting."

She hesitated "Bula, don't you need me?"

"I need you to deliver this Sharptooth." Bula's yellow-orange eyes narrowed, "It's more important, this is about family."

Sharptooth nodded. Family was very important to her as well, and pangs of loss tore at her little heart as she sighed. She would help her friend, and hopefully she could see her family again in Enruk.

Smiling, she looked at the orc centurion she had served for the last year or so. "Thank you, Bula," she said as she held her plate for one last meal before leaving on her new mission.

AT THE OTHER END OF the camp far away from Bula's plans and Sharptooth's dreams three leaders stood over a single bed, draped in clean, sterile muslin. Under the sheets was a body wrapped in gauze. The face was unrecognizable behind layers of bloody bandages but his twisted black beard suddenly shook with the booming voice of Azure.

"I will destroy them!" His voice shook the room. With a heavy sigh his breath became more labored as he coughed several times. "Those puny knights have...have insulted me!"

Cobalt leaned over his body, her claw like gloves gingerly pulling the hair from the side of his head free of the wrappings and away from his one good eye.

"Hush my brother. You must rest." As his breathing slowed, the smell of sandalwood filled the room once more as veiled nurses entered the tent, one carrying a smoldering brass censure on a chain. The warm and earthy smell was pleasant and seemed to calm their frayed nerves. The nurses worked quickly, adjusting the bedding and smoothing out the sheets, coaxing Azure to sleep.

As the last one left the room Cobalt turned to Dabria. "So tell me again, why are you leaving?"

Dabria in her black scaled armor and Una in matching robes stood stoically before the commander. Cobalt noticed tendrils of mystical vapors drifting from Dabria's shoulders, only barely visible when she was perfectly still. Una's stance echoed her dark sister's, emotionless and cold.

Cobalt's eyes narrowed slightly at the silence. She knew a trusted centurion of Dekkion's undead legions held their secrets close and for good reason, but it seemed out of place for this to happen in the middle of a long, major siege.

"Well?" Cobalt urged looking for any response.

Dabria sighed, "We are being called to the north to investigate the Netherspring. The dark lord wills it."

"Yes." Una's dark voice resonated from under the hood, mystical but not unpleasant. "The great, ancient shrine calls us. An artifact of great power. I see a staff."

Una halted and her face twisted slightly as if there was a bad smell that struck her suddenly. Shaking her head she began again, "A staff for my patron."

Dabria regarded Una with a hidden concern. According to what Una had explained to her years ago her patron was a voice inside herself from which she drew power. Una said the voice had been there since they were children, over the last 10 or so years, as far back as she could remember. A voice that provided some vague guidance, and an occasional vision. Dekkion could use these powers of Una's to see into the future, using her in dark magic powerful beyond any other necromancer she had witnessed.

Recently Dabria noticed Una becoming more distant. There were more frequent discussions with this voice and more direct demands. The voice had become more prominent and clear, not the vague ramblings Dabria was used to hearing Una recite. It seemed something had awoken once they arrived. Una looked at her and nodded. After a moment Dabria sighed and continued. Her voice was clear and concise, using words well practiced and rehearsed.

"Yes, and we will leave after we launch the first assault of the day. The undead horde will then be yours to command. Just remember they are not favorable to the sunlight." She couldn't help but smirk slightly, "Obviously."

Cobalt's eyes rolled, "Obviously." She sized up the young centurion with centuries of knowledge behind her dark eyes. Even though Cobalt was in her human form, she wasn't any less alert to the possibility of treachery. The cleric was a loyal servant of death, though, and this had been proven time and time again. Cobalt snickered smugly.

"Fine. We both know I cannot keep you if the master of undeath calls you. Leave control of the horde with Bula when you leave."

"Bula?" Dabria laughed thinking of the orc she had mentored. She knew they hated the undead.

Cobalt stared at Dabria unwavering, "Yes, Bula. That is my wish. They can control both units I'm sure.

"You would have them control both?" Dabria was awestruck at this move that was uncharacteristically ignorant of the blue dragon commander. "It's not as easy as-"

Cobalt bristled, "Need I remind you Squib put me in charge and this is MY plan? The kobolds and undead will be controlled together. Everyone must step up and do their part and we don't need to waste resources where it's not needed." She stepped towards Dabria, slowly closing the distance. She was taller than Dabria by a foot and this was more pronounced now. "After all, we are this close to victory."

"Of course." Dabria lowered her eyes. "It is your plan after all. I will leave the talisman with Bula when we leave. I will see you on the battlefield tomorrow."

Dabria turned to leave the oiled canvas tent, the icy night air biting against a scarred cheek. Her golden eyes narrowed slightly as, in the darkness, the corner of her mouth cracked upwards in a smile.

THE SUN WAS RISING BUT the battlefield still slumbered under a blanket of frost. The blades of brown grass twinkled in the golden light as if diamonds clung to their fragile ends. Skotmir smiled as he stood on the muddy battlefield.

The dwarf shook the cold from his skin, flexing his sinewy muscles and squeezing the long handle of the steel great ax in his hands. Time and a lack of concern for keeping it shaved had given way to shaggy, deep brown hair that framed his ruddy face. He took a long breath through his bulbous nose and nodded. He smelled spring coming soon. The sun would melt the frost this morning he hoped and the clear sky seemed to be a good sign of this.

He turned. The sight of the people gathered behind him was still as shocking as it had been this morning when he saw them for the first time. His own command.

"Ah." Skotmir cleared his throat nervously, noticing the handle of the ax was getting slippery with sweat. Drying a hand on his pants, Skotmir looked at the head of the ax. Dings and divots told the tale of many successful battles, and the survival of many more encounters. He looked up and out across the slushy mud of the battlefield. Taking note of their position he saw they were the reserves, meaning any charge breaking through down the center still had to get through several lines of trained knights and soldiers though the numbers seemed fewer day by day.

Squinting in the morning sun for a moment he let the light fall on his face. Feeling a warm glow, his smile returned and he turned back to face those behind him. Farmers mostly, he had guessed, based on their plain ragged clothes and ill fitting scraps of armor. Many carried a hastily sharpened longsword provided by the quartermaster but many others carried pitchforks, spears and other farming tools as proud weapons, and Skotmir noted they were proud.

The warriors of his company looked shaken slightly. There was a slight tremble in their eyes from never seeing battle but they still looked forward proudly. He hoped they would do their best to understand the gruff dwarfs' orders and more importantly interpret them to efficient actions.

Skotmir approached what he guessed to be a late teens human. His long black hair hung in locks fastened with clay beads and tied to hang behind him. His deep eyes read of many years lived despite their apparent age.

"Hey." He approached the young man. "What's your name, soldier?"

"D..Dairmid sir." The young man stammered slightly. Skotmir straightened up a bit to appear taller. Chuckling at the thought of how ridiculous he looked like he relaxed his shoulders. Seeing Dairmid smile relaxed them both a bit.

"Where are you from, Dairmid?"

"My family holds a small grain field to the east of here."

Skotmir perked up. He wasn't sure where he was going with

these questions, just that he needed to. There was something he always liked about the generals who walked and talked with their soldiers. Dairmid had set up one of his favorite topics, food.

"Ooh. And what kind of grain? Wheat, Rye, Barley?" Skotmir smiled his chipped tooth grin at the young man.

"Wheat sir."

Skotmir ruffled his back a little as if something was itchy and unpleasant under the tan, stained shirt he wore under the two thick leather straps over his shoulders. The straps held two extra hand axes in case of emergency, but offered no other protection to the berserker.

"Eh.. don't call me that." His smile returned with even more excitement in his voice, "Wheat eh? Well, do you bake?"

"Y..Yes. Yes of course. We are known for our various rolls. Great for your favorite soup, sometimes even better!" Daimid said proudly.

Skotmir beamed, "Well fight as hard as you can today Dairmid. I-" Skotmir struggled as he searched his mind for something inspirational. He remembered Benedict giving him advice once. To be inspiring one must first just 'be', as in be true to yourself. Those that can relate will. He sighed with a big grin.

"I want some of that bread."

Everyone laughed, including Skotmir. Dairmid nodded with a grin on his face too.

"Oh... ok. Sir."

Skotmir mocked frustration, unable to dampen his smile at his new friend.

"I said don't call me that... It's Skotmir. Skotmir Flintgrog." He pounded his fist on his chest proudly, "Get ready to make a tab under that name, buddy, because I'm coming. Will I need to bring my own ale Dairmid?"

Dairmid shrugged, "Well we don't really-"

"I'll bring the ale Skotmir!" an older man with hair receding back and crows foot wrinkles in his eyes spoke up. "My farm is next to Dairmid's and my family would be proud to have you at our table!"

"If you all are bringing that then... we need a stew!" another young man but twice the size of Daimid shouted proudly, driving the end of his pitchfork into the ground to steady himself. "We raise cattle just to the north of here. Best beef in the land, fed on cornmeal and blackroot they are!"

The crowd all nodded and a few cheered. The man's herds were well known in the region apparently, especially by House Venre in Darkovnia. Skotmir laughed as he put his hands on his hips.

"Well my friends! I'll see you all there!" Skotmir shouted with a fist in the sky as everyone cheered.

Skotmir was awestruck. He did it, he really did it! He had rallied his unit of volunteers and raised their spirits. He bet Benedict would have been proud wherever he might be. A big smile lit his face as he looked at his brave troops. He turned back to the battlefield, knowing if nothing else one goal of the day was to live to see a good hot meal with new friends.

THE DEAD MOVED IN A swarm to the battlefield. Limbs ending in crude, rusted, ancient weapons shook with every shambling step. The bodies barely balanced on their ancient leg bones, like the jittery legs of an old spider approaching the end of its days. They drug themselves to certain death though they knew not the purpose in their re-existence.

Squib the Crusher, overseer of Lord Pallus's forces here at the Celestine Tower, stared at the twisted dance of the dead. She scowled from the hilltop overlooking the battle, a short tusk in the corner of her mouth freed for a moment from a deep purple lip.

"Ugh... Disgusting! But effective I suppose, right lieutenant?"

"Yes... Commander." Cobalt hissed like a tea kettle screaming from a fire.

Squib had grown impatient with Cobalt's toying with the knights. She had moved herself up to watch over the opening assault one last time before leaving. They were in control of the battlefield–Cobalt had seen to that–and Lord Pallus would be pleased. Soon the knights would fall. There was no need for Squib to waste her own time anymore, or her family.

"Lord Pallus was very clear that the blue dragons would be the ones to assault the blue tower." She paused, chuckling at the irony, "He does excel at matchmaking doesn't he?"

"Like a child might I suppose." Cobalt mumbled in disgust under her breath.

Squib chuckled at her insult. Pallus could defend his own honor. It wasn't her place to defend it for him, nor did she want to. She kept looking forward. Her long black braids hung behind her slightly pointed ears, her red orange eyes were the color of the fire that burned behind them as she surveyed the battlefield.

Squib smiled, revealing more of the tusk overlapping the top left corner of her plum colored lips. She flexed a powerful arm under the spiked armor that hung at the shoulder and matching bracers. Her crocodile green skin pulled tight around large muscular biceps as eyes narrowed. Squib scowled slightly looking up to those on the horses. She hated the use of horses as simple mounts, their power and grace was put to better use with carts or better yet, war chariots.

"Well... We will be very excited to see this 'great plan' of yours today. Dabria and Una will be leaving soon as well-"

"Once they are done training Bula." Cobalt interrupted and pointed to the three of them thirty yards away at the base of the hill.

"Yes. Of course." Squib shook her head slightly. "An efficient move to task them with both the kobolds and the undead. We will see if it proves effective though."

Squib slapped a powerful hand on Cobalt's armored thigh so hard it spooked the horse into taking a step out of fear. Cobalt fumbled with the reins.

"Cobalt, your force is dwindling. Not that it means much from what I can see but I grow tired of your little games!" She drew her lips back in a snarl like a jaguar in the jungle where she came from as she hissed, "Crush them! You have wasted enough time and my people grow weary of your delays!"

"Y... Yes milady." Cobalt stammered, bowing.

Squib smiled cruelly at the formality.

"After all, you don't want to appear to be playing childish games too, do you?"

Squib looked at the man at her side. Ebon was another orc like herself, though his skin was jet black under only a fur war skirt. His massive broad chest was marked in jagged lime colored tattoos and tribal markings. His eyes held deep rubies. He smiled at her and nodded.

Squib sighed out of boredom looking back at Cobalt, "Fine then. I'll leave you to it. The day is yours to finish your... "plan." We are done babysitting you. See you back at the Obsidian Fortress. Do not disappoint me."

Her last words hung in the air like a vulture in a soft wind as it circled its prey.

"Let's go, Ebon."

Squib turned on a booted heel with her mind's thought drifting elsewhere. As she walked away her fingernails absently played with the dark brown tattoo of a war hammer emblazoned on her wrist.

DABRIA TURNED TO WATCH SQUIB walk away, her golden eyes lingering too long as she felt the fire of anger in her heart.

"She at least respects your will." Una stated

Dabria scoffed at her dark sister.

"She respects nothing. She's no different than the others. Mindless." Dabria chuckled. "Rassler has more sense than most here. Squib included."

Una cleared her throat. "Rassler. Pity you put them in the front of the vanguard. They didn't last more than a moment at the hands of the knights this morning." Bula shrugged.

"They served us well these past years. It seemed right they should find a swift death in battle." Dabria winked at Una.

"That was too kind." Una looked at Dabria with her multicolored eyes and smiled knowingly. "Well now it is time, Dark Sister. She calls us north."

"So how do I use this talisman again?" Bula said holding the bronze disk with a large black stone set in the center. The disk etched with several runes that seemed to change out of the corner of the eye like a blind spot illusion shifting along with one's thoughts.

"Simply think of the orders themselves and place your palm on the obsidian eye." She sneered deeply as she stood up straight, "It really is quite simple, Bula you-"

"Yes of course it is!" Bula waved their hands impatiently. "Just go!"

Dabria raised an eyebrow then nodded at the orc centurion. "Very well. May their death come on swift wings in your favor Bula."

CHAPTER 8

TIDE OF WINTER

Caleb's mount rode into the right flank, meeting the enemy head on. I was only a few yards behind.

"The Knightlord will guide us!" Caleb roared as he struck downward in wide swaths from his horse. Bone and rusted steel shattered under each blow, sending a musty, coppery dust into the air, mixing with the turned earth of the battlefield.

His shield was emblazoned with the Blue Crown and Sword. The glint of his longsword darted with precision, rendering the undead horde useless before him. He smiled looking back at me.

"I left you some, Keldor!" he jabbed playfully at me, "Try to keep up! unless duty still doesn't suit you."

The past few days we had spent more time together with the focus of restoring the trust of the sword with each other. Caleb had admitted to me that his outburst on the wall that night was fueled by the rage of his sister's loss and chained by years of never finding an answer. Losing life's flame for someone we are close to can drive us to the edge of insanity after all, and Caleb losing his only sister proved that. I held no ill will toward Caleb; I too grieved for Elona. Today was another step of atonement for me, today was for her.

"Ha! Duty suits me fine!" I shouted back to him, in jest.

Kicking my feet out of the stirrups I leapt from my horse and hit the mud with an impact that dropped me to one knee, briefly. Raising my head I saw the tattered ribbons of ancient armor and the skeletal face of the adversary above me. A rusty one handed ax raised up with a bony claw like hand. I drug my great sword out of the mud and at the same time slicing upward as I stood, cleaving them in two. My mount had left the battlefield and was heading back to the keep as was its instinct. I spun in the mud realizing I was surrounded.

"PEE-TAH!!" A shrieking voice carried from a few yards from me, from a living being I had either missed or had just appeared. With a booming roar, red-orange fire erupted from the ground, great columns of flame leapt toward the sky. The force parted the sea of skeletal warriors in an explosive arc outward revealing four figures.

"Clear a path!" A mage in red and gold robes raised her hands sharply as three other mages in blue, green and violet peeled a hole in the crowd gathering around me and sent them spinning into a hovering orb, the size of a wagon cart, that appeared in the air above me. They flew as if they were feathers in the cold wind, towards the glowing sphere shrouded in grey blue tendrils of smoke.

My eyes were wide as I stared upward in awe at the treacherous orb spinning ominously. It seemed to be made of darkness itself, shrouded in some sort of arcane plates. As the bodies impacted they instantly vaporized as the orb greedily consumed the undead.

I gathered myself and took the opportunity to be grateful, running towards them in the clearing. "Thank you!" I shouted as the one-eyed mage held a hand at me waving me behind her.

"Clear out!" she pointed at the green robed mage, "Moira! Over there!"

"I see them! Duck!" Moira raised her arms and rolled them hand over hand sculpting a ball of blue white fire in her hands.

"FEN SHAW!"

The ball arced off her palms and barely missed my head as I dropped to the ground mid sprint. The unpleasant taste of grit and snow splashed into my mouth. I looked up and saw blue robes briefly and a hand offering to help me up.

"Sir, get behind us please." He said as he pulled me to the side before he too shouted in some arcane language, "TEH-FA-DAH!"

I dove behind the tall bald man in the blue robes as the ground erupted in a wall of ice that darted across the battlefield in both directions, separating the horde from our army. The knights cheered.

My eyes fell on the faint crown and sword navy embroidery on his shoulder, barely visible unless up close as I was. Gasping, I realized who they were: the stone monks from the Ivory Library had arrived to assist in our cause. Our fatigued knights fell back, relinquishing the ground to the hundreds of fresher forces.

We saw blazing spell after spell roll across the battlefield, driving the adversary back towards their lines. I felt the heat as the living mercenaries fled searing flames rolling in giant red-orange arcane wheels that rolled over everything in their path. The undead stood defiantly, greeting their fiery destruction with open arms.

"NO!" COBALT SCREAMED, SPURRING HER horse into a frightened whinny as it pranced nervously at her outburst. "No! This is impossible!"

She had everything planned, everything in order. It had been so simple she was dumbfounded and shaking. The smell of the burning leather and bone was heavy on the breeze now along with the horrified shrieks of her legions. Cobalt balled her hands into fists as she trembled with fury.

"Bula! Send them back now!"

Her mouth grew slightly more red as she bit her lip in frustration. The incompetence of the centurion had cost her victory not just today, but for the entire campaign. They had to turn back. There was no other choice, and Lord Pallus would ensure she would be in a worse state than Azure's crumpled form. She was losing control of the battle, her army and herself. Spittle flew from her mouth as she screamed at the orc who had failed her.

Bula was terrified. They frantically slammed their palm into the obsidian gem, hoping for a different result, any result. Panting, they helplessly turned towards the commander's livid face.

"But I am! They aren't listening!" They wiped the sweat from their brow and tried to calm their labored breathing. Bula looked at the talisman, forcing themself to recall Dabria's instructions. They needed to be calm then they could give their commands to the stone, but they struggled to find any order within their own panic.

"Now! Do it now!!" Cobalt shrieked, wide-eyed and bloodthirsty. Her eyes began to glow from slits as her skin became more taut and leathery. She felt the back of her head ache, anticipating the horns of the dragon form she could barely keep at bay. Not yet she told herself, she would become an even larger target for the spellcasters that had suddenly appeared and they were not proving to be weak.

Bula trembled, confused and frightened of the situation they found themselves in.

"I... can't!" Bula screamed while trying to will a command, any command, into their locked mind, "Go back just GO BACK!"

Bula slammed their palm over the obsidian stone as the centurion commanded in their mind. Just like Dabria had instructed.

"There!" Bula felt a wave of relief as they panted from exhaustion. "Look Cobalt, they are moving!"

"Good!" Cobalt laughed.

She saw the skeletal army start to advance, sidestepping the wheels of fire. After a few steps the glowing blue green eyes of the undead turned towards her. Cobalt's laugh faded as, once more, her eyes grew wide in anger.

"Bula you fool!"

Soon screams erupted all around Bula as realization poured over their soul like white hot lava. They found they had been envisioning their own internalized terror while issuing the command to "go back". Bula's orders were now sending them like a tidal wave deep into their own army.

AYLA'S QUILL CONTINUED TO SCRATCH the paper while recalling her day at the trebuchet.

We watched them flee, father! It was on that 23rd day of siege when we saw them run. The smell of the blood and death seemed to follow them as we rejoiced in the coming of the Librarians from the Ivory Tower.

That evening we celebrated in the dining hall. Granted, we had yet another meal of chicken and vegetables but this one simply tasted better than any other meal. Even the stale bread trencher seemed to be made from some exotic bread from a far off land, and we got to enjoy mead together. Mages and knights alike sat and mingled and enjoyed ourselves in the hall. I saw Lord Alvar saying goodbye to some of our new friends.

LORD ALVAR STOOD BEFORE ELLOVEVE, Benedict and I as we were preparing our packs for the journey.

"Keldor, Elloveve and now Corporal Benedict." He smiled at the young man with the raven black hair before him, remembering the starry eyed squire to be from just a few weeks before. "We wish you a safe journey.

"Lord Alvar, it was an honor." Keldor held out his hand.

"No old friend, the honor was mine." Lord Alvar grasped Keldor's arm with both hands as his thin beard shook lightly. Clearing his throat he continued. "I believe someone has something they wish to say?"

Caleb stepped forward. His blue eyes were not holding any ill will behind them anymore.

"Keldor, you fought well. I am again sorry for my words on the wall the other night I-"

"No Caleb." I interrupted gently. You had every right to say them." I paused when I saw the look on his face. No further words were needed or required. We knew where we stood with one another and that was enough. He turned away from me and looked at Benedict, his nephew.

I knew he still hadn't told him, and if he didn't want to it was his right I suppose. Knowing Caleb, he wasn't sure where to start when greeting the son of his long dead sister, so he chose to greet him with honor as a knight. It didn't matter if I agreed with his method. It was ultimately his choice and I chose to honor his wish. Again I was reminded that we all carry our demons differently.

"Sir Benedict Shieldheart. I wish you success in your journey to reclaim Garnet Keep. I have something for you."

Caleb produced a folded black cloth. He opened it slowly revealing a soldier's tunic. Identical to Benedict's own but in deep red colors and the single red stripe of a Corporal.

"You will need your own uniform when you succeed." He smiled gently as a proud father might see his son. "And I know you will. May the Knight and Maiden watch you now."

ZORIN LOOKED AROUND THE MEAD hall, noting it felt emptier without his three friends. Gripping the tin tankard tight, he drew a deep gulp of the sweet brew, almost coughing a little as he felt the bubbles tickle the back of his nose and throat ache. He sighed and cleared his throat. Skotmir clapped a hand on his shoulder before turning to Sophie.

"Hey Sophie, so tell me again. Why didn't we go with them?"

Sophie sat, toying with the bracelet on her wrist while staring into the half empty goblet of red mulled wine. The warm smell of nutmeg and cinnamon wafting gently to her nose.

She spoke without looking away, "Benedict said this was something they had to do alone."

"It's a smaller group." Zorin added, holding up an empty hand as he slung a booted foot onto the table. "Makes sense if they are scouting it out to be sure. He said for us to meet them there in a month."

Cordelia reached for the glass pitcher in the center of the table filled with water.

"Yeah, no one believes there is any threat left at Garnet Keep." She sighed as she poured the water into a simple horn cup, "I'm not sure I believe them."

"I wouldn't," an unknown voice called out from behind golden eyes.

Her voice was a sarcastic tone but it was surprisingly coming from someone who wasn't Vix. It was more breathy and carried the weight of death behind it.

The friends looked up to see four veteran Knights escorting two prisoners. One of the guards looked at Zorin.

"Mister Zorin. These two were asking where to find you. We've confiscated their weapons and they didn't give any fight."

The guard opposite him laughed, "Well that one did punch Joey."

Dabria narrowed her golden eyes. "He was rude." she nodded towards Zorin. "Una. Is that him?"

Una's eyes were wide open and smiling. A smile that held no malice, no cruelty or mystery. It was a look of admiration.

"Yes! That's him, my dark sister! His heir!" she stammered with nervous excitement.

Zorin was stunned.

"Woah! Who are you and whose heir... wait." He held up the palms of his hands, shaking his head, but made no effort to sit up from leaning back in his chair. He knew by the dark armor and robes they were from the dark army. The army of his father Lord Pallus.

"Never mind that. What do you want with me?" he asked.

"We need to talk in private about a mutual... interest." Dabria smirked.

She looked at Una with her gold eyes twinkling sinisterly in the dim torchlight of the mead hall. Una smiled in return behind her dark robe, pleased in their shared success.

Looking back to Zorin she smiled like a cat toying with its prey.

"Actually, bring your friends. It'll be a party."

INTERLUDE

Winter had been dry and icy in Red Pine. The land of Wolfling was known for its cold winters and icy winds but the lack of snow was unusual. Lord Pallus brought a gloved hand to his face and sniffed the air deeply as they walked heavily towards the small raised platform of stone. Mint. The sweet smell of mint crushed in his hand filled his nose and soothed the sinuses. Exhaling heavily he chuckled.

"You've done well Maldros. Three arenas are in your control now." He smiled crookedly as he glanced at the dark man to his right. "How does it feel?"

"Good." The dark man nodded.

The charcoal armor covered him from head to foot with large horns that twisted from the thick helmet away from his face. Maldros's armored face was a horned and bearded skull with the nose peeled back like a bat's. Red eyes glowed from within showing pleasure and an uncontrolled hatred. Over one shoulder was a knotted greatclub, the favored weapon of the veteran fighter.

"-but you mean four." Maldros chuckled. ,"The trade pigs of Darkovnia haven't found a way to shut down the underground."

"True. Four it is." Lord Pallus shrugged.

Their pace slowed as they took the final steps towards the rough cut slate of the platform. Lord Pallus set a hand on the waist high stone, worn smooth in places by hundreds of feet, paws and claws of those that had fought there. Looking up he saw a fighter in his memory. An orc outcast thrown into the arenas to fight for his life and eventually his freedom.

"This one is my favorite though." Pallus smiled, "You were the best."

"Yes." Maldros slung the smooth hardwood of the club heavily to the stone. Pallus could feel the power of it vibrate up to his elbow from the impact. "Yes I was. I was-"

"The Unrelenting." Pallus interrupted without looking away from the platform and imagining the past.. "They called you that for a reason. Maldros the Unrelenting."

"True. I was." Maldros scowled. "Now they dare not call me that. They know better."

Pallus laughed and clapped a hand on the back of Maldros.

"I'm sure they do." He looked into those blood red eyes. "You are in charge now. Bloodwood, Enruk, Darkovnia and Wolfling."

Pallus nodded in approval of his own assessment. He looked back at the podium and saw Maldros, panting after his last battle, awaiting judgment. As he let his memory take over, he saw her.

Black robes were lined with silver runes and her deeply tanned cheekbones carried similar tattoos. The ghost nodded at him as she handed him the coins to pay for the warrior's freedom. Pallus lowered his head for a moment and sighed at her memory.

Ash.

Her name resonated in his mind.

Shaking his head free of the memory he turned back to Maldros, wringing his hands in thought.

"We leave tomorrow to go back to Enruk. Squib and the orc battalion will stay here in the Obsidian Fortress, but Dekkion, you and I will travel south with Fury and a new warrior for your pits."

"Oh?" Maldros's voice perked up. "Who is this fresh meat?"

Pallus chuckled, "There's nothing fresh about this one. It's Azure."

Maldros the Dark pictured the blue dragon in his former glory. Ferocious and terrifying, the smell of electricity hung in his memory like the wet air that carried it. He smiled and nodded in understanding.

"Yessss." a familiar voice hissed, grabbing their attention to a new visitor. Tattered grey robes clung to the old man's skeletal shoulders. White hair was sparse and thin around the crown of his head drifting in the air gently as he seemed to glide over the caked, cold earth.

"A warrior has requested a warrior's death." Dekkion's voice hissed as he crossed the floor.

"Dekkion." Lord Pallus nodded at the necromancer as he drew in a deep breath to cool his anger.

"We lost many mercenaries with this engagement at the Celestine Tower, Dekkion." Pallus growled, "I hope it was worth it."

Dekkion placed a talon-like hand on the shoulder of Maldros, sneering as he glided behind him.

"Lost?" he chuckled at the absurd comment. "I told you my lord.."

The cold air carrying Dekkion's voice curled in Maldros's ears.

"An undead army must be fueled by the bodies of the living."

CHAPTER 9

CHASING DESTINY

"I have to admit." Dabria smirked, "I thought you'd be... um... stronger."

Zorin chuckled. "Huh. Haven't heard that one before."

The meeting room was a 20 foot cold marble room with blue and green tapestries on the east side of the second floor. Lord Alvar believed this was the best place to discuss the strange arrival of their new guests and the curious nature of their visit. Lord Alvar noted that the long oaken table, for the first time in memory, was actually full. Sitting center of one side, in an ornately carved high back chair, was Zorin. The man he knew now as the estranged son of Lord Pallus. Zorin was also a sailor, thief, gambler and also seemed to be the focus of these two mysterious defectors from the Dark Army..

"So you are here to meet Zorin because a higher power told you to?" Sophie laughed to herself while taking a bite into a small roll of bread. Cordelia smirked, "Yeah. I'm not too sure I believe that either."

"Are you kidding?" Zorin smiled at his friends, "Even Benedict would have a hard time believing that." He paused, thinking of the honorable knight who was like a brother to him. "If he were here," he added with a sigh.

Zorin's skin itched and his heart pounded. It wasn't often, if ever, he was thrust into the spotlight. On the right of him sat Sophie, the beautiful and deadly sword for hire, who carried the soul of his best friend and her lover entwined with her own. Next to her sat white robed Cordelia with three other mages that were recognizable by their different colored robes: Rue in deep ocean blue, Moira in emerald green and Belinial in blood red.

Across from the mages sat Vix the Chaotic and Skotmir the dwarven barbarian who was now picking at the remains of a stewed chicken with his fingers. To the other side of Vix sat Una the Seer and Dabria, a cleric of some death god he wasn't familiar with. One that was symbolized by the simple goat's horn she wore around her neck.

"I would be curious as to what this voice is as well as what it says." Vix mused from behind clasped hands. "Rue, have you ever encountered something like this in your studies?"

"No." Rue sighed as his mind raced. "No Vix I haven't."

"No. Voices are rarely a good thing in my experience." Belinial gazed across the table at Vix with a single eye blazing with curiosity. A leather and silver patch adorned the other. "Have you, Vix?" she asked.

Vix closed his eyes and saw the owl in his mind and heard a harsh screech. The sound carried words though. Her soft words.

"Remember, what I told you, Vix."

The owl changed in his mind to a woman carrying a wicked and cruel spear, covered in rivulets of blood and its head was that of a raven. Her chest heaved as she stood anticipating a battle. Vix could see rain falling in the streetlights at the edge of the alleyway. The smell of wet dust and forgotten mold filled the brick and clay walls. This was the street that night several years ago when she appeared ripping from the body of a prisoner. A prisoner who once spoke of voices as well but now was crumpled at the feet of the fiend.

"Once you drink from my cup, you can't just leave."

The vision exploded in a cloud of black birds. Vix shook his head free of the memory.

"Once." He sighed. "But as you say it was not a good thing."

"Ha!" Skotmir laughed as he stared into the wooden bowl in her hands that held the last mouthful of broth. "Voices." He shook his head before slurping it away and slamming it down on the table with a chuckle.

"So again, for clarity of your purpose, you came here seeking out Zorin because of his father?" Caleb asked.

At one end of the table between Zorin and Dabria sat Sir Caleb, now decorated as a Knight Major and Lord Alvar's second in command. Who, as the host of this unlikely meeting, sat at the other end of the table, one hand calmly placed upon his chin. He regarded the dark visitors with suspicion but took care not to judge them too hastily.

They came here on their own. Lord Alvar thought. This was quite curious to him and after clearing his throat he stood up and looked directly at the new guests.

"Why would a decorated centurion of the Dark Army and their shadow oracle come here willingly?"

Dabria sighed impatiently. "I have said that–"

"Wait."Una interrupted, "No need to repeat yourself my sister. We must show them our purpose aligns with his."

Dabria nodded.

"How do you know my purpose?" Zorin questioned with a chuckle before turning to Sophie, "I don't even know my purpose."

Sophie laughed. "It's true, he doesn't."

"Jeez you don't have to be like that." Zorin mocked his hurt feelings with a chuckle. Una impatiently slammed a fist on the table as cold air rocketed through the room like a blizzard had entered the hall unannounced..

"Look at me!" she erupted through clenched teeth.

Una's eyes were wide as the warm torches of the room suddenly burned blue and green, reflecting off her eyes but also blazing from within.

"Dabria, now tell them why we walk the same path." Una's voice reverberated in the room with a hidden power.

"What path?" Zorin shook his head and he searched Una's face for answers. "What's this all about?"

"Zorin, the answer is simple." Dabria began as she stared into her cup. "Let me tell you a story. Our story."

"Our story?" It was his turn to laugh, "We have no story Dabria. I've thankfully never met you before."

Dabria's lip simply curled at the comment, but otherwise she didn't move.

"You are wrong," Una chuckled. "We know you know this topic too well."

Dabria took a long gulp of the sweet mead in the cup before turning her golden eyes back on Zorin. He felt a chill run through him.

"It's about revenge."

"FOR AS LONG AS I'VE remembered I—well Una and I lived in the far south of Trull. In the city of volcanoes, Enruk. Enruk is like a living hell of sorts. Fire and sulfurous smoke constantly belches into the red sky, a great place to live if you are a kobold or an orc.

Una and I were trained here for our roles in the army. Una was a seer; could see visions, she told me once.

'I see your dream... your 4 arms winding, turning slowly in a blue sea.'

The voice in her head was unnerving. It knew my dreams, or things about me that were true but I didn't know or remember. Maybe I didn't want to remember.

The army was my family and in this family I was trained as the feared mistress of pain. My tolerance to it was much higher than my peers and I also had a knack for tactical leadership. As the years progressed they either respected or at least feared me.

After one incident in the mess hall I demonstrated what I was capable of on someone that was attacking Una."

Dabria paused. Remembering the face of the young officer glaring at her with contempt as Una was terrified and pleading. Dabria shook her head and continued.

"I was ruthless, and the dark lord Dekkion heaped his blessings on me. I soon became close associates with one of his lieutenants. The dark eyed blade master known as Nightblade.

We were inseparable. Working in concert with each other both on the battlefield and, well, as lovers. She was everything to me that I was missing and she felt the same. Una was my best friend and the three of us were about as happy as we could expect to be. After all, we knew no difference.

We grew up there, we've known nothing else. My earliest memories were of Una and hers were off me but we can't remember anything else. No home or family, just emptiness. A void exists where our childhood should have been. The first decade of our lives scrubbed like an old chalkboard. Nightblade never spoke of her life before the army. I could tell it was a painful topic and she was 5 or so years older than me so I never pressed more. After all I couldn't remember my childhood either so we had that in common. Why mess with something that was so perfect?

Una worked with the dark lord directly. She gave him the visions he sought and over time those visions changed."

Dabria could see the stone slabs of the granite walls in her memory dripping slightly from heat and humidity. The yellow green liquid glowed from within a cauldron on the fire. A gaunt man in black armor and a midnight blue cloak lined with fur looked into the reflection on the surface with great anticipation. His own features were aged, wrinkled with papery parchment like skin pulled tight over his high cheekbones in yellow gray sheets. Clear, pale, gray eyes drew back starkly from a head of long wiry gray hair. Next to Dekkion stood Una, in her black hooded robes, eyes closed as she looked inwardly towards the future.

"Yes Una! Tell me more! If we take the Emerald Atoll will it aid in the assault on shrouded Veridian?" He shook as his eyes widened, "Is this the way to the Ferryman's Gate?"

"I see… " Una strained to make out the swirling images in her mind. "I see much death in your favor, my lord. But, the spirit tells me… " Una's eyes opened wide, staring at Dekkion in disbelief.

"NO!!" She shrieked with her eyes wide and her face pulled back in horror at the man who was her guardian, her protector. "BETRAYER!!"

"What?! What did you say to me?!" Dekkion's lips curled as his eyes darkened.

"BETRAYER!!" Una lunged at him screaming with her hands outstretched, clawing frantically for his throat.

"Bah!!" Dekkion yelled as he shoved her away, "Guards! Get her out of here!"

As the guards rushed to restrain the woman behind flailing dark robes, her hand blazed with light briefly. Falling from her hand were ashes and a crumpled blood red object that tumbled as it hit the ground. Dekkion chuckled as he walked towards her.

"Put the dog back in her kennel!" he shrieked from behind wide eyes and bared yellow teeth.

"Betrayer! Liar!" Una screamed as she was escorted out of the room writhing like a bag full of snakes. Dekkion reached down and picked up the object. Chuckling, he plucked the petals of the charred rose bud one by one before crushing it in a single clawed hand.

"That event and those following would prove to change both Una and I forever. A few days later I left with Nightblade to the Emerald Atoll south of Viridian. We were accompanied by the blue dragons led by Cobalt. I remember her chuckling before drawing her sword. She enjoyed her human form more than most.

"My fellow Dragons! Follow me!" Cobalt's voice rang like a trumpet, her sword held high in her hand. Nightblade squeezed mine, reminding me she was there with me. Always.

"Dabria, are you ready for this?" She said softly to me.

I was excited to lead my new legion for the first time. I was ready to show once again to the dread lord I was worthy of my station but more so to prove to my Nightblade. She was everything to me and her admiration was all I ever wanted.

Our assault was as Una had foreseen: bloody. I will save details of that day for another time perhaps, but I assure you it was a massacre. Those primitive people stood no chance against us, but even so one of ours fell. My precious Nightblade.

We took her back for burial. I stayed with her body onboard that ship for 20 days as we sailed back. I prayed for her rest, I cared for her peace. We as warriors, even as lovers, had said goodbye daily never knowing if this would be the time or not. It was her time, and part of me hated her for it. I was here… I was still here. Alone.

When we returned, I prepared the warrior's pyre for her. She lay in her polished midnight blue armor. The emblazoned skull of our legion prominent on her chest. Her trusted longsword held in both hands, her eyes were finally at peace. Then the dread lord approached me while I was setting heavy timbers together to form the platform.

"Now Dabria. What do you plan to do with Nightblade?" I remember his hissing voice, it was crueler it seemed, more deadly.

"She will be sent to the afterlife as a hero and warrior Milord. As she always wished." I said as I wiped the sweat from my brow with the back of a heavy gloved hand.

"But," he stared at her body intently, "why? She's perfect."

He walked past me to her body.

"You were great, my sweet Nightblade, but now." He sneered as he drew his claws over my lover's wrapped shoulder. The one person who ever loved me. "Now you will be perfect."

His eyes spun to mine, commanding and cold. "Dabria... leave this place."

I was ordered away. Ordered away from my grief, and my chance to say goodbye. Over the next few nights I pondered what was happening, what he had planned. What he had executed.

He took her from me. The battle took her once but he took her again and I hated him for it.

I hated his army.

I hated his war and saw where it started.

Pallus. Lord Pallus in his obsidian fortress.

Thus Una and I began to conspire. We heard about a son of his, one who was looking to seek revenge. This proved promising enough for us to desert our company. Of course with enough of a lead to buy us a month or two before they might realize what we had done."

ZORIN TENTED HIS FINGERTIPS IN front of his bearded face and slowly tapped them together in thought. "Huh... okay."

Zorin and the table took this all in. The story rang true. Well as far as he could tell and he was known for spinning some pretty elaborate yarns himself.

"What do you propose?" He said calmly with a sigh as he sat back in his chair.

Una nodded at Dabria. Dabria took a deep breath and pointed to a place on the map within the center of the table to the south.

"That you come with us to Whitford. From there we could learn more about what lies Dekkion and Pallus have woven and plan our next move together to stop them."

"In Trull?" Zorin questioned.

"Yes, you have been?" Una asked in return. Zorin nodded with a smile.

"I was a sailor for many years and that was one of our 3 main ports for the southland trade route." Zorin paused to chuckle to himself slightly, "Makes sense. It's the only one this group hasn't been to yet." He looked at Sophie and Cordelia.

"Well it's about time we saw more of your old haunts!" Sophie laughed. "I'd love to go, especially if it's to stop those guys."

Zorin nodded with a knowing smirk, "I do have an old friend there who might be able to help."

"Oh yes," Una interrupted, "She tells me we will find much more in Whitford. Much more." She ended with a ragged sigh that held the silence in the room eerily still.

As Una relaxed her concentration she felt a bead of sweat cross her brow as the torches resumed their yellow orange glow. Everyone looked at each other nervously. All except Rue, who was fascinated with the display of power. As everyone looked around the room the still shadow of Eralin shifted his feet as he leaned against one wall next to the sleeping form of Lorvana Birdsong. She was curled up in some blankets on a soft padded chair.

Zorin drew in a deep breath. "You are going to take some real getting used to, Una." Her expression stayed stoic as she stared into his soul. Unmoving and cold.

"Fine. Let's do it," he continued, throwing up a hand in defeat and lowering his defense.

Skotmir stood up and slammed his mug on the table. "Well you aren't going without me!"

"Nor I!" Sophie said, smirking at Skotmir. The two winked at the thought of another adventure. Cordelia turned to her librarians at the table.

"Rue, Moira and Belinial, would you accompany us?"

Vix cleared his throat and smugly dabbed the corners of his mouth with a napkin.

"Actually we were talking earlier about the possibility of my telling at the library. Correct?"

"Yes we were speaking of that." The one eyed face of Belinial was framed in dark hair and her red robes. She leaned forward clasping her hands together and resting herself on her elbows. " And the answer is no to both of you."

"What?!" Vix was appalled.

Rue smirked a little at the outburst before he too turned to face the awestruck sorcerer.

"We believe, Vix, you need to take time to see where you draw your magic from. We all draw it from within ourselves but your source." Rue shrugged, "Well my friend, that wellspring is sour. We recommend you return to the Silver Maple woods and find reflection amongst your people."

"Outrageous." Vix hissed furiously. After a moment he looked back at the room that anxiously awaited his response. "Fine. As it is on the way I will ride with this caravan of fools as far as the forest. Then we will part ways."

Zorin nodded.

"Well if we are going to stop in the Silver Maple Woods I would like to take a well earned rest while we are there." He smiled at Sophie, "They have some great wine."

THE PARTY ENJOYED THE JOURNEY to the Silver Maple Woods at the northern border of Trull. Even more so the time spent in the hot springs and sweet smelling trees. The elves of the Silver Maple Woods were light hearted and generally kind to trade and travellers, and Zorin's friends were no exception.

When they arrived Vix said nothing and simply walked into the first village they found without a goodbye. Skotmir had called out a farewell to the tall elf but it was as if his words froze in the warm breeze and carried on to be lost in the green leaves of the aspen and birch trees.

The old driver of their cart from the Celestine Tower introduced them to a tall man in a forest green hooded cloak named Vash. His hands and face showed a deep tan and a dark beard hung close to his chin and was well trimmed. He invited them to travel with him to Whitford for a few coins, which they happily accepted. Travel by foot could have proven to be a few extra days.

Vash made good on his promise and as his cart rolled down the well-used dirt and pebble road to the south, he saw the short cliffside to the east where the river cut through towards the sea from the Garnet Mountains. The smell of budding strawberries that sprawled alongside the path mixed with dew in the early morning sun. Smiling, he reached behind the wooden bench he sat on and pulled the light blue fabric that separated him from the rest of the covered cart.

"Hello back there!" He chuckled as they hit a dip in the road, tossing his shoulders to one side. His left hand cautiously gripped the leather reins a little tighter instinctually. "Woah ha! We are approaching Whitford. Hopefully you all find what you need and Skotmir didn't drink all my wine."

He chuckled with Lorvana who sat up front on the bench next to him, strumming a tune on her lute as they continued down the road. The driver looked down at his bow resting between them, noting the quiver of arrows close by, smiling in approval. One couldn't be too careful these days.

The sun beat into the side of the large covered wagon from the left of Vash as they wound the gentle slope into the town of Whitford.

The four ox at the front were bred for such weight and the combination of seven travelers and the load of sweet spiced wine and wheat was no challenge. Though one could say a weight lifted for all but the ox when Vix left the group.

Skotmir leaned back and felt a bubble form in the back of his throat before a sour belch erupted loudly.

"Ah!" He patted his stomach with pride, "Great. I would love to get a better rest than on the side of the road for once. Though Vash has some great wine for sure."

"Thanks." Vash chuckled.

Zorin sat forward with a smirk, "Ooh. Careful now Skotmir, you started to sound like Vix!"

Cordelia and Sophie burst into laughter.

"Yeah!" Cordelia chuckled, wiping the corner of an eye with her cream sleeve, as her voice softened slightly in reflection, "Yeah. Hmm, you know, it's going to take some time getting used to him not being around."

"Not for me." Sophie grunted smugly.

Skotmir chuckled at Sophie's response before he spoke.

"Yeah I know he wasn't the nicest guy but I guess he's got family there, and I wish him the best. Mentioned a brother who was a bard, and a sister who was married to a man from Whitford actually. He can be their problem now but it shouldn't be too bad for him I hope."

"They sure do have their work cut out for them dealing with that guy. Sometimes you have to choose your family." Sophie said as she uncorked a green bottle she had been nursing for a while. The sweet smell of currants and white grapes hit her nose pleasantly as she brought it up to her lips.

"That's true." Vash's voice called back. "So, Skotmir, how about you? plan on seeing any family soon?"

Skotmir thought of the parting words with his father and his brother. They probably didn't care about him. Why should he care about them? He and Sophie smiled at each other.

"My family is right here."

THAT EVENING SOUNDS OF A good crowd and the smells of fine food and drink filled the dining hall of the Severed Serpent Inn. It was known for being best in Whitford from what Zorin remembered. A smile crept across his face when he walked through the familiar beaded doorway after securing their rooms for the night. Zorin saw Boric turn and kneel before the counter, patching the dark walnut wood with a sticky tar. Boric the bartender was someone he knew well and was a friend away from home many a time.

"Boric! You ugly dog!" Zorin laughed loudly.

Cordelia was caught a bit off guard expecting an 'ugly dog' as the nearly eight foot tall androgynous individual stood and smiled gracefully. Their blue green skin was smooth around eyes of deepest purple. A soft mane of dark blue hung down the middle of their back loosely bound with a silver seashell. They wore a cream shirt with a dark black apron, but most important was the genuine smile of friendly recognition.

"I thought I smelt rotten fish entering my bar!" Boric laughed as he lifted the old friend off the ground in a big hug. Setting him down he smiled, "Zorin! What can I get you, mate?"

"Good to be back! We just reserved our rooms so now it's a round I believe!"

Boric nodded, "Only the best for you! And might I say it's good to see you. What can I get you?"

Dabria stepped forward. "Yes. Some wine please."

Sophie nodded "The same."

Skotmir smiled "Ale! I've grown tired of wine," he added with a chuckle.

Eralin stepped forward and pulled back his hood. Boric's eyes widened. "Well. What can I get you, brother?" Boric smiled. "Some wine as well?"

"Yes," Eralin said coldly. Boric held this comment for a moment as he analyzed the tall elf.

"From where do you hail from? Its rare to see us sea-born anywhere but below the surf nowadays. Bloomline? Or maybe Dragonclaw Reef?" Boric questioned with a smile. Eralin didn't move or answer, he just stared for a few seconds before Boric held up his hands with a smile, "I'm sorry I won't press. A friend of Zorin's is a friend of mine. You can keep your secrets."

Boric looked at Una gently. "And the young lady in the dark robe?"

"Um… " Una stammered as she looked nervously at Dabria. Almost as if she were a child asking permission. "W... Wine."

Lorvana happily clapped her hands together. "Oh! I'll just have a spiced wine too please!"

Boric smiled at the halfling who was enthusiastically waving her hand, the lute on her back tossing back and forth over her shoulder.

"Of course my new friend! And what is your name?"

"Lorvana Birdsong! Travelling minstrel."

"A minstrel! Excellent!" He smiled at Zorin before turning to her. "Zorin would your friend be willing to indulge this room of scallywags and barbarians with some songs about heroic deeds of days gone by?"

"Of course!" Lorvana beamed. Cordelia smiled and pulled out her old flute. The ivory dragon's head still hung from the end on a braided cord. Zorin reached over and cradled it gently, remembering his hands working it. He paused for a moment, thinking of that simpler time, before everything. Cordelia smiled at him too.

"I would love to help!" Cordelia told Lorvana, "It's been a long time since I was on a stage and I miss it so."

Thus it began. Boric began serving up drinks to their table located between the bar and the stage itself. Cordelia and Lorvana took the stage performing classic and well known heroic songs. Zorin noted the smell was what he remembered as a mix of stewed peppers and beef, sweetened by the spice wine. This overpowered the stale beer that permeated many taverns he had visited.

As the afternoon played into the evening he heard voices talking in the corners of the room. It was the hushed tones that intrigued him and drew his attention to eavesdrop.

"No, it's true." A hushed voice whispered from two men around a smoothly polished oaken table. "They are mustering now."

"Bah!" the man's companion spat out from behind a bushy blonde mustache. "Impossible, no one wants to go there, besides it's haunted."

"Well I'm going Tal. Better to die on my feet than serve like a dog!"

"Woah there Mancio! I.."

"Excuse me," Zorin interrupted, "but I couldn't help but over-hear about a revolution? May I harbor a guess it's Lord Pallus?"

The two men stopped and regarded the sailor with a wary eye.

"Y... You don't need to know." the man with a freshly shaved face spoke nervously.

The other man's mustache turned up at the sides with a gentle smile, "Mancio... come on. He knows Boric."

Boric looked over and raised their eyebrows with a smile nodding at the statement.

The man with the mustache turned his green eyes towards Zorin. "Pardon Mancio please. To the northwest of here supposedly someone is mustering a force, and rumor has it they wish to stand against Lord Pallus."

Zorin nodded with a smile and turned to Boric.

"Boric, do you know anything about this?"

Boric smirked as he polished a glass that had a faintly blue tint in the light of the wall sconces.

"I can tell you they are righteous. I can't join up but I would if I could."

"Boric. Can I talk to you for a moment?"

Zorin met them at the edge of the bar out of earshot of the other two men who were still arguing with each other. Zorin care-fully leaned over to Boric with a hushed whisper.

"Who is leading this revolution?"

Boric's eyes reflected strength and his voice deepened with seriousness. "Zorin. I need you to swear to me that you would stand up for those that would oppose Lord Pallus and all his dread army."

Zorin gasped slightly in surprise at even being asked this question. "Of course my friend. I-" he hesitated and then thought better of burdening his friend with another truth. It was better he didn't know about Pallus being his father.

"I hate that man." He continued. Boric read the sincerity in his eyes and nodded.

"Then come with me."

Boric led Zorin behind the twin massive kegs of the bar to a short hall made of old chipped brick that ended with an old iron bound door. Cold wrought iron he noted, used to keep out the fey if he remembered right.

Boric approached the door and knocked. Leaning towards the crack in the doorway he spoke.

"Red rides at dawn."

The sound of a heavy latch was followed by the door swinging open and allowing them entry. Stepping into the decent sized room Zorin noticed a map on the table and a few ledgers to either side. As he walked forward in the room he noticed they contained lists of supplies, arms and names but more importantly were the people standing behind the table smiling.

Zorin laughed.

"Benedict?!"

The room broke into jovial heartfelt laughter.

"Hello Zorin!" Benedict laughed as Elloveve and Keldor looked up from the map as well.

"Ha! you have good timing!" Elloveve chuckled as Keldor offered a warm handshake.

"Welcome Lad!"

Zorin beamed at all of us. "So you are now raising an army?" He chuckled with his hands on his hips, "Well first you take back this leader thing and then I guess where do we sign up?!"

CHAPTER 10

THE GUARDIAN

"Fifty paces north from the grinning skull of stone." Benedict said to himself as he walked a shallow forest path just past the foothills of the Garnet Mountains. It seemed he was heading roughly north with the morning sun striking his right shoulder as he strode between the sparse leaves of the aspen trees.

Three days ago they parted ways with Keldor and Elloveve and agreed they would gather up the militia of revolutionaries for an assault at the front along the long stone bridge. Benedict and the others would infiltrate the keep through an old smugglers path. A path once used to sneak illegal or stolen goods into the keep Boric knew about. Benedict was now holding the old smuggler's map and feeling they were getting close.

"How's that old smuggler's map treating you?" Zorin called out with a smirk.

Benedict sighed. "Fine."

Zorin chuckled. "Does it feel good? Like- righteous?"

Benedict laughed at his old friend. "There's sometimes I wonder if I really did miss you, Zorin."

Zorin laughed at the teasing, "well for what it's worth I missed you."

The two friends chuckled as they walked at the front of their group through the soft green trees along the path. To their right were the rolling hills they had crossed and to the left Skotmir smiled at the thought of his childhood home tucked up in the Garnet Mountains. After a few paces Zorin laid a hand on the thick armored shoulder of Benedict. The simple ring on his left hand tapped against the steel under Benedict's red cloak.

"Ah. So those old 'maps' are more like scrambled directions buddy. What's next again?"

Benedict's brow furrowed. "Something about a skull of grinning stone."

"I'll help you look." Zorin smiled.

They walked side by side up the path leading them deeper into the gentle murmur of the forest. After an hour Zorin's eyes widened.

"Hey... Look at this." He took a few quick paces up the path pointing at an opening to their left. "Back here where the path seems to branch. Look."

Benedict jogged several paces to catch up to Zorin. The heavy plate clanked against his thighs and the mail rode against the thick belt he used to take some of the weight off his shoulders. Benedict's breath quickened slightly from the exercise, and he willed his breath to slow as he approached Zorin and took the sight in.

"Oh wow," he breathed softly.

Inside a short grove of trees was an alcove with a small pond rippling gently. There was the sound of a gentle cascading waterfall pouring into it from above. The forest floor here was covered in a thick carpet of lush, lemony smelling moss, and the occasional scarlet berry was seen on rose hips along the bank. The path continued to the left along the wall to the waterfall itself. As

Benedict stepped forward along the path he ran a single gauntleted hand along the rock wall. He felt it curve slightly.

"Oh hey. Look at that." Benedict smiled.

Carved in the rock was the rounded forehead of an ancient, grinning skull.

"Well north of that is..." Zorin drew his hand up in an angle to the right. "the waterfall."

Benedict shrugged. "The path leads that way, too. Let's check it out."

Emerald and mustard colored ferns lined the steep walkway on either side keeping the path obscured to all but those actually on it.The smell of wet pine in the churning mist revealed a fallen tree at the base of the waterfall. Green pine needles still clung to its branches and the broken and upturned base revealed the network of beetles that had eaten it from the inside out.

The group continued along the path, approaching the cascade of cold mountain runoff. There they saw a five foot gap in the curtain of water. There was a cave hidden behind.

The roaring sound of the waterfall soon deafened them as they passed into the reverberating cavern. Broken stones lay haphazardly as they ascended up the gradual incline but most were small enough to step over. Unfortunately, Cordelia's foot wasn't so lucky.

"Oof! Wow... watch that rock!" She called back as she shook her foot. With a sigh she snapped her fingers, calling a floating mote of flame to the palm of her hand. Smiling, she pointed upward and the curling ball rose twice the distance above her head to help illuminate the immense cavern like a torch. Even that failed to illuminate everything, Sophie noted. It was unusually dark, possibly from leaving the daylight outside suddenly, but it left an uneasy feeling with Sophie. She knelt to fumble with the leather straps on her leather knapsack.

"Man, it's dark in here. I'll get the torches."

"Sounds good." Skotmir nodded at his friend. "I'll scout up ahead while you get ready."

Skotmir took careful footsteps outside the globe of Cordelia's light to keep his eyes adjusted to the dark. After ten minutes of travel the ground leveled and opened up even more than before, marked by blue-green glowing lights of phosphorescent growth tucked into random corners.

Stalactites hung securely from the ceiling four stories above their heads. Skotmir noted this chamber was easily a hundred yards across. The wet stones of a single stream of water lapped from one side to the other both opened with a short opening in the stone no larger than Skotmir himself. Natural and untouched by any mortal's hands he smiled. This was a natural temple of stone to the dwarf. He sniffed the air.

Only the musty smell of stagnant water and something slightly rancid came to his nose. Nothing dangerous.

"All clear!" He called back.

"Sounds good!" Benedict answered. "So Zorin you were saying about the next path. It speaks of what again?"

Zorin thought for a moment, trying to recall their last conversation, "So as I was saying Garnet Keep is just on the other side of this cavern."

"Is it?" A sinister growl boomed against the walls of the cavern. "Is it all clear dwarf?"

Everyone froze as from behind a broken pillar came a man in scarlet armor. His head had sparse patches of wispy white hair that hung framing a rotten maw of a face. The jaw was bare, showing the lower teeth and eyes black as coals burned with a hidden fire. Fear crept into the hearts of each of the party in cold tendrils of self doubt, except one.

With a deep sigh Benedict drew his blade and clutched it tightly to his armored chest in respect and wordless prayer. His eyes opened, feeling inner power course in his own biceps as he drew the blade to rest on an armored shoulder. He had come to reclaim his home from all that stood in his way and this must be the first test.

"I am Benedict Shieldheart!" His voice boomed out fearlessly, "son of-"

"Hold your tongue boy!" the rotting guardian in red armor's voice rumbled and hissed like an earthquake. "I care not who you are, only that you trespass. Seize him!"

Two massive forms charged into the light and lumbering feet shook the cavern as they fell against the rocks. Hands rotted as exposed bones gripped tree trunks not unlike the one in the waterfall outside. Their fetid and bulbous bodies revealed cloudy vacant eyes above rotten teeth.

"Ogres!" Lorvana cried as she crouched and drew her short dagger. Cordelia ran to stand by her, the globe of fire gliding as it followed.

"Worse! Zombie Ogres!" Cordelia shouted as she fanned the fingers of both hands out in front of her. "Fek-to-shae!" A fountain of fire erupted towards the leading ogre, engulfing it in searing flames that ignited the rotting rags covering its body.

Sophie met the same colossal figure head on as Skotmir charged to meet the other. Benedict slung his sword to the right as he ran towards the Red Guardian.

"Die child!" The guardian roared as it raised the blood red mace above its head to counter.

Benedict shifted his footing to lower the hilt sharply and drew his blade across the guardian's belly in a long slice. He felt several rings of chainmail separate as the sword scraped across his foe.

Raising the mace above his wide eyed head to parry a downward chop from the knight, the guardian screamed in rage. He was cut short though as three blue bolts of energy slammed into his side from the outstretched arms of Cordelia.

"Benedict, now!" Cordelia shouted to her cousin.

Benedict gripped the sword but at the last second dropped his shoulder into the red guardians chest, sending him sprawling backwards. Sophie slashed at the belly of the huge ogre as it swung at the side of her head with the remains of an old tree stump. She ducked back swiftly only to catch a flailing foot in the chest, knocking her backward. She felt the wind fleeing from her lungs rapidly. Skotmir hacked at his quarry relentlessly, ducking easily under the frantic swings of its arms. Eralin seized the opportunity and began sending flight after flight of rapid arrows into its rancid body.

Una raised her spear with both hands and began chanting a dark language. "Fal-teh-nas!" Green hissing bolts flooded from her spear to strike both ogres simultaneously, leaving black marks of charred flesh.

Benedict panted as he leaned on the heavy blade in his hands. "Again I have come to seek passage here."

Benedict walked toward his foe but was met with a bright blue green light that flashed from the palm of his hand. "Ugh! ... no.. I can't see!"

Blinded, Benedict took a step back, stumbling. The red guardian took the opportunity to cruelly assault his body with his ancient mace. The brutal weapon crushed his left shoulder, then what felt like the arm itself, and his left leg. His vision was now blurry. He swung with his right hand into the red body before him.

Lorvana and Cordelia saw Benedict falling backwards from the flurry of blows, a pit forming in their stomach. Pushing Dabria out of the way with a hand, Cordelia gripped the vibrant coast covering Lorvana's small shoulder and squeezed the stripes of coarse muslin and soft silk in her fingers.

"Lorvana! Can you use healing?"

Lorvana hesitated in confusion. "Well I–"

"Answer me!" Cordelia barked at her, startling her back to the task at hand.

"Yes!" Lorvana shouted back, nodding.

"Then hold my hand." Without waiting for a response Cordelia grabbed her friend's trembling hand in hers and began pulling the familiar weave of magic around them, "Bee-Gah!"

Cordelia imagined the space next to Benedict, as she grabbed Lorvana's hand and said the words. In an instant Lorvana saw them close the distance and appear next to a very surprised Benedict and a furious red guardian.

"What?!" the red guardian roared, "Who are–"

"Uh... hi?" Lorvana stammered waving her tiny hand at the monstrous figure.

"Lorvana!" Cordelia jerked her to Benedict's battered side. Lorvana touched Benedict's shoulder as he knelt, exhausted. Radiating energy warmed the pain out of his system, refreshing his spirit and clearing his eyes.

"Bye!" Lorvana giggled at the charging red guardian as Corrdelia imagined the spot they had left about 40 paces away. In a blink, she teleported them both back to safety.

Sophie deftly danced around the slow moving undead ogre now. Anger swelled in her heart after what she regarded as a clumsy mistake in the beginning. She struck deep into his chest as Zorin leaped from the darkness behind the rotting ogre, driving two daggers into the base of his skull and dropping him to the ground. With a few final axe blows, Eralin and Skotmir's foe had fallen into a heap as well.

"Hey!" Dabria said with a smirk, "That's what I call teamwork."

Benedict was driving the red guardian back with blow after blow. His sword driving downward in steady swings less like a sword and more like a blacksmith's hammer. Each word rung out along with each strike.

This!

Is!

My!

Home!

With a final blow, the guardian in red armor dropped to both knees on the ground. The spectral mace peeled apart into tendrils of red and black smoke. Benedict squinted and saw thousands of what appeared to be screaming faces peel apart in the mist as it absorbed into the body of his adversary. The guardian's face relaxed as he bowed to the young knight.

"Of course, Master."

The red guardian faded into the misty cavern floor, leaving a gleaming black and red two-handed greatsword pointed into the ground, where he once stood. Benedict gripped this new blade, and bowed his head in thankful prayer.

A FEW HOURS LATER THE group had found their way to a rough cut staircase of stone steps that wound its way in a wide circle several times as they climbed. The steps were short and wide, making it easier on their legs.

"It's surprisingly easy to climb isn't it?" Sophie remarked, her strong voice carrying up the stone walls quickly.

"Yeah. You can tell this is the work of smugglers." Zorin chuckled, "They made it easier to carry their loads up the mountain by foot for sure."

Skotmir laughed. "Well they must have had a dwarf or two, this work is great! Look at the wall markings. Smooth, perfect."

Zorin smiled at his grinning friend. Looking forward the torch light shone on a pair of rails on the far wall with a series of footholds carved up the final 10 feet. Above there was a trap-door flanked by a pair of worn and broken pulleys. The ropes had long since rotted and rung in shreds. Benedict put a hand on the wooden plank leaning against the wall.

"An elevator." Cordelia said. "They could use that to haul up anything from here quickly when they were ready."

Zorin handed his torch to Skotmir and climbed up the wall to the iron and hardwood trap door.

"This is it. Benedict give me a hand." Setting one foot and leaning to one side he made room for his powerful friend. Together they drove their shoulders into the door feeling the ancient hinges groan under their force. Grass and fern peeled away from around the lip as the light overgrowth tore away. Sweet grass and fresh mountain air struck their noses as a russet glow lit their faces.

The heavy trap door swung outward, revealing an afternoon sky heading towards dusk. The red orange clouds were a welcome sight after recent hours in the caves below. The air was rich with pine and fresh mountain water. As they carefully emerged, they found their backs to a stone wall 3 stories high made of a deep gray hematite with ribbons of deep red orange jasper. Opposite the wall was a massive mountain lake that glimmered like a thousand copper and silver coins in the setting sun.

The crystal clear waters cut the sunlight to illuminate the numerous fish darting between the stones. As the water darkened, further out the fish broke the surface, feeding on the flies at dusk. At the other side of the lake was a 60 foot cascade of water tumbling from another set of these hanging lakes higher into the mountain range. Skotmir smiled his chipped tooth grin as he pointed at the ripples on the surface.

"Mmm... bet that's a trout right there. A little butter, maybe some wild garlic-"

"Shh!" Zorin brought a single finger up to his lips looking back at the group. Skotmir put a meaty hand over his mouth in apology. They all nodded in understanding as Zorin pointed to the faint shadow moving above along the top of the outer wall of Garnet Keep. They made their way along the outer wall to a staircase lifting a single story to an opening in the wall. Zorin carefully ascended each step, feeling out any loose objects that may surprise his companions.

Reaching the landing, he peered around the corner and discovered this was the elevated skirt of the keep's courtyard. Scanning the area, he saw a long shadow appear, drifting towards them on the ground, its source still obscured by the wall.

"Hold up." Zorin breathed holding up a hand. "A sentry."

The short guard walked around the corner as they took its path through the corridor leading around the mead hall. The sounds of merriment echoed from the hall as what sounded like the deep, gruff voices of orcs or men cheered at some game inside. The breeze changed slightly; stale beer and filth began to permeate the air now.

Dabria noticed, once gleaming stones had fallen into disrepair and the banners that had hung were replaced by skulls of beasts on spikes bound in leather and crowned in jagged rusty iron to seem more nightmarish. She stepped around everyone to bring herself closer to Zorin.

Zorin nodded at her before peering around the corner. After a short moment he motioned for everyone to wait. Nodding quietly, they each waited their turn to pass one by one.

Taking a deep breath, Zorin darted down the empty corridor to an opening on the left. Peering his head back around the corner, he motioned for Benedict.

Benedict walked as quietly as the heavy plate mail would allow him, though he was thankful he had refused to wear the steel sabatons from the knighthood. The heavy armor that covered his boots lent some control in the gritty cobblestone at least. Soon he was safe.

Zorin looked again. He motioned for Dabria. She creeped out and walked along the wall as the others prior.

Dabria heard a small gasp behind her just before she was safely around the corner.

"M... Mistress?"

She instantly froze as she recognized the voice. Without turning she spoke in a practiced commanding tone.

"Sharptooth."

"Why?" The small kobold took a few steps closer to her old commander, "Why are you here?"

Dabria's mind raced and the cold grip of anticipation wrapped around her heart. This could jeopardize everything. Suddenly, a spark of realization crossed her mind. She turned and drew herself up into her former glory. Sharptooth responded with her awestruck eyes. It was working.

"I was going to ask you the same. Aren't you supposed to be with the army? Or did you-"

Sharptooth panicked. "No! I... I mean we-" she knelt on a red and orange scaled knee and lowered her reptilian head. "Oh no mistress Dabria... I am so sorry."

It worked better than she hoped. Sharptooth had deserted it seemed or was doing something not sanctioned by the Dark Army. The Dark Army's influence was not holding Garnet Keep, just occupied by bandits or orc warbands likely. Who knew what strange forces were here as no one had spoken of it in decades it seemed. Regardless, Dabria knew now that Sharptooth was in just as much peril as she was, possibly more.

Dabria thought deeply on this. Sharptooth had always been trustworthy to her and a friend, but even the closest of friends didn't know all her secrets.

"Sharptooth." She lowered herself to look into the kobold's gentle eyes, "You need to leave here immediately and go home. Go back to Enruk."

"Of course," Sharptooth croaked out slowly, "I... I will go back and turn myself in."

Dabria knew they would torture Sharptooth. Deserters were always used as examples to the rest of the troops. Sharptooth would be no exception regardless of the years of service or the countless skirmishes the kobold veteran had survived with her shield brothers and sisters. Fire coursed through Dabria's heart at the thought of that cruelty. Death is one thing. Death was no stranger to Dabria and she welcomed it, but she couldn't allow only cruelty.

"No." Dabria said softly and took Sharptooth's talon into her hands and squeezed affectionately.

"What?" Sharptooth questioned quietly as she squeezed her talon gently back, her eyes brimming with hope.

"I don't know why you are here, but take those that you trust only and flee this place. And-" Dabria paused again, shaking off the thought of what the army would do to her friend. "Don't go back to the army and you never saw me here. Promise me."

Sharptooth cocked her head slightly and nodded with under-standing. "I... I promise. We won't. Th..thank-"

Dabria held up a hand. She disliked being thanked. It felt like something was owed. Sharptooth smiled before she scampered off into the dark corridor. Dabria stood up and sighed before waving to the rest of the party to continue.

ZORIN AND ERALIN TOOK THE lead as they crept up the stairs to the landing of the long wall surrounding the keep. To the left was a ballista perched towards the long stone bridge that led to the keep. The faint shadows of two statues flanked either side of the bridge, barely visible from this angle. To the right Zorin saw an orc sentry several yards away looking mindlessly over the side to the lake below. He turned to Eralin and whispered, "Ok I'll take him out... but cover me just in case."

Eralin shrugged and drew his bow calmly. Zorin drew the two daggers from his belt as he swiftly and silently closed the distance.

30... 20... 10 and-

"Woah! Jeez!" Zorin dove out of the way as the first arrows sunk into the orc, silencing him before he had a chance to alarm anyone. The last one had sunk through the padded shoulder of Zorin's faded purple tunic. He spun around and felt the arrow's pointed end above his shoulder, missing his body by just a hair, he imagined, as he could easily feel the shaft against his skin. Looking back he saw Eralin simply shrug nonchalantly and shoulder his bow.

"What the...?" Benedict stared at Eralin's remorseless action with a blend of wonder and disgust for a moment before turning to Dabria in a hushed tone.

"Dabria, Una, Lorvana and... " He paused thinking of the best member to round out the team, "Skotmir. The four of you make your way to the ballista at the northern wall. They are over the gatehouse that way.

"You got it." Skotmir said as they all nodded.

"When you hear any, and I mean any action from the south, in the keep where the rest of us are going," he pointed at the broken wall where Zorin stood and then pointed opposite himself with his other hand at the ballista, "That is when you set them alight and fire them to the northeast as high as you can elevate them."

"As high as we can." Una smiled as she looked at the sky, "Birds of flame of death's wings close behind." Benedict and Skotmir silently pondered the seer's words as Dabria simply shrugged.

"Seriously Una. Please-" Benedict sighed impatiently, "This will signal the Militia for their assault. Then free the gatehouse to make way for them."

They nodded again in affirmation before turning to dart back down the wall towards the north entrance. Skotmir's heart froze upon reaching the first mounted ballista. Looking over the side revealed they were thousands of feet above the river below. The waters of the lake spilled from either side of the keep feeding it and narrowing the only entrance into the keep to the 200 yard stone bridge. This bridge connected the keep to the mountain villages and glen valley downhill. The Keep was a one way stop. Designed to protect and accommodate locals in times of need. He stood proud with a chipped tooth grin towards Dabria as he pointed at the enormous twin statues of lions standing at the end of the bridge.

"Now that is the work of dwarves."

THE WALL TO THE SOUTH led into a worn and broken stairway within the main keep. Over the years of neglect or siege, the walls had been broken down in places. The smell of grimy animal pens and dirt now filled these once great halls along with the sounds of dripping water and a hollow breeze.

Once setting foot on the ground floor they saw the entrance to the great meeting hall. One room with a broken door sat to their right as they entered the dim torchlight. Eralin became curious, wandering towards it.

"What the?" Benedict said to Zorin hushed and quietly, "Where is he going?"

Zorin sighed, "Whatever, let him check that out. Let's see what those guys are up to." Zorin pointed at what appeared to be the broad, muscular backs of two orcs. They seemed to be talking to a third but they were hidden behind their powerful forms.

The figures looked more distinguished than the orc sentry above and any other they had seen. One seemed to be speaking with the gesturing of his hands. He wore a crown of dented steel and brass twisted to cruel points. A cloak of wolf pelts draped off one mossy green shoulder.

"It's true." His deep resonant voice rumbled, "The message comes from my kin in the dark army. Now is the time to join them. They become stronger every day it seems. We can join with more orcs and have more than just this castle."

The other form shook a head of dark black and purple hair with a chuckle. A dark blue robe of coarse burlap was gathered around his waist with a cracked black leather belt. Several small pouches and a leather wrapped green glass bottle swung from his wide waist.

"Ha! Is it not good here, King Karag?" The voice gurgled mockingly, "Do you not love the wine and celebration? And the raiding? Ha! Why do we need more than this?"

King Karag's moss colored face was painted in a jagged mask that outlined his eyes and tusk filled mouth. A brutal ax swung in a single meaty hand. He was the head of the serpent Benedict was sure but the other seemed as much if not more of a threat. He clutched a staff covered with beads, feathers and a few human and dwarf skulls. They both appeared cruel and Benedict could feel the evil intention emanating from them.

"We need to leave this place. It is time." King Karg argued, "Spilge, you know there is nothing here to keep us. She knows that. Look at her."

Spilge chuckled, the bottle at his waist swaying against his thigh. "Ha! She says nothing! She knows we need to stay here."

Spilge laughed as he slammed the staff into a broken tile on the floor that once depicted part of the hilt of a long crimson sword and crown mosaic. Spilge scowled.

"Bright Oak says we stay." he added, drawing his face closer to the orc king before battle cries erupted behind them.

Benedict, Sophie and Zorin moved in perfect synchronization with their explosive attack. Zorin let loose arrow after arrow into the two hulking bodies as Benedict drove the great sword downward into his foe's shoulder. His hands illuminated and he felt energy pour through him into the orc king. Roaring in pain, Karag ripped the blade from his weakened shoulder and cried out, "Help me Bright Oak!"

What answered was a shriek like banshee's wail, high pitched and ear shattering from behind the two hulking orcs. From between them a crescent shaped blade on a long pole struck out, barely missing Benedict's thigh as he squirmed out of the way. As they fell to either side an agile and athletic form leaped in an arc over them, flipping and twisting in the air to land behind a stunned Benedict.

In the silence Benedict could hear a gusty wind picking up outside the cracked and worn walls of the room.

The creature was slightly taller than him and smaller than the orcs. Their muscles were tight and sinewy beneath a patchwork of neglected armor that loosely covered green moss and mud. Cream colored warpaint outlined crazed eyes. Gray, vacant eyes like storm clouds threatening rain, foggy and sightless.

They lunged with their wicked pole-arm again in a flurry of strikes. Moving like being carried on a gale-force wind itself tearing into his armor when it slipped by his guard. Gaining his footing and working forward, he locked them into a hold, barring their weapons from attack, bracing his blade between them and drawing an elbow under their mossy chin.

Silently, Eralin had made his way into the small room and looked around. It reeked of dirt and unnameable smells. The odor of ammonia and dried grasses was powerful to his untrained nose. In the corner of the stone room was a pile of hay that had a single dirty fur lain across it. An elk he imagined. Next to it was a wooden basket suspended on four long legs. The paint had peeled from heat and blackened in spots and there were several soft gray and white rabbit furs draped at the side of it.

"Hello," he said curiously, "what are you?

Eralin neared the basket and saw there was a small form under the furs no bigger than a cabbage or melon. Drawing back the furs he saw the tattered and stained muslin wrappings lovingly wound around the still form of a doll. The head was a crude apple carved into the face of a baby.

Suddenly startled by the shrieks outside the room he dropped the furs back into the cradle, drew his bow and entered the fray.

"DECEIVER!" THE MOSSY GREEN FACE shrieked at Benedict. He saw her gray vacant crazed eyes lock on the sword, terrified and angry as if she had seen a ghost. The facade began to melt from her as he saw the moss and mud were not flesh but a crude mask. Her once blonde hair matted into muddy locks, framing a trembling jaw. Trembling not from strain but from the sight of the sword he found beneath the keep awarded from his battle with the red guardian.

"Why do YOU carry that sword?" Her voice was hoarse but there was a gentleness behind it Benedict couldn't place, "I KNOW that sword!"

A gurgled cry erupted behind them as Spilge took a blade across the throat from Sophie. The fire illuminating his fingertips fading as he slumped to the floor.

The gray eyes began to clear. A long forgotten haze cast over them drifted away, drawing in color from the sky itself. Sky blue eyes like someone he knew so well.

Gasping, he drew in a breath of shock and couldn't help himself speak aloud.

"Zane?" His voice shook with recognition and hope.

Her eyes widened. Angrily she screamed, throwing her weight against him and pushing him dangerously backward against a broken pillar. Benedict's back arching backwards took all his strength to keep his footing. He knew she was in control now.

"First you carry my husband's sword," her voice was measured and strong as she looked into his deep blue eyes, "And now you dare speak the name of my dead son? Who are-"

Benedict didn't give her time to finish, his heart brimming with hope. "I am Benedict Shieldheart son of Lucilius-"

At the sound of his fathers name the blade glowed orange with power illuminating runes up the blade spelling out a name he was unfamiliar with, "Kettlebane."

With a great scream Elona the Fair spun to stand back to back with Benedict, the source of 20 years worth of her hopes and dreams. They struck down with swift blows, the glaive in her hand igniting with blue power as Benedict drove his fathers blade into King Karag and driving him to the ground.

The lost mother and son looked at each other and smiled before falling into each other's arms in a tight embrace. The silence of the room fell only for a moment, though, before the faint sound of distant warhorns were welcomed into the stone walls of Garnet Keep. Elona pulled away quickly when she heard the noise from outside, her smile not fading. Outside the building they heard the distant shouts of a liberating force drawing closer.

Elona laughed with joy as she held back welling tears, "Ha! My... My son-" Elona held this word for a moment in disbelief, before her warrior spirit snapped her back to the task at hand, "Ah! and are those sounds more friends of yours?"

Hot tears of joy poured down Benedict's cheeks, cutting rivulets in the dirt and blood of the day. "Keldor," he stammered shakily, "and Elloveve."

Hearing the names of her closest friends she laughed, shaking his shoulders joyously. The wellspring of tears finally allowed to flow from the sky blue pools that held them.

"Oh Sweet Maiden's grace! Of course!" She smiled, clearing her eyes with the back of her crude gauntlet revealing warm ivory behind the caked mud. "Well let's not keep them waiting!"

Time seemed to slow for Sophie at that moment as Elona and Benedict charged out of the room to meet the retreating horde by the great tree. The tree she had loved and cared for so many years ago. Eralin and Zorin ran up the stairs where they could use their bows more effectively, striking the horde from behind as planned.

Sophie drew her longsword and turned to follow.

"Sophie!"

Zane's soft voice in her mind stopped her, his emotions flooding hers as he reunited with his lost mother as well.

Wait. Look in there please?"

Sophie stepped into the room Eralin had been in and saw the crib. The memory flooded Zane's mind of a long ago fire and as she approached it could feel the heat on his arms all over again.

Instinctively she wiped her forearms of the phantoms that invisibly licked them.

She saw the doll resting in its lovingly swaddled blanket but was driven to look past it at the letters in the blackened headboard still faintly making out a single name:

Benedict

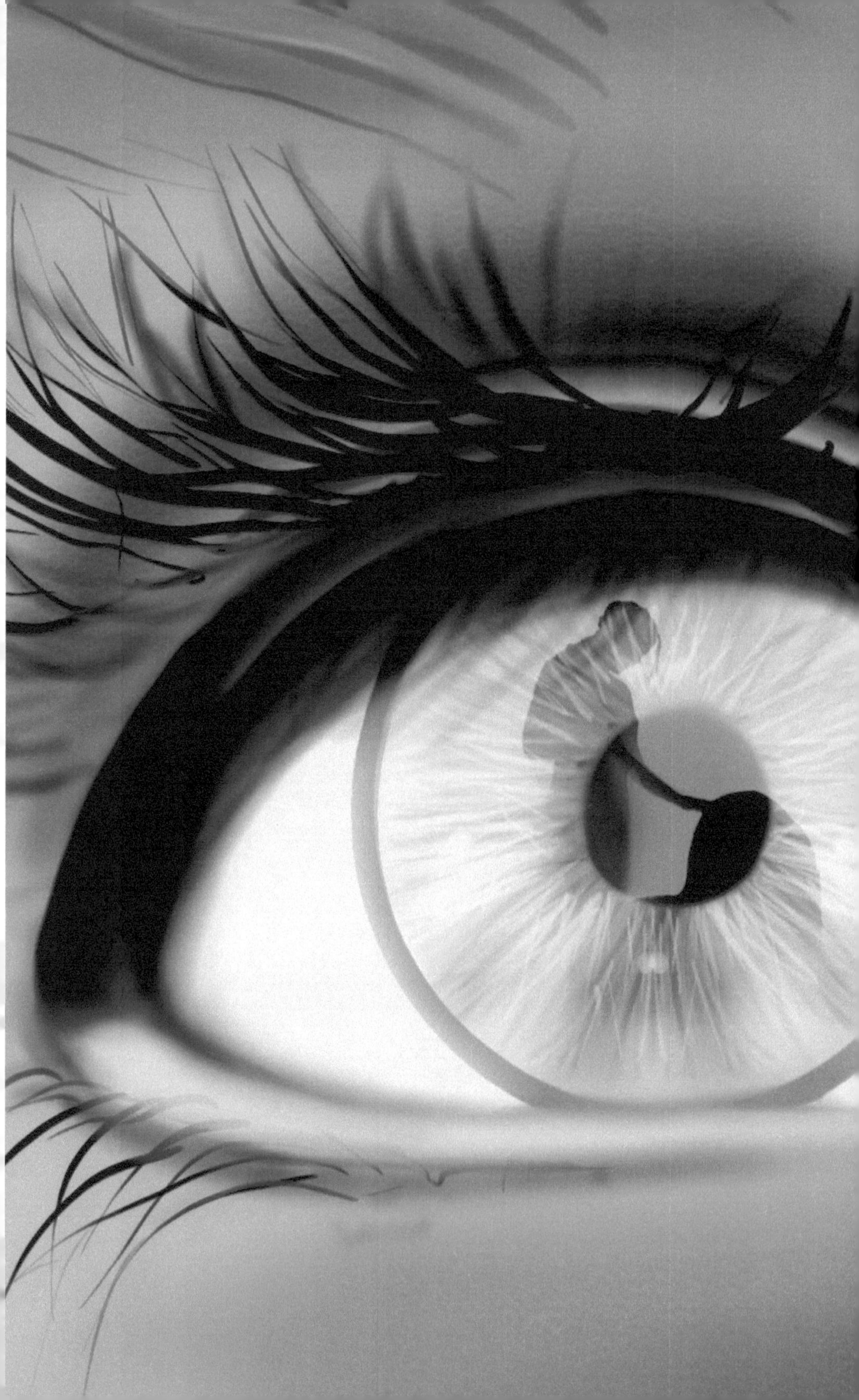

CHAPTER 11

APPLEHEAD

The battle was swift as the Mistgard clan occupying Garnet Keep had no idea what was happening. Those who ran were allowed to scatter down the stone bridge as there was little possibility for a counter-strike. The ringing of steel against iron echoed through the halls until finally all was done.

The revolutionaries celebrated in the courtyard that evening. Dancing and feasting took place in the open by old garden beds and by the great tree that stood in front of the forebuilding of the keep itself. The bonfire was lit by the old blacksmith shop the light of which danced in the branches of the strong and ancient oak. Beneath that tree stood a powerful woman leaning on a great glaive.

Her face was washed and revealed her once golden hair run through with more silver these days. Sky blue eyes of hers held a youthful fire, though the years were shown in sparse wrinkles around the worn rose beige skin surrounding them. They creased gently as she smiled, and seeing her face again brought such a warmth to my heart.

"Twenty?" Her voice was tired as reality set in, "Twenty years Keldor? It... it seems impossible."

"Yes Elona. Twenty." I sighed deeply, looking at her in the red orange glow of the fire light. Age was the most powerful of magic. It seemed only a short time ago we were all together charging across the battlefield. The six winds. Now only a breeze of our former glory to be sure. I smiled to myself to mask this unwelcome thought.

"Twenty long years old friend, but look," I nodded at the great tree as she ran her hand over the thick bark, "she still stands. As do you."

"Hmm.. yes." Elona's voice grew soft as she looked lovingly at her tree, "Yes she does doesn't she? My ancient oak. I've often wondered, Keldor, has she always stood here? When this keep was built was she but a sapling?"

"I like to think so, Elona." Elloveve's voice was accompanied by her soft footsteps, the smell of elderflowers and honey drifting over the firelight alongside her.

Elloveve had returned to our reunion under the tree carrying three goblets of sweet mead from the celebration. Elona's face beamed with happiness at the sight of her shield sister again.

"Ah! To say I missed you, Elloveve, would fall… so short." Her face trembled slightly as her smile began to fade, "I… don't remember anything. I… I thought I lost you all-"

I watched helplessly as my dear friend crumbled under the weight of two decades of a tortured existence none of us could fathom. Elloveve set her goblets down and stepped to pull her into a loving embrace, Elona's eyes pouring hot tears down her cheeks to disappear in Elloveve's fiery red hair. Elona was finally able to lose herself in the arms of safety and regain her humanity.

"There, there." Elloveve cooed gently, stroking the hair away from Elona's cheeks. "We're here now."

"Lucilius... my boys." Elona's voice broke into gut wrenching sobs that only someone who had their entire life stolen could feel. Her entire existence, all she had fought and lived for, was destroyed that night in a curtain of flames, right here in this keep.

I approached my friend and placed a hand on her armored shoulder. "Your boys are here too. Elona." I said gently, "Come. Please, sit."

I thought of Elloveve and I sitting next to the creek in Bemil, several weeks back. How she had recounted her memory with mine and regained herself. I thought of Benedict and Zane encouraging me to recall my memory of the horrible night we, the six winds, were scattered across time. The same night Elona, Elloveve and I lost everything. Our crucible moment that forged the rest of our lives. I hoped we could help her recall and confront her memories, at least then she could heal.

"Let's sit and unravel the tale together, my friend," I urged softly.

Elona closed her eyes tightly as she shuddered. "But I-"

"I'm happy to help clear up any confusion," I said with a gentle smile as I offered my hand. "Let's just see what we can find out. I'm not looking for solutions right now, just trying to understand."

Elona's face buried deeper in Elloveves arms. Elloveve looked at me, her face tormented with the sympathy of her friend's pain.

"I... I don't think she's ready for this Keldor I-"

Elona pulled back from her friend and sniffed hard with a sigh, "No. I... I'm ready. I can do it."

The three of us sat on the large exposed roots of the massive tree. The moss was soft to my hand as I eased myself down. Grunting I offered a hand to Elona who smiled, taking it politely as she sat down much more easily. One thing was certain, she didn't share the complaints I did in my lower back. She was as strong of an athlete as when I last saw her.

CORDELIA'S BLACK BOOTS STRUCK THE russet and grey marble and echoed down the ancient hallway as she walked. She had left the celebration to reacquaint herself with the home of her childhood. Cordelia was only a few months old when they were chased away from Garnet Keep but there were flashes. Bits of feeling, at least, if not full memories and she intended to seek them out.

"Wow, this place is amazing." She smiled looking around. She reached back and tied her hair with a single red leather cord away from her face in a ponytail. "Oh look at that!"

As she walked the largely unused second floor hall slowly showed less and less of the mud and iron decorations the Mistgard had used and more of the ancient banners. Banners similar to the ones in the Celestine Tower depicting historic battles such as the one before her now.

A king in solid ebony stood on a frozen battlefield. The helmet on his head sprouted two elk-like antlers and in his hand was a dark staff topped with a sphere of onyx. Lightning poured from his hands across the soldiers before him. Peering closer she saw the image of another banner in the background of the battlefield, emblazoned with the head of a wolf.

"Huh. I wonder who you are…"

"*Cordelia…*"

"What the?" Cordelia exclaimed as she peered back down the hallway to the next room. Peering into the corner chamber she saw two great ancient windows that opened up to a view of the lake behind the keep.

Moonlight danced off the short ripples on the water casting a blue white glow into the room which was disturbed only by the torch in her hand. There was a crib here and several old books on a table. All were lost to rot and time being exposed in the open room. This nursery was not to be used in all seasons of course, but provided a beautiful and peaceful place when it could.

"Summertime." She smiled as if a piece of an internal puzzle was found and fit. "We left during the summertime."

She thumbed the books on the table gently. Nursery rhymes mainly, and a short tale about a clumsy dragon. She smiled at that, chuckling softly as she lifted the book and moved it to the side revealing a single white leather tome in pristine condition. She smiled sensing the presence of powerful magic preserving it, as if immune to the elements themselves.

ELONA COULD FEEL THE COLD stone of the prison still. Mold and decay left a rancid smell that stuck to the skin and the spirit.

"Following the siege the bandits threw me in the keep's dungeon below. The one we never used. I wasn't chained, just locked up... I counted days in the number of naps I took. I never truly slept. My mind was just a pool of lost dreams and fractured memories.

I placed tallies on the wall with a small stone until there was nothing left and then gave up. I would sleep 2 or 3 times before they would give me anything to eat and even then it was hardly anything.

A cup of rice water or the end of a hambone...

A moldy piece of fruit...

The damp stones of the wall soon became greasy from my hands constantly feeling.Trying to stay busy, trying to stay sane but I just sat there in the darkness, endlessly waiting for something, anything to happen.

Until one day I heard sounds of a battle outside. The familiar clash of steel was welcome and I hoped I would be freed, one way or another. Instead I remember his croaking dark voice.

"There!" The voice panted as I saw his greasy matted hair and twisted face. His dark blue robes. "There's someone down here too! Well hello... and who are you?"

"I am-" I hadn't heard my own voice in so long all I could do was force air past the dry cords of my throat and hope. He just laughed at me.

"Well... come here my little friend and look into my eyes. Deep into my eyes."

I never should have taken that step but he was to be my liberator, my new ally. The desperate mind does desperate things. His name was Spilge. A witchmaster of the Mistgard clan. King Karag led the Mistgard. A cruel man who delighted in terrorizing his victims before slaying them. I thought I was to be slain as well but then I was reunited with an old friend I hadn't seen in a long time.

"King Karag look at what we found in the back hall!" One of the orc guards said from behind a crude helmet of twisted iron. My eyes lit up as I saw him holding Tempest, my glaive, and I let out a sigh that surprised King Karag.

"The girl knows that weapon?! Great." His eyes leered at me, "Then use it. Pergu! Nargol! Attack!"

As they threw the glaive to me I showed them a side they didn't expect. I made quick work of those two warriors right here actually, by this tree. I can still hear Karag laughing as he named me "Bright Oak" after my tree, then made me one of the clan.

Spilge had cast a deep charm on me, which grew even tighter around my reality, my very soul. Over time it made me believe I had always been one of them. I fell deeper into this living nightmare. I started decorating myself with moss and mud hiding my humanity, becoming more feral and animalistic. Embracing the clan's values of blood, war and vengeance.

I wandered to the second floor one day. No one had any interest and I just felt a bit of wanderlust. Something called my footsteps to a familiar yet unfamiliar room. In the center was a scorched crib. This discarded and ruined basket meant something to me but I didn't know what. I wandered back to the mead hall and rejoined the feasting. Then I started having dreams.

I dreamt of the children. I could see Zane taking cookies from the baker's racks and looking at me innocently when I scolded him. I saw Lucilius smiling behind his dark beard at the baby in that crib.

In these scattered visions the crib had no marks, no burns and that vexed me.

I woke up that night unable to go back to sleep. It seemed, then, this false reality Spilge had woven was beginning to crack. I walked back to the second floor and to the front of the forebuilding where I found the crib and I carried it downstairs into my room. Over the next few days I found an old baby's gown, and began twisting old gray rags into a body shape, stitching it together loosely.

I realized I had formed a body shape that matched the hole in my heart. I placed the gown over its soft terry cloth shoulders. I cradled it in my arms, pulling it closely to my chest. This was familiar. Joy over such a small thing burned inside me. It was helping me realize what I was missing in my torn heart, but the palm of my hand felt empty.

Incomplete.

Days went by as I tried stones by the lake in my hand and even pinecones but it was in the feasting hall where I found it. I sat next to Spilge who grabbed an apple from the center of the table.

I snatched it from his hand as he just laughed at me. I ignored him as I stared at the apple imagining something perfect. I took it to my room and began removing the pieces from the apple with my dagger that didn't belong to my vision. After a few hours I happily placed it on the doll's body and then held it.

Perfect.

The hole in my heart began chipping away at that spell. I remembered events or emotions briefly, but most importantly, I thought I heard names.

Your names.

The clan had become restless. Talking of an incoming invasion. Many members snuck off into the night deserting the clan. I stayed. I would stand my ground for this building and the memories it held as I was realizing that hidden inside these walls was the real me.

I would outlast them all.

Then the invasion came.

"And you my friends," Elona's tear rimmed eyes and smile broke through the night like the rays of dawn, "And so did my sons!"

We all embraced under the great oak as the sounds of dancing and merriment would carry into the evening.

Elona the Fair had returned to Garnet Keep though physically she had never left.

Cordelia's voice, bright and unexpected, cut through the quiet hum of the distant celebration. We all turned to look at her, surprise evident on our faces, and then we couldn't help but chuckle at the startled way we had reacted.

"Oh, hey there," I managed to say between laughs, "You. You didn't scare us at all..." My voice trailed off in a sarcastic chuckle, amusement dancing in my eyes.

"I'm not interrupting anything important, am I?" Cordelia asked, a hint of playful concern in her voice. She tilted her head slightly, her eyes scanning our faces, as if searching for any sign that she'd arrived at an inopportune moment.

"No Cordelia!" Elona sniffed, smiling as she wiped the tears from her eyes. "You look so much like Lora. Doesn't she?"

"Yes." I nodded as Elloveve chuckled.

"I have thought so many times."

"Oh well thanks but," Cordelia drew out a white leather book from her belt. "I found this in the old south nursery. The one outside where the fire was."

"A book? It looks familiar." I took it from her hand and opened it, "but it's blank to me. Maybe an unused journal"

Elona's eyes narrowed with a smirk. "Wait." She took the book from me and handed it back to the young fire mage, "What do you see Cordelia?"

"Only my mother's name on the back."

Elona's laughter bounced off the large oak, her eyes twinkling with amusement as she looked at my bewildered expression. Her mirth only seemed to increase as I continued to stare at her in confusion.

"Oh, come on," she finally managed to say between giggles, "Don't tell me you two forgot about Lora's spellbook."

A wave of realization washed over me, and I couldn't help but join in her laughter. "That's right!" I exclaimed, "She had it locked down tight! That's why we can't see anything."

Elona nodded in agreement, her smile softening as she turned to Cordelia. The warmth in her eyes was unmistakable, a mother's love shining through as she gazed at the young woman.

"Cordelia. Your mother used a single word to lock that spellbook."

"How would I know what word to use?"

Elona chuckled at her gently, "It was the one thing that meant everything to her in the entire world when she made that spellbook. I bet the answer was in that room as well, at that time."

Realization washed over Cordelia as she held the soft white leather book in her hand. She watched the smiling faces of the three elders in her life. She smiled and placing her left hand on the book spoke softly:

"Cordelia."

The book flared and in an instant was gone. Cordelia panicked "But! ... I was sure!... I oh no..."

Elona laughed gently as she stepped toward the young woman. Her voice was a warm sound that eased the tension from Cordelia's face.

"You were absolutely correct, child," she said, her eyes twinkling, "Now, tell me, where would our dear Lorahana keep a spellbook?"

Cordelia's brow furrowed, her mind racing as she tried to recall any clues or hints about her mother's habits. She stammered, "I... I don't know. Maybe in her chambers? Or perhaps a hidden library?"

Elona's smile deepened, and she reached out to gently take Cordelia's hands in her own. "The answer is closer than you think, my dear," she said softly. As she turned Cordelia's hands over, a gasp escaped the young woman's lips.

Elona held Cordelia's hands gently as she turned them over revealing the tattoo of a White Book on her left wrist.

Hush now, don't you cry
little applehead

A sky of blue, over you
a blanket as you sleep

Wrapped in white
close your eyes
you're all that mommy needs

The fire light,
burns tonight
lost within a dream

A kiss goodnight
turn out the light
lying in your bed

Hush now, don't you cry
little applehead

INTERLUDE

"Take my hand Maldros." The voice of Ash De La Rosa reverberated in his memory. "You have won your freedom."

The gladiator shifted from one leg as he rose. Powerful thighs pulled at sore knees as they drew straight and standing. His blood red eyes closed and as he drew deep breaths. The smell of the pine trees and mossy stones mixed pleasantly in his mind as if he were still there that day, The smell of freedom.

He saw Ash in her black and silver robes, a surprisingly kind smile on her face as she looked up at his muscular frame. He smiled, too, behind the thick armored faceplate covering his face, hinged by a pair of bolts to the helmet that wrapped around horns. Beyond her he saw the long, midnight blue hair of Pallus draped over a wolf pelt on his shoulders. A well used longsword hung at his side as he paid the pit boss off with a satchel of coins.

"You know this is less than what I'd make off him in a year." The bald man frowned, weighing the coins in the palm of his hand. "I shouldn't do this for a champion like Maldros the Unrelenting."

"Oh but you will, Felias." Pallus's voice boomed slightly even when he whispered. Like a distant thunder in the jungles of the Deadlands, the home of Maldros and his people. "Or I won't take that little friend you've been complaining about with me. How will you feel in a few days as it continues to claw at you? Inside and out?"

Pallus, his expression a mixture of pity and impatience, gestured towards the small leather bag that hung around Felias's neck. The cord had rubbed the skin raw, a stark testament to the burden it carried. Felias, his face etched with pain, nodded and reached for the bag with a trembling hand.

"Just get it over with," he whimpered, his voice barely above a whisper. "It's agony."

"Ash," Pallus said, turning to the woman beside him with a forced smile. "If you would be so kind."

Ash smirked, her eyes glinting with a strange light above the thin band of runes in black ink gracing her cheekbones and the bridge of her nose.. "Adap-teh-fer-bo-teh!" she chanted, her voice weaving a spell that conjured tendrils of green-blue smoke. The smoke coiled around the pendant, lifting it gently from Felias's neck. The moment the pendant was removed, Felias collapsed to his knees, gasping for breath.

"I'm free!" he cried out, tears streaming down his face. Ash watched him with a mixture of disdain and amusement. He had been a slaver, a dealer in human misery, and now he had become a slave to his own greed. The irony was not lost on her.

The pendant, now freed from its captive, pulsed with a dark energy. It was a sinister artifact, a tool that should be handled with caution. Pallus held out his hand and Ash placed the pendant carefully in his palm. He wrapped it in a cloth, sealing away its malevolent aura before she flicked a wrist slightly, returning the wrapped object to float in the air between them.

Felias, still on his knees, looked up at Pallus with a mixture of gratitude and shame. "Thank you," he croaked. The raw chafed line of his throat shaking with his voice.

Pallus shook his head from the display of weakness and turned away.

"Hand him to me." Maldros's red eyes glowed slightly in anticipation. Nodding to him and with a wave of her hand, Ash passed the satchel to glide upon the breeze gently to rest in the palm of his hand.

"It's good to be back with you, my friend." A familiar voice hissed in his mind. He closed his eyes and answered back, internally.

"Can we trust them?" Maldros concentrated on the words in his mind while answering the voice.

"Yes," the voice wheezed, *"Ash and Pallus can help you free me. Remember your promise, and I will remember mine. Those who sold you will pay for it. But we must use them, and beat them at their own game."*

"What of Felias?"

"He is nothing, but let me at least give you a taste of vengeance now. Don't let anyone say I don't reward those who are faithful to me."

The raspy voice cackled in the mind of Maldros He nodded as he drew the satchel over his neck and Felias looked on in horror.

"What is it?! Who are you really?!" he gasped as Maldros stared at him with cruel malice behind his eyes.

"He has a final gift for you, slaver." Maldros grinned, his red eyes narrowing behind the helmet. "I'm no longer your slave. I am no longer Maldros the unrelenting. I am free!"

"Yes! You ARE free, my child. Now hold me where I can remind this worm of who he is. Of the darkness he held us in for too long!"

As Maldros held the pouch out from his chest gently, a wave of black bolts rocketed from the satchel around his neck and into the wide terrified eyes of Felias. With a scream all that was left were two empty sockets where his eyes once were. Frantically his hands went to his face.

"I can't see!" he screamed "My eyes! Th- the dark!" he cried.

"Thank you for my freedom, maggot." Maldros nodded, smiling cruelly, "I hope you never *see* me again!" Maldros laughed deeply.

"Come Maldros. Or should I say *'Maldros the Dark.'*" Ash laughed as she took his hand. "There is much to do and little time."

Maldros emerged from the depths of his memory, his eyes fluttering open to the hushed stillness of the arena. The stale air of the evening hung heavy, undisturbed by the usual clamor of combat and cheers. The only sound was the soft echo of his own breathing, a stark contrast to the thunderous roars that typically filled the space. He was alone here

From the sand, he looked up to the vast expanse of the arena that seemed to stretch into infinity. The rows upon rows of empty seats were a silent testament to the countless battles that had unfolded within its walls. The sand, usually stained crimson with the blood of fallen warriors, was eerily pristine, a chilling reminder of the violence that lay dormant, waiting to be reawakened.

Lost in thought, he turned and walked back through the stone archway, down the gently sloping ramp. A guard nodded respectfully, but he didn't notice. He saw the gated cells and the still bodies lying in the hay.

The gladiators' quarters, normally abuzz with activity, were shrouded in an unsettling silence. The only sign of life was the occasional soft murmur or rustle of straw, the restless sleep of warriors haunted by the ghosts of impending combat. The air was thick with tension, a palpable reminder of the ever-present threat of death that loomed over their existence.

He smiled knowing they were his gladiators, and these were his games.

CHAPTER 12

THE PLAN

Una's sleep was restless. Her legs felt uncomfortable when she was awake, and readjusting her position in the soft bed didn't help. Frustrated, she peeled back the covers and sat up, rubbing her eyes. Her feet touched the cold stone floor, sending shivers up her spine as she pulled the blanket close around her body.

Una...

She sighed as the familiar voice cooed in her head. It was distant but lately seemed to be drawing closer, more understandable.

"Yes, master," she whispered in the cold night air. The smell of charred wood and rose petals drifted in th

rough her open window. Una knew why the voice called her, as it had done so many times before.

Come to the fireplace and look beyond the flames.

She walked toward the stone hearth, where the fire had burned low while she had been trying to sleep. Una glanced outside and noticed the sky starting to lighten, but it was still hours before dawn. Standing in front of the fireplace, she felt the radiant heat of the coals as she gazed into them.

The coals began to slowly shift, creating a pattern, then a glowing image. Una saw two dragons facing each other; the one on the left was calm and strong as it stared at the other, frozen in rage. The fire it breathed created a crashing tide in which two lovers sat, staring into the distant unknown across the sea. They sat on a beach made of the hair of two sisters, bound by family and facing a great enemy within. To their left was a mountain made of a giant skull where five mysterious figures were approaching, but to the right, two fighters scrambled in a vast arena. Below all this, she saw twin mountains spewing fire above a broken city and a fallen dwarven warrior with an axe in his back.

The ethereal voice hissed like water over hot coals. It was hard to hear but she believed she made out some words.

Do you see?

"Yes," Una nodded quietly, "We must return to Enruk."

THE ANCIENT MEAD HALL THAT stood during the time of Benedict's father echoed with voices of merriment once again. The heroes had returned to the halls of Garnet Keep. Over the following week, we had rebuilt what we could to make the keep livable, and tonight was a time to celebrate. While everyone joyfully carried on throughout the night, we, the party of adventurers, met in the war room. When I entered the room, I noticed my armor gleaming gold in the candlelight. Elloveve entered behind me dressed in leather armor emblazoned with the Sword and Crown, befitting a decorated Scout Archer. She was with a young woman from the ranks of our forces; a mage, if I remember right, and also a fellow elf from the Silver Maple Woods in the north of Trull.

"It has come to our attention, my friends," I began to address the room, "that we must infiltrate Enruk, the City of Fire. Isenatha is here to assist in planning this dire mission."

Isenatha, the young elf, looked at us all carefully as she took in a deep breath and closed her eyes.

"In the," she hesitated, and I could tell something bothered her in that room, or possibly someone, "south of Trull is a-"

Eralin cleared his throat nonchalantly. "Ahem. Excuse me."

Isenatha's eyes widened angrily as she saw the crude smirk on the sea elf's face. "Do I bore you?" she asked venomously.

"Woah, you haven't even started yet." Eralin held out both his hands defensively, smirking as he glared at her. "But I'm laying money on it."

She snorted. "Figures. Of course, you would. Money is everything, am I right? You and the rest of your kind only care about yourselves and staying out of the way of progress. Tell me, Eralin," She leaned in closer with her arms crossed, "where have you been?!" She leaned closer as we all stared at her, confused and lost in her anger.

Eralin chuckled and shook his head in disbelief. The man rarely showed any emotion, and this time we saw a bit of a rise that I think even surprised him. Cordelia held up a hand.

"Wait a moment, Isenatha; is that really necessary to-"

"It-" Isenatha held her breath tight for a moment before she sighed. "You are right, Cordelia. My apologies."

Looking around the room, she saw the faces of her new friends. These weren't her enemies, she reminded herself, as she continued to slowly let her blood cool, pointing at a small dot on the map at the southern tip of the Garnet Mountains where they met the sea. She smiled slightly, trying to regain her composure as well as realizing the need to tell them everything - at least as much as she knew - then finally closed her eyes, resolute and calm.

"This happened many years ago in the city known as Enruk. Enruk is surrounded by twin volcanoes and is known for its-"

"Pits." Dabria interrupted. The room shuffled nervously as Dabria confirmed what we all dreaded. "Gladiator pits."

"Yes. Their beloved blood pits," Isenatha looked up at Dabria, her eyes light yellow-green sparks of hazel in the firelight. "But more importantly, I know of some allies currently imprisoned there who can help us."

Isenatha's fists clenched into balls as she listened to the former officer of the dark army speculate on the fate of her friends with such indifference. She still wasn't at ease with Dabria or Una's presence. A moment passed as she thought about Dabria's last words before drawing a breath to continue.

"You may have known much as a commander of Dekkion's Dead Army, but I fear you didn't know everything." She narrowed her eyes at Dabria coolly. "Dabria, we MUST assume nothing and investigate."

If I didn't know better, something in those words confused Dabria. I saw her stone-cold visage quake slightly, but not as much as what took place next.

"She's right." Una shrugged, looking at Dabria, her green eye and grey eye both pleading with her to reason. "There were many things kept from us, my sister. My guide tells me much of his... love for secrets."

With a slight gasp, Una straightened, leaning on her spear as if it were now a staff. The dark hood of her robes cloaked her scarred face in shadow, frozen save for the tremble of a single corner of her mouth. Her eyes opened wide, staring into the fireplace. The smell of the ash and pine burning seemed to dull in that moment as the fire's color faded to a cold blue-green.

"I'm..." Una's voice became as distant as her gaze, reverberating off the cold walls as darkness lapped at the edges of the light. I could feel the powerful pull of necromancy from somewhere, but not Una. Like she was only reading it from beyond our four walls.

"I'm being told we must return to the doomed city. It is key to his unraveling."

"Dekkion's?" Dabria asked with a somber note, her voice becoming strikingly serious again.

"Y...yes," Una stammered, her eyes clenched tight as she struggled to make sense of the whirlwind of images and voices in her mind, "Th...the Dead Lord himself, but also Lord Pallus."

Zorin didn't look up, but I felt his body tense at the mention of his hated father, the one who had selfishly destroyed so many lives. Dabria gasped, and the fires returned to their normal red-orange glow. Drawing a ragged breath, she looked at her dark sister.

"We must seek the truth. The truth beneath the temple."

"Well, that's all I needed to know." Dabria looked at Isenatha and crossed her arms. "When do we leave?"

Sophie smirked as she also turned to their guest. "Isenatha, do you have a plan for this?"

"Yes. Thank you, Sophie. We must divide into two groups. One group will travel south along the Garnet Mountains toward the sea and through the North Pass." She leaned over the map, drawing a line with her hands as she spoke, one for each team. "The other will gain passage and sail out of Whitford, around Trull itself, and into the bay. I will lead the group coming into the North Pass, and we will proceed to the Temple."

"We believe it is somewhere beneath it that the prisoners are being held. The other party, a much smaller party, will dress like human mercenaries and infiltrate to find out what Lord Pallus plans and if there is any chance of driving a rebellion from within."

"I know the Temple." Una said softly. "I served much time within its walls when we were training."

"This is good. You and I will be together then, as I seek to free these prisoners." She turned to Eralin. Not a note of apology was on her cold face. "I can only hope you won't be as selfish as I think you are, but I need to trust you to help us. I want you to help lead the smaller party coming in by ship since you and Zorin know the sea so well."

"Of course we do; consider it—"

"Not to mention," her voice pitched up as she halted his outburst, "your skill at 'deception.'"

She turned to Zorin. "Zorin, no one knows your father like you do. You should go with Eralin, but you will need a guide. Dabria, one of his most trusted commanders, will do nicely. You will also need a light in the darkness to go with you. I recommend Benedict."

They all nodded in agreement with her team-building. She turned to the rest of the group.

"And with us, Skotmir and Sophie will be our defenders."

At that moment, I looked around for Benedict and remembered he was in his prayers.

"Maybe it's best I tell him about the change in his armor," I said apologetically. "He may not take it so well."

LATER THAT EVENING, THE PARTY went to the armory to outfit and get more equipment. As Zorin was browsing, I saw Benedict enter the armory to see where he could help or assist with the various gathered equipment and weapons. This was an interesting approach as I think he was having issues actually accepting his role here. I suppose this was all the more reason he needed to go on this mission. His heart wasn't ready to just lead. He needed to affect it directly.

"Milord! What are you in here for?" the blacksmith called out from a smile of a few missing teeth. His sparse gray and black hair was pulled back in a ponytail.

"I wish to simply help, not purchase." Benedict answered. He was eyeing some of the damaged and bent longswords in a pile in the corner. That's when I went to him.

"Benedict, there's something I wish to tell you about your upcoming journey." I shrugged to hopefully diffuse any negative reaction he might have. "You will need to wear a disguise."

"What?" his eyes narrowed at the thought of the act of deception.

"Son, you must change out of your treasured and accepted armor into a set of…well, it's only a disguise of sorts." Clearing my throat I put my hand on his shoulder, "You must dress like an evil officer of the Dark Army."

He stared at me, thinking. I knew he wouldn't like it.

"I hate this idea, Keldor. But it does make sense if we are infiltrating. May the Knightlord forgive me."

I chuckled, "The Knightlord will forgive your fashion choices I'm certain, Benedict. Despite what you may have heard, clothes rarely make the person. It is weighed only on your actions."

"Yes." He shrugged with a smile, "I will accept this as just another challenge, Keldor. No problem for me." He turned to the blacksmith. "Now I would like to ask you, good sir, if you wouldn't mind me throwing some hot steel around? I do miss the craft."

"Of course!" the blacksmith beamed, handing the hardwood handle of a hammer to the knight. "Step right up milord!"

LORVANA WAS IN THE GARDEN looking up at the stars and humming her old traveler's tune. She loved the night sky and it was nice to have something this peaceful to look at.

Ho-ei-oh! Here we go!

We dance across the skies.

Walking through the poorly maintained garden beds she made her way toward the old tree. She smiled as the moonlight danced on her old trusted lute. As her feet went one in front of the other, Lorvana absentmindedly twisted the instrument slightly to catch the blue white glow of the moon and stars across the bronze and sinew strings. The deep cherrywood created a violet tone in gentle waves across the fretboard. Elloveve sat on the exposed roots of the ancient tree, smiling at her little song in the shadows, toying with the silver horse head cuff adorning one pointed ear.

"Oh!" Startled by her friend smiling in the darkness, Lorvana stopped playing and stood still.

"Oh don't stop because of me! I truly enjoy you playing that tune." Elloveve pleaded gently.

"Really? Oh." Lorvana smiled shyly, "Excuse me, um. Elloveve. I really wanted to tell you."

She paused. Truth be told she was enamored with the strong elf woman. She was a legend who lived in songs and poems she had heard for many years. Even better yet was one she could actually talk to.

"You." She paused, sifting through the words in her mind. She let out a deep sigh and smiled wide, "Are just amazing." She giggled.

Elloveve laughed gently, "Oh you are amazing, too, Lorvana! Thank you for all you've done. If it wasn't for you, I may have never found my way back." Her smile warmed as she pointed at the tree trunk next to her. "Sit here with me a moment please?"

"Oh yes! Of course." Lovana said eagerly as she grunted and groaned to climb the root. Elloveve smiled at her smaller friend gently. Although a decent seat for those of Elloveve's height, it was a bit out of the way for Lorvana's three and a half foot stature. She offered a hand to help her into her seat before placing it on Lorvana's shoulder gently.

"Little one, I have something for you." She said in a motherly tone, "First is this gem. If you hold it up at the light just so it can show the edge of most secrets. There," she pointed, "You see over there? The wall?"

Lovana held the small blue and white gem to her eye and squinted through it.

"Umm- Oh! I see letters... or... or something. Blue ones!"

"That's it!" Elloveve said happily, confirming it worked for her friend. "Those are the words of magic. Old magic, but it still serves its purpose. And then there's this. This arrow has been part of my quiver for many years, and it now reminds me of you."

"Oh wow!" Lorvana gasped as Elloveve produced an arrow made from a rose's thorny stem, straight and true. Lorvana remarked, that the head hooked back almost like a glaive on one side but perfectly balanced on the other with a swooping point. The fletching was black with purple tips from some magical and unknown bird.

They could hear another voice in the distance of the courtyard. Zorin's voice. He sounded frustrated, voice grunting as he struggled with something.

"Oh come on... just... latch.... new leather. Always such a pain. Ugh! Where's some water?!"

Elloveve chuckled. "Well I better give him a hand."

"Thank you Elloveve. I love it." Lorvana said with stars in her eyes.

"I'm glad you do. It will hold your quarry in place with thorny vines at least for a moment." Elloveve smiled as she stood up dusting off her armored thighs quickly. "Good luck tomorrow."

Elloveve walked to Zorin who was going over some of his new weapons. She could tell by the look on his face he was picturing them buried in his hated father, Lord Pallus.

"I hope you find closure Zorin." She paused, looking at the new rapier in his hand. "That's different."

He shrugged, "Me too. Er...oh, you mean this?" he patted the twisted steel of the basket hilt gently. "It's not as balanced as I'd like and the blade has way too much flex-" He sighed gently, "It's not like her."

Elloveve cocked her head, "Her?"

"Oh!... ah... There was a sword I thought I held once that was-" he sighed, "Never mind. This will do just fine."

Thrusting into the open air, he remained focused on the outstretched, sharpened tip of the steel blade, imagining a look of surprise or, better yet, fear at the other end. She gently turned his chin. Zorin remembered her doing this when Zane and he would need 'instruction'. He could smell the flowers and honey that always seemed to follow her, and the embroidered vines on her glove pressed gently to his face.

"Be calm though, don't let impatience and hatred take the best of you away." she smiled gently, "I always viewed you like a son and I always will."

"You've always been there for me," He wrapped her in a big hug, his pulse slowing in her arms. His vision became clearer as the feelings of anger slowly melted away and he regained control.

"Thanks for being you."

BENEDICT WALKED THE STONE WALL circling the keep. He noted how he was reversing the steps he took when he first came to the stairs. Peering down, he remembered telling Una and the others to go to the front. That's now where he was heading, to the front overlooking the great canyon below. Even though the rubble and filth had been cleaned up over the last week, he could still look back at broken walls and their jagged scars.

The glassworkers and blacksmiths were now replacing windows that were broken. Masons cut new bricks and stone to replace the old. The Mistgard barricades made of skulls and furs had been either burned, melted down for re-purpose or thrown over the side of the long stone bridge, falling a thousand feet to splash in the river below.

Benedict helped by overseeing the design and reconstruction of the keep. He oversaw the development of the rooms' design in the main keep itself and the barracks. He rebuilt the smithy and began rebuilding the chapel to the Knightlord. The stables were patched up first and the horses were grateful. As he walked he noted there was still so much to do.

Standing by the left forward ballista stood Elona the Fair. She was staring at a point into the distance northward, looking past the bridge to the large meadow on the other side known as Bear Trap. From here she could see where the path disappeared down the far side of the mountain. In the far distance the rolling foothills gave way to the vast Glen valley.

"Hello Mother." Benedict smiled gently, "Good morning. How are you?"

She turned towards him, the cool wind catching her gold and silver hair gently in the breeze. It was now cropped at the shoulder, the way she always wore it, at least how Zane would describe her to him. Elona's armor was polished now and a white tunic of a knight major adorned her chest with 3 red stripes. She was the one in charge and given what she had been through no one questioned it. Elona's trusted advisors were Keldor and Elloveve and the collected input of the keep itself.

In her hand, the familiar tall magical glaive stood polished. He could make out the name *Tempest* across the oiled hardwood pole. Elona's blue eyes smiled in the red gold of the dawn's sunlight. She lingered there for a moment longer than what would normally be comfortable, taking in that moment of thankfulness for what it was.

"Good morning my son." She turned back to her gaze into the distance, where Benedict could make out wisps of clouds snaking between the rocks and crags of the mountain in the golden light of the dawn. "You've done much in this week."

"Has it only been a week?" Benedict sighed. "It feels like-"

"A lifetime for me." She smiled at him, "A life that you returned to me. I can never thank you enough. Your memory kept me alive until you returned to me. Thank you."

Elona steeled herself for her next statement. Benedict spoke urgently.

"I... I wanted to tell you that I can't stay right now that-"

"Shhhh..." Elona placed a gloved hand on his shoulder. "You are a knight now. The son of two warriors." She chuckled at this statement gently, "Two warriors, I might add, who made their own path. Two warriors who never said goodbye, not even-" She stopped herself for a moment, thinking of seeing her beloved's body on those steps, lifeless. She winced slightly.

Benedict could sense her pain, "I didn't mean to-"

"No," she wiped away a tear forming in her eye as she looked upwards into the expanse of gold tipped clouds turning to cream, "this is good... Benedict." She chuckled with a gentle sniff. "Now I can truly grieve, but where I thought I lost everything, I found you."

She turned to him and cupped her son's cheek in the palm of her hand.

"My angel I was so sure I lost you, too."

Benedict brought her close in a warm embrace as Elona gently pulled her face into his shoulder he felt his chest grow warm with her tears.

WE ADVENTURERS ALL ANXIOUSLY PREPARED their horses, ensuring their supplies were carefully tied off behind each of them as Dabria began.

"We will ride together southeast for about a fortnight until we reach the fork to Whitford. And there we will part ways." She realized something she may have overlooked as she turned to behind her to the rogue in dark robes. "Zorin, are you familiar with the Black Skiffs?"

"Fastest ships in the world, from what I've heard. They were the ones that would take our supplies out of Whitford to Enruk in a matter of days. The shallow reefs south of the old country wouldn't allow the larger frigates and merchantmen. I sailed on to travel that way."

"Why not just use them instead to begin with?" Sophie chuckled mockingly.

"You can-" Dabria laughed, "But they become a leaf drifting on the ocean, violently tossed and re-tossed until they were nothing but toothpicks and drowned dead."

Sophie snorted, "Well make it your goal, Dabria, to bring my brothers back safe."

"Fine." She paused, smirking at Sophie, "You do the same for my sister."

Una and Dabria laughed at the absurd thought of needing help as Elloveve, Elona and I watched them all mount. Little Lorvana handed Elona a small purple flower and giggled as she climbed into the saddle of a small pony alongside Skotmir. Elona smiled and nodded at the bard as I bid farewell to these brave adventurers.

"Godspeed my friends. We will expect to see you return with the next moon!"

"Goodbye!" Cordelia called out. Something struck Benedict as he looked at everyone in that moment and suddenly he understood.

"Actually Cordelia. We don't say goodbye."

Elloveve, Elona and I looked at each other, three remaining members of the Six Winds, and we smiled.

ON THE THIRD DAY, UNA and Dabria parted ways. The harsh heat in that noon hour helped kick up dust in the muggy road. They didn't seem to notice though. They solemnly nodded at each other before Dabria snapped impatiently.

"Eralin, Zorin and Benedict. Let's go."

As the two groups split here as planned, Sophie knew something was about to change, and some of them were not meant to come back the same.

Another week's journey passed as Una and Isenatha led Cordelia, Sophie, Skotmir and Lorvana deep into the violent hills of southwest Trull. The grass was dry and smelled of dust and sour springs. Skotmir mentioned the Garnet Mountains as they headed beyond their hidden passes. His voice was soft and reverent.

"These mountains hold the halls of my ancestors. They always seem so solemn... and lonely."

Isenatha looked up as she continued to ascend the broken rocks, placing one heavy foot in front of the other.

"Una... those dark clouds-"

"Yes," Una's voice was raspy and winded, "that's where we will go. Climb up, up ,up... into the mountains. Into the storm."

Sopie saw the dark clouds, but they seemed more black than normal, "Is it... rain?"

"No." Una looked at Sophie and smirked, "Fire."

DABRIA STOOD ON THE DECK of the black-sailed ship with her companions as they cut swiftly through the waves and air. Sleek and streamlined, the Minotaur captain grinned menacingly as he held the helm steady with a stone solid and gray muscular arm. She saw the dark clouds thickening on the horizon.

"Mistress Dabria! In three hours and a turn we will be making port. Best make your preparations!" He began shouting to an old sailor unfolding a knife in his tarred and chapped hands. "Fasten lines and check the wake!"

"Aye aye Captain! She's running shallow and smooth."

"Good! Let's bring her home then!"

He pointed to the forming roots of the great volcanoes at the foot of the Garnet Mountains. Those rocky peaks ended here, disappearing into the sea. Gradually the mountains grew as the speedy craft approached.

Dabria turned to Benedict. He was dressed as a human officer of the dark army in a uniform that was collected from the Celestine Tower's dead, she assumed. Zorin and Eralin, on the other hand, looked like low ranking mercenaries. She had seen hundreds of their kind, and they should also go unnoticed here. Even the tall Eralin was enough of a cold blooded individual to pass with his elven features. Elves were less common than even Halflings as mercenaries for whatever reason.

Benedict walked to stand next to her, emotionless, making a conscious effort to not break his new character. Dabria cocked an eyebrow and nodded in approval at him. Looking across the waves she spoke softly.

"Enruk is a cesspool of the world's forgotten and forlorn. Those that walk that twilight between life and death thrive here." Dabria chuckled as they swiftly sailed towards the growing pair of volcanoes sprawling in front of them.

"Before Pallus came it was ruled by kobolds who traded with the local Orc clans to the east, some Dwarves to the north and the mysterious Chikarans to the west. When Pallus came he taught them to no longer be simple kobolds by showing them how to thrive in commerce."

She hesitated for a moment, thinking of Sharptooth and their last words. She sighed with a faint pang of hope as she continued.

"They began to view him as a savior, one who promised to lead them into a new and wealthy future. Maldros the Dark brought fighters from Bloodwood to train here and they opened up their own arena."

"Zane spoke of the pits in Bloodwood." Benedict said under his breath, "Were these-"

"Worse. Much worse. In Bloodwood, even occupied Bloodwood there is bureaucracy from the fighters and the trade barons that even Maldros himself couldn't completely overcome. Here he had thousands of either bloodthirsty volunteers or those willing to do the unspeakable to turn a profit. Sacrificing them to the sport answered his dreams. Soon, the bloodpit came to rival any other, standing as the most impressive arena in the world."

Her fist balled up angrily. "Built on the shoulders of the dead gladiators he committed to the bloodstained banner of entertainment."

She turned her gaze out over the ocean where, in the distance, a deep gray haze lay on the horizon. Unclenching her fist slowly, she took a breath and continued.

"During the day a small amount of sunlight, filtered like red orange fire in spots by the heavy clouds, illuminates the city with a ruddy twilight. The city itself is sprawling brick and clay not larger than two stories but only featuring two major buildings. The arena and the temple. There are now a few rough taverns and inns that treat the officers of his great lordship quite well. It is recommended that you all watch your backs. This town is more than rough. It is evil and-"

Benedict coughed as the smell of sulfur assaulted his nose, sending burning sensations back into his throat. She smiled crookedly, her gold eyes cutting through the thickening haze.

"It is also what I called home."

CHAPTER 13

THE CITY OF FIRE

The sails of faded black were pulled back as the ship docked easily in the harbor of Enruk. A warm, thick haze hung heavy and low, smelling deeply of the burning brimstone nearby. Minotaurs, ogres and humans moved about the dockside, carrying very large crates or barrels from the docks to carts leading to the marketplace. Benedict looked up.

"Dusk is setting in," he murmured as he shrugged his shoulders uncomfortably. "Ugh. This armor chafes." The seams of the leather plates under his shoulders pinched the skin under the shoulder blades if he bent over too far. Zorin chuckled and pointed at the sky.

"How can you tell that?" he whispered, "It just looks slightly dimmer to me."

"The sun is fading to the east past the mountains meeting the sea." Eralin said hushed and reverently, "I feel it's fading." the powerful legs of the captain stomped across the deck towards them.

"There you be." He nodded with a pointed finger to the docks. Turning to the rest of the crew he began to call out, "Make ready lads, we leave in an hour!"

Dabria heard him mumble as he added softly, "Don't want to stay here longer than I have to."

Dabria shrugged as she turned to her companions, "Come on. Follow me, there's a place we can get a room just outside the docks. It is a bit quieter."

She led the three other darkly dressed companions up the docks. The smell of copper, salt brine and vinegar struck Zorin's nose as familiar.

"Well someone's pickling fish today." He smiled at Eralin.

"Disgusting." the tall elf replied, his eyes showing a bit of unexpected horror. "Like vegetables? That's revolting."

Zorin laughed, "You haven't had the good stuff then. Can be pretty welcome on-" He paused for a minute at what he was going to say, deeply curious about Eralin's offhand remark and dismissal of what he knew to be welcome food for every sailor he ever knew. He stared at his friend curiously before continuing, "long journeys."

The footfall of huge hulking bodies vibrated the wooden planks under their feet. Looking across the docks they saw four ogres making their way toward them.

"Well what do we have here?" One voice boomed. "Dirty Mercs?" He closed with a deep laugh through broken teeth. A ragged leather cowl was draped over his sweating bald head.

"Let's go make some friends shall we?" another said a sparse goatee of coarse black hair wagging in three strands from his chin as he spoke. A shoulder was covered by a crimson leather pauldron, made from thick elephant hide that was boiled hard.

A smaller ogre began laughing from behind thick black goggles. Rows of spikes like them connected to a crude iron helmet. "Oh sweet sweet little friends they be too! All the huggin' hahaha!"

Dabria held her hand up, freezing them in their tracks and keeping them at a distance to observe and not interfere. Her golden eyes glowered at them as they passed by, ignoring the visitors. Their bodies stood twice as high as Eralin and dark black leather scales hung from pale waists, draping over muscular thighs. Rudely they forced themselves through the packed crowd, who clamored to get out of their way for fear of being trampled.

The smell of sweat and ammonia followed them, making Benedict's eyes water. They walked toward a group of six smaller humanoid mercenaries. Likely a mix of human and elf based on their height, Benedict imagined.

"You carry what's mine!" The cowled ogre said grinning mercilessly.

"Yours? Hear that boys?! We have a donation!" The dark clad mercenary pulled a scarf over her nose and mouth, only revealing a pair of almond shaped purple eyes. Elven eyes. She stood up on the crate she was perched on like a raven, her dark cloak emblazoned with a half skull and hourglass in faint silvery thread.

"What? What donation?" The lumbering ogre's confusion etched across its round face.

Another one of the mercenaries stepped forward, the cruel curved dagger of dark damascus tossing lazily in the palm of his hand as he slowly explained.

"Yeah. See, you hand over your stuff and we... liberate you from the tedious mundane task of ever having to carry it again! Real simple."

A smaller mercenary, probably the height of Lorvana, stepped forward with a dark cowl and drew a blackthorn bow. "Real simple." he repeated.

"I not simple!" The ogre in the red pauldron protested, shaking a fist.

"We no donate!" The cowled ogre stood up straight and grabbed a wooden shipping crate in its hand like a child would a ball. "We take!" he roared as the ogres careened into the crowd like the crashing waves of a tsunami, powerful fists raking the shorter bodies below.

As innocent individuals in the crowd were mowed over, the blackened steel of one the mercenary's helmets helplessly caved in, its wearer thrown to the side lifelessly. The remaining mercenaries bolted as a single force, darting between the thick trunk-like legs of the ogres to strike at hamstrings and open flanks. Screams erupted as the ogres frantically searched the crowd for the quick assailants.

The smaller ogre groaned and fell off the dock side into the water with a large splash. The other two stopped and looked at each other, fire in their eyes dwindling.

"Filthy pests! Keep your gold!" the cowled ogre yelled, "Let's go!"

"Bah! It's no good anyways!" The ogre with the red pauldron said as he glanced one last time at the body of the smaller one floating in the bay.

As they left, Benedict noted the bodies were roughly tossed to one side to clear the path as the crowd began bustling again. He looked 20 yards past where they were and noticed the remains of three other bodies in a heap by some old shipping crates. They were old, rotting bodies probably from a few weeks prior. The crowd moved around the gaping faces and cloudy eyes without paying any mind. Benedict was appalled.

"Does... does no one care about the law here?" he trembled as he complained under his breath to Dabria.

She smirked at the paladin in disguise, "What law?"

"They were murdered!" Benedict said louder, drawing Dabria's ire but luckily no one's attention.

"You!" She hissed behind her cold eyes, and clenched teeth, "You are wearing that law right now, and that law is hate, lies" Dabria pointed at the bodies, "and murder. Do you understand?"

Benedict nodded hesitantly. Dabria looked at Zorin and Eralin, who also nodded awkwardly in understanding. She turned her golden eyes to Benedict. He noted they seemed cold like golden rings found in a forgotten glacier.

"Just- walk the walk Benedict." she sighed while adjusting the hood of her cloak over her head again, "Come on."

There was a faint, sweet smell that mingled with the tang of blood and sulfurous brimstone in the thick air as they continued into the heart of the quarter. The deep red sky reflected the pools and rivers of fire that surrounded this ancient holy city of the kobolds.

As they walked down the cobblestones, Eralin repeated the harsh conversation with Isenatha in his mind, her accusations of selfishness and greed stinging with the same impact he felt when they parted ways.

What did she mean "your kind"?

He thought back to the ruby cage he was trapped in. Forgotten for how many years in that twilight world beneath the hills, beneath the kingdom of the dark dwarves. Did she know more about his lost memories? Was she some sort of key to unlocking them? Sighing, he realized he had many questions for her once they returned. If they returned. Emotionless and resolute, the ranger stuck to the rear of the group and continued, one foot in front of the other, clutching the pendant at his chest.

Turning a corner Dabria pointed across the broken curb of a dust intersection, "There."

They continued to walk towards a boxlike brick building. As they approached, they noticed there was nothing remarkable about the rough red and black brick other than a lack of markings on the two story building.

"Yeah…" Zorin stared at the building, investigating the appearance with his eyes. "So, this looks like a warehouse."

"I agree. Are we sure this is-"

Dabria rolled her eyes with a deep, audible sigh, "Gods- fine! Watch if you don't believe me."

Almost in response to their commentary, confirmation was given as the door to the dingy, unnamed tavern burst open followed by six mercenaries, staggering out into the street, cursing and shouting.

One orc looked at Eralin and his friends, scoffing. "Well look at these weak bloods!"

They all laughed as they drew closer to the group.

"Nice cloak, rich boy." the Minotaur said disgustedly from a grey-blue muzzle. "It looks like it could use a bath. Well, so could you."

Benedict shook his head slowly and cracked his knuckles, never taking his eyes off the imposing figure.

"Hey girlie." The minotaur's voice was slow and venomous. "I'm talking to your friend. Maybe you can tell him to show some respect"

"Yeah respect!" A kobold cackled. "Weak bloods need to show some respect right Snake-eye? It's something they don't know cuz they ain't got it."

"Shut up," the minotaur said as he slapped the back of the kobold's yellow green head. The smaller creature slinked behind him, rubbing the pain from the scales around their crown.

Dabria's blood boiled at this crude display of power but she simply laughed. She recognized this thug.

"Ah. Snake-eye." She crossed her arms, daggers forming in her eyes. "I've heard of you. Shouldn't you be back at the dock bringing us more ale? Or is it cleaning the waste pits again?"

Snake-eye's smirk melted as he felt the weight of her insults land in his drunken mind.

"What did you say?" He hissed. He felt anger rise and he wasn't going to just weather insults by those lesser than him.

Dabria pulled the loose hooded cloak back from her face and crossed her scarred arms. Scars that found home somewhere in this dark city's past, no doubt. The Minotaurs' eyes fell on her like moths to a flame. Recognition and horror swept across their faces as the golden eyes of Dabria narrowed.

"I- meant no disrespect to the mistress. Please!" The orc bowed gently.

"Mistress?" the kobold questioned, their eyes growing larger with realization, "Wait- oh no- Forgive us dark mistress!"

As Snake-eye's companions fumbled over themselves with apologies, his muzzle trembled slightly with restrained rage.

"Run. I have no time for you-" Dabria said cooly. As they stood frozen in place, she sighed. "I said run!" Dabria gestured at the cruel whip on her belt. This was her namesake and weapon of choice. The mercenaries scrambled down the street drunkenly, tumbling through an old cart filled with foul smelling refuse. She pulled the thin velvet of her cloak back over herself, gently covering the raised jagged scars of her arms.

A memory shot through her mind as she winced slightly. Training had made her immune to pain, and a loveless world cemented it to her like a second skin. She was the mistress of pain to those that served her, and to others she was the angel of death.

Without gesture she began to walk across the street to the heavy iron handle of the door.

"Come. Let's go inside.

SOMEWHERE IN THE NORTHWEST AREA of town the other group made its way through the city closest to the temples and the barracks. Cordelia and Isenatha worked together to weave an illusion, making them seem like mercenaries. One of which looked pretty awkward as it plodded down the road.

Short legs and two heads behind the dark armor revealed a halfling perched on the shoulders of a surly dwarf. Una looked back at her companions.

"We still must be careful here. This is the Ogre perimeter and they don't care for mercenaries, let alone the rest of us small folk. Even Dabria and I didn't walk here alone.

Sophie nodded in understanding as she walked next to the dark-robed oracle.

"Bah! What's with all the dark armor and shrouds of lies?"Lorvana joked, "Not fitting for me to hide behind this trash. Rather behind a good boulder or maybe a keg of ale, right Skotmir?"

Skotmir chuckled at her mock bravery. "Easy for you to say. I'm trying to blend in with you on my shoulders."

"Oh you're fine! Look!" Lorvana smacked the top of his head with a mighty slap. "You're tough!"

Skotmir laughed under his breath afraid of who might hear their playful banter, "Well you're heavy! Maybe you need to lay off the pastries."

"Oh stop it!" she said childishly, "No need to hurt my feelings."

Skotmir chuckled, "Oh I'm sorry. I was just playing. You're making this more fun honestly, and now we are twice as high!"

Lorvana beamed at the thought, "Well- I am at least!"

"Wow, look at that!" Cordelia gasped.

The row of structures to their right ended, revealing a pristine white building. The red orange glow seemed to diffuse when it hit the white marble walls shining on its own like a proud beacon.

"The Temple of the Sun." Isenatha spoke reverently, "The kobold's ancient temple."

Sophie looked up to the cloudy dark sky, red orange networking in slow drifting veins between them. To imagine a sun was impossible.

"How can they worship the sun in a place like this? How can they see it"

Isenatha laughed. "It's- symbolic. It's true they don't see it, but many of us don't see the gods we follow, correct?" She waited a moment before continuing, "The sun and the moon are two of the most powerful sources of power to us in this world. All things have good and bad. Light and dark."

Una smirked, looking back at Isenatha, "Evil and good can be learned from the same teacher."

Isenatha smiled softly, "Yes." She hesitated as she let her answer linger in the air for a moment, "And culture, too, is a powerful teacher."

Sophie saw Isenatha bow her head in thought as they walked and wondered what made her answer that way.

Excuse me. Would you have time for an old man?

At the sound of a kind voice, Lorvana looked back to see a man in a dark robe leaning on a tall staff. The hood coiled over his head, leaving two eyes the color of deep oceans over a soft smile.

"Oh of course! How can I help you?" She said happily.

Skotmir looked around for evidence of who Lorvana was talking to.

"Wha... who are you talking to?" He stopped puzzled at finding the dirty alley empty save for them and the smell of old trash and mold.

Suddenly deep voices could be heard approaching as two ogres came from the open walkway between the rough stone buildings.

They were laughing at some unknown joke until they saw the group of weaker dark army soldiers before them. One of them smiled a crooked grin below beady black eyes.

"Smelly smelly! Loot these troll dungs bodah!"

"Yessss." The other grinned cruelly, showing his front teeth were filed to points. "Out of your place little bugs! Get em!"

As the two lumbering ogres charged Sophie drew her sword and smiled, "Come on Skotmir, lets go!"

As Sophie and Skotmir broke away from the ranks and ran headlong into battle, Lorvana's mind slowed down time. Details rarely escaped her and this would prove to be one moment she would never forget.

She saw the old man she had been addressing slowly look at Sophie and smile. As if suspended in some sort of thick syrup they ran towards him as he stepped forward and held two hands out in front of Skotmir and Sophie. Greeting them warmly as if they were long lost friends or family returning.

She noted they didn't react to him being directly in the way as they drew their blades. Lorvana's heart raced as she realized she still sat squarely on the charging dwarf's shoulders. He must have forgotten her!

"Oh no! Hey! W... Wait, he's right in front of you!" She stammered as they bounced towards the ogres. A flash of light and a deep low rumble of the world left her looking directly at the old man for a brief moment.

"It's time, little one," he said softly in her mind, "Be brave."

As time resumed, a ball of fire engulfed the entire group in a flash. Lorvana felt no heat, yet when their eyes adjusted the ogres were gone.

She could barely hear Cordelia screaming, "What happened?! Lorvana? What happened?!"

Lorvana looked around, trembling, trying to parse the last few minutes in her mind.. She saw Una, Cordelia and Isenatha but the old man and Sophie were gone, as were the ogres.

"Oh." Her tiny voice shook with worry as she looked around wringing her hands. "Um, Skotmir?"

She stood trembling on the hard ground where the powerful shoulders of Skotmir once were.

THE AIR SEEMED SLIGHTLY CLEANER, having some thick stone and an oaken door between them. There was a welcome smell of old beer and herbed cheese that pushed back the heavy smolder-ing scents outside. The dining room was sparsely populated, as Dabria had expected and hoped. This inn was a favorite for sailors, not soldiers and that probably contributed to the warm welcome of the thugs outside a few moments before. Though she herself would be recognized without the cloak, it wouldn't necessarily be a bad thing, just not her intention.

There were a few older human merchants at one table, and the surly barkeep sitting behind the cracked and worn dark bar top smoking a rich, chocolate-smelling pipe. Benedict turned to her, his eyes kinder than his armor looked. She hoped he wouldn't let his morality get in the way of their success sneaking into the town.

"Those mercenaries really were frightened by you."

"Many are." she said, peering into the goblet of dark red wine in her hands, tilting it slightly to watch rivulets of the liquid separate and flow back into the bottom.. Zorin gulped his ale greedily.

"Ah! Hmm.. Well... She was in charge of the Undead Legion right?"

"Yes" Dabria sighed.

"Well minotaur are terrified of the undead." he sat back as he wiped his chin smugly with the back of his sleeve. "Something about it being an affront to the glory of a proud warrior's death and all that."

Dabria now glared through Zorin, daggers passing from her eyes.

"I mean… I uh… " He stammered as Eralin shook his head in embarrassment.

"Yes." Her voice was cold as she continued to stare, "Something like that."

"Um-" Zorin frantically searched for a way to change the subject, "well this place seems to have pretty normal patronage. Maybe they might be able to give us a local scoop."

Dabria nodded. "I figured this is a place we can start at least. But not with me as I'm too well known as not being one of the people."

She looked away and back to her wine, watching the ghosts of her past swirling somewhere behind the sour liquid.

"I'll go."

Without waiting for permission, Benedict took in a deep breath and strode over to a table with four older merchants dressed in rich colored silks trimmed in fine furs. One of them was regaling everyone with a tale. His white mustaches wagged as he spoke and were well below his chin. Benedict noted how they waved similar to a banner in the breeze on the battlefield.

"Yes indeed they are," his voice was hushed as Benedict approached, "and so I'm sure everyone will get their sick enjoyment out of the 'parade' tomorrow. Pallus can't be-"

"Excuse me." Benedict interrupted with a commanding tone. The merchant's eyes grew wide for a moment in surprise.

"Oh! I ah-" the man with the mustache stammered as he lowered his head in a short bow.

"What do you know of this parade?" Benedict snarled. A look of fear washed over the man as he saw the unexpected dark army officer looming over him.

"My lord I...I... " The man stammered as he looked to his friends for support.

"He meant no disrespect, my lord." His bald friend smiled wide with strong hands held out apologetically. "Supporters we are! Right?"

The woman in blue and black nodded quickly, her dark hair spilling around her shoulders. "Yes! Hail Lord Pallus!"

"Silence!" Benedict slammed a fist onto the worn and heavy banded oak table top. "Imbecile!" he shouted.

Dabria raised an eyebrow at the outburst as Zorin leaned over to her with a smirk.

"Hey. He may be able to do this yet." he said under his breath.

Benedict placed two heavy hands on the table and leaned into the man's coarsely shaven face. He could see the mustache tremble. His faded green eyes darted side to side, unable to lock with Benedict's icy stare.

"You." Benedict's voice was cold, quiet and intimidating. "Answer my question."

A deep sigh came from the man before he began, "The parade tomorrow will welcome a new special batch of prisoners. Everyone's excited, milord."

"Why?" Benedict mused smugly. "What makes this so special to you cretins? My Lord Pallus can easily take prisoners with our army's might."

"But it's the usurpers, milord!" the bald man interjected.

"Usurpers?" Benedict questioned.

"The- the prisoners are from some ragtag army to the north." he offered, nodding quickly.

Benedict laughed heartily, "Yes! And then to the dungeons, correct? Just to be paraded around and shown off like the pigs they are!" He clapped his hands and stood up straight, letting a cruel joy sweep across his face, like a cat with its wounded prey.

The merchants gave each other an uneasy glance before the man with the mustache continued, "Milord, they will be taken to the arena for the Lord Pallus's enjoyment, as well as the entertainment of the rest of Enruk."

"Of course!" He nodded at the merchants as he straightened the cloak at his shoulder. "That will be all." Benedict turned to walk back to the table, barely overhearing them continue.

"That's no ragtag army, Donovan! ...word is they took back Garnet Keep!"

Dabria saw his eyes open slightly wider, meeting hers.

SKOTMIR FELT THOUSANDS OF CLAWS in the darkness, pulling him apart.

Then a sensation of being carried away as if lifted on several arms from a battlefield, and then, finally, nothing.

"Woah... wh... where am I?" He groaned.

Rolling over to a side to help him sit up he found himself in a dingy cell. The smell of dust and ammonia lingered in the air like a neglected circus cage. Small mounds of hay and straw used for bedding, or who knew what else, were piled in the four corners of the cell. To the back from the gate, one rough cut stone wall existed accompanied by three sets of crude ancient iron bars.

Skotmir could see this was one of many cells in this row. Lying on the ground in the cell to his right was Sophie. Her chest heaved with arduous breaths but at least she appeared to be alive; passed out, maybe, but alive. He was relieved. Looking at the wall, he noticed scratch marks, like tick marks for counting off calendar days. Skotmir squinted his eyes at the scrawling letters that seemed to form.

EvErytHinG haPpenS fOr a rEasoN

He rubbed his eyes and the message was gone. Skotmir heard another groan and noticed a small crumpled form in the cell opposite of Sophie's to his left. He heard another slight moan as a bloodied hand reached out to crawl to a seated position, or at least to lean on an elbow.

A distantly familiar face rose as it looked at Skotmir from one closed and bruised eye. He could see a familiar glint of dwarven pride.

"Skotmir? Is that you?" The voice trembled as Skotmir crawled towards the bars. His legs were weak and his arms barely obeyed him. Skotmir was puzzled, but couldn't help but crack a smile when recognition snapped in his mind.

"Yes, it is I," Skotmir chuckled weakly, "Thotmir."

Thotmir chuckled as well, matching Skotmir's. "I... I found you my brother."

Skotmir was stunned for a moment. Their last words were in anger, not love, and Skotmir left his family believing them all to be uncaring and ignorant to who he truly was. Now he saw the genuine, though weakened, smile on his brother's face. The dark past feud had died somewhere behind Thotmir's welling eyes, it didn't matter anymore.

"Father will be so happy." Thotmir's joy dropped as the sharp ache in his ribs held his breath tightly. He took in a deep laborious breath and smiled, holding out a powerful dwarven arm. Ignoring the pain of the past and his present weakness, Skotmir thrust his hand through the iron bars to clasp his long lost brother's wrist. The two dwarven brothers laughed weakly from behind ragged beards in their foul smelling dark cells.

Their reunion was cut short as a booming voice echoed down the hall along with storming footsteps. The footsteps became louder, stronger as they approached.

Around the corner a tall dark man stepped forward in black fabric clutched tight around a muscular body. What appeared to be a horned helmet poked out from beneath the hood of his cloak, his face wrapped in dark black gauze. He leaned on a crude great club, the wood dark with years of use and blood.

"I look forward to meeting all of you in the pits tomorrow. MY pits!" the booming and unnatural voice dripped with cruelty, "Hmm…. I wouldn't bother sleeping now, boys. Tomorrow you'll either sleep forever or sleep for days!" Laughing, the man turned on his heel to walk off, followed by the pair of cackling blue and yellow scaled kobolds accompanying him.

After the footsteps faded away, Thotmir cleared his throat.

"That is Maldros the Dark. He runs this place and has been a champion for as long as anyone can guess."

"Yes. I know." The voice startled the two dwarves, who turned to see a very awake Sophie, her eyes staring down the long hall, following Maldros. Behind her eyes was the spirit of Zane, trembling no longer in fear but in anger.

CHAPTER 14

THE ARENA

Zorin walked out of the inn and onto the street, stroking his chin in anticipation. He hadn't seen his father since the fall of Port L' For, and just the realization made him feel anxious. The small breakfast of pasty gruel and salted eggs from the inn was trying to make its return in the back of his throat. It felt like a hot ember under his quickly beating heart, deep within his chest. His jaw was drawn tight from the quaking anger, much like his short bow.

Eralin and Dabria, who passed by making their way to where they found a place for them all in the growing crowd followed Zorin. Not too close to draw attention and not too far for the same reasons. He felt Benedict place a hand on his shoulder, giving him a quick look of reassurance. This was going to be a horrible reunion.

Eralin looked up at the sky trying to not let the lack of sun show it bothered him. He imagined it was mid-morning and took a moment to stare eastward, hoping to catch a glimpse of the life-giving sun as it passed beyond the clouds.

A murmur rolled down the crowd, helping to announce the procession well ahead of the parade. Soon, a plume of fire erupted from five multicolored dancers leading a column of dark armored soldiers marching down the center of the street. The dancers breathed plumes of fire as they juggled both fire and blades, weaving their way to clear a path.

Zorin noticed they were dressed in colored scales mimicking five different colored dragons. As the dancers passed, the marching military soon followed, some shambling and undisciplined as opposed to the more senior troops who drove the crowd back from sheer terror; orcs and men mainly. Immediately following the soldiers bobbed two figures sitting on a dark platform.

"Oh my god." Benedict gasped in horror under his breath.

Dabria shook her head, "Not in this city."

Men clad in dirty rags groaned as they carried the black and gold platform on lacquered poles across their shoulders, six to a side. Weeping wounds from fresh lash marks graced their backs and bruises marked their once proud cheeks. Two figures sat defiant on the platform. Lord Pallus sat in a dark wood chair at the front with his arms crossed, a cruel smirk crossing his face. To his left, a gaunt man leaned on a staff from his chair. He was icy, cold and unmoving.

"That's Dekkion." Dabria spoke to her group carefully.

Zorin recognized the dark cleric. He was the same man who struck down Zane when they were children in OallEnAkhan, and who stood with Lord Pallus and Squib during the destruction of Port L' For. The destruction of both places he had ever called home.

"Hail Lord Pal-lus! Hail Lord Pal-lus! Move and bow before his excellency you worms! Hail Lord Pal-lus!" Rasped the lead orc, and the crowd repeated back in awe and fear.

"Where are they going?" Zorin asked as he continued to look across the parade, keeping his head low and allowing the hood of his cape to fall over his eyes.

"The Arena." Zorin noticed a tinge of contempt rolling off her tongue. She looked into his eyes calmly. "Wait here."

Not fully understanding why, but feeling it to be right, Dabria hung her head and quietly worked powerful magic, gripping the goat's horn at her neck. She didn't know whether he was mocking her or not, her dark god answered her.

Dabria felt her energy surge with a gasp as she drew from her life force and slowly passed her own essence to the poor men carrying the chariot. They felt the pain leave slowly, but were careful to not show the relief.

Dabria's veins grew black from the fingertips like a runaway infection. Her eyes became jaundiced and her cheeks sunken. The pain was unbearable, but she welcomed it. Time itself seemed to slow to a crawl.

She raised her eyes weakly to see a child. A child she remembered from a dream so long ago, her blonde matted tresses softly moving in the wind. Four massive shadows spun in concert behind and around her slowly, silhouetted by the light. The girl held a wooden bear in one hand and a single white and black feather. Her blue eyes, that once poured tears cutting paths through soot stained cheeks when they last met, were now clear. In fact, as she looked, she saw the girl stronger, beautiful and caring. She held her hands out and smiled.

You are on the right path. Keep going!

Dabria gently wheezed as she felt time and her vision returned to normal.

"I got you." Benedict's voice resonated in her ear gently as he braced her body from falling over or attracting any unwanted attention. She quietly sighed, allowing herself for once to lean on someone else.

Dabria prayed quietly to her dark god once more that no one would notice the Paladin hiding in dark armor holding the infamous mistress of pain.

RISING IN THE MORNING FROM their Inn at the far end of town, Lorvana and Isenatha watched the armies clear the camps for the parade. The view from the window of the second floor room they had rented was actually perfect for viewing the army, and the horrible Temple that was their destination.

"Una, what is this temple for?" Cordelia asked, playing with the thin cord around her wrist. She was trying to take her mind off of the thought of Sophie and Skotmir's disappearance. She didn't know why but she felt they were alive and that's what Cordelia told herself to hold onto. She had to.

"The Thorn, or The Prince of Righteous Vengeance." Una sighed, "At least it was until Lord Pallus turned it into another base of operations."

The group left the Inn without looking at the other guests in the main room. Cordelia and Isenatha had disguised them once again as Dragon Army soldiers but it was only a thinly veiled illusion.

Lorvana's stomach growled as she saw the plates of meat and some sort of pasty gruel. She sighed.

"Probably doesn't taste very nice anyways." she told herself as they walked out into the hot dusty street again.

"Stay close and don't raise any suspicion. Cordelia's spell can only do so much to disguise you." Una said quietly before pointing to the northeast, "There. See there. We must pass between those two observation towers."

After a few hours they felt the sun climbing in the morning sky behind the clouds. High above the parched landscape leading to the temple, an elven guard leaned over a giant war horn in the tower. Spotting something, his eyes narrowed before a cruel smile twisted from a corner of his mouth. He motioned for the other guard to see something.

"Hey. Check this out. Is that… ?" he said pointing at the group of figures below.

"Yeah… Mistress Una. Looks like the seer has some friends with her today too." the guard leaned back in his chair lazily, "Whatever."

The pointing guard chuckled. "Look at that one, looks like a kid."

"What? Oh… hahaha! Good for them. Make them work for their gruel, says I."

The guards laughed to themselves, thinking the tiny form of Lorvana was simply a servant child. They returned to scanning the horizon. Any other guards usually posted would be absent at this time given the parade and games later today, Una was certain of this.

Pallus was arrogant and she remembered how he would insist his secrets were those that could guard themselves. Una's lip curled at the thought.

"We will see." She chuckled as she opened the great brass door leading into the hall. The handle was an ancient sculpted dragon that flowed upward along its edge. Cordelia noticed the dragon wasn't bearing teeth and seemed peaceful, welcoming.

They entered the great hall of worship. A dark wooden throne now perched on the dais where once sat an ancient altar. A deep echo seemed to amplify their footsteps as they walked no matter how hard they tried to muffle them.

Cordelia pointed to the mural on the wall depicting a man holding a crown with a star and moon symbol emblazoned on it. To his right was a helmeted knight carrying a cruel battle ax, smoldering with red and black smoke. Behind them was a tall slender man with blue eyes holding a staff topped with a grinning skull.

"Who is that?" she asked. Una sighed, "I asked the same thing and Dekkion would just laugh. The old man even tried to tell me it was himself there in the picture." She chuckled darkly shaking her head under her hood. "Later in my years I learned this is only three of the gods, the others must have been lost where the wall is now broken."

She gently drew her hand across the broken stone wall that carried out across the wall to the left noting the numerous marks and impacts that appeared to have removed the others.

"I know it's back here." Una said to herself loud enough for Lorvana to hear.

Once behind the throne itself Una felt the wall behind the crimson velvet draped there. Her fingers remembered the secret door, which matched the wall so perfectly pressed against the left side firmly. The door swung open with a subtle grind of stone. Inside was a large hall. No visible doorway marked the 4 walls. As her eyes narrowed, Una pointed directly across from the doorway.

"That's a secret door leading outside into the mountains behind the temple. Somewhere in here is a way down into the dungeons." She peered at the wall and drew her hand across the stone surface. "I never came this way though. I only heard Dekkion speak of it, once." She shrugged.

"Una, I-" Isenatha's voice was quick and quiet, "I'll wait here to guard the escape if needed. From here you will need to delve deeper and I may prove to be more of a distraction. I'm not very sneaky." she shrugged.

Una considered her offer, "Interesting proposal." Something was bothering Isenatha and though Una was curious she also knew a guard wasn't a bad idea. "Yes. Yes, you should wait here. The three of us can move more swiftly then."

"Wait." Cordelia stepped back to the door they just passed through. Drawing her hand in the angular pattern of a star, a faint yellow glow blinked from around the frame and disappeared. "Ok,

I placed a spell on the door back out to the throne room. If someone approaches this door you and I will know, Isenatha."

"As if we had had the same mind, Cordelia," Isenatha smiled. "Brilliant." They nodded at each other in acknowledgement.

Lorvana pulled out the gem from Elloveve and peered through it at the secret door leading outside. Magic letters sprung to life.

"Yay!" She exclaimed. " That is so cool! Hey- wait a minute, look at that! Una I think I found it!" Holding the stone so Una could clearly see the glow of magic letters outlining yet a third secret door.

A THREE HUNDRED FOOT STONE wall faced the approaching crowd. Lines of people weaved the multiple switchbacks leading up to the top. As he stared upward it made Zorin's head reel.

"Woah- This must be the arena."

"Hmm."Dabria nodded, "Benedict and I can pass as Officers but you two will draw too much attention and possibly too much risk." She looked at Zorin.

He nodded in acknowledgement. "Eralin, let's find our own way in."

The tall Eralin nodded from beneath the dark hood framing his pale face and platinum hair. It took but a moment for them to disappear into the surrounding crowd, like waves on the sea.

"Show your support, drop your coins here!" A voice rumbled out like an earthquake from one of two ogres taking money from the crowd of people funneling in.

"Donations are encouraged!" Taking the queue from his partner, the other one leaned down to a short cowering man with curly hair and a green cloak, "Hey! Do it tiny!"

The ogres laughed at the joke. Joining the laughter was Dabria's familiar laugh.

"Ah... um-" the ogres looked at each other uneasily as they recognized her, "Ah- Go ahead mistress." The large ogres at the gates nodded to Dabria and knew better than to question the presence of the unrecognized officer at her side.

Dabria held an infamous reputation they were well aware of. A centurion of Dekkion, Master of the Undead is terrifying enough but her disturbing focus around manipulating the pain of others was feared, or at least respected by most of the Dark Army. According to local legend, she ripped the flesh from another officer and turned them into an undead servant, for no reason. It was done simply because she wanted to, hence her nickname of the "Mistress of Pain".

They made their way up the huge ancient stadium rows. The stadium was able to seat hundreds of thousands of people and towered in the air as the highest structure in the city, with nothing else coming close. A marvel to behold, it held row after row lined up all the way to the top. The highest sections were where the lower classes were forced to sit far away and so high that the unaided eye would likely see nothing. Those final rows were not even given a wall at their back to brace them from a tumble backwards to a gruesome death below. The rich were granted seating lower, and the army's guests and officers were allowed the best seating, alongside a booth in the center. This was a suspended platform, jutting out 25 feet from their row for Pallus himself.

The arena floor was made of sand, with the wall towering three stories around the perimeter, slightly angled outward and topped with long bladed spikes to prevent any unwanted climbing. Benedict's eyes grew wide at what potential combatants could be here today.

"This could-" he sighed nervously and turned to her, "Dabria, do they bring dragons into this arena?"

Before Dabria could answer, the crowd erupted with the sound of deep horns as Lord Pallus stepped forward on the balcony. Following closely was the frail necromancer, Dekkion to his right. His arms outstretched, he welcomed his bloodthirsty and beloved crowd to his games.

ZORIN AND ERALIN MADE THEIR way down the dark, damp alley between the barracks and the arena in a light and quiet jog. The smell of old wet refuse and decay faded as they drew closer to the operations of the arena. Looking closely at the stone wall, Zorin found a small opening in the cut stone they could squeeze through. He took a moment to carefully peer in.

"Ok this looks like some sort of... storage?" As they entered the room they saw several tall and strange shapes sticking out of crates and barrels. "What is- wait- is that a palm tree?"

Zorin pointed at the two dimensional wooden cutout as they heard muffled high pitched voices approaching.

"Oh jeez, Eralin hide!" Zorin whispered as they quickly tried to hide themselves.

Zorin ducked back in the shadows easily. Eralin's head darted back and forth frantically, trying to find something to hide behind. Zorin tried to guide from the shadows.

"Hey! That barrel! No, not in it you idiot! Get behind the crates around it. Yeah!" the voices were almost in the room, "Now don't move." Zorin's voice trailed off like a lost breeze and disappeared.

As the kobolds milled around the room gathering supplies for the arena, Zorin was able to move freely in the shadows, making his way to the mouth of the arena itself. Taking a moment to look around, he now saw that the room was filled with facades of scenes on wheels painted like trees, or stones.

Some small buildings with ropes to move windows from behind the slats were lined up, pointing out the huge door itself. As he drew closer Zorin could hear the deafening roar of the crowd above and he sighed as he slunk back into the shadows silently.

"This... is going to be a huge production."

"AN HEND AHSEE PALAN AWAUI o nin!"

An orb the size of a small orange appeared, floating in the air before Cordelia. It glowed dimly with a ghostly blue light, but not enough to draw too much attention.

"Wow! What's that?" Lorvana's eyes were as wide as her grin.

"A magic eye." Cordelia answered proudly, "I can see what it sees. For now it will scout ahead for us. Um, what did you find?"

"Oh, I found some glass bottles. Nothing in them but I got a few right here just in case."

Una nodded, "Mm-hmm. Wise. Let's continue on."

"Wait.. what is that? Oh wow!" she had a hand on her temple as she concentrated on the eye's vision in her mind, "I think it's safe, at least I hope so. Let's press on."

They walked swiftly to keep up with Cordelia's excited pace. The musty smell of the lower level echoed stale water despite the surface's dry, cracked earth. Entering the next room, it opened to a doubled and vaulted ceiling, featuring a faint mural depicting dragons and kobolds feasting together. Cordelia's magic eye hovered slightly at the end of the room. A hulking mound shivered in the dark recess of the room from under what appeared to be a red orange sheet of thin metal. As a slow breath entered its great lungs, a deep voice boomed forth.

"Whoever you are, come no closer."

"We... mean no harm or intrusion oh great one." Cordelia trembled as she spoke but her smile shined with hope.

"Great one?" the resonant voice chuckled in deep rolling waves, "You certainly have nice manners young one."

The form raised from the ground, a shimmer of light now dancing over what was suddenly shining copper scales. It stepped into the light, revealing a thirty foot long dragon. His scales gleamed like a copper penny, though age and wear may have dulled them slightly. A huge chain clattered across the stone floor from a single leg. The faint outline of a great doorway could be seen on the other side of his body. He lowered his powerful head down to the group, and though they were awestruck they noticed they didn't feel overcome with fear like with the other dragons. Lorvana stepped forward, smiling.

"Wow... you are so pretty!"

Again the dragon chuckled, "Well... so are you my little friend."

"Oh! Call me Lorvana. Please. What is your name?"

"Chalkos. It's not often I get many visitors as kind as you, Lorvana. It's quite refreshing."

"That's such a nice name!" Lorvana said as she clapped her hands together with excitement, "Sorry my friends are so quiet. We never met a nice dragon before."

Chalkos's eyes seemed to dull slightly with sadness for a moment at this.

"I'm sorry that has been your experience."

"May I..." Lorvana stepped forward with pleading eyes, "Um... if it's ok with you I mean."

Lorvana held up her tiny hand, palm outstretched in front of her kind and harmless eyes. Chalkos was stunned for a moment. He could not remember the last time he was greeted with such reverence. He drew his head closer and felt her hand on the side of his muzzle. He smiled warmly.

"Thank you." his voice trailed in a purring rumble, "That was nice."

Cordelia stepped forward with her hands held open, showing she was no threat. "Chalkos, we wish to pass. Would that be ok?"

"Yes, my new friends, I have been bound here to protect those held here from leaving." He saw their curious eyes and continued, "Beyond here are held the betrayers of the kobolds."

"Can we not free you?" Lorvana ran her hand across a massive metal link, "That chain looks so heavy and mean."

Chalkos looked at the heavy iron, five inches in width bent into two foot reinforced links. He turned his head to see the smallest member of the group. She could see years of pain, tempered with a strong resolution behind his eyes. Lorvana could tell that even not remembering fully the reason for his fate, he would stay here. He would die here. He would guard this with his life forever.

"No." His voice dripped with sadness, "No, little one, I must stay here. If nothing else, I know I cannot let them leave. They hurt my family, killed my friends and they took my memory." Chalkos closed his eyes as he tried to recall them to his mind.

He let out a deep sigh, "You may pass, but promise me you will not release them. They must continue to stay here for as long as I have breath in my body and life in my heart."

"Oh, I promise you Chalkos. As your new friend, I promise." Lorvana stood up straight with her hand over her heart proudly.

"Hmm!" Chalkos nodded happily, "Yes! Yes, I believe your promise is stronger than this iron chain my little friend. You all may pass."

The group made their way quietly down the hall past ancient sculptures and monoliths erected in the worship of what appeared to be dragons. Numerous different versions, with varied numbers of horns either curved to the front or flared behind their heads.

Some were singular lines from the snout or several others formed a crown or possibly a beard.

"I see every dragon here." Cordelia said as she looked at the murals, "The good dragons like Chalkos and the evil ones like Fury alike. Altogether."

Una nodded. "Isenatha. She said good and evil are taught."

"Hmm." Cordelia looked at Una. "Yes, she did, but I don't know if she really knew what was-"

Una snapped a hand between them sharply, "Hush!" her eyes darted as she scanned the air for something in the quiet. The sound of a hollow, stale air was all anyone else could hear, possibly the faint rumble of the volcano that they were near.

"Wait. Hear that?"

They began to hear a dark forgotten language. As they proceeded towards the source it grew louder and louder.

Ash kulkodar ob uluk kulkodar. Ash mabrotnosh azat burz gaddur. Mir kulkodar lump ishi ghash shakamub. Bumbullaum agh balt. Zau dot agh vuras shara. Broshan pallus! Broshan dekkion!

The faint dark words repeated over and over again, reverberating off the stone walls like the sound of dripping or the scurry of a rat's legs.

"Let's wait here." Cordelia motioned for them all to stop. She held her hand out to the orb floating by her side, "Go." The magical eye darted up the hall as she placed her hands to her temples and closed her eyes.

"I... I see two hidden, um. Cloaked... yes cloaked people around a slab of dark stone... They stare at a person on the altar, chanting. Wait there's someone else there."

The man chuckled darkly as he wrung his hands in front of his fire red beard and wicked smile.

"Well, Mortas and Stockuk, I can feel it working." he drew a hand over the body on the altar, "Yes, the prisoner is ready. The Dark Queen has opened his life force to us. Now. Take it!"

"A red haired man." Cordelia said.

"With a red beard?" Una offered quietly, "is he thin and wiry?"

"Yes."

"Fury."

"Wait- Lord Pallus's mount?!" Sophie looked shocked.

Una smiled at Sophie's words, "Ha! Don't let him hear you say that. He will never believe he is Pallus's servant. Though we all know he is."

Cordelia continued, "On the altar is a man. His beard is braided in a different way than I've ever seen... with bronze beads. The men have paused chanting and one is holding some twisted brass scepter up to a stone dragon's mouth. Wait, it's not a scepter, it's a tall vial or vase, dripping... liquid fire!"

They heard a scream erupt down the hall

"The man is in agony as blue white energy pours from his mouth and eyes, charging the large gemstones in the room with his own life." Cordelia's eyes opened as she looked at Una in horror.

"Una, they are pulling the spirit from these prisoners!"

THE HEAVY IRON GATES GROANED in ear piercing concert with each other as the four guards stood waiting for Sophie, Skotmir and Thotmir.

"Move!" one barked as the others chuckled, "Death awaits all of ya!"

"Yeah! Don't want to keep the crowd waiting." one grinned cruelly as another chuckled darkly, "Or Maldros!"

The guards all laughed and snorted as Skotmir, Thotmir and Sophie were ushered roughly out of their cells by the Guards, finding themselves walking up a long ramp with a dozen other men.

The men were covered in a network of bruises, especially around their battered shoulders. The smell of the prisoners' unwashed bodies assaulted their noses. As they walked they could hear a dull rhythmic rumble growing louder.

"Hey!" Thotmir exclaimed as one of the taller guards drove an elbow into the side of his head, driving him into Skotmir.

"Woah!" Skotmir wrapped an arm around him to keep Thotmir from toppling over, "I got you brother."

As they were shoved up the hall, a shudder ran through the brothers at the sound of a bloodthirsty crowd. The music grew louder and louder. Rumbling sounds that were once dull became clearer as they approached the gated mouth of the ramp. Realizing it was announcing their procession for the arena, Thotmir turned to Skotmir and Sophie.

"The forge watches over us today, my friends. Fight well."

Entering the red glow of the day, they saw hundreds of thousands of spectators roar at their arrival. The stone brick and sandstone towered in every direction from the high wall, as far as the eye could see. Pillars and stands alternated in a dizzying pattern swirling hundreds of feet into the air.

"Move!"

Sophie felt the kick in her back knock her forward. She was shocked by the scene around her. The sound of the bloodthirsty crowd numbed her senses and chilled her blood. She knew these people wanted to watch them die, and the more horrible the better. She closed her eyes and willed her ears to muffle as she looked inward for the only sanctuary she knew.

Hey.

The sound of Zane's voice called in her mind.

Your heart hurts.

"They are all so horrible." her voice was trembling as she spoke to herself, "All of them."

Listen to me. Don't focus on those outside the ring. Just- just survive. Do what you do best Sophie. Fight.

Pallus and Dekkion stepped forward on the tall balcony reserved for them. Dekkion nodded at the crowd briefly before his voice magically boomed into the arena and hushed the crowd.

"Who are these wretches brought before his magnificence, Lord Pallus?!" the voice reverberated over the crowd and filled every ear as he spoke, "I shall tell you! They are those that shall face your judgment in the ring of fire and blood!"

The crowd exploded in well rehearsed cheers, ready to watch the next spectacle of entertainment.

"Die well! For your lives are now not your own." he snarled as his voice faded once again into the deafening cheers of the crowd.

Looking around, Skotmir saw the newest captives, some terrified, some resolute in knowing they were at death's door. He spat on the ground in disgust, his proud dwarven blood boiling. These were innocent people committed to a dark unfair fate.

"Maldros! We commit them to you, King of Gladiators!"

From the opening came Maldros the Dark, cloak flapping behind his hulking form, red eyes glowing. Sophie froze as a wave of memory hit her.

She found herself in an arena not unlike this one, holding twin daggers in her hands, feeling acrobatic, confident and a bit cynical. Across the arena was Maldros, clutching a wound at his side and kneeling. A wound delivered by the crude orcish daggers in her hands. Or were they her hands? Was this even her memory? She turned her head in the arena to see Zane standing next to her, with the same daggers in his hands. Blood cutting through dirt and dust on his cheek, and sensing her gaze he turned and smiled.

"I never finished that story on our way to First Port did I?" Zane laughed as he looked down at the daggers. "You know, I like being able to share them now. Share my memories with you."

Zane stepped towards her and cupped her cheek in his hands. She felt its warmth as if he actually was there. Her eyes closed but her smile grew as Sophie found peace for a moment with him. Zane drew her face gently to look into his smile one more time.

"Hey, I got this." He laughed. "For once at least, trust me. I'm with you, Sophie- always."

The vision faded and Sophie opened her eyes to see Skotmir's puzzled face.

"You alright?" He said to her softly, his chipped teeth sitting behind his dirty matted beard.

"I.. I know him." Sophie sighed, "Well not me, but Zane does."

"That's still you from what you told me sister." Skotmir grinned as he slapped his hand on her back, "But hey! Good to know he's gonna help us too!"

High in the stands, Dabria and Benedict sat watching Dekkion and Pallus intensely. How they nodded to each other cooly while pointing at the crowd in larger than life gestures. The horns sounded and as the prisoners stepped forward, Dabria sighed.

"It's them." She said softly, "The first sacrifice to the blood pits."

Benedict's eyes grew wide as he saw the men from the death march set to fight each other. When the deep war horn blasted in the arena, one bald man immediately cut the throat of another next to him, a gentle man who only yesterday had saved another soldier's life on the battlefield. Panic entered the eyes of a young man with tousled hair who ran in terror from them all. Another dropped to his knees, dropping the weapon on the ground, arms outstretched refusing to fight as an anguished cry erupted from his cracked chapped lips. Weeping, another man drove an ax into his back, ending his nightmare.

"This is horrible, these were our men." Benedict whispered in horror.

"Yes, they were, but not today." she said quietly as she stared forward.

"But, this is madness!" his hands were clenched as he held back the well of anger in his throat as protested in a hoarse whisper.

Dabria turned to Benedict, "Benedict, our goal was to find out what he plans to do next. Don't you see? Look!"

"See what- wait. Oh no!" A wave of realization poured over his soul like the quench of a fresh blade. These prisoners were his soldiers, and they were found as usurpers to the Dark Army. They had found what they came for: Lord Pallus was going to strike Garnet Keep.

"We need to get out of here and get back to warn-" His voice was cut short by the sound of the warhorn. Glancing back to the battlefield he saw them all motionless on the ground, including the bald man holding his own blade deep in the pit of his stomach as a final action.

"Behold the slain before you all! They die for all your enjoyment." the unseen voice boomed across the crowd. It was a different announcer than Dekkion, a strong commanding voice.

"Who is that?" Benedict whispered. Dabria chuckled.

"That is the commodore. I'd recognize his voice anywhere. He runs a fleet of pirates out of Enruk out to Dragon Claw Island. Word is they work for a few of the trade barons but no one knows which." She shrugged. "We worked with them several times while

I was in the army. Transport and such. They knew how to get our groups in and out in a hurry."

Benedict nodded. Looking over the crowd he thought he could see a black hat with a red plume of feathers bob just on the other side of Dekkion as the voice continued to boom out.

"Next we bring you two brothers, dwarven sons of the Garnet Mountains!"

Benedict's eyes widened as two dwarves walked into the dust together. "Skotmir!" he said between clenched teeth.

Dabria shook her head, "I have a feeling your mind has changed about leaving, then?"

"Not without him. I swear it."

"Good." She smirked, "We finally agree on something. Let's see if we can get where they leave the arena. I have an idea. Once the match starts we will-"

A deafening roar filled the stands, startling the two. Dabria's gasp was lost in the roar of the crowd as the next challenger entered the arena. A massive blue dragon. His scales were battered with wings torn and bent to odd angles in places, but more notably his face was destroyed and only had one eye. Dabria's heart dropped as her eyes widened.

"Witness the mighty Azure! A lifetime of battle served, he wishes to continue to kill for your enjoyment!"

Azure's gurgled growl murmured slowly as the crowd's voice lowered to a dull silence. He chuckled as he raised his head to speak, his lips curling back from sword-like teeth.

"This is my honor and fate to die for you in this glorious arena! And I will do so happily! BUT!" He shouted letting the last word of defiance roll across the crowd. Azure dropped his head low to stare at the two dwarves with one massive black-rimmed yellow orange eye. This was his time to be honored. Azure knew he would never fly again and he would have a glorious death this day. Lightning crackled between the teeth of his drooling maw.

"Not today." he chuckled at the weaker beings before him, "And not to you worms!" Azure shrieked as the dwarves ran forward with axes held high, roaring their own battle cry.

CHAPTER 15

BLOOD AND DRAGONS

Steel slammed into scales as the two dwarves attacked ferociously, shaking off fear and replacing it with deep dwarven rage, hacking into the dragon with their axes. Thotmir was lifted off the ground by the gaping maw, teeth biting into his chest and sending shock waves of electricity though his body as he was flung to skid across the dusty ground.

Rising back to his feet he charged again, his roaring battlecry not any less powerful. Thotmir's feet quickened underneath him as he closed the distance, the thick plates bouncing on his shoulder like the snares of a marching army. He grinned behind his ash blonde beard as his ax rose in his hands to strike the heaving belly of the dragon. The ax found its mark, lifting a set of large scales the size of small plates up, allowing the blade to slip in. Dark red blood poured across his arms as he continued running, this time away from the beast.

Azure roared as he swung his head to face the dwarf. "Time to suffer!"

Skotmir ran to the rear leg to strike like felling a tree but it was too late. Azure's mouth erupted in a crackling network of light that hit Thotmir full in the steel breastplate.

"No!" Skotmir cried as with a scream Thotmir's arms threw themselves outward. Sparks radiated across blue armor as Thotmir fell to the ground unconscious.

STEP BY STEP BENEDICT AND Dabria made their way down the ramps. The echoes of battle resonated with their armor as other voices filled the halls. Vendors purchasing provisions like lizards barbecued on sticks or large insects. Ale and mead were poured from huge barrels taller than the kobolds tending them and the soft jingle of coins rattling filled their greedy ears.

"Come this way. I bought us some time." Dabria said as she chuckled softly.

"Sure... wh... what did you do?" Benedict asked as they walked through the crowd.

Dabria smiled deviously. "I sent an old friend a message. Well, just a suggestion really."

She chuckled again as they made their way around a small wicker booth carrying balls of rice covered in some dark, sweet smelling sauce.

"A small message to Dekkion suggesting the match was boring. As we were leaving I saw him complain to Pallus who apparently agreed. I saw him tossing his goblet."

"Good thinking!" Benedict laughed, "that should draw out the match a bit while we get down there."

As Benedict and Dabria quickened their pace down the hallway, high above Pallus nodded to the announcer with a smile.

"Bring out the human warrior!" the Commodore shouted as the crowd roared.

Far from Dabria and Benedict's sight on the arena floor Sophie didn't hesitate to assist her chosen brother Skotmir. Running towards the dragon, she jumped to grip a low shoulder and swung her body upward landing on his jagged spine. Producing Zane's two daggers she plunged them into the dragon's back.

Howling in pain the dragon swatted the annoyance with his tail, sending Sophie tumbling to the ground. Pallus stood up, furious, tossing his arms around like a stage director as he shouted at the Commodore under the roar of the crowd.

"Wait! Fighters! Belay yourselves! Stop!" The Commodore shouted, the red and black coat of his arm flailed wildly as he called for their attention.

The match slowed to an awkward pause, led by Azure's respect for the command. He and Sophie stepped back out of range of each other for a moment. They heard the crowd grow silent save confused murmurs of anticipation as the stirred dust settled beneath the jagged spikes lining the walls. All except Skotmir. Seeing his brother's crumpled and unmoving form on the ground, he remained stuck in his fury and continued to charge the dragon. Before Sophie could grab him, Azure swatted a paw down, pinning his body to the ground.

"Time to wait, you impatient insect!" Azure purred as his maw dripped over the struggling dwarf.

"Skotmir! Save your energy!" Sophie called as she too looked at Thotmir's form on the ground, her heart pounding in anticipation.

Just beyond the wall from Sophie, the quick footsteps of Benedict and Dabria approached an isolated gate with a single guard. Dabria nodded and the young officer stepped to the side with a quick bow, his head low.

"The dark lord is coming. Stay out of his way and ask no questions or it will be your skin!" She hissed.

"Y-Yes milady!" The young man held the gate open for them as they passed.

"Close the gate." she commanded coldly, "Don't want them thinking you are letting out the pets, correct?" The man nodded and latched the gate behind them.

"This is where they hold the gladiators." She whispered under her breath as they entered a long entrance room with an iron gate on one side and a descending ramp on the other. Beyond the gate they could see the dusty arena floor.

The pair slipped into the shadows, to the right of the same gate the gladiators had entered from and ducking behind a few crates. Dabria held up a hand of silence to Benedict as she saw Lord Pallus, flanked by four guards and a very excited Dekkion, enter the light of the same room. Waiting for the gate to open, they stood mere feet away from their would be assassins in the shadows.

Dekkion's hoarse and frail voice cackled, "Yes my lord. This will prove to be most exciting!" Lord Pallus's deep booming voice joined Dekkion's in cruel laughter as the gate's chain clanked and groaned against a rusty iron pulley.

From the other side of the arena, Zorin saw the gate clank open and his father's entourage step out to the arena floor.

"What are you doing, old man? Wait…"

Pallus motioned a hand in Zorin's direction.

"He calls for props folks!" The Commodore's voice rang out, "Their deaths shall be framed in a glorious and bloodsoaked setting designed by our great leader!"

Suddenly, facades of palm trees shot out onto the arena floor from the prop entrance, Zorin dove into the shadows to remain unseen as a few dozen mercenaries and servants moved in to move everything into place at the call of their dark lord. Finally, building facades came out and much to Zorin's horror six kobolds began dragging the crates hiding Eralin.

They grunted and groaned as the wheels began to turn slowly out the iron gate. Zorin looked past the staves of a broken barrel to see a single wide purple eye darting nervously.

"Oh no... stay down you idiot!" Zorin could feel his heart pounding in the pit of his stomach frantically trying to think what he could possibly do next.

BENEATH THE ANCIENT TEMPLE, UNA approached one of the glowing torches in the hallway.

"You better answer me."

In response to her words, it quietly spat a green flame in the shape of a rose that morphed into a skull and finally green fiery embers before flaring into the shape of a faint face.

"Why haven't you freed me?" The voice in her head shrieked out in layered unearthly voices. *"You must grow stronger and find me in Strath!"*

Una sighed heavily as her eyes clenched shut, "I will- my master- but first I need to know how to rescue these prisoners and get them out of here."

"Maybe there's more power in them than you know. Just like you refuse to recognize the power within yourself."

Una shook her head, "I don't understand."

"Una, Chalkos is being lied to. These aren't the betrayers in his tragedy, but I assure you they were in the play!" The voice became softer, clearer and almost motherly, *"Maybe, my little Una, they actually need to rescue you."*

The torch flared and sputtered, returning to a normal orange glow. She turned back to the group.

"Well?" Cordelia asked Una.

"They are the friends... of Chalkos."

Cordelia gasped, "They could be… " Her excitement was barely contained as she wished and hoped in her heart her feelings were true, but also worried at what that could mean. "We need to tell Chalkos but…"

"I'll do it. He." Lorvana stood with one hand in the air. "He's my friend."

Cordelia knelt next to her friend, "Lorvana, you are so brave but if something were to happen you are so small could you-"

Lorvana shook her head smiling, "Cordelia, actually I think there's someone even smaller than me to help us. Watch!"

Lorvana whispered a song under her breath. Faintly they could hear a scurrying across the floor as a dusty gray mouse ran to her, its nose twitching as it looked up at her questioningly. Lorvana bent down to whisper to the mouse, smiling gently.

"Hiya! Can you run that way and tell Chalkos, uh- so he's a big ol' copper dragon but he's not scary! Tell him we see a terrible thing about these prisoners. All of them are being destroyed but they are actually friends of the kobolds and we think they could be his friends. Tell him we need his help, and hurry!"

As the mouse ran off Lorvana stood up proudly and dusted off the knees of her baggy green pants. She smiled and nodded to a smiling Cordelia.

"Ok! Let's go make some more friends!"

Continuing down the hall they snuck past the altar room. Moments later, they carefully approached a large room with several cells. Framed in rusty bars caked with centuries of neglect. Inside the cells were the forms of three people.

"Who are you?" a man with twin braids that fell from the corners of his mouth spoke softly. The other two were silent, one a bald man with a goatee tied off with a single bronze bead and the other was a woman with long warrior braids.

Cordelia ignored him as she spoke hushed but urgently, "Una, spring the lever at the far end of the wall. That should let them out. I'm still watching the chamber with the dark altar. "

Cordelia was struggling to keep her overwhelming feelings at bay. She was overcome with hope but knew she first had to get them out of there. The gates swung open as Una reached out a hand to help the man stand.

"Let's go."

They were human and elf, if they were to guess but something was different. Eyes were brighter. Powerful muscles rippled under robes. Despite their weakened state they held an unquestionable power behind their eyes.

"Liars! Thieves! Deceivers! Betrayers!" The sound of Chalko's anger echoed deeply, shaking the temple's foundation. They could feel the stone grinding as he ripped the chain from the wall down the hall. Cordelia saw the three figures exchange a glance before darting out the door in the altar room to investigate, leaving the weakened man alone.

"We are trapped!" Cordelia cried as she dispelled the orb.

"No." Una said, "We can try to flee deeper into the volcano this way. Follow me!"

Cordelia nodded, "Take them, I will catch up but I'm going back for the last one."

Lorvana clapped excitedly "I'll help you!"

Una and the prisoners ran one way down the wide hall while Cordelia and Lorvana ran back to the altar room. Soon after, a roar erupted down the hall and was quickly getting louder. Lorvana helped push the man up from the stone altar and into Cordelia's arms.

"Go! Take him back! I-" Lorvana took a deep breath, steeling herself for what she knew in her heart she must do, "I need to save Chalkos."

A raspy voice came from the old man, "Chalkos? He... still lives?"

"Yes- Please Cordelia!"

"But you-"

"Just go!" she shouted at the much taller people with her. Cordelia nodded as she scooped an arm around the weakened man and then began to stumble down the hall.

Lorvana ran as fast as her little legs could carry her, back towards the roaring Chalkos, wondering if she made the right decision but knowing in her heart she did. Turning the corner, she saw Chalkos hunched but still able to run towards her in the wide hall, his form barely clearing the opening. He roared when he saw her.

"Run! Run little one, and climb on!"

Bending a wing low, Lorvana nimbly bounded up to sit astride his neck as they barreled down the hall. Looking behind her, the glow of fire erupted as she realized there was another dragon close behind.

PALLUS PACED IN THE DUST, admiring the scene before him. Four fabricated palm trees stood in the center along with the facade of an ancient temple. He was particularly nodding at the cutouts of some terrified villagers. They were caricatures of people, exaggerated on purpose to look cartoonish and comical.

"This is fine work! Isn't it?" Pallus looked at Dekkion with dark eyes below the twisted crown.

"Yes, my lord!" Dekkion wheezed, smiling, "It's perfect. The Cheerless Swamp no doubt?"

"Yes. Back in my younger days, before you and before we learned of the Dark Queen." Pallus laughed, "When I was so ignorant."

Eralin felt Lord Pallus draw closer, but as he did something familiar pulled at his neck. Suddenly it felt like he was being pulled slowly towards him, like a magnet. Peeking from behind the barrel, he saw Pallus mindlessly caressing the dragon turtle pommel of the sword at his hip.

"Wha...? What is this?" Eralin thought as he looked at his necklace. The blue eyes began to radiate, mimicking the ebbing and flowing tide of a rolling sea. Looking out he saw the red eyes of the sword answer, softly glowing in the same perfect rhythm.

He felt a sharp pull in his mind as a wave of memory washed over him. He saw himself restrained on a stone altar, his being poured from a screaming mouth as the small red stones filled with all he was, all he remembered. He saw three cloaked men draining him into the ruby.

All went black for what felt like years compressed into moments. Lasting until he heard his voice, Zorin's voice when he had found him, or at least part of him, in the underworld. Imprisoned in a ruby cage.

Suddenly one word sat at the front of his mind. A forgotten name, his forgotten name lost until now.

"Watch out, my lord!" Dekkion was surprisingly quick as he stepped in front of Lord Pallus and called curling black smoke to form a wicked mace in his hand.

Lord Pallus laughed and curled an eyebrow as Eralin stood up from the crates. Pallus's laugh began cruelly as he regarded the new combatant, before his eyes grew wide in recognition. His eyes fell to the necklace in horror.

"You!" he shouted, "Stay back!"

Dekkion's icy eyes grew wide in his dark and hollow sockets. "What? No... NO!"

A great pull generated from his sword to Eralin's necklace itself. There was a flash of light, and Eralin's necklace was gone as were the eyes on Pallus's Sword. Dekkion was enraged as he scrambled away howling.

"No! Not you!" Dekkion's hands shook as he screeched, "Impossible, we watched you die on that altar!"

Eralin stepped forward smiling, as he felt whole again. Looking up, he smiled at the sound of his own name passing his lips once again.

"Rood-o-nen."

Instantly, Eralin felt a familiar change as his body grew, expanding outward. The skin on his back hardened and his hands became scaled flippers. The front rows of the crowd shrank back in terror, for before them was a hulking twenty foot high dragon turtle.

"Yes! Come at me, my cousin! This is a glorious day!" Azure's voice roared as he charged at Eralin, driving him into the wall of the arena. The rows of benches just below jumped up in fear but the great stones withstood the impact. Sophie bolted to Thotmir. Both of them ran as fast as they could to the sidelines far away from the pair of massive creatures, staring helplessly at Skotmir trapped on the other side of the creatures. They watched Dekkion and Pallus split towards the other side back behind the iron gate leading to the storage area.

Eralin faced the dragon as his throat erupted a cone of superheated steam in a shrieking deep roar. It hit Azure with its full impact, peeling the flesh from one side of Azure's face and revealing the skull beneath. This was the battle he longed for, this would be the hero's death he craved so badly. He tried to summon his breath, but coughing found that he had to resort to claws and bites. The blows glanced off the hard spiked Dragon Turtle's shell, protecting most of its body.

"Die!" The blue dragon roared as he climbed up on the back of the Dragon Turtle, slamming his exposed head into the sand beneath his claws. Eralin bucked upward and threw Azure to the ground, sliding into the high retaining wall surrounding the arena. Long spikes drove like skewers into his wings.

"Let us end this!" He roared as, in one massive heave, he tore them free, ripping the fragile webbing that once caught the air with so much grace.

As Azure charged towards him Eralin breathed in again. Exhaling sharply he blasted him a final time and Azure crumpled to the ground. The great wyrm was slain.

The Dragon Turtle collapsed as well, heaving as his body shrank rapidly. "Ugh- Can't breathe-" Eralin heaved, "Skotmir!" Returning to his humanoid form after finding himself out of breath, Eralin rushed to Skotmir's side only to be greeted by several dozen guards.

"Hard to take your form out of water isn't it? What was your name again?" Dekkion wheezed as he grinned wickedly wringing his hands. "Ah yes. Eralin. How you came to escape the realm of the dead is curious. Very curious-" he paused as his old eyes glanced at the tall sea elf before him. "Well no matter. I caught you again didn't I, little fish? Take them away."

Skotmir carried the limp form of his brother over his shoulder as they were all escorted back into the gate leading down the ramp to their cells. Dabria and Benedict tried to position themselves to intercept them. Ten guards surrounded them and there was no way they could see to offer any subtle action. They looked at each other helplessly.

Benedict's voice was barely heard in the shadows after his friends walked by, but not over the roar of the crowd outside.

"Knightlord, please give them strength." Benedict's hushed voice shook a little in the darkness behind the gate.

"Mistress Dabria, please follow me." The voice croaked in a familiar high pitch from the deeper shadows behind them. Dabria spun around her hand on the whip at her side defensively.

"What? Wait." her eyes grew as she smiled in recognition, "Sharptooth?"

The red-orange reptilian snout illuminated as she stepped carefully into the light but the rest of her scales were hidden under a black muslin hooded cloak, "Yes. Please, my friend, follow me." She pulled on their hands and tried to drag them with her into the darkness, "We need to go now."

Benedict resisted, "But Zorin and-"

"No time!" Sharptooth protested as she began to plead with them, her eyes filled with worry, "Come and live to fight another day. It's the only way. They will soon know you are here."

Dabria sighed heavily, "It's true. Dekkion will be able to sense me, I'm sure of it- and if Azure is here that means Cobalt has possibly exposed our lie now. It's only a matter of time before Una and I are hunted."

Sharptooth nodded at them before she gave a gentle tug on their limp arms again, "This way."

As they disappeared deeper into a tunnel hidden in the shadows, Benedict turned back.

"I'm sorry. May the Maiden guide you, my friends." and with the sound of soft feet on gravel fading into the inky darkness, he was gone.

"RUN!"

Cordelia's yelling voice echoed as she ran frantically, trying to remember a spell as they burst into a glowing cavern.

Magma fell around the chamber three hundred feet away on all sides as they ran along the thin rock bridge spanning the heart of the volcano.

"Ugh!" The alarm spell went off in her head as Isenatha's voice called out to her.

Run my friends, they are coming! Go! I will meet you back at the keep!

Suddenly several kobolds of different colors in black cloaks swooped in out of nowhere on long ropes to land on the bridge.

"Come with us!" one with green scales under a black cloak shrieked.

"Who are-" Una questioned as she helped the man with the braided mustache jog.

"No time!" another mustard yellow one with fiery red eyes called back as he grabbed Cordelia's hand, "Look!"

The bridge rumbled and shook as Chalkos landed in a heavy run behind them.

"They are behind us! Go!" He called in his deep raspy voice. The bridge shook as the copper dragon slammed one foot in front of the other on all fours. They were half way across when the giant form of the red dragon Fury burst onto the bridge. He roared in anger as he took flight to hover in the massive chamber, allowing the smaller guards to pass beneath him in pursuit.

"Stop them, you fools!" he let out another furious roar, "Chalkos!"

"Hold on, little one!" Chalkos called back to Lorvana who was gripping tightly to his back and burying her head in her arms as well.

Sensing Fury draw breath into his mighty lungs, Chalkos threw one broad fanlike wing up as a shield over himself, Lorvana and effectively the rest of the group, who had now reached the far exit.

With a roar, the blast of dragon fire slammed into his wing, driving him closer to the exit. They were only mere steps away but the guards of the Dark Army were closing in fast.

"Look up there!" Lorvana called out to Chalkos. Without dropping his wing he looked up, and saw how fragile the rocks above are. Keeping the wing up to the blast he dashed to the exit.

"Goodbye, Fury!" He laughed before Chalkos suddenly angled his wing to reflect breath into the loose rocks above as he blew acid across the bridge. They dove into the exit as everything crashed down, sealing them in the hall.

"Nice work!" Cordelia panted as her chest heaved with a smile towards the dragon.

"Thank you!" Chalkos bowed, "I like to think of-"

"Please come!" the yellow kobold interrupted. "Your friends await you ahead, there is no time!"

They continued running down the hall for what seemed like several minutes before coming to a large cavern with hundreds of kobolds milling about.

"A village?" Cordelia asked Una. Una shook her head. "I never knew of this place."

They were approached by several other kobolds but two more familiar faces stepped forward.

"Cordelia!" Benedict called out with a smile.

"Benedict!" Cordelia called back to her cousin as she wrapped him in a warm embrace.

"Ah!" Una smiled at Dabria as she walked to her nodding, "Hello dark sister." She looked at the familiar kobold next to her. "And Sharptooth, correct?"

"Yes Una." Sharptooth bowed before gesturing to the village with one red-orange talon. "We are the Shadowclaws. We wish to return Enruk to what it was before the dark army came. Before the arena and the greed we are slaves to. Come now, you must flee."

Following Sharptooth through the village, they eventually slid a large rock that blended with the cave entrance behind them. Benedict noted they effectively were hiding from any pursuers that could come their way. Sharptooth took them to one of many exits on the opposite side of the cavern networked there. Each had rocks poised to keep this place a secret for however long was needed- or even forever, they imagined.

Sharptooth nodded to Dabria, "Here. This will take you through the mountains to the east. Into Chikara. Take the ones you rescued home from there."

Sharptooth bowed at the four prisoners. They looked at each other uneasily and smiled weakly before the old man as well offered a bow. The man with the braided mustache followed as did the bald man and the woman with the long braids.

Shaptooth nodded happily before she sighed looking back at Dabria, "Please take these healing salves and food for the journey. And-"

She looked at Dabria and smiled. "My friendship and prayers... forever."

HOURS LATER AND DEEP UNDER the arena, the sound of evening silence filled the halls, barracks and prisons. The end of the day, and only the occasional footsteps of a guard were heard in sparse but regular sequence. Now hidden amongst the rats there was another shadow lurking the halls, free outside the cages. He was free still but now alone. In his mind he sighed as he slunk along the walls just outside of the orange torch light.

"Well, here we are again Zorin." He smirked at himself and thought of Elloveve when he felt lost as a child. When he would look at her and ask, "Where are we going to go now?"

CHAPTER 16

LOST SECRETS

Zorin was alone.

Wandering the dark, old smelling halls under the arena was lonely but in the inky darkness he felt a familiar home. He heard voices periodically, causing him to instinctively duck into recesses in the cracked stone, brick walls or behind the occasional supply crate lining the halls, shrouded in the shadows.

"Can't get to them now." Zorin sighed.

He had seen where Sophie, Skotmir and the other dwarf had been roughly caged.

"At least not tonight. Let's see what we can find about what dear old dad is planning shall we?" He chuckled inside as he thought of how ridiculous that sounded to make his cold murder of a father seem human, "Why yes Zorin! What a smart man you are! Yes yes I know. Stick with me, and you'll- whatever."

He sighed as he stopped to get his bearings. He had things to do and he couldn't let his feelings get in the way. This was too important.

"Ok- if the crew is being held down those stairs, that should be the dungeon. Which means up those stairs would be the barracks.

So then down that hall would be likely any kind of office- if I were to guess."

Zorin made his way down the hall, dimly lit by a single oil-burning lantern. He looked at the well on the lantern briefly and saw it was three quarters full. A ring of sediment on the bottom was mirrored by one barely a finger above it. This was a common line for it to sit as he noted.

"They won't be back this way to fill it tonight. Looks like it's snuffed out in the morning at the same time every day. Good."

He turned the corner and found several darkly stained oak doors, closed, each with matching wooden signs burned with a single name. The hall appeared smooth and a dusty crimson and charcoal rug ran the length of the floor. He smiled slightly, thinking Zane would have been proud. He remembered them sneaking into the village store-house in OallEnAkhan. Zane had pointed out the most important items were always kept somewhere next to the office, and the office wasn't too far from the rest of the finished goods.

"Some people love being near their work. And since the most important things are usually- right next to each other," Zane chuckled in his mind's eye, "Don't look too far away to start with."

Zorin smiled at the fond memory before the weight of seeing Sophie on the arena floor today with Skotmir lowered his mood in the darkness.

"I'll get you out buddy- I promise. Ok this is," He looked at the name plaques on the two adjacent doors, "Stocuk- and you are Mortas. Hmm... really?"

He stared at the third name for a moment, part of him knowing he shouldn't be surprised. Soon, curiosity getting the better of him, he gently set the latch with his thumb and slipped into the door.

"Ok, Lets see what you have here, Dabria. Anything that you might have forgotten to tell us?" Part of him questioned if it was truly their companion as he began to investigate. The room was very clean and tidy. Various implements of torture lay organized in an open box. He shuddered slightly.

"Ugh- what are you?" He thought as he looked at the various picks, blades and pliers lined up neatly on a leather mat. "This is awful but- but I saw you yesterday."

He remembered her face at the edge of the parade. More importantly Benedict saw something in her, a goodness. He chuckled, "Well Dabria, you and Benedict are off somewhere probably having a meal, and hopefully not trapped sneaking around with half the Dark Army above your head." He sighed as he scanned another table, "Oh. Hello. What's this?"

His hand found a leather Journal. Opening it, his hand landed on an entry from 2 years ago. This was her handwriting, he was sure of it. Calculated, precise sweeps of red sangria colored cursive ink danced across the yellowed parchment of the page.

> *23rd day of Harvest fifteen twenty.*
>
> *My partner is leading our dead legions to the Emerald Atoll, a little island with nothing of importance as far as I can see but Pallus and Dekkion are convinced it is of future strategic importance. It's only a primitive human settlement of fishermen, led by a single shaman. One that holds some heathen spiritual significance.*
>
> *An old magic I assume, but I don't care. Nothing that can stand before us. We must strike following the closure of the trade routes for the winter to not raise any suspicion from the neighboring elves or the merchants of Port L'For. I have requested I accompany*

her as well and it has been granted. I must admit I look forward to our journey alone together.

For once there is something I crave more than the battle that sets me free.

Soon we will be away from it all. Away from him. I despise the way Dekkion looks at her.

I will ensure Kartilaan watches her back.

Zorin froze.

"What... Kartilaan? Sophie's sister?"

A flood of memory as he remembered the last time Sophie spoke of her.

"My sister traveled a lot as a sellsword... It would be weeks if not months before we would see each other again. She mainly protected caravans crossing the desert back in Kur. She just never came back. If she did... well there's nothing left of home anymore for her to come back to, is there?"

"I-" He was stunned as he stroked the back spine of the book gently, "I have no idea how I'm going to tell her this. Well Dabria may want this back."

He closed the journal and tucked it in his knapsack. Seeing nothing else in the room but dark memories, he nodded in respect one last time at where Dabria had come from before leaving the room, returning to the dim hall of doors.

"Hmm. What's this?"

Further down the hall he spied a room slightly ajar but that appeared to be unoccupied. There was no sign on the outside, possibly a shared room of some sort.

"Ugh... looks like his office back home."

Peering in he could see the foul and obscene marking of the dark army draped on the wall with an 8 foot map laid out on a large conference table. Thirteen chairs were tucked around the giant rectangle, an echo of the unseen attendees in this War Room.

Zorin leaned over the thick parchment on the heavy table. He began noting where large Obsidian beads were placed, they appeared to hold some interest and not just left there haphazardly.

"Let's see here. Enruk, Kur and Port L'For. Then there's southern Bloodwood, Wargrave. Really? I knew the Mines of the Bloodwood dwarves... but the arena there as well actually- that's making complete sense looking at this place. Hmm, he never did get Viridian according to this, just the Emerald Atoll. Ok, let's look over the pond here in the new country. Yes of course here in Enruk but one more in Wolfling. The... Obsidian Fortress." He paused while mumbling to himself and closed his eyes.

As they had all feared, at least according to this map, the Obsidian Fortress was under his dread father's control.

"Gods... wait. What's this red marker?" The northern half of the new world continent was split amongst three areas only known as The Shattered Lands. No one went there, as it was the birthplace of the darkest of legends. A land cut off from the rest of the world and draped in shadow, it was best to leave it in books and stories to scare children into behaving, or to entertain in the dark of the night around a campfire. It was at their southernmost central border with the northern glen valley. A gateway between two lakes.

"The Netherspring. Ok Dad, what else... well... Garnet Keep has a red marker too, I could have guessed that one. Better get the hell out of here soon so I can tell Benedict how my dad is gonna take over his dad's place. That will go over well." He looked around the room and saw the tall shelves holding scrolls but also a handful of books. "Ok, time for the shelves."

The smell of worn salt-tanned leather and molding pages greeted him. These were records, likely containing historical significance if nothing else. Thumbing past a few dusty scrolls that were past ledgers of financial transactions and folded up leaves of yellowing musty parchment with sketches of different room layouts, he found a midnight suede journal.

The familiar skull surrounded by five dragon heads within a red triangle was burned and painted into the flesh. This had to be from an insane follower of the dark queen herself.

"I totally want to wash my hands after this. I don't want to know what leather this is ... yuck. I don't even know how to read half of this, must be magic or something. Wait. No, it's a journal." He found a name in the inside page scrawled with "Mortas".

"Hmm," he thought as he thumbed the first few pages. "Looks like the year is fifteen twelve. Wait, that would be-"

Realization powered his hands as a finger trembled, framing this date. His pulse quickened as his heart pounded in his chest.

"That was the same year as OallEnAkhan, that was early spring, where were you that night?"

As if willed from his mind that was the day OallEnAkhan was sacked by his father. When it all began.

10th day of Spring Blossom, 1512.

Just the mention of this month makes me want to vomit. Blossom, how putrid. Oh so pretty they say, as they dance! They danced so pretty for me on fire they did! Yes you foul pixies, I so love to pluck off your wings like a child with a locust. Nothing can hold such beauty that pain cannot extract, before it becomes mine. Perfect.

The Dark Queen calls us to our purpose and I will answer this call without hesitation. Dekkion tells us that she is his bride, but she is still trapped in the underworld. A shattered soul in the twilight realm between life and death. She must be freed!

She is the Dark Queen, the widow of death itself and she will fly on swift wings to destroy this world and recreate it in her image!

Dekkion says we must find one of her ancient followers in the Bloodwood Mountains but first we need to retrieve an artifact of great power. All of this seems so simple but we keep encountering delays! I cannot fathom my dark lord's will, I realize that, but why do we keep stalling!

Searching the parched deserts of Kur for some lost temple, the months spent in the maggot infested deadlands, all of this seems pointless. Until yesterday. We burned the village of OallEnAkhan and took back Lord Pallus's power. I saw them dance.

Those pixies danced and screamed and I... felt joy.

Today as we searched south for some refugee children Pallus wanted captured, we found a windmill by the coast. Ash Delarosa and I found only an old man and a young girl there.

Dekkion refused to approach the windmill, sending Ash and I to retrieve the girl. Even after flaying the old man he never told us of those missing children from the town.

Then Ash presented the girl to lord Dekkion as the dark lord had requested. That girl has a power I don't understand. She is connected to death in a way I wish to know more about! The way she just stared at the old man and how calm he became in his last moments baffles me. She was cold, almost at peace.

His skin fell from his sides in bloody rags and as I laughed he didn't move.

He didn't move! He felt nothing! Like he wasn't even there. Dekkion just leered at him the whole time. They both never took their eyes off each other.

She stole this from me!

This was to be mine, my dark queen demands their suffering and now it is just lost? No, I will find a way to reclaim it.

Dekkion just laughed at me, saying I was too dull-witted to understand. Ash laughed at me.

She laughed at me! One day it will be I who laughs at you Ash Delarosa! I will laugh at your putrid corpse.

I was told this girl will travel with us now and I am to guide her in our ways. Fine, she will be my little angel of death.

In fact I will name her 'Dabria'

Horrified at the words on the page, Zorin almost didn't hear the voices up the hall approaching. After closing the book in its original position, he darted out the door and hid in the alcove across the hall from the unmarked door. A pockmarked man rounded the corner. Dark robes falling at his side, he spoke to someone behind him.

"Such arrogance!" he shouted, "Lord Dekkion is most displeased and I blame him not! Those guards will find themselves serving in the undead legion for sure."

"No matter anyway, Mortas." the other man was hidden in dark robes, "They had to have died in the volcano's heart with those kobolds when it caved in. To hell with all of them and their horrible little hearts. I only wish I could have tasted their blood- at the end of my knife." His voice was deep, raspy and wicked. Mortas laughed.

"Yes. indeed dark brother. Come."

Zorin noted the sores and boils around the bald man's neck and head as the door came shut, and with it, silence. He hurried back down the hall, his curiosity satisfied but now filled with a dull and forgotten ache in his chest.

"N... not now... not yet... oh god... no..." Zorin fought wave after wave of emotion crushing his heart as he ran silently in the shadows. He found an unused stairwell and crawled beneath it as far as he could. He felt a few small pebbles grind under him. The cobwebs gave way, tickling his nose briefly, but he ignored them. "Here... just. Here-" He whispered to himself.

Zorin curled up under a cold stone stairwell far away from the regular path of the patrols. Trembling, he tucked his hood and cloak around and lost himself in its warmth. His breathing slowed, and then he allowed himself to remember.

He remembered the shock at seeing Zane, his best friend, struck down by Dekkion himself. His father killing Erebus and

Lorahana Shieldheart. His father, who was Lord Pallus. Zorin remembered their hearts were low and left their home in OallEnA-khan so many years ago with Elloveve.

Five lost children on horseback.

Zorin remembered passing the windmill with the old man and the young girl. He remembered their eyes, her golden eyes and how they silently pitied those refugees which he was part of. Zorin remembered the sound of the waves on the coast, the feel of the misty rain on his cheek and the fiery glow of their homes burning behind them in the rain.

He remembered the haunting song Elloveve sang as they rode towards Port L'For to start a new life. How Zorin then hated that girl for her pity, for her happy life with the old man far from his family's struggles.

"I'm... so sorry." His voice was hushed and ragged as he let the white hot lava of guilt, sting his eyes and wash over his heart.

In that moment Zorin realized, six children, not five, were changed forever and Dabria was their missing sibling. A sister sired also from that long night.

On this night, alone in the darkness for the first time in over a decade, Zorin finally wept.

SOPHIE DREW THE BLADE BACK from her enemy's dark green gore. An enemy that moments before had chattered angrily behind wicked fangs and mandibles. Its multiple shining black orbs for eyes leered at her as it swung a jagged ax in one spider-like limb. Leaning over to catch her breath, the roar of the arena dulled for a moment as she spoke to herself inwardly.

"Ugh... you promised me a dance... or at least a nice dinner... not... ew... eddercaps."

"No I didn't," Zane protested, laughing in her mind, *"you know I can't afford that! But I hoped for something better than this. At least one of those stale cakes back home they would put outside for the beggars. Only the best!"*

Sophie chuckled as she pulled her sword out of the dead body of the bloated humanoid creature. Its wicked spider-like mandibles twitched slightly even in death.

"Ok, I guess you are right. That's pretty gross."

Sophie laughed to herself as she drug the end of her sword in the dirt from a limp arm. She was resting it for a moment while she could before it was called to action again.

The crowd chanted above Sophie in the arena. Hers was the first battle of the day. Eddercaps were wicked things, she remarked, always looking to ensnare their opponent with webs. Like a spider. Like those giant spiders she saw in the underworld. She shuddered.

Sophie recalled how she was rudely awakened on the second day of the games. A swift kick to the ribs, as the kobolds just laughed at her. While every fiber of her being told her to fight back against her captors, Zane's calm voice kept her in check. He repeatedly assured her their time would come.

She had been fed a soupy bowl of flavorless pasty gruel alongside many fellow gladiators, which now included a silent Eralin. He sat across from her that morning, mindlessly stirring the gruel with an iron bound hand. She noticed everyone's head was down too, and quiet. Skotmir and his brother weren't in their cell when she woke, or at the table.

Sophie was called to the Arena first, making her ascent up the stone ramp alone save a single guard opening the iron gate. She had been met with a cascade of boos from the many members of the audience, chilling her blood.

She looked around now, rolling over the dead eddercap with her black leather boot as the crowd's cheers dulled. They were her audience, though she didn't want them as much as they didn't want her. She glowered at the endless rows above, filled with cruel leering faces.

"You have to play them." Zane called in her mind, *"The show has to win."*

"Why should I care about the show?" she protested.

"Something I was taught long ago." *If the crowd isn't entertained they will send more things to keep them entertained. You need to prove you can be the bigger thing."* Zane sighed, *"The show has to win for you to win. We have to win to survive. You got this."*

"Ok fine." she clenched her teeth as she stood up straight, screaming, "Who's next?!"

"She wants more, my good people of Enruk!" The commodore's voice rang out across the crowd, bouncing off the walls, "Here to finish her off is a favorite of yours and mine the legendary- Ibn Dragonheart!"

"Wait... who?!" Zane's voice was surprised at the mention of the name.

The gate to the ramp opened and out strode a warrior in sparse green and black armor over a dark riveted chainmail hauberk. It covered the thighs, right shin and one left shoulder. His helm was a simple blackened steel sallet sitting over a chainmail coif, the single slit allowing his eyes to see but leaving his lopsided smile exposed. Sophie's heart dropped as she took up her blade again in a defensive stance.

Zane chuckled, *"Well hello, Ibn."*

"Friend of yours?" she chuckled.

"Oh we go way back, actually liked the guy once upon a time. Watch his sword. The guy likes to poison the blade and paralyse his

playmates. Wait-" Zane's voice hesitated as Sophie kept her eyes on the new fighter, *"is Maldros watching?"*

Sophie looked towards the edge of the pit and saw Maldros. The unmistakable, shadow-like form of a horned gladiator stood there with gauze covered powerful arms crossed and two blood red eyes staring out from behind the blackened helmet. Unnerving and intentionally staring at her, analyzing every move.

Sophie chuckled nervously, "Oh yes."

"Strike Ibn with a spear toss first, then don't use your sword. Instead, use my daggers."

"Ok, but-"

"Let's send a message."

Sophie thought of how Maldros had tortured and twisted Zane. Years they spent alone, and away from each other. Today they were now together and whole. No force on this world or the next could pull them apart ever again. Zane's vengeance on the man who kept them apart was also hers. Sophie smiled nodding.

"Yes. Let's." Sophie picked up a spear from the arena floor and with a screaming battle cry threw it at the charging warrior. He swatted it aside with his armored arm, missing the mark. He continued charging forward with his sword, swinging wildly at her as she stepped out of the way in a swift graceful motion, swatting upward to the sword's crossguard and the fingers beneath with her gloved hand.

Startled, he missed with such momentum that the weapon flew out of his hands. In a continuous motion, Sophie drew Zane's daggers and slashed like a windmill in six quick slices across his body, driving him backward, warm blood oozing between his fingers from his exposed abdomen..

"Gah! Those daggers! ugh... Impossible!" He drew a handaxe, striking at her midsection. He missed as he stumbled, blood soaking the chainmail across his chest where the links had separated from the blows.

"Yield or die!" As she yelled Sophie lost her footing and failed to land the hit. Her moment of weakness opened up the opportunity for her opponent to grab his sword and hit Sophie with one of two strong swings, cutting deep into her forearm. She felt a numbing creep along her arm from the blows.

"Bungle Poison!" she felt the numbing creep rapidly weakening the arm up to the shoulder. She didn't have much time. "Haven't felt like this for a while but I gotta act fast. Sorry Zane, it's my way now."

Knowing she had moments to fight against the poison before she would be helpless, she entered a panicked rage, dropping the daggers and pulling out her longsword. She swung weakly once and Ibn dodged. Using the force of the swing she brought the sword back around and over quickly, landing her hit with a sickening 'thunk' into the top of the fighter's helmet, splitting it to the visor.

The crowd went wild and the body of the great Ibn Dragonheart slumped to the ground.

Sophie felt her blood run cold as the numbing pain of her arm faded into nothingness. She used her other arm to awkwardly sheath her sword.

"This victory feels hollow and makes me want to puke. How can they cheer such a needless death?"

"*I know,*" Zane's voice rang in her ears soothingly, "*I feel the same as you. Come on, let's just go.*"

After regaining Zane's blades, Sophie turned to the edge of the darkened sand of the bloodpit in which she stood and saw Maldros staring at her intently. She looked down at the daggers in her hands, then smiled at Maldros. She stood straight and held them aloft in the air in victory, spinning them across her palms before bowing. A move she felt she had done before, in a different life, at least.

"Your victor! Sophie!"

The crowd started chanting her name in a slow perfect rhythm like a heartbeat, "So-phie! So-phie! So-phie!"

Sophie left the field as the crowd continued to chant behind her. The sand looked blood red from the thick dark crimson and black colored clouds of Enruk. She passed the now open iron gate and walked a few paces down the stone ramp towards her cold dark cell. Sophie was escaping away from all this madness as far as she could.

"You!" A familiar deep resonant voice roared in the passageway followed by quick heavy boots. She knew without turning, it was Maldros.

She could not pretend that this man didn't scare her to her core. He grabbed her collar and drew her close to his hot breath spilling from the mask and red glowing eyes. Zane's voice filled her head, blocking out his sharp words and reassuring her.

"I'm here. Don't let him intimidate you. He scares everyone, but he's nothing. Nothing but an angry slaver, Sophie. He's scum."

"Tell me one thing, Maggot. Where did you get those blades?" His voice was measured and powerful like molten metal pouring into a form.

"They're mine." She said producing one of the jagged blades for him to inspect for himself. "Orcish make. I was given them."

Maldros laughed as he snatched one from her to verify his eyes weren't deceiving him. "Orcish? I know orcs and this isn't their make! Besides, I knew their owner once and it's not you. At least." He saw her stand in cold defiance, and he chuckled, "It matters not. Sleep well, and you will die well, maggot. You will die well." Maldros leered from behind the dark helmet before storming away.

ZORIN REMARKED ON THE SECOND night that it seemed easier to move around with fewer guards, and he smiled to himself. There was a network of tunnels that seemed to be largely ignored throughout the facility, ancient pathways built by the original kobolds for some purpose, but not used by the larger humanoids who would need to stoop in many cases to use them. One he found earlier that day was actually right at the arena entrance.

"If we time it just right and if we can get rid of the guards for a moment, we could slip into the shadows there and escape this hellhole." He shrugged, thinking to himself.

He was hiding behind a crate and able to see Sophie, Skotmir and Thotmir's cells behind two orc guards in dark rough forged iron armor. There was only one way in and there was nothing to hide behind. Besides, he didn't even know where they had the key.

Zorin sighed to himself, "Can't do anything tonight. I'm sorry, my friends- but tomorrow. I promise tomorrow we will escape." He whispered an apology under his breath as he dipped into the officers' area once again. After all, they had a mission: find out what Pallus had planned, or was planning.

He returned to the unmarked war room. Digging in the other books he found a bound collection of loose pages, notes of some sort. It was in these there appeared to be an index for the books on the shelves. He placed the index on the table under the light and looked. Running his finger down the list, one title caught his eye.

Research - Una.

Searching the shelves he found a thin box holding several sheets of paper loosely standing on end. He thumbed through the old dusty pages. They described various experiments testing clairvoyance, page after page filled with dry data points and tables. Frustrated, he went to return the box when he saw something sticking out tucked in the back, folded differently than the others.

"Huh- some old note." He thought as he carefully unfolded the dry paper in his hands. It wasn't brittle but it felt thinner than the other papers and with a torn edge, ripped from another book he thought.

> *Una is some sort of seer, supposedly able*
> *to predict events of the future in strange*
> *visions only she can see.*
> *The rest of Amberreach are like dogs. Yet,*
> *that seems appropriate for what Ash has*
> *done.*
> *She and Dekkion are both amazing and*
> *horrifying to see work with each other.*
> *I must learn much from them.*

He folded the paper back up and placed the box back on the shelf. He returned to the map filled with markers at various locations on the table. After a few moments he found a small town at the edge of the Giantlands just a few days north east of the old mine, through the Bloodwood Mountains.

"Amberreach." He whispered, touching the map with his finger, noticing there was no marker. He looked west again.

Investigating the marker on the Netherspring revealed a number *"6"*. Looking on the edge of the map he found reference.

Operation Blue Fire.

"Wait. That was in that index. Yes-" he looked at the index and it called to a small green book on a lower shelf. He opened it and scanned the pages.

> *There's an artifact deep in the Netherspring's ruins,
> from before the destruction of the stone. Legend
> claims it can destroy an entire army but be wielded
> in a single hand or by a single person, the text is
> vague. There is supposedly an ancient portal also
> within there that can only be opened by someone of
> the "original bloodline". We do not know what this
> means.*
>
> *The prophecy states that this person will travel with
> two pairs. Two lost souls from the sea who are actu-
> ally two halves of the same coin. Also two brothers
> by marriage joined from a common tragedy. This
> sounds ridiculous but Lord Pallus and Dekkion are
> convinced we can just force it open with the right
> tools, or ritual. He's one of the few that has ever been
> there so he must be right.*

Zorin closed the book in thought, "We... We need to get there first but Garnet Keep is likely his first target."

Feeling confident this could be what they came for he quickly slipped into the shadows, now focused solely on planning their escape.

SKOTMIR'S BREATH HEAVED IN HIS chest as he looked up from the hot dust of the arena floor.

"The sun must be high. It's already a long day, my brother."

The brothers of the Garnet Mountains stood side by side in the red arena, looking up past the far bleachers to the sky itself. The dark clouds, separated by cracks of deep red and orange, were menacing. Only now that they became accustomed to the gloomy sky, they saw it for something else entirely. Ebbing and flowing like the bellows of a great forge, it was creation itself. They smiled inside at peace, it was freedom.

"Did you see your friend this morning?" Thotmir said softly.

"Yes. She was right behind us on the ramp."

"Oh?" Thotmir chuckled, "That lightning bolt the other day scrambled my memory as well, I think."

They both laughed as the commodore's voice rang out, announcing the next fight of the day.

"The dwarven sons of the Garnet Mountains are back folks, and today they will be facing one of Dekkion's finest apparitions! Formless and angry!"

Back at the gate Sophie watched the brothers prepare for battle. She glanced at the chalkboard.

"We aren't on for three more matches, Zane. Good."

"Those not fighting should return to the mess hall for rest!" the slender guard barked at her from the other side of the gate.

"No. I want to watch this match."

The guard laughed mockingly, "Oh! Hahaha! Those are your little friends aren't they?"

Sophie glared daggers of warning at the guard from behind her dirty matted blonde locks. The other eight gladiators shrugged as they made their way down to the mess hall. Thinking better of taking any action against the two orcs guarding the gate, she turned back to the arena while leaning on the iron gate with both hands. They didn't notice her position, her hands around her face, to hide the welling tears.

"Yes." she sighed softly

The second guard clapped a hand on his back. "Leave her. Let's go get some food too, eh? Not like she can go anywhere."

The guards laughed, "Yeah! See ya later- girlie. Hahaha!"

After a moment Sophie drew in a deep sigh as she pressed her head against the cold iron bars, losing herself in their touch. Time slowed for a moment as a tear rolled down her cheek. She couldn't help her chosen brother on the arena floor. She couldn't help Skotmir. She looked at her dirty hands.

"Some good you are right now." She sniffed as Sophie felt the faded threads of the friendship bracelet on her wrist, absently fidgeting with it, with trembling fingers. She momentarily lost herself in a fond memory of Cordelia giving it to her when they were children, promising to always be with her. Her best friend for all these years and at this point Sophie was afraid to ever remove it.

"Hope you are better off than us right now." she sighed brushing her wet cheek with the back of her hand, "Gods I miss you."

"Hey."

The voice shocked Sophie as she spun to look in the shadows where it came from. She saw a familiar bearded face barely visible in the dim light.

"Wha... Zorin?!" her outcry was hushed as hope filled her heart.

"Yeah, over here, but don't draw attention to me, keep your eyes out on the arena. Look, there's a tunnel back here in the shadows. It's not very high, probably for the kobolds but I haven't seen anyone use it. When they come off the field we are going to duck out through it."

Sophie's heart soared. Freedom was here at last and again, just as it did in the deep elven prison, Zorin was here to help. She heard footsteps coming up the ramp. Turning, she saw the form of Eralin walking alone up the ramp. He approached the gate next to her, and stood silent.

"Hey." she said, fighting to hold back any clue of what lay in the shadows.

"Hello." Eralin sighed deeply. His depression seemed to have spiraled even further since this morning.

"You ok?" Sophie whispered looking around for anyone else coming. They were alone.

"I'm fine." Eralin closed his eyes as he repeated his rehearsed response. "I'll be fine."

Sophie smiled at the tall ranger, "Got a surprise for you."

"Oh? And what's that?" he sighed exhaustedly.

"Me, tall and ugly." Zorin chuckled, "Who saw you come up?"

"Zorin?!" Eralin's eyes brightened, which was the most surprised look they had ever seen him appear. "Ah... no one." Eralin shook his head.

"You sure?" Zorin said with his hands out to not appear threatening, only cautious.

"Yes, now that I've returned to being a dragon again, I- I can tell. They will be there awhile. They have no interest in me as a gladiator." he shrugged, "I believe they will try to capture my soul in that sword again."

The explosive sound of crackling air and steel resonated from the arena as the Commodore shouted again, "Ouch! a colossal hit! His axe was shattered by the force of the lightning strike, folks! He's not moving!"

Sophie snapped back to the arena. She saw the ghostly form of some armored wraith circling the two brothers, but now Skotmir stood over the crumpled form of Thotmir, his axe held high in his hands.

"No! You will be destroyed, demon!" Skotmir swiped madly with his ax, separating the shrieking blue and white wisps that made up the form of the creature. Its face curled back in a scream as it disappeared, and the crowd exploded in cheers.

Sophie turned back to Eralin but he was already gone.

"Come on, let's get ready. Eralin is probably halfway home by now!" Zorin chuckled, "I probably shouldn't have shown him the exit yet." Sophie and Zorin smiled as they shrugged in the understanding that Eralin wasn't ever the best at teamwork.

The gate groaned as it ascended. Skotmir walked in carrying his brother's unconscious form over one shoulder.

"Hold on Thotmir." Skotmir sighed as he plodded one foot in front of the other.

"Skotmir! Over here, quickly!"

"Zorin?" He said in shock.

"Yes, there's no time!" Sophie pleaded from the shadows, "We are escaping!"

Skotmir started towards the dark recess next to the gate when he heard voices coming from down the ramp.

"No. I'm sorry." He sighed as he shook his head quickly.

Sophie's eyes grew wide as her heart clenched, "What? Why? Come on!" she pleaded.

"Thotmir won't make it. We... we will have to find our own way out."

Sophie's voice began to break. "No... Please?"

Skotmir's face was troubled but she could sense his mind was made up, "Sophie, We will slow you down. Go. We will meet again someday, but I have to do this. He came back for me."

Sophie looked at the two brothers and knew this was goodbye. She stepped from the shadows briefly to embrace Skotmir.

"He did." She sniffed behind clenched eyes. Hot tears streamed down her cheeks and into the dwarfs dirty, matted brown locks. "He did. I love you... my brother."

"Forever and always the stone. You and I, Sophie. Forever and always, I will be your brother."

"Here." Sophie slipped a small coin into Skotmir's pocket. "Still owe you that drink."

"Goodbye, pal." Zorin said as he pulled Sophie into the tunnel. Skotmir nodded and continued down the ramp as his friends plunged into the darkness below Enruk, knowing in his heart they probably would not meet again in this life, but hoping he was wrong.

IT TOOK ONLY AN HOUR for Zorin, Sophie and Eralin to stumble across a few of the Shadowclaw kobolds, who happily showed them the way out to the north, setting them on the path back to Garnet Keep which was a week or so away.

After 2 days' travel, they had set up camp at the foot of the Garnet Mountains and seemed to be very close to the familiar waterfall that shrouded Smuggler's Path. Zorin was cooking some venison that Eralin had hunted on the way.

"This is going to be the finest dining." he chuckled to himself as he moved the meat over the coals to the right of the fire, just outside of the direct flame.

"Oh really?" Sophie laughed at his brazen confidence.

"I always paid attention to Elloveve's cooking," he bragged.

"Through your stomach, you mean!" She jabbed at her old friend.

"Best way to learn!" Zorin laughed.

Eralin shrugged, "Well, it smells good."

"Really?" Zorin's sarcasm dropped from the compliment.

"Yes." Eralin nodded emotionlessly.

"Well thanks!" Zorin smiled happily "Who?" Zorin's attention was taken to the edge of the campsite where she heard the crumpling of dried leaves rusting underfoot.

"Hello?" A woman's voice called. Stepping out of the shadows into the campfire light was a familiar face, dirty and mud soaked from the road.

Sophie rose with a warm smile, "Isenatha?"

"Sophie!" Isenatha ran to embrace her tightly. "We thought you all died in the fireball, but I knew! I just knew you were ok." Isenatha pulled back for a moment, holding Sophie's hand. Smiling, she patted the bracelet on Sophie's wrist and nodded. Sophie was taken aback slightly.

"Hey Isenatha uh-"

"I'm so happy I found you." Isenatha interrupted. "Do you mind?" She stared at the cooking fire hungrily.

"What?" Zorin looked puzzled for a moment before he chuckled at his own foolishness, "Oh! Of course, sit down and prepare for a taste sensation! That's what Una would say."

Sophie laughed at the comment, "No she wouldn't!"

Zorin stared at Sophie for a moment. "Really? Huh."

Zorin's heart dropped as he realized something was missing.

"Wait. Where is Una and everyone, Isenatha?"

"Yes. Are they behind you? Or?"

Fear gripped Sophie's heart as she saw Isenetha's worried face.

"They were escaping the Temple underground through the heart of the Volcano when it collapsed. I-"

Sophie's eyes brimmed with tears, "No... are they gone?"

"No! I believe they escaped."

"How do you know?" Sophie asked, looking for further comfort to settle the tightness around her chest.

"I just do." Isenatha's voice was soft as she looked into Sophie's eyes, "I just do Sophie. You will have to believe me. Where is Skotmir?"

Sophie sadly shook her head. "He's still trapped in the prison below the arena. Zorin got separated from Benedict and Dabria too."

"Yeah. They disappeared after the first day I was trapped. Never saw them again in the stands either. Hope they didn't get caught elsewhere, it's not like goody two shoes to disappear if he knows his friends need him."

Isenatha sighed, "Well, let's not give up hope."

"Yes." Sophie looked out into the stars at the sliver of moon barely visible, and felt her heart make a wish, "Let's not."

The next day, their return to Garnet Keep was a syrupy dream. They came to the same crossroads where they had all parted ways once before. When they were all together. They stood there for a moment when Eralin stopped staring down the road to Whitford, away from Garnet Keep.

"The sea calls to me."

"Oh? Are you leaving us?" Sophie didn't know what to say. It was so abrupt but nothing was normal about the tall elf. She smiled as she shook her head, letting go of the burden of trying to understand.

"I'm not surprised." Zorin chuckled, "Well say hi to her for me, and take care of yourself, Eralin."

"I will see you again, Zorin. I know this." Eralin turned to face Zorin, "Our paths will cross again. Send me a call of the sea, and I'll be there."

"Call of the sea?" Zorin asked quietly.

Eralin stared at Zorin's furrowed brow awkwardly for a moment before nodding with no further answer as he turned away. Holding onto the memory of the young mariner silently was his way of bidding them all goodbye. As Eralin turned his path towards Whitford, Isenatha smiled.

"You did good, Eralin" She muttered, "You did good."

SOPHIE DIDN'T BELIEVE IT FELT real. Here was home before her. Her friends Keldor and Elloveve gave her hugs in greeting and Zane's mother kissed both her cheeks. Her heart was locked in place though, unable to free itself to soar and fly as she expected.

Slipping into the shadows of the celebration, she made her way quickly to her room... and sitting on the edge of her soft bed she allowed the boiling emotion to surface.

Thinking of brave little Skotmir, now alone as she had been.

Sophie cradled her face in her hands and cried.

CHAPTER 17

THE EXPEDITION

The smooth gray and deep crimson marble steps reverberated with the sound of several different boots cautiously entering the room. Ribbons of garnet cutting through the granite walls from the previous hallway faded into the dim void of the expanse, ominous to be sure but the expected familiarity helped to ease these seven figures. One stepped forward further into the darkness as the rest of them instinctively stood back. Zorin was in his early twenties. The rich brown of his curls and close cut beard were blackened by the darkness but he could smell the musky scent of the lamp oil as he drew closer to the flask. As his hand found it the copper and his own sweat mingled the smells not unpleasantly.

"Ah. Here it is…"

Smiling, he turned back to the patient gathering still standing behind him. His eyes fell on the one in the front. A large half-orc unusually dressed in bright brass armor, armor that looked similar but newer than mine. He had the emerald and sapphire turtle shell on the neck of the large guest in front of him.

"You there? Zev wasn't it? Do you mind handing me that tin lantern?"

Zev took a single step gracefully to the wall to his immediate right where a small lantern hung. It was old, he thought, but well made and showed it was even more well used. The tin was worked repeatedly with the ball end of a hammer with precision and the hood could be adjusted at the top to direct its light from the hand punched holes. Feeling the smooth tooling he grinned with a single white upward tusk poking from the corner of his mouth. This was good work. Turning it in his hand, a finger dipped slightly into an indentation he didn't see on the back, when he heard Zorin chuckle.

"Yes, the one with that small dent in the side." Zorin interrupted Zev's short-lived admiration of the lantern. His crimson eyes laughed gently as he nodded and walked the few steps to the swashbuckler. A long dark braid fell from the top of his mossy green head and danced across his back, bound in a single gold bead that bounced gently as it caught the last light of the hallway behind them.

"Thank you." Zorin smiled, "Heh, it has the flint and steel I left here last time in it. Let us warm this room up a bit, can you bring me some of those logs while I set up the tinder?"

Walking to the center of the room Zev found a large fireplace. He could begin to make out intricate relief sculptures and designs in the dim light from the lantern as Zorin set it down on the slate threshold. Zev pulled a few of the logs from their neat resting place to the left of the hearth and handed them to Zorin. The silence of them working in concert with each other was soon broken by the sound of steel and flint in rhythm with the soft pumping of small leather bound bellows.

Soon red gold coals began to glow. Footsteps of our friends followed as one by one they entered the warm glow of the fire and sat in the soft cushioned chairs that formed an arc outward but turned facing it. Zorin stood up from the fire and gripped the arm of a nearby chair himself. The wood was ancient but not weak. If anything it was stronger than the beams of some ships he had sailed, the oiled teak almost like soapstone to the touch. He turned to the curious faces that were looking to him for guidance and sighed.

He felt pressure in his chest, not heavy but just slightly unnerving. The role of leadership wasn't something Zorin ever actively sought out, but here he was.

"Well I guess…" He said with a groan as he shifted in his chair draping a leg over one arm. He plucked a small orange from a pocket in his faded purple tunic and drove a thumb into the flesh gently. The smell of citrus filled his nose welcomingly.

"Let's kick our legs up in this den and talk… err… a moment. Keldor, do you mind starting us off?

I nodded, straightened up and walked to the fireplace, placing a hand on the hearth. I drew my thumb over the relief carving. It was of the Knight and Maiden standing in a field looking to a distant mountain. A mountain with sharp jagged peaks that didn't seem quite natural.

"Not at all my friend." I said as I turned my head to the group, "Thank you for lending your sword arm to the cause and now with this very important expedition. It will be a few hours before dinner is served in the hall, and Zorin has asked me to give a bit of background here"

I extended my hands towards the fire momentarily, feeling the flame warm my hands. Standing back up I was wringing the heat from the fire in the palms of my hands, before continuing with a soft chuckle. "Heh, but I guess he may just want me to tell you a story of how we got here in this most important of moments. And, well, we have a bit of time now. Let's see, where to begin… "

I paused for a moment as I slowly reeled back a memory in my mind. I looked for the end of the yarn that was our tale and struggled to find the best place to start. Zorin held up a hand with a smile, politely attempting to aid my memory.

"Darkovnia. Actually, how about after Darkovnia…and of course after we woke up."

I nodded with a grin. "Ah yes… the road back to Bemil."

I felt the air of the sweet trees and smelled wild currants hiding somewhere behind us as I drove my memory back, recalling our adventure so far for our new friends. Hoping it could give them what they needed to succeed.

AFTER A FEW HOURS I had filled them in covering the call to action at the Celestine Tower, Our recapture of Garnet Keep and the infiltration of Enruk.

The group sat in silence as they digested everything I had said, I hoped. In reality my fear was that it meant nothing to them and I had simply wasted their time.

"Hmm," The tanned ranger with the shaggy black curls nodded, "So that's how Zorin came to be in charge now? Wow, that was a long-winded story."

I saw his smile and knew he was simply joking to make me feel at ease, "I agree, it was… maybe a bit more elaborate than needed, Mierak," I smiled as well, "but I'd rather you all be prepared for what may lay in store. The Netherspring is a mysterious place, not much is known about it."

Mierack chuckled, "It's fine, Keldor. Just giving you some grief is all. After all, we all know Zorin's not actually in charge of anything but a pastry." The room laughed, including Zorin.

"Thank god I'm not." Zorin mumbled.

"Sounded to me like it was Sophie." Zev stated.

Mierak nodded. "Hear that."

Isenatha cleared her throat, "Well Keldor, Elloveve and Elona are the ones that keep this place running."

"Yes they do, and they do it well and we are grateful. But if the question is about our little group though, Za-" he paused to clear his throat, "Sorry, I mean Sophie has always stepped into that role in my eyes, if everyone was needed."

The group smiled at Zorin as he nodded with a short laugh. "Ah! Family. What about you? Do you have a family?"

The dining room filled with awkward silence as the seven of them looked at each other. The past few hours we had told our own stories, as requested by Zorin, from after Darkovnia and leading up to now. It was just yesterday when Sophie, Isenatha and Zorin had returned alone. Zorin and Isenatha requested this meeting and these six other people had answered Isenatha's call from within our small community. Garnet Keep was growing but it was still small.

It was out of courtesy and our curiosity that Zorin was looking for their stories as well. After all, I knew them only as volunteers, both for our reclaiming of Garnet Keep months ago and for this quite harrowing and daunting task.

Isenatha had sought them out specifically based on what Zorin had told us about what he had found in the dark war room of Enruk. She swore these diverse members would be the ones to open the Netherspring.

"Hey, dinner is ready!" A voice called out from the long hallway. "And the ham is really good!"

We all looked at each other hungrily. Zorin stood and clapped his hands with a smile. "Let's pick that up after we get some food in our bellies. I'm starved!"

AN HOUR HAD PASSED SINCE our supper time, the once filled bowls stacked on the table still smelling of the sage and pepper that dressed the ham. The room was silent save for the crackling fire burning warmly in the hearth.

We stared at each other as Zorin's question lingered in the uncomfortable silence now.

"So where were we?" Zorin smiled as he picked his teeth with a short wooden splinter, "Ah yes, family. Do you have a family? How about you Virion? You haven't said much today, do you have family?"

They all looked at each other in a way that made Zorin wish he hadn't said that.

The slender, gaunt man who answered to the name chuckled, his chin length, dark hair shaking from his head and shading his eyes. "Heh, what good is a family when it just leaves- a hole in your heart."

He was one of two brothers who sat next to each other. The other was an elf but the one speaking was a human. Zorin became more curious about their story and there was something familiar about the blonde elf's eyes but I couldn't place it. The elven brother placed a hand gently on his brother's shoulder.

Across from them sat Meirak and Edde. He was six foot, deeply tanned, with dark eyes and long curly dark hair. She was easily half a decade younger than him. She was like a reflection of him, with long curly blonde hair and bright blue eyes. I remember thinking they were sad eyes. Eyes that kept some dark secret. They were rarely seen outside each other's company. She was unsettled by Virion's outburst, no matter his intention. Her eyes trembled slightly.

"It's ok, Edde." Mierak soothingly said as he pulled her shoulder towards him protectively.

"Really? But our family is right next to you, Virion." Zev said. His olive green skin was more unique now that the Mistgard Clan of orcs that were here before had been run off, and it must be noted that his help was instrumental in both taking the keep and helping to heal and tend to the wounded. A talented Cleric of the Hag, though different, wasn't something that was considered evil to me. She represented the elements themselves, those building blocks of everything that were neither good or evil.

"He... doesn't mean it really." Virion's brother said compassionately, "He's just been-"

"Oh shut up Reinold!" Virion snapped at his brother, " This is-" Virion clenched his jaw, fighting back words that may cause more harm than good.

"I'm going for a walk."

Reinold was stunned as Virion stormed out the door and down the hall. After a moment silence fell on the room as did everyone's eyes on Reinold. He took in a deep sigh, never taking his eyes off the hallway where Virion had disappeared.

"He's been really struggling since my sister's death. She was his wife. He blames anything and everything now but later feels bad about it. To answer your question, yes. I hail from my people in the Silver Maple woods. There, I have a family but now I am taking care of him." Reinold smiled gently, "at least for the time being. We came here to try and see if we could start again with so many others trying to do the same."

"I'm... I'm sorry to hear that." Zev said gently, his short tusks were tucked behind his warm expression. Reinold shrugged.

"Oh don't be. We are happy to be here, trust me. And now that my true brother has returned home it's his turn to take care of our immediate family's needs."

Zorin smiled, "That's nice of him."

Reinold laughed, "Oh, you don't know my brother. He isn't nice. I spent most of my time traveling around playing this old lute for coin where I could, met everyone in the Silver Maple Woods for sure and most of Bellz. Partially so I didn't have to spend time with him when he came around. He was outcasted from our people too for a time. Apparently my self righteous brother and Lord Hyro had a falling out I was told. My sister, on the other hand...her grace was unparalleled in all of the forest." he smiled as he wiped his hands on his soft emerald green pants. "What about you, Zev?"

"I love my family. Though I haven't seen them in a long time." Zev sighed, "My tale is longer than my relatively short life would reveal though."

He and Mierak chuckled together. Mierak gave a prompting nod to his friend, "We met when you were a sailor. How did that become your work?"

Zev smiled.

"My story begins just south of the town of Whitford in a small apothecary shop. My mother's shop. She sold tinctures and balms to help heal and strengthen those who purchased them and collected their components from the nearby woods. She told me it wasn't easy since she was born without sight, but my mother was far from being hindered by it."

"She could see more by listening than you and I can see with our eyes. She could sense past their words to someone's true intention. She could tell the difference between a scared and angry threatening creature."

"One day, many years ago, two visitors came and one was very sick. The other asked her in a rough but pleading voice if she could heal his brother's fever, as he was on death's door. She agreed and set him up in her small guest bed. She could tell he was larger than the bed, but he didn't complain."

"She cared for him night and day, spooning a thin broth made from salty chicken with local mushrooms and savory green herbs. Which was her specialty."

Zev chuckled, "I remember it fondly myself as a young lad. Eventually one day he became better. He also grew to love my mother and she, him. He was a kind man and had an elegant way of speaking."

Zev felt the tusks on his face and smiled, "She told me he had short tusks that came up from his jaw. Like mine. He was embarrassed, claiming it meant he was weaker in the eyes of his clan, but my mother loved him regardless. So he stayed and helped my mother gather her herbs, and even taught her the orc names for them."

Zev paused as he looked into the fire, "As you probably guessed, months later my mother was with child. They were very happy, but his brother was not."

Zev's lips pursed as his eyes narrowed, "The orcs called my coming an abomination, and they threatened to kill all three of us, even with me not yet born to this world. My father devised a plan to protect me, and left. My mother and I moved north, just south of Silver Maple Woods along the eastern coast. It was here I grew up never knowing my father"

"I'm sorry lad." I said to Zev. He looked at me and smiled. I could feel our hearts were made of similar stock and he valued life like I did.

"Thank you Keldor, but I still honor him. I knew I'd never find happiness with the orcs or man but the sea always called me. The way she ebbed and flowed was like the gentle wave of a close friend in greeting. I would spend hours early in the morning watching the surf on the sandy beach as the sun rose in the eastern sky."

Zev closed his eyes and imagined those rolling hills and the crashing surf below. He could hear his mother calling as if in a dream.

Zev! Come home, son! I wish to speak with you! There's someone here to meet you.

He smiled remembering that day.

"I was given a chance by Captain Bugle of the Southern Star to come aboard as a deckhand. I said goodbye to my mother the next day and I sailed with him from Whitford. I served with him over three glorious summers, coming home periodically to see my dear mother, and make sure she was alright."

"I took to the duties aboard ship naturally, grew to be welcome and trusted for many positions about the merchant ship. In the storms I found a strange sanctuary and, talking with some of the older crew, they taught me about The Hag, the four elements themselves and her four bastard children: lightning, magma, mud and steam."

His hands opened as he smiled. Recalling the joy of finding how to make his spirit soar.

"I learned that the chaos of the elements still followed the great laws of the universe like the reeling of a ship on the waves of an angry sea. I learned that, in some ways, we all are her bastard children. Sometimes angry or sad but it's in those peaceful times we find our true selves."

"Well, now I had a new love of faith, and found myself a purpose. I didn't have to run from my anger, I now could accept it, use it and move past it. This was even more freeing than my journey aboard the Southern Star."

"I had made up my mind that it was time to set out in a new adventure when next we returned to the new country, but we had just landed in First Port." he looked at Mierak, "It was thereafter I met Meirak and Edde, who were starting again I believe."

"So they came aboard and we sailed back to Bellz. There we heard about the mustering of an army to take back Garnet Keep from a clan of orcs and bandits. This seemed like a worthy cause to fight in. Mierak and Edde offered to make the journey with me."

Mierak smiled at Zev. He turned to Edde next to him.

"Edde," his voice was deep and soft, "Go up to the tavern and treat yourself to some of that sweet cake you like. Use this."

Mierak pulled a silver coin from his pocket. It was worn and old but still held value.

"Got it today splitting wood with Deacon. I'll be there after this."

She nodded and smiled at him before leaving the room in a happy jog. Her long cream colored dress waved in a trail behind her down the long hall. Once she was out of earshot, Isenatha leaned in to speak carefully.

"Mierak, about Edde- She doesn't say much, does she?"

"She-" His voice broke a little. He took a moment to cough and clear his throat, "She can't."

"She- can't speak?" Virion asked quietly with his eyes filled with concern.

"No." Mierak shook his head, "Hasn't in the past few years."

He leaned forward and rested his elbows on his buttery doeskin leggings. "Edde and I come from the Emerald Atoll. A small island off the coast of Viridian. Up until now it was more than an Island, at least to us it was everything we knew. We rarely saw outsiders in our village and when we did they were usually elves trading from the mainland for our fish, dyes and oils that came from the rich shallow ocean there."

Mierak chuckled as he heard the echo of a memory from long ago.

Come on Mierak! I'll race you to the wharf! Hahaha!

"My best friend was Pike, Edde's brother. We were about the same age and being raised together by the clan after our parents were lost at sea many years ago. The hurricanes were devastating that year on our fishing boats."

"Sure, we were three orphans but we were happy. Our community was tight knit and provided for each other happily. Pike and I were helping to repair the nets and occasionally diving for clams in the harbor, as we could hold our breath for almost a full five minutes. Edde was only twelve when the dark ships came."

"Clouds seemed to follow them in, but that could just be my memory. Huge galleons with dark sails- a crimson skull surrounded by dragon heads painted on the largest."

Zorin and I looked at each other. "The Dark Army" Zorin sighed.

Mierak nodded. "Yes. We knew nothing about them or their cruelty then. We welcomed them into our home."

"After they landed we all gathered in the center of our village to greet them. A pale man in black robes approached our elder. She looked at him, leaning on her shaman's staff, feathers of seabirds gently swaying in the wind around the limb of an ancient tree carved in the shape of the moon. She was the strongest of us."

Isenatha shifted uneasily in her chair as she listened to Mierak continue.

"I don't know what was said but the man raised a single white, claw-like hand and green bolts of energy ripped into her body. I saw smoke rise from under her hood of coarse wool. Thus began our waking nightmare."

"Pike and I were hiding behind some crates when they struck. Our village fought bravely against what we believed were men- until I saw they were probably once men. Rows of shambling dead were killing our friends and family with rusted weapons and empty eyes."

"We ran." Mierak closed his eyes tight to recall the memory and make sense of the dissonant noise in his head, "We darted between our houses and buildings, the rough wood tearing into our arms as we brushed against them. When we- found Edde."

He stopped and rubbed his red rimmed eyes and coughed nervously.

"When we found her, she was kneeling in the center of a shallow pool of mud, eyes wide in terror. Circling around her trembling body were six wispy blue and white- translucent forms. Ghosts or banshees, I knew not then, but their mouths peeled back revealing shark broken teeth and the inky tendrils of smoke that came from their eyes. Edde saw us and I heard Pike whisper to her not to move."

Edde! Don't... move...

Mierak shook the echo of Pike's voice from his ears.

"Edde's chest heaved, her lips trembling behind her muddy face. Her chapped lips cracked and torn as her mouth ripped open in a scream- a scream I will never forget. The spirits circled more earnestly as if they were living off this terrified child. Suddenly Edde threw her arms out and- a shockwave erupted from her- and all went silent."

Isenatha looked at him with compassion and curiosity.

"They were gone, Edde had collapsed in the mud. I ran to her and scooped her up. The three of us ran to the boat house at the edge of town and, hiding behind the barrels of fish, we continued to hear the massacre of our people."

Mierak's eyes closed as he fought back stinging tears.

"They killed all of them over the next few days. They asked for our allegiance and when it wasn't met they killed us. We watched them tie our people to boulders six at a time, then a dragon would drop it in our shallow harbor. Shallow or not it proved to be enough. Our people drowned mere feet from the surface."

Mierak's hands clenched as he opened his eyes looking upward. Zev patted his shoulder compassionately. Mierak smiled at his friend as he clasped his hand seeking comfort.

"Once they believed we were all gone they left us and finally we were alone. When the food supplies we could find finally dried up, we worked together to salvage what we could from the sea. Our haunted sea."

"I thought I could hear the voices of our people in that harbor, and many times I'd find Edde just looking out across it. She was silent now, her voice completely lost to that horrible memory. One day, after a year passed slowly, I met up with Pike to look at a project he was working on. He had begun lashing three small boats together in a triangle."

In this boat we can leave! Hahaha! We can leave and start over, Mierak. It will be strong enough to get us North to First Port in the heavy waves. You I and Edde! Hahaha! Oh my friend we will soon be free of all this! And Edde- Edde can find her voice again!

Mierak smiled thinking of his friend. "We worked on the boat night and day for weeks then- Pike became ill and there was nothing we could do as we helplessly watched him get worse"

"He caught a fever, and finally died. We wrapped him in the blue blankets reserved for the heroes of our people and loaded his body onto the boat. I had to make sure he escaped with us, just like he planned."

"We sailed out past the harbor and Edde curled up next to me. For the first time ever I saw her relax and allow herself to dream."

Mierak stared into the fire, hearing the gentle crackle mixed with the groaning of the creaking boards on the waves. The red orange firelight was the soft dusk sun casting itself across the western ocean and with it a gentle breeze. After a moment he shook his head gently and took a drink from his mug.

"We were picked up by the Southern Star while we were drifting. Zev brought us aboard, and well you know the rest."

"Forgive me, but what about Pike's body?"

Mierak smiled gently at Zorin, "We are children of the sea. After Zev picked us up, I watched his body and his boat that brought us our freedom, carry him off to the next life under the light of the moon."

We sat there with nothing more than the soft sound of the fire crackling in the fireplace for what felt like an eternity. The story sharing had been a lot for us to take in and the silence was welcome and respectful, at least for a moment.

"What about you Isenatha?" Reinold took a sip off his chalice of tart wine. She looked at him slightly bewildered.

"Oh... I've... traveled a lot. Odd jobs, that sort of thing." She cleared her throat, "So just the five of us? Is that all that will be leaving in the morning?"

"Yes. The rest must stay here to prepare for the assault on Garnet Keep. With Benedict gone-" Zorin coughed, "I... I mean absent, currently, we will need all hands available to make ready."

I looked at them all as I gestured to the old map on the coffee table. "You five volunteers will set off to ride north across the Great Glen Valley, past the Celestine Tower to the edge of the Shattered Lands. There a grim monument stands. Legend has it that it was one of the last of the great giants from two millenia ago, before they were lost to time."

As they all left, Zorin asked Reinold to stay back for a moment. "Yes Zorin?"

"Isenetha. Have you ever met her before?"

"N... No." Reinold stammered confused, "This is the first time we have met, why?"

"Oh... no reason, just curious." Zorin smiled at his new friend, "Well, sleep well. Long day tomorrow."

"Yes, you too."

As he left, I too became curious. "Zorin. What was that about?"

"Something is bothering me about how Isenetha knew so much about Enruk, and was magically the only one to return from her party. No Cordelia, Una, Lorvana. Sophie and Skotmir somehow ended up in the arena and they can't explain it either- but one thing is coming to light though."

"What's that?" I asked

"Keldor." His eyes were narrowed, "She's not from the Silver Maple Woods."

This is the journal and recording of Zevitar Fallow-spire, cleric of the elements and member of this expedition to the Netherspring.

Though the travel across the Great Glen Valley by horseback these last 17 days was largely uneventful, it was breathtakingly beautiful. Rolling hills as far as the eye could see covered in a blanket of kelly green grasses and sprinkled with delicate meadow flowers the colors of sunrises... the sunrises back home.

Four days ago we passed through the Whispering Mountains. If any stories are true it is that these mountains possess a strong old magic. At night we could feel ourselves being watched. Not... menacing, though. Just being observed from the inky shadows. Mierak was unnerved and couldn't wait to get out.

The final night we were sitting around the campfire when Mierak came back from scouting around our perimeter cautiously.

"These woods have ears we cannot see... That is certain. I'll help again with the first two watches... I won't be able to sleep anyways until we are out of it."

"Are we there yet?" said Virion in a sarcastic tone. Reinold hit his brother with a small stone in the chest, "Really? Well right now we are camping."

"Yes I know... but... I'd appreciate you just answering the question." Virion's sarcasm cut the air and if they weren't so exhausted may have actually been insulting.

"We should be there soon." Isenatha said with a yawn.

Mierak nodded, "It will be impossible to miss, given this pass in the mountains is the only way north. We will press on in the morning- right Zev?"

"Yes. We should be there by midday if we get a good start in the morning, looking at the map."

The morning came without any further events of note, just the dim Sunrise from the flat eastern horizon. I assumed this was the vast and distant Thunder Lake sixteen or so leagues away that I could locate on the map. The largest lake in the world, almost its own small sea, was tucked away here in the lost and forgotten north of the new country but away from our eyes at this position.

We continued our travel north and, as expected, midday rose but the sun was hidden behind some dark storm clouds forming in the sky. An afternoon thunderstorm no doubt was common at this cooler latitude. I must be honest though, I only note the weather from my memory as the next events will perplex and haunt me till the end of my days.

Coming out of the forest into a large basin, we saw it. Rising out of the ground was a skull, mouth agape as if shouting at the sky above that its empty sockets stared at. Time had made the skull part of the landscape to be sure, the foliage and greenery blending it into the landscape. If it weren't a small mountain seventy feet high from the base to the grass and moss covered brow I would have thought it to once be... human.

"Behold... the Netherspring." Isenatha said in awe.

"Is this...?" Mierak was wide eyed, "Were they...?" Isenatha looked at him and smiled gently.

"Giants? Yes. This is what remains of one of the ancient races before the fall of the stone. I have heard these giants still exist. Though now driven under the waves."

"Or further north." Zev added, "In the old country giants rule and trade there. Though I've never seen one this big."

The wind picked up and carried a distant sound. An unnatural and hollow wail of sorts that unnerved us all.

"Wh... What was that?" Reinold stammered as he looked into the cold night air.

"I'm not waiting to find out." Virion said as he began to run towards the stairs leading up the face of the skull. Mierak saw a dark misty shadow that began chasing Virion and then disappeared. Looking behind them he saw an eerie green glow spill from the trees faintly.

"Run to the stairs!" He shouted

We ran to the worn and old wooden stairs that wound up the throat and to an ancient door at the jaw of the hill. They creaked and cracked under the newfound weight of us all. Looking behind, the storm clouds were descending and a gray green mist was pouring out of the woods towards us.

Virion grabbed the latch of the door, expecting it to be locked and had a lockpick already poised in hand... when it opened on its own.

He looked back at us shocked.

"This... this can't be good..." Virion said wide eyed to Isenatha. She grabbed him and pulled.

"Quickly! Inside the door!"

"Move!" Mierak shouted as he ushered us through.

Mierak and I shoved the door shut behind us. We expected the wave of mist and cloud to slam into it... but it never came.

"What the... Virion look." Rienold said in a hushed whisper but their eyes told him where words failed.

Slowly Mierak and I looked at each other, eyes wide in disbelief. We had our hands on the door. I... I swear we had our hands on the door! I felt it as we turned to stare down a barren and empty... dirt road.

The sky was overcast and the woods surrounding us seemed dark and menacing. In the far distance we could see the towers of some citadel or castle perched on an outcropping like a large black bird...

We turned back and there was no Mist...

no howling wind of the storm...

and there was... no door...

INTERLUDE

*C*ome *Una over here! Look, it's the silly dragon!*
Una could feel her little legs running slowly–as if suspended in syrup–with her friends. She saw them all barely ten years old laughing and chasing each other towards the old sawmill. She felt a hundred laughs in her belly as they watched the wheel creak over in the stream.

A brown haired boy with freckles smiled at her, holding out a piece of bread. She happily took it and floated it in the stream watching it disappear under the wheel of the mill. The boy pointed up as she felt her spirit soar uncontrollably upward on the wheel. She grew afraid as her friends called out to her but now she felt distant. Like a single dandelion seed caught in a welcome summer wind.

Una felt her dreams begin to carry her far away to where she was standing on a high balcony in the north. Only this wasn't her. She was someone else.

She felt her eyes clench tight as the storm brewed above. Distant thunder and the smell of the wet woods was soft to her senses as she remembered part of an old nursery rhyme. One passed around Una's village to all the young ones.

Long ago there was a wayward prince,

who left his throne with his friends.
One a knight and stout of heart,
who always was there to defend.

The unlikely pair they left that day,
to travel far and wide.
it was there they met a ferryman,
and the druid who was his bride.

The woman opened her eyes and saw her pale hands on the stone railing, glistening from the sprinkle of misty rain continuing to fall. She sighed as she heard the sounds of ancient steel clashing and the roar of dragons around her. Standing up straight the sounds faded into the night air as she gently stroked the stone railing and felt the wedding ring on her hand skip along its surface.

She saw his blazing blue eyes in her mind for a moment before they began to fade teasingly. She clenched her eyes tight attempting to recall his face, but there was nothing but pangs of lost love ripping at her heart as she clawed her way through the labyrinth of her mind..

Only a grim staff appeared behind her clenched eyes, topped with a blackened skull. Her heart tightened again at the sight of it, menacing and mocking her. A wheezing laugh resonated in her mind from the vision. She reached for her chalice and peered inside. It was empty, but upon feeling her touch, it slowly filled from the bottom with sweet red wine. She was thirsty.

Come. Drink.

It soothingly called to her with a voice not unlike her own.

She took a deep sigh as she heard voices on the road. New guests in her domain, and maybe they could help her.

She tipped the goblet back and felt the liquid pour down her throat. Cool and sweet, she smiled.

The liquid reached her belly and she felt the warmth turn to daggers, as she screamed in pain. Suddenly fear cut icy blades through her heart as she remembered enough to recognize her mistake, and this wasn't her first time in this dread cycle.

"No, not again." She sobbed between clenched teeth. Her eyes opened wide upon hearing her voice match the one moments ago from the chalice, "I was so close this time. I almost remembered!"

Visions screamed through her mind as she saw images of people fighting dark shadows and huge dragons, people she felt she knew. Her feelings soared as the images came quicker and more rapid. Finally she saw a man with blazing blue eyes sip from her cup as his spirit faded. Dead at her hand.

The visions faded into a growing darkness of her mind. Waves of guilt peeled back her heart and mind in an instant leaving her shrouded in darkness. A darkness she lost herself and sense of self in immediately.

She could hear her heartbeat fade into her ears. Her fingers clenched as she felt breath fill her lungs again. Her mind filled with dark, cruel voices. One was laughing and, as she brought her hand up to her temple to ease the throbbing headache, she felt her hot breath. She was the one laughing.

She opened her eyes, grinning menacingly and looked over the road below. There in the short distance she saw five figures walking towards her. She chuckled as she sensed the tragedies of their lives illuminate in auras around them.

Two brothers who lost someone they loved walked behind two men of the sea, both lonely sailors that sailed seas of loss and pain. Finally there was a woman, who actually wasn't a woman at all hiding the truth from herself and others like her. More importantly she could sense she carried the first bloodline within her veins.

The woman chuckled as the only fragment of some poem or rhyme she could remember played itself repeatedly in her mind.

> *It was there they met the ferryman,*
> *and the druid who was his bride.*

Throwing her head back she laughed.

> *With a kiss she had betrayed him*
> *And with a drink his soul had died.*

Her lips pulled back in a cruel grin, as she willed her hands into wicked talons, razor sharp and seeking to rend flesh from bone. Her voice became raspy and cruel as she heaved a ragged breath with a cackle.

"Come my new friends, it will soon be time to dance our wicked dance of a thousand steps within a hundred betrayals. You can call me *The Widow.*"

CHAPTER 18

UNEXPECTED ALLIES

The faint vision of the woman on the balcony was swept up in the inky vapor of Una's dream. It faded into the recesses of her mind as Una slept, replaced now by a more powerful voice in her mind. An all too familiar voice called to her in the dark corners of her sleep, ensnaring her thoughts in a cacophony of sound, and once again Una felt herself dancing on the razor's edge of madness.

He found her once before, my little Una, if
only in the twilight of a dream.
There and yet NOT there, he must find her
again.
Help him find her and put the pieces together.
Pieces like hidden memories and forgotten
dreams, not just steel and brass.
Tucked away along with the truth... Your
truth Una... OUR truth.
Help him and it will help me... then... you can
find me.
...Now... wake...
and remember the first thing you sense...
as your first clue...

Una smelled the sweet lilies at the water's edge as she opened her sleepy morning eyes. They fell on the beautiful lagoon outside the straw hut she had called home for the past few days. The sky was clear here and the soft air was filled with the song of small peaceful birds.

The dark sky above the southern tip of the Garnet Mountains and the volcanoes of Enruk were but a small shadow to the east behind them. Now the voices of several pleasant conversations came from the waterfront where she saw her companions smiling and talking with a few of the prisoners and their clan.

Sitting proudly at the waterfront's outskirts was Chalkos, the huge copper dragon who had helped them all escape, his scales shining like a blanket of polished coins in the light. She reached for her spear at the bedside and used it to gently prop herself up on the side of the bed. The dream still echoed in her mind, gently reverberating as she gathered her legs under her dark robes to stand.

She caught her reflection in the little hand mirror left by some other occupant on the small table, the only other furniture found in the small room. Una's emerald green eyes and straight blue black hair framed her soft face. Her eyes softened for a moment as she brought a single hand to her cheek. She closed her eyes, thinking of this moment in this beautiful place. Secretly wishing it wouldn't end. As if sensing her need for respite, in this moment the voice in her head ceased its demands, and allowed her... peace.

"Good morning, Una."

Una's eyes opened and saw the man she first met in the prison beneath the temple. He smiled gently behind twin sandy blonde braids that hung from the corners of his mouth above the short cropped beard on his jaw. His shoulder length hair was pulled back into two braids on either side of his head. He now wore a simple leather tunic that was black with dark green trim, topped with what appeared to be traveling boots. Different from the tattered muslin the freed prisoners were all dressed in when they first arrived. He looked not only stronger but something was powerful about him now.

"I hope you slept well?" he smiled gently.

"I... Um.. Yes." She stammered as she cleared her foggy mind, "Yes Kopyrus."

The man chuckled, "Kogyrus. Kopyrus sounds pretty nice too... but my name is Kogyrus."

"I'm... sorry Kogyrus."

"It's ok!" he smiled and laughed, his eyes twinkling with yellow and red flecks that sparkled "So back to my original question. Did you sleep alright?"

"Yes." Una nodded, returning the smile. "Yes I did."

"Good. Come. Get some breakfast. I believe we owe you and your friends some answers."

Cordelia and Dabria sat with three other people at the stone meeting table by the water's edge, enjoying various fruits and cheeses from a large central silver platter for breakfast. Lorvana was energetically talking to Chalkos, no doubt telling him some wondrous tale of adventures she had heard, which he very much enjoyed. Considering his smile and focused nodding, this tale was no exception to that.

Benedict stood with a shining purple apple in his hand, enjoying the tart fruit one bite at a time as he noticed the unlikely pair approaching the group. He smiled. He noted how Una's dark shadow seemed to have melted away over the past few days. She still acted slightly awkward but everyone was very forgiving and kind to her new steps. Like a family with a newborn learning to walk.

Community elder Arianell smiled at them as they approached.

"Welcome Una. Come my dear, join us. Sit. We have much, as you can see. Apples and grapes and some wonderful soft cheeses. Enjoy," she gestured to everyone who was sitting in the small grove around the ancient stone table and benches. "Now that we are all here, healed and well rested, I believe now is the time for us to deliver our promise of the truth to you, of whom we owe so much."

She placed a hand gently on Cordelia's and patted it assumingly as she smiled. She was a caring and loving matron of this village.

"You rescued our people from the enslavement of this Lord Pallus but I'm afraid the threat is deeper than you know or realize. You see, I knew Dekkion."

The sheer mention of the name in this beautiful place, and coming from someone as pure as Arianell, felt profane to the companions at the table. The shock seemed to dull the senses slightly, as they didn't hear the footsteps approaching the table in the soft grasses.

"As did I." The old man they had rescued from the dark altar approached in white and gold robes that shone brightly in the sun.

"Aryat. Please, will you join us?" she gestured to the table

"Of course, Arianell. Excuse me Cordelia, is this seat taken or can an old man sit by your side?" he smiled at the young mage.

Cordelia beamed excitedly at her new friend, "Please sit, Aryat! Always good to see you." As he approached she hushed her voice to continue, "After this I want to talk to you about that dancing fire spell you showed me."

Aryat chuckled, "Oh that old thing? Great! Yes please, after this." Aryat groaned as pain in his hips erupted, lowering him to his seat. "Ah! That's better. What's this? An apple with my name on it, how delightful."

Kogyrus chuckled at the elder of his people, "Time for eating may need to wait, wise one!"

"Really?" The tanned bald man next to Dabria protested in a deep voice. "Are you actually doing this now?"

Aryat chuckled, "Calm down Ymir!" Bringing the fruit to his mouth he bit into the firm and sweet fruit., "Heh, delicious. You see, Cordelia, how the apple crunches perfectly to the bite?"

"Sure Wonderful." Dabria leaned forward impatiently, "Are you quite done? We have questions that you owe answers to."

Dabria stared at the old man with twin white and gold mustaches that trailed from the corners of his mouth. They weaved and swayed gently as he chewed the bite of an apple, considering what she just said. Ymir sat with his arms crossed, his deep brown chinstrap of a beard fell into a single braid clasped by a bronze bead. Below his bald head were angry impatient eyes and tight lips.

Across the table sat his twin sister, Cemri, whose platinum and charcoal locks were braided in eight warrior's braids. The fact they ended in bronze beads as well was probably the only thing that showed any similarity to her twin, at least they were told the two were twins. She was quiet, reserved and smiling at Aryat's carefree attitude with a hand on a graceful chin, as was Arianell.

Aryat let out a deep disappointed sigh, as he lowered the apple to the table. "Fine. You see my friends, some of us are old and old people tend to know each other because the longer you last in this mortal coil the more chances you have to run into each other. With patience-" He glared mockingly at Ymir and Dabria before chuckling and shaking his head. He took another bite and struggled to talk with his mouth full of the juicy fruit, "There's a good chance you'll meet everyone someday."

"When did you meet him?" Cordelia asked, "We first saw him in OallEnAkhan eleven years ago."

Aryat shrugged, "Well we, Arianell and I at least, both met him-" his eyes rolled up in thought and calculation as he took another bite of the apple, "Let's see that would be... over fifteen hundred years ago I suppose."

Dabria threw herself back in her chair at the absurd comment, "Impossible."

"What? How?" Cordelia was bewildered and confused.

Arianell laughed as she patted Cordelia's back gently, "It's ok, child! I suppose it can be shocking."

Aryat grinned at her, "But... I look good for my age though, don't I?" he laughed teasingly, "To be truthful that's because of you I look so healthy my friend."

"I-" Cordelia burst into laughter at the dear old man, before she patted his shoulder in mock assurance, "Sure. Sure you do Aryat. "

Aryat laughed and pointed across the table at surly Ymir who sat defiantly with crossed arms.

"See? I told you, "Ymir, stress will make you age much faster."

Ymir just grunted and shook his head in response.

Benedict leaned forward "Amazing! but that would mean you were both alive during..." He paused as his eyes grew wider, "the war of the stone?"

Arianell nodded, "Yes Benedict. The others are a bit too young for that event but Aryat and I knew it well."

"What part did Dekkion play in that war?" Dabria asked as she glanced to read Ymir's stoic mannerism.

"Dekkion helped lead the western army of the Eagle to capture the stone. He believed it would help immortalize him. Rising to challenge the gods themselves. This was what pitted them against nearly the entire world. We helped defend our friends the kobolds, believing this was a war only for the humans. Soon the dwarves and elves of both continents took up arms to battle against the banners of the Eagle. The banners led by the dark lord Dekkion's insanity."

Aryat sighed as he looked at Cordelia, "To be honest we should have joined sooner, as by the time we did we bore little help from here to the center of the valley where the stone stood." He looked apologetically towards the rest of the table, "By the time we got there the stone was destroyed."

"You said you knew him though?" Lorvana asked, "He wasn't a close buddy was he?"

"No, I said we met him before." Aryat smiled, "You see, this land of Chikara stretches to the sea... to the south and west, separated by the Garnet Mountains to what is known as Trull and its northern border consisting of Wolfling and the Obsidian Fortress. But most importantly, this is where he was likely born."

"Here?" Cordelia was shocked, "In this lagoon?"

Ymir laughed, "Ha! I should hope not!" Cemri nodded at her twin before adding, "I... was told it was a village to the north in the great desert. Now lost to time though. No, Cordelia, this lagoon is our home and rarely do we host the various people of the world here."

Cemri sat forward, looking gently at Cordelia. Her green and gold eyes behind her deeply tanned skin reflected strength and wisdom beyond what appeared to be the middle aged woman's frame. Arianell smiled and nodded.

"We have discussed the current dread that has fallen over the land and realize it is time for some of us to join you on your journey. We do not wish to repeat the mistakes of the past by delaying any longer."

Ymir and Cemri rose from the table. Kogyrus patted the black shrouded shoulder of Una gently and with a smile and stood up. She saw the shimmer of glitter in his amber eyes briefly as he walked with the others to the clearing.

Aryat grunted, "Ah... Cordelia, can you give me a hand up?"

"Of course." she smiled at the charming old man.

"Thank you." He groaned as he found his feet again, "Ah! Such a lovely girl you are. Such a wonderful heart."

Aryat smiled and, leaning on his staff, made his way with the others to stand in the large clearing by Chalkos. Chalkos took a few steps back with his giant head bowed in respect.

Arianell stepped to the edge of the clearing to speak. "My friends, you have delayed yourselves to ensure the safety of my people, and for that we are ever in your debt. The dark magics in Enruk being worked in the shadows took some of us dangerously close to death and for others took something precious."

Chalkos looked away. The once proud dragon felt humbled at this statement as it reverberated through him.

She continued, "Garnet Keep is in danger and you will not be back in time to save it. Unless we help you. One of us has pledged to assist in taking each of you there."

Aryat smirked at Ymir, "Age before beauty, I suppose."

Aryat stepped forward and dropped the staff on the ground. He raised his arms to the sky quickly and they seemed to continue upward and outward until a dragon much larger than Chalkos stood. Cordelia's eyes shimmered as they brimmed with tears.

"I knew it. I just knew it!" She shook happily with her hands over her face in joy.

Towering above in blinding gold, the tendrils of his twin mustaches visibly wavered as he spoke. His voice came to Cordelia's mind as if he was sitting next to her again.

Cordelia, I am Aryat, the Fierce. And I have chosen you.

The twins looked at each other before their serpentine forms of sleek Bronze, similar in size to Chalkos. Their heads came to the shoulder of the towering Aryat, who had now carefully stepped to the back of the group behind Chalkos.

Dabria... I am Ymir, the Swift. Together, you and I can do... great things.

Dabria smiled and nodded, stepping forward in response towards one of the bronze dragons.

Benedict... I am Cemri, Protector of the Sky. You and I shall defend your home.

Benedict saluted her, overcome with shock as he made his way to the other bronze dragon, now almost a mirror image of her twin.

Kogyrus smirked at Una, "Well-" he chuckled sarcastically, "we saved the best for last."

Una saw him change into the reddish gold of brass, thin and appearing almost smaller than the others, but simply just thinner with shorter limbs and more powerful claws. Two rams horns adorned either side of his head. Una was shocked to see her new friend.

"Kogyrus?" She smiled at the dragon behind her dark hood. In the sun, her eyes now appeared both gray.

Yes, Una.. I am known as Kogyrus, the Protector of the Weak. You and I will scout ahead of the group.

"Arianell." Chalkos's voice boomed out in stark contrast to the telepathy of the dragons and their riders. "Will you allow me to take Lorvana back to Garnet Keep as discussed? Hope you don't mind the little one... if you prefer someone else's company I..."

Lorvana looked at Chalkos, a smile stretching across her happy face.

"Oh yes please! That would be wonderful, Chalkos!"

Arianell took a moment before responding. They looked magnificent in the light dancing across their metallic scales. Chalkos was eager to do this task and she noted how close he and the halfling had become. Perhaps she could help him find himself again.

"Loyal Chalkos... Yes... Yes I believe this could do you some good and possibly can regain what you have lost in this journey." She smiled behind her silver gray hair and pale eyes at the group, "Go now, my friends. We wish you all well and may the winds be at your back!"

FIVE SHAPES BURST THROUGH GOLDEN clouds in a champagne sky. The glitter of a million metal scales reflected the soft orange and pink hues of the sunset surrounding them as they flew on high above the hidden earth below.

Benedict, Cordelia, Lorvana, Una and Dabria sat astride their dragon mounts as they flew northeast, finally crossing the Garnet Mountains after four days of traveling north along the western slope and its rocky foothills.

Rhythmically the huge wings beat against the cool evening air, a sliver of pale crescent moon now becoming more visible in the clearer skies. The smell of mountain pine in the thin air was a welcome change from the humid mineral and sulfur of the hot springs previously in the valley. Benedict saw the faint outline of somewhat familiar angular pillars on the mountain slope as the faded ancient road snaked its way down the cliffside to the valley in the distance.

"Is that a dwarven ruin... or maybe a mine?" Benedict thought.

"Not a mine, my dear Benedict, but THE mine." Cemri said to him, "This is the great mine of the Garnet Mountains. Known in your tongue as the Southstone Caverns, the dwarves know it as KadreUnrol."

"Skotmir."

He thought of his friend Skotmir and hoped he and the others had made it out alive. As if sensing this concern in the air, Cordelia felt a thin braid of faded colors now pastel from the sun around her left wrist. Peach and periwinkle, once a strong red and blue over a decade ago, were braided in the child's friendship bracelet given to her in trade by her best friend Sophie.

She felt a calm come over her, not directly but just a feeling that again, her friend was alright.

At the front Kogyrus darted in and out of the clouds quickly, until something caught his attention in the distance.

"Hmm that can't be good." Looking behind them briefly, Kogyrus saw something else on the southeast horizon. Several dark shapes came up through the distant twilight clouds, suddenly bursting into familiar and unwelcome blue and red colors.

He sighed, "Thus it begins." He began to shout back to the group, "My friends, we have some visitors coming at us due east, it appears. A large red and five escorting blues."

Cemri gritted her teeth, "Not the odds I would have hoped for at this time."

Ymir nodded, "As much as they make my blood boil... it would be suicide to engage with them now."

Chalkos looked at his friends, "Lorvana and I will try to draw them higher."

Aryat's deep voice growled, "Agreed... we cannot afford to waste time fighting them! We must get to the Keep and confront them there. Fly, my friends!"

Through the evening, they found themselves followed by five blue dragons and the hulking bodies of two additional red ones in the cold clear moonlight. The riders tried to sleep on the backs of the tireless dragons but found it impossible.

Hour after hour went by as they flew steadily through the night but to their dismay they could see the following dragons slowly gaining their position. A slow, calculated advance. The sun began to rise 30 degrees to their starboard or right side, Cordelia noted in her head. She looked and saw they had reached the valley on the other eastern side of the mountains below.

Here the dragons banked together, following Kogyrus's lead, and began changing course north. Cordelia looked behind, her heart pounding, as she saw the pursuing dragons were now within a hundred yards of them. Now she could make out a rider on one of them in dark armor, carrying a crooked magical staff that glowed green in the dim dawn. Her eyes narrowed as she noticed something missing.

"Aryat, don't- don't stop, they're very close but I only see three blue dragons now."

He growled, "What?... But where did-"

"They are flanking!" Kogyrus interrupted.

"Dabria, do you see them?" Ymir called out.

A blue shape in the dawn's light drew above Dabria, blending with the sky save for its mustard yellow underbelly. Dabria tensed as she saw it and drew closer to Ymir's back.

"Above!" She shouted in the rushing air.

"Die!" the blue dragon screamed.

Dragons of blue and bronze collided for the first time in centuries high above the plains of Trull. Ymir and Dabria spun around moments before the blue dragon met them with all four claws in a powerful strike downward into the clouds.

Ymir could see beyond the blood red eyes of his adversary, peeled back bloodthirsty and cruel. He smirked as he knew this dragon.

"Not this time!" He groaned, "Midnight!"

With a roar, Ymir ripped free of Midnight's grip and quickly ascended back to the group, climbing higher to gain vantage as they sailed through the sky. Swooping quickly to take his place was the swift Kogyrus and Una.

Passing by the slower moving dragons Kogyrus opened his mouth, expelling a pinkish purple cloud into the face of the blue and a large red who was close behind. They reared back, roaring in protest once before their bodies went limp and fell out of the dawn sky.

"Night night, friends! Hope the hills below don't wake you up suddenly! Woah!"

Suddenly, the hulking form of the other larger red dragon moved into his path. Kogyrus strained as the force of the turn threatened to shatter his mighty bones from the quick maneuver. Recovering quickly, he noticed their group weren't their intended target as the red dragon laughed, hovering with the gold Aryat.

"Been a long time Aryat! I see your soft heart is still a problem? Still hugging your precious trees?" She mocked cruelly.

Aryat's voice growled in his chest like an earthquake, "Blaze. I should have guessed you would still be a slave to your abomination of a Dark Queen."

Aryat's golden body reared back as they both answered each other's insults with a cascade of fire streaming from their mouths. The red dragon drove him and Cordelia backwards but the fire reflected harmlessly from his golden scales. Ymir turned to the brave Dabria.

"Take us below them." she commanded.

"Gladly, hold on." Ymir drew in his great bronze wings and transformed back into his human form.

They dropped like a meteor from the sky. The wind rushed past Dabria's ears in a welcome, anticipated rush as she clung to his back. Her blood lifted gently as they fell between and unnoticed by the huge battling forms. Only the sound of the air and his powerful heartbeat was all she could hear and in this moment Dabria felt alive and free. Smiling gently she drew herself closer to Ymir feeling his muscles suddenly tense as they threw his wings out 30 feet below the pair of greater ancient dragons.

Dabria clutched the goat's horn at her neck. "Bless his strike in this moment, dark one."

A shockwave erupted from Ymir as it rippled across the sky, slamming into the much larger red dragon. Blaze roared furiously. "Oof! Why you little- hahaha!!" her anger rolled into a fit of laughter. "You fools choose to side with these ignorant humans instead of embracing your own magnificence!" She shook her head.

"Until next time Aryat!" Blaze turned and dove into the clouds and out of sight. Aryat watched his old adversary depart, surprisingly finding part of himself smirking inside.

"She always was so... hot headed. Impetuous." he sighed with a chuckle, "If she would just relax, take in this wonderful dawn before us like- wait!" a shadow grew quickly in the clouds, "Watch out! Cemri!"

Another blue dragon slammed into Cemri, pushing her and Benedict downward to the thick blanket of clouds. The moist air ripped across their bodies as vision became shrouded in mist like a waking nightmare. The cruel dragon raked Cemri's wing with a mighty claw, leaving it tattered and torn, flapping uselessly in the wind. Cemri roared in pain as she twisted to face him. She drew breath but paused as another form came into view above bursting through the thick blanket of clouds.

"Cemri!" Chalkos yelled to his friend as his wings flapped furiously in the air in an attempt to catch up.

"Chalkos!" Groaning, she wrestled her opponent's grasping talons. "Go back!"

"No! I can't lose you!" His voice panted as he felt his heart pound in his chest. Powerful muscles drove his wings forward. "Not again!"

The blue dragon laughed as they squeezed their talons deeper into Cemri's body. "Your friend can't save you!"

Time slowed for a moment from the pain as Cemri saw the look in Chalkos's eyes through the fog. Panic of being unable to help save their plummeting bodies. His eyes trembled in helplessness. A forgotten memory erupted in her mind.

She remembered him in his human form, long, bright, red orange hair tied back in a series of five braids, one larger one on either side with three small ones down the middle. He was standing in front of a door in the lost temple of Enruk. The thunder of an imminent collapse of rock and stone was growing.

"Back this way!" Kogyrus called back as he ran, "Hurry, Cemri!"

Cemri looked behind her and saw Chalkos draw a broad scimitar from his belt. He nodded to her, "Go now! I'll protect the passage until the kobolds come. Run!"

Cemri could feel her heart pumping in her chest from running, her breath heaving, "No Chalkos! Come with us, don't just wait here for death!"

Chalkos lowered his head solemnly, "I won't lose you my friend. Now, run!"

Cemri opened her eyes from the memory, the path now clear before her. She watched the glow of the approaching sunrise and sighed deeply.

"Please!" Chalkos pleaded as he struggled to gain distance from her, "Cemri!"

Cemri smiled calmly at her old friend, "You won't. Now please save them like you saved us! Get them to Garnet Keep!"

Summoning all her strength Cemri pushed the blue dragon off her with one mighty shove of her hind legs and blasted a shockwave similar to her brother's, knocking the dragon back into a waiting blast of corrosive acid from Chalkos' open maw.

Chalkos swung a powerful claw across its jaw as it shrieked from the burning liquid sprayed across its rippling neck and shoulders. Chalkos gripped it in his claw and grappled, raking a few powerful hind claw attacks across its exposed belly, before it broke free, blasting a crackle of hot blue powerful energy over his shoulder, barely missing his wing. Chalkos struggled to recover and once he did he saw the blue dragon disappear into the fog, flying away from them all.

The sound of the cool dawn wind and his own slowly flapping wings was the only thing he could sense. He looked around in the silent air, his eyes beginning to sting as his heart dropped.

"Cemri."

She was gone. He paused for a moment, thinking of her last words. He nodded at her last wish before explosively pursuing their friends above. A few moments later, he joined the rest of his friends in the clouds above the golden dawn now turning to familiar and clear blue skies.

Aryat saw the look on Chalkos's face, dreading his answer, "Where is Cemri?"

Ymir knew his twin's fate before Chalkos could answer.

"She fell. but I do not feel my twin's-" He paused. The twins were born from one egg. A rare and magical thing for Dragons. They could share bits and parts of feelings and senses. He felt a wash of reassurance and then a call to action.

"She wants us to go!" Ymir shouted, "There is no time."

"This sortie was a sure sign that the keep will soon be attacked, if it wasn't already, and it is still a few hours flight to the north." Kogyrus stated as his breath slowed. He looked at the heartbroken Chalkos. "Come, Chalkos my friend. Fly with me, please."

Chalkos looked at his friend and sighed, nodding. "Of course."

Aryat nodded at the smaller dragons, "Let us fly! We must hurry to Garnet Keep."

As the conversation of the dragons echoed telepathically in Cordelia's mind, she thought of Benedict in the fog below, helpless and lost. The great gold dragon banked hard into the matching golden clouds of the dawn followed by the three other smaller dragons. Ymir looked at her. She thought she saw his strong icy eyes tremble for a quick second before he shook his head, roaring to pass them defiantly.

She felt warm tears stream down her cheeks as she gripped the harness on Aryat's back, drawing herself to him seeking comfort and hope.

CHAPTER 19

WINGS OF FIRE

An old shepherd stood on a quiet hillside northeast of Trull. He had been watching the creeping shadow of the Dark Army approach the ruins of Garnet Keep for the past three days. Though seeming slow in their preparations, there was a method behind their madness that concerned him.

He had warned some friends joining the rebellion a few days ago that he had seen them building up for an attack. Hopefully Benedict Shieldheart, the heir of Garnet Keep, was prepared. He thought of those old days when Lucilius Kettlebane and the six winds watched over the land, before those they protected turned on them.

The farmer sat in his creaky old wooden rocking chair. The dawn country air smelled of grasses and dew kissed meadow flowers. He heard the familiar padded footsteps of paws tapping their nails on the wooden plans slowly. Reaching a hand down without taking his eyes off the golden clouds he felt the warm wet muzzle of the pet jackal. He scratched the dusty tan and gray head as he chuckled, "Hmm, them were the best times. Weren't they boy? Yes, I know." He stopped stretching as he shook a hand back towards the open door behind them, "Go on Toby. Go fetch your master Shimi, I want to talk with them about it."

Toby barked gently looking up at the sky. A faint distant rumble rolled in the air.

"What? What is it?" His voice trailed off as his eyes drifted back to the sky as well, "Oh... my!"

A brilliant glint caught his eye in the clouds reflecting from the rising sun behind him.

"What is it?!" a tall ranger in green leather and deeply tanned skin through open the door out of the small house. His eyes opened wide in wonder.

"Look Shimi!" the old man pointed with a shaking finger.

Bursting from the lower cloud bank he saw what appeared to be a brilliant greenish gold ball that glittered as it plummeted towards the earth a few miles between himself and the Dark Army.

Thin wisps of trailing clouds followed closely, like a falling star.

BENEDICT REMEMBERED FALLING. CEMRI'S GREAT wings, tattered and torn, flapped aimlessly behind them and the rushing air deafened him. She lifted him from the harness on her back and pulled Benedict into her arms like a mother would a small child. Cemri's voice echoed in his mind as they plummeted down through the endless skies.

We.. we will be ok. Trust me Benedict. I swear... I... will not fail you.

The air seemed to swell in an instant, along with a crushing squeeze, then all went black.

Several hours went by before Benedict opened his eyes from a dreamless sleep.The smell of the crushed grasses beneath him was sweet-smelling, mixing with the settled dust on the breeze. The sky was now darkening as he slowly turned his head to see the soft meadow they lay in.

Crickets were beginning their song in the tall grasses surrounded by scattered birch and aspen trees. Looking past the edge of the trees' natural line, he could see the warfires of the camp now a mile or so out, he guessed. Beyond that was the setting sun over the mountains. More importantly Garnet Keep was now mere miles away and up the pass on the other side.

He held his breath to listen.

Judging from the relative silence surrounding them along with no movement, that meant no scouts, he hoped. A labored breath came from behind him. Lying there in her human form was Cemri. Her wise and kind face was marred by the scars of battle. Her breath was heaving and raspy.

Benedict crawled to his knees, feeling the ache of both the crushing impact he was protected from but also laying motionless for these past several hours.

"Oh Cemri."

Her chest heaved slightly and shook with each breath. Realization set in heavily. Her life was leaving her, he had to act quickly. He gently placed his hands on her dirt and bloodied cheeks and lowered his eyes in prayer.

"Knightlord. Please heal this servant of justice. Protect her as she protected me."

The air twinkled around his fingertips in warm yellow sparkles as he felt life giving power pass through his body to hers. Cemri's breath steadied and her eyes gently fluttered open, revealing the yellow green flecked irises adjusting to the dimming light around them.

"Oh... oh I..." Cemri smiled gently at him, "Hello. Benedict." Cemri groaned as Benedict helped her to stand up and survey the land.

"Well, I suppose there could have been worse places to land in. And they-" Cemri pointed at the distant camp, "didn't take notice of our little sky dive." Cemri chuckled, rubbing her sore shoulder.

"We will need to get to Garnet Keep soon. They will be there by tomorrow, I imagine." She took a deep breath and tensed. Frustrated, she stormed away a few steps and tried again. Sighing, she turned to Benedict.

"I cannot return to my natural form with these injuries, Benedict. We will have to get to Garnet Keep by foot. Hopefully Aryat will be there. He... he can help me, he knows the way."

Benedict nodded, his healing skills were spiritual but only very basic. He shrugged with a smile, "Understood. I wish I could do more but I know nothing about dragons."

They chuckled together. Turning around, Benedict could see Cemri's back was covered in large dark red scabs. No longer bleeding but still painful looking.

He felt a wave of deep fear enter him as he remembered her words.

"We are going to have to sneak past the entire Dark Army." He chuckled as Cemri smiled nodding. "Zorin and Zane should laugh at this story, if- I mean when we make it home."

THE COURTYARD OF GARNET KEEP was alive with the laughter of children and lit by the smiles of their parents watching.

"Hello! Ha!" the deep voice of Aryat boomed gently across the crowd.

Cordelia laughed softly as she leaned over towards a young girl smiling with wide bright blue eyes.

"It's ok, little one, go ahead!"

The wide eyed girl stood with her mouth agape as Aryat lowered his great golden head to her. Despite the draconic visage his characteristic mustaches wavered from the corners of a gently smiling maw. His golden eyes were still kind, despite the head being much larger than the young girl.

Cordelia smiled, "It's going to be ok now."

The fire mage looked around, remembering the last few minutes since they landed in the courtyard mounted on four large dragons. She saw Elona and Elloveve, mouths agape as they moved the awestruck crowd out of the way, but Cordelia knew the looks on the faces of the children are what she would remember the most.

All eyes fell on brilliant metallic scales of the dragons that made everyone gasp and stare wide-eyed. All of us but the children.

"Come on!" one little boy called out to his excited friends. They all began to run, laughing happily.

"Daniel! No! Come back here!" his shocked mother called out in vain to him. The children just laughed and fearlessly danced to them, giggling and smiling, ignoring the quiet protests of their parents. Enchanted by magnificence and grace.

Now Cordelia was standing with one, in particular, who had a tribal design of brown henna across the bridge of her nose below her blue eyes and blonde tresses. She had approached Aryat with wonder, holding up a single hand, Aryat dropped his huge head to look at her with his characteristic smile on one side of his face. Cordelia smiled as she bowed slightly while standing next to the teenager.

"I felt the same way too. He's here to help us."

The girl just beamed, wordlessly smiling at Cordelia before turning her gaze back to Aryat.

"What's your name?" Cordelia asked gently but there was no answer. She heard only the footsteps of an approaching friend.

"Her name is Edde, she.. doesn't speak." Zorin smiled at Cordelia, "Go ahead Edde, he's a friend. Welcome home, Cordelia!"

Cordelia wrapped Zorin in a big hug, "Oh Zorin! I missed you."

"Me too kiddo!" he said as he squeezed her tightly.

Edde placed her hand gently on the muzzle of the gold dragon. His eyes closed slightly before he politely pulled back and transformed into his familiar human form. Edde gasped slightly in shock. As did the other children.

"Wow! Cool!" the child named Daniel called back grinning ear to ear happily.

Aryat smiled, "Hello, Edde. Wonderful to meet you but if you'll excuse me." Producing a long staff from gnarled wood he walked towards Zorin slowly. "Zorin? We bring ill tidings, unfortunately. I-" Aryat looked at Cordelia's face as the happiness melted away, leaving the cold reality in its place.

Cordelia held up a hand as she closed her eyes, "Aryat, don't." Opening them she continued as her voice was soft and carefully measured. "I should tell him myself."

"Tell me what? It-" He looked around. Two other dragons slowly took on human forms and walked by their riders, Dabria and Una. The Copper dragon remained in his form, chuckling as children climbed on his back and neck while he lay prone next to a laughing Lorvana.

"Um... Where's Benedict?"

THE VOICES CARRIED THROUGH THE night air from the nearby camp. Two shadows were working their way around the perimeter of the encampment, trying not to draw any attention to themselves but far enough of a distance to where they felt as comfortable as possible in such grim company.

Man, ogre and orc were feasting around the many campfires, the heavy and familiar smell of a thick stew carried alongside it. Benedict's stomach growled. Cemri smiled gently.

"Benedict, what is that wonderful smell?" She said softly. They were well out of earshot but it was best to remain cautious.

"Just beans and ham if I were to guess." The thought of food was becoming tiresome as the last thing he had was an apple yesterday.

Cemri chuckled to herself, "Ah. That makes sense. It has been a long time since I have tasted ham. I did enjoy it so very much–before they all came." She motioned at the army encampment.

Benedict looked at her, "Cemri, how long were you imprisoned in Enruk?"

"It felt like a long time to be sure, but only a decade in that dark dungeon according to what we've been able to piece together. Though they took their time. They set that trap slowly and carefully."

He furrowed his brow, "How do you mean?"

"Well, it started well before that fateful day, when you found us of course. Possibly a quarter century ago I believe?" She chuckled. "I imagine that would be... a few years before you were even born, dear Benedict."

"Benedict shook his head with a smirk, "Yes. I actually just turned twenty not too long ago."

Cemri smiled. "I'm quite a bit older but I hold no disrespect." she sighed, "We were guests and protectors of our friends, the kobolds. Not rulers, mind you, but guardians. It was our service to travel to Enruk periodically, and assist them with what we could. Guidance or the occasional building, we were treated as the experts and they all looked up to us, but–"

Her voice trailed off as she heard cackling from the camp. Memory washed over her mind briefly, unpleasant memory of that cell they lived in for so long. The greasy walls and hot humid air they shared clouded her emotions, leaving a hot pit in her heart. Benedict, sensing her uneasiness, allowed some silence to pass for a few moments, before prompting quietly.

"But what, Cemri? Please go on."

"There's no denying, my friend, that we–" She took a deep sigh, "We were treated like royalty and we grew accustomed to it. When Maldros came, he showed them another way. A way of money and commerce."

"They opened up trade routes with the barons, and the minotaurs of the north found a way with their shallow drafted ships to navigate to that once isolated city. We saw the signs, Benedict, but we ignored them. It was their actions and only affected them after all, not us. It was easier for us to ignore the threat and go about our way."

"We left and returned the following year as planned. The arena was being built where one of the many temples once stood. No matter. We had other temples erected to us, dragons we didn't need that one. Soon they began to hold games there. Feats of strength and dexterity, and one day, an accident on the field as two kobolds locked in sparring led to one's death."

Cemri sighed as she looked at the night sky.

"The crowd cheered, yet still we ignored it. We were reminded it was not our way. A way that only cost a few lives, it seemed. No big matter. Over the years our visits were met with less and less enthusiasm from our friends. We slowly faded out of their favor to this new arena, but there were a few dedicated people who ensured we enjoyed all our previous luxuries. Unfortunately this kept us blind to what was happening around us over those years."

"Then Pallus and Dekkion returned, with that crown and our wicked hearted cousins.

She paused for a moment as they carefully stepped through the soft meadows well outside the campfire light, shrouded in darkness. They could see the outline of huge hulking bodies now, on the far side of the camp thankfully. The unmistakable red and blue scales moved as they too enjoyed their feast before what they saw to be the eve of another great victory.

"There is no love between us as dragons Benedict. The metallic dragons took oaths long ago to uphold justice and balance throughout the land where we saw fit." She chuckled, "You see how comfortable we are in our other forms? Honestly, I rather enjoy it, getting to walk with someone such as you and discuss things in the world or share stories without it being awkward."

She closed her eyes and took in a deep breath of the night air, the smell was comforting.

"Hmm, I have to say. If this wasn't the dire situation it is, with the current disagreeable company we have close by and despite this searing pain in my back." She chuckled, " I'd say this is a great evening- walking with a great friend."

Benedict nodded smiling, "I agree, thank you. So what of the other dragons, do they have human forms as well?"

Cemri looked in the distance at the dragons of the Dark Army. "Oh yes, Benedict. We all have another form. Though not all are human specifically. It just depends on the dragon and the people they interact with."

She held up her hands to show how much they looked like his.

"You see, my home and elders believe the form is a gift. So we are actually weaned off our dragon form at the time we enter this world."

"How?" Benedict asked. Cemri closed her eyes, remembering a not too pleasant memory.

"Well, actually, you saw something similar in the defiler's chamber beneath the temple. Through magic, the dragon essence is removed. The dark clerics used a similar method based on what they found out about our way, but whereas we just put to sleep that part of our being- waiting for the right moment to be discovered- they tapped it and tried to remove it altogether for their own purposes."

"Our cousins believe, to my understanding, that the form is a weakness and they prefer to use it only for stealth and deception. We believe we should walk the land with the various peoples for a time before being granted our true form. To teach us-"

"Humility." Benedict finished, nodding in understanding.

"Yes."

"That explains why each of you is so unique. Ymir is so different looking than you."

Cemri chuckled warmly, "Ha! Yes. My brother spent much of his time in northern Kur, embracing the desert nomad culture. I actually stayed on this continent, enjoying my time traveling throughout the Glen Valley and Darkovnia- but this was all hundreds of years ago."

The weight of that statement listed on the night breeze gently as the two companions continued their journey. Then something shot through Benedict's mind briefly, something familiar but long forgotten until now.

"You said a crown. That Pallus had a crown. What did it look like?"

"It has five gems, each representing one of our cousins: ruby, sapphire, emerald, diamond and jet. They are all twisted together in snakelike tendrils of metal. The followers of the dragon queen believe it is the mark of her champion, and those dragons that follow her would gladly serve the bearer. There is no mistake, Benedict. It is the cursed Crown of Dragons."

She hesitated to continue as she saw his face pale as all warmth left it.

"Have you seen it?" She asked gently, fearing the answer.

Benedict closed his eyes, remembering his friends in the old mine outside OlanAkKhan. When Zane placed a crown they had found on his head, froze up, panicked, and finally threw it off his head. His younger self had looked at his older brother.

"Are you alright Zane?"

"No one, I mean no one should put that on. Come on, let's go."

Zane had strapped the crown to his belt, he remembered, and carried it up until he had confronted Dekkion.

"Come child and let me show you the darkness of my queen!"

Zane had fallen at the feet of Dekkion and Pallus that fateful night. Benedict could see the crown lying next to him now, in the rain and mud as they ran away. As the cold rain and soft footsteps faded in his memory he sighed looking up at the stars pleadingly. After a moment he took a deep breath and turned to Cemri.

"Yes." Benedict lowered his eyes and shook his head with a sigh, "Yes, I have seen it before."

THE TORCHES BURNED ON THE hard granite walls of Garnet Keep as we each leaned over the great table covered in a few maps and blueprints we had found. Some were dusty schematics showing how things were built in the first age of the structure, during the dawn of the knights over a millenia ago. Only one seemed to be updated, and I recognized Lucilius's handwriting.

"This is the smuggler's path." I chuckled, "Looks like Lucilius knew about it and kept it secret from me as well."

Elona shrugged, "I don't remember it either, don't feel so bad, Keldor. He had his reasons I'm sure."

Zorin nodded, "Yeah. He sounds like a smart guy. I was always told if you tell one person a secret it's ok but tell two and you might as well tell everyone." He looked at Lorvana.

She looked perplexed but nervous. Battle wasn't something she was good at, he wagered and to be fair, he felt the same. He smiled and realized they still had a place in this where they could help.

Lorvana and I aren't much good in an open conflict. Anyways, we will take a few others into the smuggler's path and just ensure it's defended.

"Sounds great!" Lorvana chirped, "Hey, I can try out that alarm spell Cordelia taught me!" She weaved her hands around them and posed a few times trying to seem like a great wizard. Zorin laughed as Una shook her head.

Ymir cleared his throat. The shadows that were stronger on his side of the table illuminated everyone's hair but his bald head. that glistened in the torchlight. He motioned to the map of the northern perimeter he was looking at. It was the only way they could assault the meadow and the keep itself.

"I suggest these trenches here we ensure are trapped and hidden. It will funnel their ground forces through the canyon." he growled confidently with his braided chin wagging as Dabria ran a hand over her burr cut head.

"Agreed. Knowing their tactic, they will lead on the ground first before bringing in the Dragons. Their hope will be to come back here." She gestured to the mouth of the meadow at the base of the Canyon marked as Beartrap Meadow, "The ballista will be the biggest threat to them in the air."

Sophie leaned in, her long blonde hair falling over her shoulder. "I will help guard those."

"Excellent Sophie." Elloveve smiled, her lavender eyes glistened as she turned to me. "I'll take Lamprey and the archers up the canyon wall on this flank. We should have a solid view of the meadow below."

"Good." I nodded, standing up. The cotton jerkin I was wearing was soft and warm, but my shoulders were anticipating the weight of my plate armor again. "Sounds like we have the best plan possible now."

It was silent as I looked around the dim war room. It was great to have so many of us back and the advantage given with these great dragons who came to assist us in this time of need was immense.

One was missing though, as was one of our members. My eyes fell on Elona. Her sandy blonde hair framed her blue eyes as they met mine. Wordlessly she could sense my thoughts as a rose colored lip trembled slightly in opposition to her clenched jaw.

"Excuse me." She whispered as she turned on her heel.

I watched Una, Kogyrus and the rest of the group step away to allow her to leave the room.

Who could understand what was going through her head? The siege on her home? Her missing son, Benedict?

All these terrible memories now manifesting themselves again like a terrible dream. My heart went to her. I waved my hand.

"We can all disperse overnight." May the Knight and Maiden watch over us on the battlefield tomorrow. and above all else, do not lose hope."

Everyone began to leave, but I noticed Zorin standing by the window looking out upon the courtyard. The giggles of children could be heard faintly as the parents gathered them to rest as well. I stepped next to my friend as I peered down to see Chalkos speak kindly to each one, wishing them a good night. I leaned on the window frame, feeling the cold stone on my fingers as dusk sun fell on my face. It was getting late, and tomorrow would prove to be a long day.

"He's got the right heart to defend them. You made a wise suggestion, Zorin, keeping him here."

"Thank you. Keldor. I appreciate it. I'm not used to making decisions." He turned from me towards the door where everyone was leaving, "Kogyrus, do you have a moment?"

Kogyrus turned from leaving the room with Una, placing a gentle hand on her shoulder. She nodded in understanding as he strode to join us. His hard soles of his dark brown boots clacked on the floor gently.

"Yes? What do you need?"

"Chalkos." Zorin nodded out the window, "Is there a reason he refuses to change into his human form?"

I saw the mood of Kogyrus darken slightly as he looked out into the twilight of the evening.

"He doesn't refuse to my friend." Kogyrus looked compassionately at the gentle dragon. "He would if he could."

"What do you mean?"

"When we polymorph between our forms, we speak something very special. A word only we know. We learn it as we go on our journey as young ones. We clad ourselves as humans or whatever people we wish to associate with. My baby sister, for example, last I heard was traveling in the forests around the Silver Maple Woods searching for her word. No doubt dressed as an elf."

"You see we have to learn to coexist with you all. It's not a mere suggestion, our culture dictates it. The word comes to us when we least expect it. It just- is, and it's ours, and only ours, individualized for each dragon."

Zorin looked at Kogyrus, "And what happened to Chalkos?"

Kogyrus's eyes softened slightly as he looked at his ancient friend, the last light of the sun dancing in the metallic flecks of his eyes.

"Chalkos stayed behind when we tried to escape Enruk many years ago, when Maldros and Pallus turned the kobolds against us. They captured him with some new dark magic, leaving him in his draconic form, wiping his mind of everything, but his will was too powerful."

Gently one of the beads on Kogyrus's mustache rose up in a smile, "-and he was able to hold on to one thing. Not a word, but a concept."

"What was that?"

"The last thing he promised anyone. That he would defend that hall from any enemies."

Kogyrus sighed as his voice became softer.

"When Chalkos was overrun he was told we had all died. In guilt and grief from failure, he swore allegiance to the kobolds and their new-" His voice began to shake in anger, "friends."

"Chalkos agreed to stand watch and never let them escape. Those who he believed killed his friends. Killed us! But not know-ing-" His voice broke as he lowered his head. Kogryrus sighed as he closed his eyes tightly, feeling the sting of old tears blossoming. He heard the children's voices below, distant voices of joy as they played with their new friend. His eyes fluttered open and fell on Zorin and I pleadingly.

"Zorin, can't you see? W..we thought he died. For ten years we thought our brother died, and we were actually only separated by a few yards and the stone walls of that dungeon."

Kogyrus watched the children say goodnight and walk away as the shining form of Chalkos curled up on the ground alone once more. Resting his head on his tail he watched the sky dim and the stars begin to appear softly. I saw the great copper dragon's chest heave with a heavy sigh.

Kogryus wiped his eyes on his sleeve. "As it turned out I guess, he thought we had, too."

CHAPTER 20

THORN OF THE ROSE

Sunlight began to shine through panes of stained glass, casting sky and rose colors on the clasped gauntlets before my eyes.

"Protect us, Knightlord, as we protect those who cannot protect themselves. In this we pray."

I stood and looked at the temple. A stained glass knight holding a shield at his feet, emblazoned with a red sword and crown, his helm bowed slightly in reverence. A depiction of the Knightlord, bowing himself to the divine each of us holds in our hearts. I walked to the doorway, stopping by the font of water. I peered inside and saw my face, tired but ready. I drew my long sword and, holding the blade down, placed it against my chest.

"Blessed be this blade on this day. May it strike true if our duty proves to be virtuous."

Placing two fingers into the small fountain, I drew a single bead of fresh spring water that broke the light like a perfect diamond. Placing it at the hilt I bowed in respect as it ran the length of the fuller from hilt to point. I stood and walked out the temple door to the courtyard of Garnet Keep.

The sky was shimmering with gold and violet hues as the sun rose beyond the walls of the Keep. I made my way across the courtyard, passing by the great oak tree. I smiled at its magnificence and absentmindedly nodded at the old friend as if she could hear me, and part of me wished she could.

"Keldor, we have prepared the trenches and readied the ballista as ordered.

I knew Demtri's voice enough to recognize the young knight was addressing me but it didn't break my gaze from that ancient oak.

"Good," I said absently.

"Anything else sir?" His words rang in my ears as I paused for a moment to gather my thoughts. I stood there in the center of the courtyard, the tree, temple and the keep itself now behind me. Beyond the young officer I saw the smithy, quartermaster, supply and the stable.

The same stable I lost my faith, friends and a former life in so long ago. How far we have come.

"Sir?"

"Oh! I'm sorry, Demitri." I shook myself loose of the ghosts of my past momentarily, No. No, there's nothing more, thank you."

"Yes sir." He turned to walk away.

"Wait. Demitri."

"Sir?"

I held my hand up in a blessing to the young man. "May the Knight and Maiden guide you and your charge today."

He nodded and I could tell this pleased the soldier, "Thank you, sir."

I saw him smile slightly as he straightened the black and red tunic he wore over heavy chain and splint armor. The plate was heavy, but even the chain and splint the infantry wore was quite the burden to move in.

As I made my way to the stables I recalled Demetri was a young Knight and great horseman from the Celestine Tower. He had family in Kur and had requested to join us once the keep had been reclaimed as it put him closer to home.

I approached the worn wooden gate and pushed. The sound of old ancient hinges groaned as it opened, and I chuckled to myself as it echoed my own aging joints. I saw a forge mark on the hinge and my chuckle turned to laughter. Erebus had forged this hinge when we all lived here together.

I heard the young bray and snort of another friend waiting to greet me.

"Well hello, Feather Breeze." Walking to the center of the stable, I brushed my hand over the head to scratch the ears of my horse, being groomed by two young squires. I continued to coax my steed. "Yes, good to see you too. What's that? A carrot? Of course!"

I held a carrot to her muzzle, which she gently took from the palm of my hand happily. I placed my cheek against the white star marking on her chestnut forehead and smiled. I ran my hand down the side of her powerful neck.

"Are we ready young one?" I asked her in a hushed whisper, "Shall we ride off into storybooks and legends together? You and I?"

She gently pulled back with a bright whinny, her ears alert and forward to me. I chuckled.

"Well let's not keep destiny waiting. Squire Tully?"

I called to one of the squires wearing a chain coif.

"Yessir? A... Are you ready for us to suit her up?" She said to me with warm brown eyes.

"Please, and thank you."

I waited a moment as I saw two other squires wheel in the heavy tack she would be wearing, both to protect her and keep me in proper position. Plate and chain formed protection for her head and an ornate chest plate depicting a single eagle's feather in the center. Not anything menacing, but I smiled as it reminded me of her spirit. I saw my saddle, one of the only things showing the leather it was made from; and the muslin skirt and matching chain and plate to keep us mobile but protect her flanks. I nodded slightly as I left them to their duty.

Walking out into the courtyard again, I made my way up the stairs to the outer wall and stone battlements. I walked towards the ballista perched in its corner like a large bird of prey. As my feet plodded on the high stone wall I noticed a familiar group of friends below me huddled up with Chalkos and a young boy who had brought them all a gift.

"MMM! Truly delicious!" Chalkos boomed deeply.

Aryat laughed as he leaned on his staff, "Seriously! Taste it! Ask the children Kogyrus." He sighed before he turned to the young boy, "Little Daniel, is this not the most delicious apple you have ever tasted?"

The child laughed, "Yeah! It's great!"

Kogyrus joined in the laughter, holding up his hands in surrender, "Fine! Fine! Wise one. I'm sure it's amazing!"

The dragons had said they were ready and now stood in the courtyard in their humanlike forms with Cordelia, Una and Dabria, who would accompany them into battle. The hulking shining form of Chalkos was there too, though he and Elona would be guarding the Keep. They would retain order behind these high walls and protect those within who were unable to defend themselves.

As I drew closer to the Ballista I heard Sophie addressing the other fighters who were the most skilled in operating the devastating weapon.

"Yes, the skies. We will save the first wave for them." She paused, seeing my approach. "Keldor."

"Hello Sophie. All is well?"

"Yes, we are ready as we ever will be."

"Excellent. May the Knight and Maiden guide you today."

She smiled at me slightly and looked back at the ballista. I could tell she was not handling this well. "And you too. I guess."

"Hey," I said softly to her, "You know what, I remember standing right here long ago. Nervous as you are, before we rode out to join in the battle of the Cheerless Swamp. Erebus met me here and placed his hand on my shoulder."

Mirroring what I remembered, I placed a hand on her shoulder. *Keldor, what say you old friend?*

I paused. I could hear his deep voice in my memory as if he were right here again standing next to me. Ready to meet the challenge together as we had so many times before. I looked into Sophie's eyes and she smiled as if she could hear him too.

"STEADY NOW!"

The roar of horses' hooves and heavy armor filled our ears as Dimirtri shouted to the nine riders to our left.

"The Knightlord rides with us!" I answered and relayed to the nine riders to my right, "Push them back!"

Twenty of us rode out on horseback to assist the hundred or so souls on foot in our first attack on what remained of their mercenary vanguard. Before our galloping charge we could see the battle line approaching the thirty foot twin lion statues at the edge of the bridge leading back to the Keep behind us. They stood rampant, facing each other, their front paws locked in some eternal wrestle that created a unique archway, greeting those who would be friends and also narrowing any ground assault to the Keep, funneling them to the only choice. The one hundred foot long, twenty foot wide stone bridge across the deep chasm that we rode out on.

"Now fire!"

Sophie's call and the sound of the ballista rocketing overhead snapped my attention to the skies, and away from the dark shadow of ground troops we soon would engage with at the front line.

My blood grew cold as I heard the roar of dragons. I saw the blue and red dragons swooping over the far cliffside onto the former meadow from the jagged peaks. Men fell out of the way as the ballista fire drove the would-be assailants from landing their first attack.

Reaching the end of the bridge, our troops parted, allowing us the ability to splash into the first several ranks of their troops, carving a path with our swords and the heavily armored bodies of our brave horses.

I heard the whistling rain of feathered arrows as I swept my blade into the surge of attacking warriors. I saw their left flank fall in a flurry of arrows as cheers erupted from the cliffside.

As planned, Elloveve stood to our left on the high cliffside one hundred yards away with her group of longbowmen. They began launching volley after volley, driving the group further to our right and eastward.

High above, Kogyrus slammed into a blue dragon, blasting its face with a fountain of fire as he clutched it in his powerful front mitt-like claws. The fire washed over its face and back, engulfing the armorclad rider in the red orange flames.

Terrified and screaming, the surprised rider fell from his mount, his arms flailing helplessly as flames trailed behind his plummeting body. With a deep growling roar, Ymir flew past, raking the ranks behind pouring out of the canyon with lightning. A familiar blue dragon swooped in from above blasting Ymir with crackling white hot energy of its own.

"Dabria, watch out it's Midnight!" Ymir shouted in rage.

Lightning streaked across the sky. Ymir, who was struck in the left wing, shook it off.

"Hello again, cousin!" He bellowed as the two dragons collided briefly in the air with teeth and claws. As they struggled a nine foot wooden bolt ripped into the Blue dragon mere feet from Dabria. She looked wide eyed back to the keep at the shrugging Sophie, who was faintly standing proud by the war machine.

Dabria smirked with a chuckle, "Good shot."

Midnight fell from his home in the sky into the vast ravine, his powerful wings unable to obey him as his life escaped from the wound in his throat. The once great veteran of many battles found himself tumbling hundreds of feet to the icy rapids below.

We cheered as their remaining vanguard ran back to regroup. Almost as soon as silence fell across the meadow it was replaced by the echo of resonant warhorns. A single note reverberated across the cliffside.

Our hearts sank as we heard the chilling sound of the marching horde of shambling forms now appearing out of the canyon. Lines and lines of the animated dead, mindlessly marching into Beartrap Meadow from the path cut in the faraway canyon.

"Milord! The dead have set upon us!" I heard Demitri's voice tremble as he shouted to me from his mount.

"Steel yourself Demitri!" I called back, summoning courage and strength to meet this next foe without fear.

The sky was darkening now. The clouds in the sky were driven by some dark, powerful magic, shielding the dead from the life-giving rays of the sun. I looked at my blade, past the dark blood now staining it. I concentrated on the blessing I had placed upon it this morning.

"Knightlord, please guide my hand. Help me to send these rest-less souls to the ferryman's realm where they may find peace-" My prayer stopped short as something caught my eye in the distant right flank, along the cliffside.

Two sprinting figures held each other up as they navigated the rocky slope down to the valley alongside the dead army.

The army kept its rhythmic march without noticing the pair and something was different about them besides just being alive.

"Archers! Ready!"

I wasn't the only one who noticed them. Elloveve stood on the cliffside opposite them all, archers waiting patiently and disciplined for her command.

"Who are you?" She spoke under her breath, "Not orcs, is that one a mercenary?"

"No, that's the armor of an officer Captain!" Lamprey called back to her. "Should I take them out?" he drew back the bowstring and locked his shoulder and elbow, waiting for her orders.

"Yes a dark army officer but the other is-" Her eyes narrowed focusing on the faraway pair, "He is helping to carry an unarmed woman? Wait!"

A memory ripped through her mind. She also stood elevated but surrounded by flames, her children running to safety as she protected their escape on the streets of Port L'For. She saw Benedict running beside Zane, and he was running just like this officer was.

"Wait" She yelled, "Archers hold your fire!"

She pointed at the shambling infantry and those undead closest to the fleeing pair on the meadow.

"There! Protect them!" Answering her own command she drew a pair of arrows and with a shout shot them into the horde, dropping two rotting corpses to the dirt. More arrows followed suit, dropping them one by one and making a path for the fleeing pair as they touched the meadow grasses and ran holding onto each other.

Each one was holding the other up in a fatigued run. I saw them now, I saw who it was and I wasn't the only one. I heard Cordelia's voice from above call out, "Benedict! Beneeeeeediiiiiict!!!!"

The huge gold form of Aryat raced overhead as Benedict and Cemri tried to outrun the thousands of undead pouring slowly into the grassy meadow. I felt a drop of rain strike my cheek. Then another, in those seconds.

Aryat snorted as he summed up the situation quickly, "Hold on Cordelia! Trust me."

With one huge golden claw he reached back and plucked her gently from his back, bringing her underneath his broad chest as he swooped quickly downward over Benedict and Cemri.

Landing heavily on the ground he swept his giant wings in an arc and drew them back, over his body and his three friends, creating a dome to protect them. Mindless zombies and skeletons attempted to drive their dull and rusty weapons into the form, swarming over it like ants would a careless grasshopper.

The remainder of the dead army continued its assault towards us.

"To battle my friends! Charge!" I called as again we continued to assault their legion. I felt searing pain as a rusty spear drove through my left calf, knocking my foot out of the stirrup and tossing me from Feather Breeze to the hard ground.

Though the ground had taken my wind I rose quickly, leading with my trusted shield to push them back and clear a way for my next sword attack. I chopped hard across the shoulder of one skeletal warrior who shrieked, disintegrating into ancient dust and ash and leaving nothing but the remnants of the rusty chainmail upon the ground.

Pressing forward my blade bit hard into the next skull, eyes empty save a faint blue green glow deep within. It drove its jawless head downward before they too evaporated. I stepped to the new clearing I had created with new, stronger footing to face a familiar figure. Teal warpaint surrounded his eyes and pulled down a rotting alabaster face into twin points like assassin's daggers. I knew this was Loukas, the warrior Benedict had fought in single combat at the tower.

Just like I had seen him that night from the nightwatch's wall, His red copper hair hung to the shoulder and he wore the midnight tunic emblazoned with what appeared to be a smeared dark blue teardrop, but inverted as if flowing upwards. As I drove my sword downward across his body, releasing him of his curse, I noticed the tattered blue and black tabards of fallen Celestine knights behind him.

My now undead brothers and sisters were mixed with the rotting bodies of the undead dark army. To my horror they had all returned like the crawling rebirth of a former battleground we were too familiar with. Now they were all my enemy. How long I could keep my guard up against this tide of the undead would only be a matter of moments, I knew.

I willingly pressed on into the fray. I could see Demetri still mounted and mobile twenty or so yards away. Then time seemed to slow as shrieking unearthly sounds filled our ears in the green mist that was rising.

I saw a dark rider appear a few ranks back, slowly marching upon a dead black mare. The rusted and broken armor of the steed fell and waved slowly around exposed ribs like cloth on a wind. Her mane matched her rider's blue black hair, moving in the same dread breeze. A graceful hand held an unholy longsword clad in blue fire, eyes burning like blue white embers shining behind her face. A face like you and I, one that was once possibly very beautiful and somewhat familiar.

I heard her voice. It was dark, raspy and cruel. "In the name of Lord Pallus, die!"

Horror set in as I saw her wading through her soldiers to strike downward into Demetri's shoulder. The burning blade found its mark, driving him and his steed to be lost in the dark surge below. Her eyes fell on me.

"You. Paladin. Your time has come to pay the Ferryman."

I was frozen in fear. A darkness shrouded my heart and eyes, a darkness without the light of the Maiden's grace. The skeletal warriors stepped around me, obviously ignoring their dark commander's new quarry. All hope left my heart as I pulled my shield closer to my chest.

I was absolutely doomed.

"Dabria! Now!" Ymir shouted, snapping my eyes upward to the sky.

As if answering my prayers, a shape had descended above me. Ymir swooped low to where Dabria leaped fearlessly towards the dark rider. Her armor shone brighter in the light, her arms outstretched. My darkened eyes cleared in that moment to witness her like a dove's approach to land. I saw her twist in the air to mount behind her target, grasping the reins and her hand.

"What? Who?!" the dark commander protested as Dabria reached around her for the reins..

Dabria smiled at me as she pulled those reigns, plunging them back to be swallowed by the tide of the undead.

AS THE SHROUD OF THE skeletal army washed around them, separating them from the battlefield physically, Dabria willed their minds and spirits to a single shared space. A familiar space for both.

A black sand beach under a rose-gold dawn.

She felt the sand and water around her feet as she sat at the edge cradling her lover in her arms while they looked out across the glistening tide.

"Hello, my sunbeam."

Nightblade's eyes opened and were clear again, filled with life. The smell of the surf was sweet on the cool breeze. They were alone and together again.

She trembled in Dabria's arms, "I... I remember."

"Shh... please. One more moment." Dabria's soft voice was warm against her cheek, "Let's just wait. One more moment. Please?"

Dabria inhaled deeply, smelling lavender oil in Nightblade's black hair mixed with the salt sea. She placed a cheek upon a soft shoulder, committing the embrace to her treasured memories. Then, as if remembering her duty, she pulled back and smiled.

"I've missed you."

"And I you-" Nightblade's lips pulled back in a soft smile Dabria remembered too well. "but... Dabria- why? Why did you leave? Leave us? Leave this?" Her voice broke slightly as her once silent heart pounded again in her chest.

"I've realized he's not the savior we thought he was." Dabria closed her eyes bracing for the impact her words might bring.

"What?" Nightblade shook her head, long black hair spilling over her shoulder. "No... you are mistaken."

Dabria looked into her lover's deep blue eyes. Eyes that matched the ocean behind her. Her devotion to Dabria was only matched by her devotion to Lord Pallus. The man who supposedly saved her from sharing the fate of a destroyed village and lost family. Then Dabria's heart broke, as she recognized these same eyes.

"Good shot." Dabria mumbled as she shook her head gently.

"What?" Nightblade questioned. Dabria just smiled as she held her shoulders in the palms of her hands and looked deep into her eyes.

"I know you feel differently but, hear me out. I have found some that have seen him spread darkness across the land. Lord Pallus is actually helping those that took everything away from us, and Dekkion-"

"What of him?" Nightblade interrupted sternly. "Dabria, you know my village was destroyed and Pallus saved me. And Dekkion? He's a wise old man only determined to give the world a better place. A place without death."

Dabria paused, knowing she had to choose her words wisely. Nightblade would likely not understand or share her feelings about him. Dekkion the Dark Cleric was able to control and twist the truth... it would likely set them against each other.

"Do you believe he ended death for you?"

The sound of distant thunder from an approaching storm was her only answer.

Nightblade looked at Dabria with a sadness behind those eyes, as the scene around them slowly began to fade. Her eyes were now replaced with those glowing blue white embers, and her skin became taut and papery as the sky grew dark.

"No. I didn't mean-" Dabria's voice cracked weakly, as she pleaded, "Not yet. Please?"

Dabria drew back a tear as the last wave hit the black sand shore only to become the outlined shattered helmet of a passing undead soldier.

The battlefield was an unwelcome change for both lovers now standing on the ground. Nightblade looked around and sheathed her sword.

"Dabria. I-" She sighed as her unearthly voice rasped out from behind the glowing blue eyes, "I'll give you this day."

She stared at her before closing her eyes, the blue light twinkling for a moment.

"Thank you for sharing one more moment with me."

Nightblade turned to the shambling mare and mounted. Thrusting her hand upward the horde began fading into a teal colored glow. We witnessed thousands of skeletal warriors and wraiths change into this singular mist.

Dabria also held a single hand outstretched to Nightblade. To her sunbeam. Nightblade took it gently without hesitation, smiling while interlocking their fingers.

"Goodbye."

I saw them as the last thing on that now empty battlefield. Two lovers locked in an eternal struggle to free their entwined souls from their shared burden. Each trying to save the other.

As the final skeletal figures disappeared, and the sun began to peek from the fading clouds, their dark commander was the last to leave the battlefield.

Dabria stood there in sudden silence.

As we stood there motionless we heard another distant horn sounding.

"K... Keldor? Is that more of them?"

I ran to him with new found hope, "Demitri! Oh thank god you live. I... don't know. Make ready!" I shouted to the troops that were still standing.

I nodded as our surviving force flowed together, regrouping and anticipating this next wave. Weak and breathless, they bravely came to each other's side.

I saw a few more horses approaching from the keep. Riding one of them was Sophie.

"Keldor you can't keep me out of this one," She shouted as she galloped up to me, "as fun as that ballista is this is where I belong."

All re-grouped save one.

"What is she doing? Dabria! Don't be a fool!" Sophie shouted.

Dabria hadn't moved from her position in the last ten minutes. She just drew her whip in solitary defiance, as if preparing to meet this army herself.

We could hear the rhythmic drums and disciplined, marching footsteps growing louder as the army appeared in the canyon, but it was not what was expected. Instead of dark and sinister colors, the standards of twin axes were seen on red, blue and green banners. Huge carts rolled behind rhinoceros and at the front they were led by a unit of dwarves riding armored warpigs.

We all began cheering, recognizing them as the dwarves of the Garnet Mountains came to help us. Sophie's deep blue eyes washed in hope.

"Oh my god! Can it... can it be? She grunted as she spurred her horse into a fast run. "Yah!" Tears streamed down her cheeks as Sophie galloped across the meadow, now bathing in bright sunlight. The army was a welcome sight but she rode towards one figure. His unwashed face with its bulbous nose peeled back in a wide grin.

"Hahaha! Sophie!" Skotmir shouted with his fist high in the air, "My sister!"

Grinning, Sophie dove off the horse, tackling Skotmir off the large boar he rode. Laughing, the two reunited friends rolled on the ground as we all cheered.

THE TAVERN WAS ALIVE WITH much joy that night. Cordelia sat with Arayat and they discussed their love for magic. She laughed as he displayed small cantrips across the table.

Elona laughed with Benedict, as he told a story about Zane's antics. A mother and a wife who had, until recently, thought she was no longer either was with the boy who survived the fire in her memory and the journey across the battlefield.

Cemri and Ymir listened to Kogyrus and Una talk about philosophy and theory. Neither quite understood what was being discussed but Ymir smiled at his twin and gingerly placed an arm around her, avoiding the mint-smelling bandages on her back and neck.

Keldor and Elloveve had been pulled apart by faith and duty, but even after her supposed death they were finally together, loving each other as only those that shared their years of pain could.

Lorvana snuck off to bury herself in her room of blankets, finding some trinkets as gifts she would show Chalkos in the morning.

Behind the keep, on the parapet overlooking the moonlit lake, two figures stood. The sounds of the tavern behind them were drowned a little by the raging waterfall.

"Sophie. I haven't been completely truthful to you." Dabria spoke softly, "I just didn't know how to say-"

"No." Sophie held up a trembling hand, "I saw. I wondered if, and I hoped but I saw her. Didn't I?"

"Yes."

"So Nightblade-" Sophie hung her head and sniffed, "That's what happened to my sister... Oh, Kartilaan." She sobbed.

Dabria placed a single arm across Sophie's shoulder as they both felt the release of knowing and realization wash over them. As the moon spilled her light across the gentle water of the lake, Dabria and Sophie thought of their love for the same woman.

The woman that raised both of them, one as a sister and mother where else there was none; the other as a mentor and lover in a dark life within the army.

In the pale light they looked out on the water together, washed in the memory of the one that, despite everything they knew, they still loved. The one who ended the bloodshed today because of her love.

Dabria and Sophie held each other on that cold stone wall realizing, love's flames can never die and its power truly has no boundaries.

- Una's Vision -

EPILOGUE

Maldros held the Satchel in his hand as he sat on the broken slate boulder.

Come Maldros, why so sad?

We are captured. Why shouldn't I be sad?

It's not that bad. We know those that hold you… Look, their emblem is a snake on a black shield with a gold bend. That is the Kettlebanes.

The sound of footsteps echoed in the temple's great hall pulling the warrior from his memories. Maldros looked up at the throne where Lord Pallus once sat but now stood next to it feeling the intricately carved armrest with his hand.

"Maldros." The powerful voice rolled in the hall, "We need to return to the Obsidian Fortress. We leave tomorrow."

Maldros thought of the arena, grunting in annoyance.

"Fine."

"The arena can run without you, Maldros." Dekkion's voice hissed behind him, "You should take the chance to check up on the pits in Wolfling anyways."

The cold deathlike hands of the necromancer patted his shoulder as he passed by. The smell of myrrh and aloe filled him, reminding Maldros of entombed bodies.

"What drives us there now?" Maldros growled.

Dekkion chuckled and looked at Lord Pallus. Lord Pallus stepped off the dias and strode across the floor to Maldros, his face dark.

"We have received word that the Green Heartstone was shattered in the underworld."

"How?" Maldros's eyes widened under his helmet. "That means-"

"Yes." Dekkion sneered, "because of these fools the ancient darkness is rising, but-"

Dekkion chuckled as he wrung his talon-like fingers together, "It also has allowed some spirits to be set free, some of whom still owe me a debt I absolutely plan to collect."

Dekkion giggled eerily as he held the palm of his hand out. Wisps of green black smoke formed the hull and three masts of a ship he animated to bob as if on the ocean.

Maldros snorted, "What of my revenge?!" he growled.

Dekkion raised an eyebrow as he dismissed the apparition, "Patience Maldros. Those that enslaved you will pay dearly, I promise you that, but first they must be used."

Lord Pallus chuckled deeply as he adjusted the Crown on his head, the serpentine forms of dragons writhing as they stepped outside into the humid heat of the Enruk day. A massive red dragon waited outside, his chest heaving impatiently. Pallus smiled up at him.

"Fury. It is time."

Fury simply growled as he bent low allowing Pallus and Maldros to climb up on his massive back. Maldros looked back to see Dekkion standing in the same place they had left him, looking up at the sky.

"Dekkion! Why do you delay?" Maldros shouted down to the frail shadow of a man.

Dekkion chuckled darkly, the hoarse voice rattling and unsettling, "I have my way."

Dekkion raised a hand to the sky as dark clouds swirled directly above him blue white lightning crackled as the clouds burst with the skeletal form of a dragon, both horrible and familiar to Maldros.

"Breathe the air once more, Azure! The coward ferryman does not get to claim you today!"

Dekkion cackled as the dragon swooped down to pick up his dark master. Blue scales and torn wings matched the single glowing eye in the dragon's skull. His once proud flesh hung in tatters along the jaw as he mindlessly roared. Dekkion climbed on the undead beast's back and grinned. Gesturing to the sky they rose with great plumes of dust driven across the parched earth below.

As the roars of the dragons rose in harmony, they flew into the skies like a gale force wind. Only taking moments before their powerful bodies were swallowed by the blood and fire rimmed black clouds swirling above the temple.

ACKNOWLEDGEMENTS

This second installment in the Chronicles of Avinol series holds a special place in my heart, filled with cherished memories. As I've mentioned previously, this tale sprung from our tabletop role-playing game, shaped and molded by the players' actions as I presented them with various scenarios.

In the previous book, we encountered a dragon turtle that was born from a conch shell I had lying on the table, intended as a quick prop. In this book, we're introduced to Zorin's *"Stinky Lockpick,"* which began as a jest and evolved into a legendary item. The origins of this item lie in Cody's playful refusal to definitively answer how he kept the lockpick hidden. My mistake was not asking for specifics, only requiring a dice roll to determine if he successfully concealed it.

The more the other players pressed for details, the more Cody leaned into the humor, suggesting that this object could be hidden anywhere. The imaginations of those at the table took over, fueling the legend of the Stinky Lockpick. The possibilities were endless, and the air was thick with speculation. Was it tucked behind an ear? Hidden in a boot? Perhaps it was even concealed in a more *unconventional* location, the mere thought of which caused uproarious laughter around the table.

"The Stinky Lockpick" became a running joke, a symbol of the unpredictable and humorous nature of our tabletop adventures. It also, and more importantly served as a reminder that even the smallest, most mundane objects could take on a life of their own in the world of imagination and role-playing.

The fall of Azure when the trebuchet took him out of the sky is a table legend as well. To help you understand this I should tell you about how the majority of the first half of "Children of the Flame" was played. The Battle for the Celestine Tower was an all day game where I built a full size to scale model of the tower at 1:300 scale. This scale is where 5 feet is roughly 1/4 inch.

I built a simple system where 1" squares of cardstock were individual units of 16 soldiers. To mix it up I made Dragons to this scale and small cards balanced on top of a 3 inch stand to give the feeling of flight.

In the game we played two phases with each phase having a strict 30 minute time limit. The party itself was very large so we split up the group a bit. We knew Benedict, Keldor and Elloveve would be on the battlefield, but also Skotmir volunteered. We assigned all four of them to individual tiles on the battlefield. Then the players split into two groups, one controlling the dark army and the other controlling the defenders of the tower.

I allowed everyone to discuss what they would like to do and had a few options prepared to throw at them as well. One was bringing in the trebuchet. Now again this system I built wasn't fool proof at all. In fact it had a lot of loopholes so I should take a moment to thank as well as apologize to the players for putting them through such a half baked scenario.

Phase two was where we used theater of the mind, inside the tower as they searched for a way to support the group outside.

The phase one gameplay was turn based with the number of forces on either side rolling dice equal to the forces in the skirmish and resolving on a table. This is like any battle system honestly, including the classics like *Risk* or Axis and Allies. If the cards depicting major characters were involved and lost half of their casualties we would pause the phase timer and zoom into the melee with normal miniatures to remind the players there were lives of their favorite characters at stake.

I even had random rolls for fireballs or other artillery striking the grid and affecting multiple soldiers. Some of which could be friends or even themselves.

With this background, the significance of the following events becomes clearer. The defenders decided to construct a trebuchet, sacrificing some of their infantry to operate it. When the dragons entered the battlefield, the defenders rolled a natural 20 to hit a dragon, and I ruled that it was knocked out of the sky.

The players controlling the dark army were outraged, especially Phil, the player controlling Vix the Chaotic. Phil, a highly intelligent individual with a love for science, argued that there was no way a trebuchet could hit a dragon. I conceded that there was only a slim chance, but luck played a factor. This disagreement escalated into a heated argument.

As the gamemaster, I ultimately won the argument, though at the cost of some tension at the table. However, this incident inspired the ongoing joke about Vix's disbelief in the story. My reasoning was that the defenders had launched a large projectile into the dragon's path, and while the dragon could have easily dodged it on a good day, luck was not on its side. Additionally, I never downplay the significance of natural 20s or 1s, regardless of the gaming system. A 5% chance is rarer than some people realize, and both successes and failures can contribute to a compelling story.

Another memorable moment was when one of the 30-minute phases was spent entirely on arguments, resulting in a wasted day's action. Cody expressed his frustration, and I reminded him of the timer. The dark army had failed to accomplish anything that day due to their infighting.

Following this incident, Phil and I agreed to play a different game together. Not every game is suitable for everyone, and this particular game wasn't the right fit for Phil, who preferred a more strategic and tactical experience. He excels at chess and can often predict his victory within the first few moves.

Being a game master is interesting because you control both many things and nothing at the same time. It's not like chess. That's the fun of this story though, I couldn't just sit down and write this without the table breathing life into the world and making it truly live. The character starts as a concept and then they come to life in a world filled with other lives. It's truly wonderful.

A player can mention something, not even thinking of the impact and it sparks the mind. The return of Elloveve in the first book was spawned because when Kara joined the group she asked to play an elf ranger with red hair. I had an extra mini for her to use which was previously Elloveve's. To her credit she didn't really know who that was at the time and this was before I started the show so only those that played previously would associate it.

While sitting there at the end of the session with the ambush where she first appears she mentioned to Joleen (Cordelia's player) "I like this mini! The name on the back isn't me but I like the character."

I smiled in my head as I thought, "What if?"

As the game progressed I tossed in some dreams of her background and she liked all of the story building. Finally I took her aside and we discussed it. I never forced the idea but offered it up with the opportunity to play another character. She took the opportunity happily and created Lorvana, a character all of her own now that she was more familiar with the game.

Elona's return was another "What if?" where as they were taking back Garnet Keep and they saw Spilge and the King arguing I thought "What if their lost mother is actually still alive? Better yet, what if she's one of the bad guys now?"

The creation of Benedict's sword and the Red Guardian was a spontaneous decision, driven by my desire to pit him against an equally formidable adversary in a one-on-one duel. I wanted Brian, the player controlling Benedict, to experience a true challenge. To simplify the process, I took a copy of Benedict's character sheet and essentially "reskinned" his abilities, transforming them into darker versions. The Red Guardian was, mechanically, the same character as Benedict, just with a different aesthetic—a change in "color," so to speak.

The Red Guardian, once a simple sword, has now become a character in its own right. The prospect of delving into its origins, its history, and the intricate details of its existence was exciting to me. As the narrative unfolds, you too will have the opportunity to uncover these mysteries and explore the depths of the Red Guardian's lore. I look forward to your journey of discovery as we continue this tale together.

Real life, as we have seen, can be a harsh and cruel teacher. The loss of a child is something that is so deeply traumatic that only those that have experienced it can really know what it's like, and even then it's different for every person. In my own journey through grief, I found solace in writing the backstory of Elona and Benedict. It became a way for me to process the devastating loss of our son, who passed away before he had the chance to enter the world. His absence created a void in our lives that remains unfilled, and I suspect it will forever remain so. The pain of his loss is a wound that may never fully heal, a constant reminder of a life we were all denied.

Like with most of life's struggles one must not succumb to the dark thoughts that dwell in the corners of our minds and instead we must actively feel for those handholds to crawl out of the pit of despair before it becomes us. It's not easy, nor does it seem like sometimes it's even possible, but it is necessary.

Elona's journey through grief, as she gradually freed herself from Spilge's dark influence, mirrored my own experience. It was as if I had been trapped in a deep abyss of despair and had to confront and conquer the inner demons I had unknowingly created to move forward. Time, relentless and unforgiving, continued its march, and I had to find a way to balance my grief with the necessity of taking those first, tentative steps towards healing.

The realization that our son's death wasn't my fault, that there was nothing I could have done to change the outcome, was a turning point. It wasn't anyone's fault; it was simply the cruel hand of fate, weaving our individual threads into a shared tapestry of sorrow and loss.

The pain of losing him was a constant companion, a shadow that followed me even in the brightest of moments- but this group and our story helped me to navigate my feelings and deal with the dark clouds of depression.

We tried again, and were blessed with Ari who is my angel of hope.

Chalkos became friends instantly with the bubbly Lorvana played by Kara Danvers who repeatedly made high rolls of persuasion as she praised the ancient copper dragon guarding the prisons. After a while I couldn't justify him as anything else. She had totally won he and I over as the perfect match for Chalkos. She had completely won us over as the perfect match for Chalkos.

Another particularly memorable moment of inspired roleplay occurred during the Battle of Garnet Keep. JD, playing the character Dabria, made the daring decision to leap from a dragon's back onto a moving horse when she recognized the rider as her former lover. As the Dungeon Master, I called for a skill check, and to everyone's surprise, she succeeded.

The real magic happened when, due to her natural 20 roll (a critical success), I asked JD what she wanted Dabria to do next. Her response was unexpected and deeply moving: "I want Dabria to talk to Nightblade."

In the midst of this chaotic, high-stakes battle, we were presented with a poignant scene: two former lovers, their hearts burdened by past grievances and misunderstandings, attempting to find reconciliation. In a world where magic was commonplace, why couldn't emotions and relationships also defy expectations? As the gamemaster, I felt it was my duty to facilitate this interaction, rather than hinder it with rules or limitations.

So, I transported Dabria and the horse's rider into a shared memory: a tranquil black sand beach bathed in the soft light of a rose gold dawn. This was to be a place of peace and mutual understanding, a sanctuary they had both cherished together in happier times.

The Chronicles of Avinol delves into the lives of many NPCs, with Maldros the Dark being a significant one. Maldros symbolizes my internal struggle with rage and depression. He represents the looming darkness that threatens to consume unless kept in check by love and guidance.

The players, including Storm S Cone, Joleen Fresquez, Colten Janssen, Jordan Thompson, Brian Dowling, Kara Danvers, Corey

Pfhauch, Hayley Muñoz, Laney Flannigan, Becky Atchley, JD Rose, Phil Brown, Daniel Nichols, Rachel Herring-Luna, Rori Christenson, Liz Hunninghake, Elena Rebholz, and Cody Miller, have been instrumental in shaping this narrative over nine years and six intertwined campaigns.

Daniel Nichols, through Good Ham Productions, has been a crucial partner in expanding the universe of Avinol by interweaving it with his Chronicles of Eridul. The stories progress with bridges connecting these two worlds, creating a richer, more complex tapestry.

Different campaigns occurred at various points in the timeline, featuring diverse characters. This book aims to unify those narratives into a single epic. The expedition, for instance, allowed me to participate as Mierak. Arianna briefly joined as Edde, but her involvement led to an interesting backstory development.

Edde's story will continue in a separate horror-driven series, "The Shattered," where she and her companions navigate the darkness of The Shattered Lands while facing the twisted spirit known as The Widow. Despite their harrowing experiences, they play a vital role in the fight against the Dark Army, operating from the shadows.

This book aligns with seasons 3 and 4 of the podcast "Dice Tower Theatre presents Dawn of Dragons," a period of significant growth in production quality and cast size. The immersive arena atmosphere was captured on location, and even a team of 20 voice actors contributed to the layered sounds of battles.

Thanks to the talents of Joleen Fresquez, Cody Miller, Sarah Jenkins, Colten Janssen-Olsen, Brian Michael Dowling, J.D. Rose, Matthew Bianchi, Daniel Nichols, Rebecca Atchley, Jessica Atchley, Harlan Guthrie, Kara Danvers, Stormy Cone, Hayley Munoz, Brian Dowling, Timothy Rowland, Scott C. Brown, Barret Giant, Benjamin

Corley, David Tilstra, Nikki Richardson, Patrick Mendelsohn, Jordan Thompson, Storm S. Cone, Ian Wilkinson, Piper Cleaveland, Shannon Roby, Phill Usher, Heath A. Martin, Jesse Phillips, Laura Jerdak, David S. Dear, Lesley Beckmann, Arianna Atchley, Chris Herrera, Sam Weigel, Mike Kienker, Patrick Cramer, Tyler Caldron, Ellie Gossage, Sam Wiegel, Michael J. Rigg, Sabrina Patten, Melissa Kersh, Scott Blankfield, Jordache Richardson, Ned Donovan, Tal Minear, Saoirse Brown, Melinda Barkhouse, Kaitlyn Athoff, Shannon Roby, Ryan Van de Kamp, Byron Thompson, Melanie Petry, Cheyenne Bramwell, Adam Kidjoaka, Jesse Davis, Abigail Richardson, Elizabel Riggs, Stephen Farruggia, Corbin Miller, Bridgett Farruggia, Daphne Bichler, Brad Colbroock, Chris Herrerra, Joshua Thomas, Gin Walker, Steve Rausch, Jaccie Kitts, Jesse Davis, Chris Ponds, Gryffn Foote, Casey Kennedy, Brad Zimmerman, Hannah Mullen, Maddy Searle, Daniel French, Elizabel Rigg, Bhavneet Athwal, Brian Penaloza, Abigail Richardson, Alex Gilmour, Steph Dewey, Trevor Rupe, Jeff Ogden, Larisa Bishop, Chris Hart, Aicila Lewis, Lec Zorn, Valeri Gray, Layne McCaleb, Sunny Alyssa Wolf, Joseph Duncan, Darla Miller, Logan Miller, Janet Atchley, Clyde Sacks, Genevieve Gionet, Laura Atchley, Jordan Thompson, and Maddy Searle.

The songs "Applehead" and "Ignite," written and recorded with Rebecca Atchley who plays Una, further enrich the Dawn of Dragons experience and are available wherever you stream your music. We wrote the song "Applehead" together where I wrote the melody and arrangement along with the lyrics and sent it to Becky to see what she would do vocally to it.

"Ignite" on the other hand was almost entirely her and I said "perfect! I want to use it"! I then used her recording to layer more instruments on top of her already powerful piano and vocals. I felt it gave closure to this book ending with Dabria and Sophie staring across the mountain lake as a falling star streaked across the sky. A single owl hooting from the forest, maybe.

Maybe it could be Vix's owl afterall.

A final note, this book is dedicated to Ian Wilkinson, a great friend who passed away a few years ago. One of my oldest friends who accompanied me on many adventures in my young life. When I was starting out in the middle of Wyoming wanting desperately to be a spooky performer like Skinny Puppy or Alice Cooper he was there with me. He was there while I rolled around in a straight-jacket screaming in a microphone while helping run a CD player with some strange movie samples.

We grew apart over time and he went on to build a life elsewhere as did myself. About 10 or so years ago we met up again in Casper, more specifically in *Sonic Rainbow,* a local record store we had many fond memories of. Still hanging in the back was a poster with my young face on it as SHADE, a former music project I did in the 90's. Forever screaming in a microphone. It was wonderful to see him.

We restored our friendship and he happily took the role of Lord Pallus when I offered it to him. His booming voice was well known on the radio for a while in the Chicago area. My favorite moment with his involvement was right after delivering the death blow to Erebus Shieldheart in the very beginning of the story. He called me and said "So I had this guy make me a sword and then I just killed him with it? That's cold man!"

I still laugh at that one. Everyone knew him as a wonderful person, a big flameheaded 7 foot high biker with a heart of gold.

Stay tuned my friends as *The Chronicles of Avinol* saga continues soon with our ongoing adventures, and the third book promises even more excitement.

Until next time...remember the oath!

ABOUT
THE AUTHOR

Mike Atchley, born in the heart of Wyoming, is a multi-talented artist who weaves immersive worlds through sound and story. As the narrator and producer of the award-winning audio fiction podcast, "Dice Tower Theatre presents Dawn of Dragons," and its companion novel series, "The Chronicles of Avinol," Mike brings decades of audio engineering expertise to his craft. His voice has graced numerous audio productions, including "Fate of Isen," "Aethuran Dark Saga," and "Chronicles of Eridul," showcasing his dedication to the audio community. With over 30 years of experience in audio engineering, music, and foley artistry, he creates rich soundscapes that transport listeners and readers alike. A passionate advocate for the audio medium, Mike also contributed to the live immersive theater experience "Avistrum" as the ghost of the unknown soldier or Scorpio the Werewolf and cherishes the opportunity to ignite the imaginations of children. Connect with him and explore the world of Avinol at GoodHamProductions.com.